THE WAYS
OF THE OWLS

A novel

MANOUSH GENET CASTAÑEDA-VIZCARRA

BOOK PUBLISHERS NETWORK

Book Publishers Network
P.O. Box 2256
Bothell • WA • 98041
PH • 425-483-3040
www.bookpublishersnetwork.com

10 9 8 7 6 5 4 3 2 1

Printed in the United States of America

LCCN 2009913404
ISBN10 1-935359-27-4
ISBN13 978-1-935359-27-2

Editor: Julie Scandora
Cover Designer: Laura Zugzda
Typographer: Stephanie Martindale

To those who know their value.

Dear Michelle,

I hope you enjoy my novel.

Remember to listen to your heart.

Manoush Castaneda

03/24/2010

ACKNOWLEDGEMENTS

To my abuela María who taught me the love of books and learning. To my abuelo Fernando who knows how to make me laugh. To my parents, Jose Luis and Marlene, who are the best in all senses of the word, and my little sister, Maximianne, whose personality inspired Maximiana's character in so many ways.

To my uncles, aunts, cousins, nephews, and nieces for all of their support.

To Natalia Brambila, Mexican soprano singer, who is my older sister at heart.

To my editor Giovani Amaya for helping me all the way in making this novel a reality and who is the older brother I always wanted to have.

To Jackie and Susan Walsh who led me to Sheryn Hara and Julie Scandora. Julie, thank you for your patience.

To my best friends Edna, Shennan Juliette, Daniel G., Madhya and Haydee, Lucas, Arianna, Xandra and Daniel K.

To Damon Jay Cunningham who sees inside me without asking questions.

Last but not least, to my classmates, teachers, and staff at my high school in Seattle, Washington.

I am very lucky to have all of you in my life.

Forever thank you.

PREFACE

The summer of 2004 marked a special time in my life. My parents took me to a small town in the countryside, twenty-six kilometers east of the city of Mazatlán, México. The 150-year-old town's name is El Roble. My first memory of El Roble is that of a piece of countryside paradise, where the sun reflects itself on a close-by river called the Presidio. The area where El Roble, which means "the oak tree," stands used to be full of oak trees. In the past, when people from the gold mines of the Sierra Madre traveled to Mazatlán, they would rest at the *roble* trees. Today, two streets cross at the exact place where they would stop, and that corner is located across the street from my grandparents' house.

No one could anticipate how my life would change as a result of that visit, nor could I have imagined how the world of stories from long ago would enter my life when I walked, for the first time, into the town's old abandoned hacienda, the once-called Grand House. Several owls flapped their wings at me when I pushed the heavy door to enter its water tower. Something mystical and unexplainable happened inside, and I emerged, transformed from within, ready to bring many souls back to life with the pen, and I began writing in my diary nonstop.

Manoush Genet Castañeda-Vizcarra
Just diagnosed with dystonia
Fall 2006
Seattle, Washington

1

Earlier than sunrise, I walked through the huge door that led to the entrance of the great Sarmiento house when the sweet aroma of fresh gardenias hit me. I moved around for a while, not knowing where I was going on my first day working there.

"Are you the new servant girl?" a voice behind asked. I turned around, and in front of me stood a girl a little older than I was.

"Yes," I replied, concealing my shyness.

"Well, I am Raimunda, and you probably already know that," she said sharply. "Your sister used to work in the fields with me. I'm one of the many other servants here … seventeen in total. I heard that you were going to come. That's good because we need a lot of help around here, and the chores never end. Follow me. I'll show you to the kitchen."

Obediently, I tagged along Raimunda who continued talking in a quick and squeaky voice that denoted nervousness. We walked through a short hallway that led to a long corridor, extending throughout the back of the house. On the way I looked at the beautiful design on the floor of the hallway. The pattern in colors of red, blue, white, and gold made it look three-dimensional. I had never seen anything like it before. We arrived at the kitchen, which occupied a separate building in the rear of the house; different scents came out of it, a hungry person's paradise.

"I believe that you will be doing all of the chores here ... but I am not sure. We have to ask Doña Luisa; she is the lady in charge. But first, I will show you the hacienda. Right now Señor and Señora Sarmiento are sleeping, so we have to be very quiet."

I nodded while following Raimunda out of the kitchen and back into the house. We passed through the short hallway, and Raimunda explained that the door to the right took us to the dining room and the door to the left was the parlor. The parlor room was the place where Señora Sarmiento sat to have tea and do embroidery and knitting with her friends whenever they visited from Mazatlán. We turned right into the dining room.

"Look, either one of these two doors takes us to the great room," she said, pointing to the crystal doors with wooden decorations on them. "But, the room that is next to the dining room is Señor and Señora Sarmiento's bedroom. You see? There is the door to their bedroom."

I nodded.

Raimunda continued, "Then there is a spare room and one of the washrooms." We passed through the small hallway again to land on the back corridor one more time. "We are not allowed to go inside the sleeping quarters since everyone is still asleep. But, the bedroom with the balcony is Orlando's, and then it's the twin girls' room, and the last room on this side of the house, in other words, next to the parlor room, is Alejandro's. Domingo's bedroom is outside the main house, over there ... see?" She pointed to a two-story building on the side of the main house.

I nodded my understanding again.

Back in the kitchen, Raimunda listed some of the chores for the day, and I grabbed the broom and started sweeping the endless corridor. While working, I observed the bustle of servants who came and went, unified in their domestic care of the house but isolated in their individual tasks, oblivious to their comrades. The gardener, a man named Carlos, was working next to the water tower on a sunflower plant, its bright yellow colors contrasted with the greenish texture of its leaves. I tried not to distract myself from my chore, but it was almost impossible with so many new things in front of my thirteen-year-old eyes.

⚓

I heard noises coming from the great room and saw a little girl go into the dining area. The girl knocked on the door of Señor and Señora Sarmiento's sleeping quarters; the door opened, and she walked in. I longed for one of them to appear so at least to know what Señor or Señora Sarmiento looked like, but I had no such luck. I had seen only their backs before, at Sunday mass. The Sarmientos had built the church for the people in town. It was the only church in the entire county, and when its cast-iron bells rang, the sounds echoed throughout the countryside.

After I finished sweeping the corridor, I went back into the kitchen, still looking around all the novelties surrounding me.

"Take these plates and go set the table. The children will come out soon for breakfast," an old woman said.

That must be Doña Luisa, I thought.

Of course, I did what I was told but had no idea what to do with so many plates, forks, and spoons. At home we used only one plate and no silverware but our hands and tortillas to scoop up food. I looked at Doña Luisa with a puzzled face and walked into the gigantic dining room. It had an enormous table that could probably seat fifty people … well, maybe more like twenty.

"Once everyone is out of their rooms, you will go in to pick up dirty clothes and do beds. Armanda does the floors. Also, knock before you enter, just in case there is someone still in the room," Doña Luisa explained to me with a candid voice.

"But, what should I do? Just make their beds? Clean up a little?" I asked clueless.

"Well of course! And look under the beds for dirty trousers," she replied, amused.

I went through the hallway, and after crossing the grand room, I arrived at the front garden. Next I walked straight towards the bedroom with the balcony. This bedroom had a huge porch with red tiles on it. I knocked on the door, and after waiting a couple of seconds, I opened it with caution. Inside a big bed and a desk with many papers on it occupied one side; there was also a piano. I had never seen a real piano before. My fingers tingled with desire to touch the shiny keys. The windows, tall and dressed with long cloth curtains, were open, inviting a breeze that filled the room with the fresh aromas of gardenias from the garden. In another corner stood a wardrobe with a mirror. I felt so amazed by the beauty of the room that I almost forgot why I had come; dust rag in hand. I moved towards the desk and looked at the papers—pictures and, I assumed, letters.

If I could only read what they say.

I turned around and walked to the mirror. Its frame had carvings I had never seen before—mystical-looking designs that made me think of somebody who practiced magic. I stood for a minute and looked at myself. My braids hung on the sides. I smiled and opened my brown eyes widely, closed one, and quickly moved away from the "magical mirror" that I would look into from that day on every time I entered the balcony room.

The room was not messy at all; I only had to fix the huge bed. The cover was heavy; I climbed onto the bed in order to straighten it. Then I dusted the room a little bit just so it would look better. I felt a wave of fresh air coming through the windows and closed my eyes. The smells of the garden entered my nose. I opened my arms wide to have the wind go through my thin clothes, but a different aroma came in, a scent I had never sensed before. I opened my eyes, turned around, and saw the door behind me closing. I walked towards it and opened it slowly. As soon as I peeked through it, I saw the other door in front of it close quickly, catching only a glimpse of a hand. But the scent of a human lingered behind, haunting the room and my senses.

I stood there, looking at the perfectly rectangular doors that followed one after the other, giving the effect of a canyon and overwhelming me with a sense of profoundness that made the distance seem greater than it must have been. I entered the next room; pastel colors suggested a girl's room, as did the toys scattered about. Dolls with hard faces littered the beds, and different toys that represented a girl's world of tea parties and days filled with play lay on the floor. I quickly fixed the beds and looked under them.

The next door was closed, so I knocked. As I grabbed the doorknob to open it, I heard a voice from inside.

"You may come in."

I walked in and saw a young man sitting on the bed.

"I will come back later, Señorito," I responded, avoiding his eyes.

"No. I'm about to leave." The young man walked out through yet another door, but before disappearing into the parlor, he said, "Thank you."

That must be one of the Sarmiento boys.

Next, I entered the most amazing looking room I had ever seen and realized that throughout this day I had seen "amazing rooms I had never seen before" several times. A huge window draped with red curtains dominated the room, and a cream colored sofa with a shiny wooden table sat in the middle. On the largest wall, there hung a huge picture of something that looked like a clock, prominent in its gray hues.

I was about to walk into the dining room when I heard Raimunda approaching.

"Where are you going?" she asked.

"Into the dining room so I can get into the rooms next to it," I answered.

"NO! You are never to walk into the dining room while they are still having breakfast! You must wait for them to finish, then walk in, and take the dishes. Only then go into the other rooms!" she scolded.

I was speechless. She had screamed at me as if I should have known such a rule.

"Didn't you work before?" she asked, annoyed at my ignorance.

"This is my first job doing anything like this."

"Aren't you fifteen already?" Raimunda asked.

"No … I'm thirteen," I answered, hesitating, unsure if I should answer my real age or not.

"Well, no wonder! Just come into the kitchen with me."

Once again, we went into the kitchen and waited for the Sarmientos to finish having their breakfast.

"Señorito Alejandro wants more juice," a girl said as she walked in the door. Raimunda gave her a cup full of juice, and she headed back outside.

"How many children are there, five?" I asked.

"Yes, five: three boys and two girls. The girls are twins, but don't ask questions about them," Raimunda answered.

I just nodded and waited for Raimunda to tell me when it was fine to go clean the other rooms.

After what seemed like ages, Doña Luisa finally told me that it was time to go into the dining room with Raimunda to get the dishes. The hours passed quickly, and I started to feel a hole in my stomach; however, I did not dare ask if I was allowed to eat something. But as the day went by, a feeling of despair weighed heavy within me. The sole thought of having to come back tomorrow and the day after to repeat all of these chores gave me a sensation of wanting to cry my eyes out.

I'll just do that last, I said to myself when the gigantic bed stared back at me, waiting for my exhausted arms and back to dress it. While dusting the biggest bedroom in the house, I noticed on top of one of the wardrobes a couple of pearl necklaces. I just glanced at them because I had heard many stories from my mother about people claiming that servants in the house had stolen their possessions, and justice showed no mercy when it came to the rich Sarmientos. When I finished dusting, once again, I stood in front of the bed, which now seemed to be laughing at me.

Why do these people need such a big bed in the first place? It does not make any sense, especially because the weather is hot most of the time. Lying on the floor feels better—cool and fresh.

El Roble was so hot that sweat would roll down onto your eyelashes and burn your eyes directly if you were not careful. We were in January; at least the humidity of the hot days was under control.

Finally, after much effort, I finished making the senseless bed. Since it wasn't my job to clean the washrooms, I went straight back to the kitchen.

"Are you all done?" Raimunda asked me.

I nodded, with what felt like the last breath of energy left in my body.

"Now you will go wash clothes."

Left speechless again and so shocked by her words, I didn't even feel when Raimunda dragged me out of the kitchen, my heart sinking with the idea of doing even more work. We walked behind the water tower building to meet the laundry ladies.

"You will be washing clothes here. Each one of you takes a spot. They will tell you what to do."

Raimunda walked back slowly to the kitchen. I could tell that she was very tired. Her arms were burned from being constantly under the sun, her feet were scratched, and her back looked as if her shoulders could not hold it any longer. But even in her weariness, her long black hair tied back in a thick braid made her beautiful. I looked at her, imagining my hair looking as beautiful as hers.

"Girl! Girl!"

I turned around to see the unfortunate one the voice attacked. Shamefully, it took me a while to figure out that she was talking to me.

"You have to stop wasting your time like that because you will get yourself in trouble and not get any work done," a woman with a hoarse voice said.

"I'm very tired … Can't I sit for a little while?" I asked, adding one more mistake to my list of the day.

"No, if somebody sees you, you will get in trouble. Push yourself against the washing stone. That will help you rest a little bit. It's your first day, but you will get used to it," she said, pointing to a basket. "Once the basket is filled, Lupita will take it to Lucina, and she will hang the clothes on the clothesline."

I nodded and started right away. I felt relieved to know how to do at least this job, and the talking and laughing of these women made time fly faster. The fresh water was fun to use, but when I was done with my second half of clothes, my enthusiasm began to fade away. My back ached and so did my feet. I looked up and saw the green valley that extended all the way to the mountains. Even though I should have had no time to look up, I hung on to the moment, filled with such beauty and magic. Right in the middle of a large stand of trees at the valley's edge, I fantasized I had a small cottage, a place where I could have many books and that I could actually read them. I lowered my eyes again to continue washing those heavy skirts and trousers that did not belong to my family while my mind played with the memory of the distant sight. A light breeze blew through now and then, a reminder of the vast expanse of greenery and liberty so near yet unattainable.

"Maximiana, you can go into the kitchen and have some lunch now. But once you are all done, come back out here and help us some more."

I heard Margarita's words and slowly walked back into the kitchen. As soon as I entered, my legs collapsed me onto the first chair in front of me.

"Are you hungry? We have red rice, and get a banana to accompany it," Doña Luisa said. "I think that I have seen you before. You are Ignacio and Lupe's fourth one, right?"

"Yes." The affirmation came out in a tired tone.

"It is a disgrace what happened to your sister."

"Yes," I replied in a still lower voice. Somebody in the fields had abused my older sister Otilia. Now nobody in town spoke to her because she was seen as somebody with a stain on her face. When that happened, my papá stopped talking to her for days, and mothers in town did not allow their daughters to speak to Otilia anymore. According to their stupid ideas, my sister had become a bad influence. Yet my heart ached when I thought about Otilia and what had happened to her. My face was turned away from Doña Luisa's to hide the sentiment that was showing because I remembered that day. I had helped Otilia wash her skirt, and I had wanted to hug my sister and tell her that both of us were going to run away to a faraway place where no one could ever find us. But I had been only twelve at the time, and Otilia had just turned fourteen.

"Nobody will marry her, you know," another woman said.

I started eating and did not speak again but to say thank you as I left the kitchen. As I walked back to the washing place, I wondered what a conversation would be like if for *once* someone didn't mention what had happened to my sister.

"Good thing you're back. I need you to wash this little pile of clothes, and then you are done," Margarita told me.

"Done? I can go home?" I answered excitedly.

"No. Done doing laundry. You will go find Raimunda after this, and she will tell you what to do next."

My hopes sank. As I washed the remaining clothes, I took notice that neither children nor adults were anywhere to be seen. I had imagined them running around or screaming in play. Of course, I didn't know how old any of them were. I speculated that one of the Sarmiento boys was about seventeen or eighteen if he were the young man I had encountered in the corner room.

When I had completed the job, optimistically, I went out to look for Raimunda but secretly hoped that it would take me a while to find her. I wanted to explore the place a little bit and see if despairing souls in agony truly haunted the hacienda. I was too curious to let that opportunity pass by. The hacienda had many enormous buildings clustered around the property that they made it look like a town inside another town. One, the servants' quarters with a red tile roof held a long file of rooms. Flowers grew everywhere and spilled into the main house; apparently Señora Sarmiento loved to have the house full of different bouquets. Unfortunately, Raimunda caught me short in the middle of my exploration and sent me to the ironing room.

※

"Raimunda said that you would tell me what I have to do next," I stated in a quiet voice but secretly wished to hear the words *"There is nothing to iron today"* come out of her mouth.

"You have to iron these clothes. Lupita took down the clothes that are already dry. You iron the clothes in the water tower. Go. Bernarda will tell you what to do."

From that moment on, I realized I was a "living hot potato," tossed from the hands of one servant woman to another.

The inside of the water tower felt hot and stuffy, made worse by the charcoal fumes of the stove for the irons that seeped into the room. The cramped room made it really uncomfortable to be inside. No ventilation, for mercy … there were no windows inside! I started to wonder what sins I had not confessed that God was punishing me this way.

"You, go to that table over there and start heating the iron. Once it's hot enough, start ironing the clothes," a girl with empty eyes said. I dragged myself over to the table and put the iron on a stove to let it heat up. Raimunda came in just to inform me how interesting it was for me to be so tired when it came to chores but not at all to go exploring around. My face felt as hot as the irons on the stove.

When I had finished in the heat chamber, Raimunda announced that I could go home. Slowly I walked out to the front door. The sun was beginning to set, and the sky had turned into a sea of orange, pink, purple, and gray. On the street, children were running around barefoot, oblivious to the hot pebbles under their feet. Usually, I would have played, too, but not today. Now I felt tired even when I breathed.

While walking towards my house I saw my friend Daniel coming towards me. He was with a group of boys and men, returning from the fields.

"Maximiana!" he called.

I smiled at him, understanding how every bone of his fourteen-year-old body felt. Daniel had been my friend since we were very young, and since I can remember, he had always been energetic and in a good mood.

"Hey," I answered back while he waved good-bye to his group and ran towards me.

"How are you?" he asked in his usual enthusiastic voice.

My honest answer escaped in a single word. "Exhausted!" I replied. "I started working today in the Grand House … Trust me I *know* what they mean by 'grand.'"

Daniel laughed his heart out, but he could not conceal the tiredness in his body any more than could I.

"So how did 'the ghosts' treat you?" Daniel asked, making spooky noises to my face.

"They were very friendly, actually, and asked about *you*." I just loved to outsmart the boys. Yes, we had energy enough in our bodies to kid around a bit.

When I arrived home, Mamá was making our usual dinner of beans with cheese and tortillas.

"How was your day?" she asked without looking at my face. I knew Mamá felt bad that we had to work, but there was no way out of it. We all either worked for miserable cents or starved to death.

"It was good," I said looking away to avoid giving more explanations that I didn't want to share. "I will go get Natalia." As I got up to get my sister, I felt my back bend with soreness.

During dinner, Natalia asked about the Grand House. Otilia quietly listened to Natalia's questions, and I knew they both wanted to see it through my eyes, but I didn't want to talk about it. There was no point in describing something that they would likely never see. My appetite slipped out of my body when my soul realized the little detail that I had to go back to that place the next day.

After dinner I went to clean myself. The bucket of water felt heavier than ever. Otilia came to help out and watched for peeping Toms. Our "shower quarters" was a four-pole square with curtains in the back yard; we could never shower alone because the wind might come up and raise the curtains, showing our bodies in undergarments to the world of El Roble. Then our reputation would go directly to the deepest water hole in the county.

At night, I lay on my cot, and a memory from earlier in the day came to light.

Whose hand had I seen going into the other room? Perhaps Daniel was right, and ghosts did inhabit the house. But do ghosts hold the aromas that that one distinctively left behind … an aroma so different yet so familiar and beautiful …? Beautiful … Why did I just say that …?

And then a deep sleep took over my tired body.

"Today you are working in the library," Raimunda announced. I had been waiting three weeks for the moment of finally entering the library. The chores that day seemed like playtime for me just because I was going to walk into the most beautiful room in the house. I had peeked into the library through the windows and had seen the lines of colorful books in perfect order. The library was a building apart from the house; it had its own entrance and exit and was right next to the big gate that took you to the street. Every night I had gone home, wishing for the next day to be assigned to dust those books. My curiosity killed me to open them and see the pictures that I imagined filled their pages. I could just see in my mind those paintings of landscapes and places so far away from El Roble that it would take me a lifetime to get there by foot.

"Snap out of it, Maximiana! Get the broom and GO!" Raimunda shook me out of my daydreaming while throwing the broom at my hands.

"Yes," I answered in a hurry to get there as soon as possible. She opened the two side doors for me, and we walked into the library. We had the place to ourselves.

"I can do it by myself if you want to," I announced, hiding my intentions.

"Just don't trip on the stairs," she answered.

"So … do I dust every book in the shelves?"

"Of course not. You are only cleaning the floors, so stop talking and hurry up. We still have much to do," Raimunda mumbled on her way out. Nobody could believe that a sixteen-year-old girl could behave as a fifty-year-old. But that was Raimunda.

Relieved, I closed the doors behind me and walked towards the first bookshelf to my right; I took a book in my hands and opened it slowly. There were pictures and so many squiggles that made me dizzy.

If only I could read what it says.

The shiny ball on the stand in the corner got my attention. Spinning it seemed like a good idea, and I sat a moment turning it round and round. It had blue and brown colors and lines with squiggles on them. I stood there thinking about what it could be when a sensation came over me that someone was watching. I stopped the spinning, asking myself if I should hide under the desk, fearing I was in trouble. Realizing I could not escape, I turned around. But at the door was a boy, not much older than I, looking at me, half smiling. I stood up, startled, and quickly grabbed the broom to start sweeping. I continued sweeping the floor without turning my face towards the boy, but I could hear his steps coming to me. My heart pounded, and I felt a rush of heat moving up to my face.

The tone of his voice was gentle when he said, "I'm here just to get a book."

"I'm almost done," I answered, and without being able to take it any longer, I turned my face to look at him, certain my cheeks had turned crimson in that instant. A full head of brown curls contrasted with the paleness of his face, and a sweet line on his lips showed me a smile. But his eyes had no light in them. Yet, he carried a humbleness in his manners that made me feel safe with him.

"Don't worry about it. Take your time," he replied while passing his fingers over the books. Through the corners of my eyes, I followed his movement.

And then he looked back at me and asked, "Would you like to borrow one?"

His question took me by surprise. I just couldn't imagine a boss offering to lend a servant a book. But most of all, it mortified me, having to tell him that I couldn't read.

"Thank you, Señorito. But no," I politely responded.

"There is no problem, really; you can borrow one," he insisted.

"I cannot read," I said in the lowest possible voice, hoping that he could not hear me.

"Don't call me Señorito. My name is Orlando. What's your name?"

I stopped sweeping, and looking directly in his eyes, I said with a proud voice, "Maximiana Valdez."

"Why don't you know how to read?"

I just couldn't hold back my shock at his question. The answer was obvious—at least to me. How could he not know? I felt tremendously uncomfortable having to reply to such a question coming from somebody like him. What was I supposed to say? That I cannot read because poor children don't have teachers to teach them? That the only reason *you* know how to read is that your family owns half the town? Orlando read the answer in my face, and for an instant I felt his eyes filling with shame. Or did I only imagine it?

"Would you like to learn?"

"Yes, I would," I stated proudly, but added defensively, "but, I guess that's impossible."

"Why?" he asked.

"Because I don't have a teacher or books to learn from …"

"I could give you the books. We would only need to find somebody to teach you," *We?* I thought, *Who's "we"?*

"Do you know somebody that knows how to read?"

I was about to answer no when I thought of Beatriz. She had learned to read while working with the nuns in the town of Agua Caliente.

"I know someone."

"Hold on. I'm going to go get you something." He ran out of the library, leaving me speechless and not believing what had just happened. Orlando Sarmiento had offered me books to learn to read!

I continued sweeping, making time for him to return before Raimunda would come get me. But my plan failed. Raimunda came a few minutes after his departure to see if I had completed my chores and asked me to follow her to the kitchen. With a drawn heart, I went after her. But to my surprise, while doing the dishes, the kitchen went silent when Orlando walked in with three books in his hands. He stood there, looking at me, and I turned around, dried my hands on my apron and took them from him while being showered with the intrigued looks of all of those around us. In an indifferent way, I put them on the table, said "Thank you," and continued with my work. Orlando walked out, and the silence became a whisper of comments behind my back among the women in the kitchen.

I couldn't wait for the day to be over and go home with those precious books and look at them. I knew Beatriz would help me learn how to read and write. A tender feeling tugged at my heart when I thought of Orlando Sarmiento; he had been so nice to me, even though he didn't know me. I felt ashamed because up to that day, I had felt that the Sarmiento family were heartless oppressors who didn't care about anybody but themselves. Yet, Orlando showed me he cared about my words and my thoughts.

1904. Numbers. I can read the numbers, but what does it say under it?

I passed my finger over the letters, wishing to have magic powers that would tell me what it said under the number "1904." It was taking a long time for Beatriz to come home, and sweat began to trickle down the small of my back as I sat on the hot porch in front of her home.

"Maximiana, what are you doing here?" Beatriz asked when she arrived.

"I'm waiting for you because I want to ask you a favor … a big one."

"What is it?"

"Do you think you can help me learn how to read and write?"

"Where did you get those books? Let me see," she replied while taking them away from my hands and examining them.

"Orlando Sarmiento let me borrow them, I think …"

"You think? What do you mean by that?" she asked with an astonished tone of voice.

"Yes, 'I think,' because he didn't say if he was giving them to me or letting me borrow them; he just handed them to me. But I'm taking good care of them either way."

"Orlando Sarmiento?"

"Yes. Orlando Sarmiento."

"You talked to him?"

"Yes. Today in the library … and he offered me the books."

"Really?"

When she said "really," I began to realize that she doubted my story and that perhaps the idea of "stealing" was crossing her mind.

"I would never steal anything, Beatriz," I said with a proud voice. "Are you implying that?"

"Of course not. I'm just confused that he talked to you and offered you books. You know how those people are. They don't even look at us, and they most definitely will not talk to us, except to give orders."

"Well, he did. And I want to ask you to help me with this. Would you help me?"

Beatriz sighed. "I do not have much time, you know."

"Anytime you can, I'll be here. But please help me. I really want to learn how to read and write."

After thinking for a moment that seemed eternal to me, she finally said, "I will. But not today; I'm too tired. And I bet you're tired as well. Go home now." And she patted my back.

I stood up quickly.

"I will. But first, please just tell me what it says here."

I pointed to the words under the number "1904."

"It means that this book was made in 1904. So it is three years old."

"Ah! Three years old. It is almost new," I said, smiling.

"Yes, Maximiana, I know. Now good night!"

"Good night. And thank you so much!"

I walked home with a sudden enthusiasm that invaded my soul, knowing that I was embarking on a journey that would forever change my life. I wanted to skip my steps, but I was too old for that and, instead, just carried the light-hearted feeling on my face.

When I arrived home, I found Daniel waiting for me with a bag full of guavas. I told him my story of the day, and he was curious to look at the books also. For the first time, he asked me about the house, how it was inside.

I answered the truth, "It is huge, an enormous place full of unnecessary things that make no sense to me …" Images of the house ran through my mind. Daniel kept quiet for a while and did not ask any more questions. He knew what I meant because we had lived under the same circumstances all our lives. "Except the library," I amended.

"It sounds so beautiful," I said. "It rings in my ears like a song."

Orlando chuckled when he replied, "Songs are poems."

"But I didn't know that you could read them like this."

"Poems are like songs except spoken. And there are places called theatres where you can go listen to people recite them."

"Mmm." I was mesmerized, thinking about being in a place like that. Orlando talked about so many amazing places to see and about different things that I didn't know happened in the world. After almost three months of Beatriz's help plus all of my enthusiasm, I could now read quite well. Stories that I had only imagined before, I now began to enjoy in the books Orlando allowed me to borrow. Even though, at the beginning, those around me found it strange that I borrowed books from the Sarmientos' library, they got used to the idea. People knew I had Orlando's permission, but those around us never realized I shared anything with him beyond the books; they never saw us talking together. Our conversations were secret.

"Can a song in a piano be a poem?" I asked, truly intrigued. Orlando was taken aback by the question.

"But there are no words."

"So?"

"Ha, ha, ha! I guess you're right. I just never thought about that before."

"So every time you are playing that piano of yours, you are reciting poems to the world."

He looked at me as if saying, *You come up with the weirdest ideas.* But I enjoyed having the freedom to say those things to Orlando because he was my true friend and I trusted him.

"I think I should go now; it's late," I said as I stood up.

"Yes, I know. But I wish you could stay longer," Orlando replied while standing up. As usual, he opened the door of his balcony and quieted the dogs so I would be able to leave. After he helped me up and over the railing, he said in a whisper, "Poems are usually written to express a person's feelings towards his or her loved ones."

Without replying, I waved good-bye and jumped the fence onto the street, losing myself to the starry night.

As on every Wednesday, I was working in the laundry with Margarita and listening to her usual chattering when I suddenly completely blocked her voice from my mind. Someone was playing the living room piano, and the melody of the music reached the washing stones. I knew it was Orlando; I didn't have to see his hands on the keys to know. Only he was capable of playing it that way. I lost myself in the moment until he stopped and made me come back to reality. Wrapped up in her endless monologue, Margarita did not notice my momentary diversion or the admiration in my eyes.

That night, as I sat on the floor of Orlando's room with my head resting on the side of his bed, I said, "I heard you playing the piano today."

"I played those poems for you," he answered, looking at the floor.

I didn't know what to answer to that. My silence became too quiet for both of us.

"I wasn't sure if you could hear me," Orlando stated.

"I did. But I almost didn't because I was in the back doing the laundry ..."

And another awkwardness came between us, as it did every time we were reminded that I was one of the servant girls in his house.

"I have been thinking about something. Do you believe it's hard to write a poem?" I said to break the moment.

"Yes, it is. I don't think I am capable of writing one."

"Maybe it will be easier if we write one together," I muttered with a smile and stared at his brown eyes.

"Ha, ha, ha! Mmmm … Let's try to write a poem then …"

I wished the room had more illumination than just the little coming out of the oil lamp to show the expression of his face better. I saw his dark figure reflected in the magical mirror when he rose to get paper and ink.

"How should we start?" he asked.

"*Secretly they meet every night … like owls in disguise …* You continue," I shyly said.

"*To hold each other without falling, in arms …* Now you continue …"

"*Saying words with no sounds … however, spoken from the soul of those who feel …* Your turn …"

"*That music is a poem without words …*"

"I like it! Let's say it out loud together," I proposed, and showing a hint of embarrassment, Orlando agreed.

> *Secretly they meet every night*
> *Like owls in disguise*
> *To hold each other without falling, in arms,*
> *Saying words with no sounds,*
> *However, spoken from the soul of those who feel*
> *That music is a poem without words.*

His sweet and wet lips caressed the side of my neck, sending shivers down my spine. I closed my eyes, feeling the trembling of my inexperienced heart palpitate to the rhythm of my mind. His hand reached my waist and pulled the side of my body towards him; I could react but by touching him with the same tenderness. I felt his hair on my face when his warm lips found mine. Endlessly we kissed and passionately, beyond the innocence of our age. We submerged ourselves in our feelings of the moment, without regard to the reality we both knew existed between us. I did not want to reflect about it. I just sought to lose myself in his arms and believe that he cherished me as much as I cherished him. Again, I wanted to think it was possible for true love, regardless of age and in spite of differences in money or status, to exist and survive any threat. I trusted Orlando Sarmiento with my heart.

"I have to go now …."

"Stay longer … Don't go yet … A little bit longer …"

I wanted to stay. I wanted to lock myself with him in that room and continue writing poems for the rest of eternity by his side. But I rose and walked towards the balcony one more time, as I had been doing for months without ever being caught by anyone.

"We are like Romeo and Juliet … but I am Romeo …," I said with an enormous smile on my newly kissed lips. Then I jumped off the balcony while Orlando held the dogs and, embarrassed by my statement of calling him Juliet, looked away.

Oh, how I desired the sweet lovable daylight to arrive. Yes … tomorrow seemed too far away to wait to see him again.

The next morning, everyone was shocked by my lack of usual talkativeness.

"Are you sick?" Raimunda asked, concerned by my strange behavior.

"No." It was the same answer I had given my mother that morning.

"You sure are quiet today …," she said with a hidden meaning while I walked away as if I hadn't heard her and started my daily chores. I went to the twins' room to clean it and heard someone behind me. I knew it was he; I could smell his scent, but when I turned, he was gone. Throughout the day, unconsciously, I kept expecting to see him appear as he always did, but he did not.

Should I come again tonight? I asked myself over and over again. Disappointed and confused, I walked home, knowing that somehow our friendship had been ruined and what had happened the night before was a terrible mistake. Those thoughts depressed me, and thinking of the end of our special relationship made me feel empty and alone. Despair invaded my mind and soul; it had been an especially trying day, walking around that house expecting to see Orlando at any moment—and disappointed every time.

The memories from last night were engraved in my conscience. My stomach felt uneasy, but worse was the expression on my face that everyone seemed to notice.

❧

That night I turned on my cot without being able to lull myself to sleep. The roosters' screams woke me up too soon after I had finally fallen asleep. The idea of going to the Grand House made me feel uneasy. I needed an excuse not to go and stay hidden from the world, at least this day.

"I don't feel good, Mamá."

"Let me feel your forehead. Come here." Mamá walked towards me, touching my forehead and neck.

"I feel dizzy. I don't think I can go to work today," I stated tragically.

"No, you should not. I will send Natalia to tell Luisa you are sick. Now go and lie down. I will bring you tea," Mamá said in a hurry.

I had told the truth; I did feel sick from lack of sleep.

After she brought me tea, I pondered the events of two nights before while Mamá went to the corner store on our street, one of the two stores in town. The other was located in the Grand House, and most workers bought their everyday needs there; they would get their debt discounted from their salary. The workers never had money left, and most of the time, they were months behind in grocery payments. A strict man owned the corner store, but he had three daughters who had good hearts. Mamá used to go and buy leftover foods, which were the cheapest, and the eldest daughter, named Luz, would always put an extra piece of something when nobody was looking.

At the corner store, Mamá commented to Señorita Luz that I was late for work because of my "illness." Señorita Luz was concerned and offered a remedy. However, Mamá noticed the other women in the store exchanging suspicious looks.

Little did I know at the time that my nightly escapades, jumping the balcony to read and learn under the guidance of Orlando

Sarmiento, were general news in town. What a town! Gossip spread like an overflowing river during cyclone season. My minutes alive were being counted at the time by each one of the inhabitants of the town of El Roble. They were imagining the worst. Honestly, I couldn't blame them; it had *looked* very bad even when it was not.

Only much later did Mamá relate to me the chatterings of the ladies in the store; she said nothing of that when she returned.

Meanwhile my stomach churned with thoughts of not jumping Orlando Sarmiento's balcony anymore. The allure of continuing my once-a-week, or more, visits of the last couple of months no longer looked as adventurous nor did our display of affection seem as romantic as I had thought before. Feelings of regret filled every inch of my body.

How could I have been so stupid?

I just could not believe myself. Not only was Orlando not going to be my friend anymore, but if he felt as bad as I did, he might have me fired!

What would I tell Mamá and Papá about it?

We needed those three pesos and fifty cents a week desperately. I designed a plan to fix the mess: I would talk to Orlando and tell him that I was really sorry for what had happened, that I wanted just to be friends again, and that I would not come to my lessons at night anymore.

Yes, I will do that. That will fix it and the sooner the better.

I took the last sip of my cup of tea and got up. Mamá was surprised with my rapid recuperation and eagerness to go to work. I rushed out to get there as soon as possible.

Once inside the Grand House, I grabbed the first opportunity to sneak myself into the twins' bedroom. The girls were not in their room, so ignoring the beating of my heart in my palms, I walked into Orlando's room. He was still sleeping, but cautiously, I pulled his cover down from his face.

"Shhhh …," I whispered, hoping he would wake up. "Orlando … wake up." He turned around and looked at me with sleepy eyes.

"Wha …?"

"I want to talk to you ...," I hurriedly stated.

"About?"

"I'm sorry about the other day ..."

"Why are you sorry?"

"'Cause that was wrong. Can I still borrow your books?" My statement made him turn completely around and sit up on the expansive bed; he looked at me with a puzzled face.

"What books?" Orlando naïvely replied. At that point I did not know if he was too asleep to understand how I was trying to be tactful in changing the subject or if he thought I was making fun of him.

"Your books ..."

"Is that *all* you care about? The books?"

No! Of course not! I care about YOU! my mind screamed with a heart thrown to pieces.

"If I don't borrow them from you ... I have no other way of reading and learning. You have taught me ... you ... and your books ..."

Orlando was astonished at my statement, his newly discovered manliness hurt to the bone.

"Oh ... pardon me; I'm too stupid. You see? For some reason I thought you cared about *me*," Orlando replied, pushing the heavy covers off his legs and turning to get off the ridiculously gigantic bed.

"I care about our friendship, you have been very nice to me, and I don't want to ruin it," I said with a smile, but secretly fighting back tears.

"*Ruin it?* You are talking about ruining it and—"

"You know what I mean," I interrupted.

"Lower your voice ... somebody might hear us," he said in a whisper, pulling me by the arm to the corner of the room.

"You see? This is what I mean. We have to hide our friendship because señoritos like you are not supposed to befriend servant girls like me," I replied.

Orlando was fighting logic to convince me of my mistake even though he knew how right I was.

"But I like you a lot, Maximiana."

Why deny it? His words flattered me immensely. "I like you, too," I said.

"I'm always thinking about you," came his quick response.

And I am always thinking about you, I answered in my mind. "I don't want to get in trouble and be fired; if people know about all this, they will kick me out and then … I will never see you again." The last phrase came in a murmur.

"And then you will not be able to borrow my books?" he ironically replied.

I faced him in silence. He stared at me but could not hold it longer and turned around. I walked out, fighting tears with all of my will. Orlando stayed, utterly confused.

I went to talk to Doña Luisa and told her I needed to go home; my monthly visit had come, and I was not ready. She saw the trembling of my lips when I pronounced the carefully chosen words and noticed that something was very wrong.

She asked, "What is going on, girl? Did somebody say something to you?"

"No," I immediately replied. "No, I just don't feel good." A tear rolled down the side of my eye. The trembling of my lips could not get under control.

Doña Luisa got my chin with her old hand and pulled it up. Then she grabbed me by the shoulder to take me to the storage room, adjacent to the kitchen, and asked in a secretive voice, "Did Señor Sarmiento try to …?"

My body was trembling.

Which Señor Sarmiento is she talking about? I asked myself in panic.

"The old one?" I replied, hesitant.

"Or any of the three young ones."

I hardly knew Alejandro and Domingo, so I shook my head, evading Doña Luisa's face.

"You have to be very careful around here with those things, Maximiana. They are not only men but they are men with power and money.

Girls like yourself are usually used for the worst reasons and end up with ruined reputations and usually with a child. Do you understand what I'm saying?"

"Yes," I replied.

"Señorito Domingo and Señorito Alejandro are not young boys anymore; they are nineteen and eighteen. Señorito Orlando is already sixteen; he is not a boy, and you are not a little girl. What is all that business of Señorito Orlando letting you borrow books? Señora Sarmiento is not so happy about it. Did you know that?"

"No."

"She's not. She doesn't want the boys mingling with the servants, but Señor Sarmiento seems to get a kick out of it, so I heard. I have been here all my life and know that man like the palm of my hand. He is probably enjoying the fact that his boy is having fun with a girl … Do you understand that?"

My breathing accelerated with the thoughts of what she was saying. But I knew that Orlando was not like that. He would never harm me. He was noble and sweet, and he cared about others. Orlando Sarmiento was my true friend. He had even said he liked me. *We are owls in the night,* I reminded myself.

"I understand," I replied respectfully. However, I did not believe it.

"Go home now."

I walked out through the back gate, passing by Orlando's bedroom. I did not look at his bedroom's windows, but I heard the piano playing on the way out. The twins, Lourdes and Isabel, were having fun in their bedroom and said good-bye to me with their five-year-old hands. I waved back and lost myself on the street again. I felt relieved of my conscience. Perhaps I had not fixed the mess totally, but at least I had clarified our relationship.

The fresh water on my skin contrasted wonderfully with the beating vapor of the sun. Often, just looking at the Arroyo de Constancia's running water relieved one of the relentless heat. That was the name for the tiny stream that ran behind El Roble. It was born at the Sacanta Mountain and ended up in the Presidio River two kilometers away.

Otilia, our younger sister Rosaura, and I were down by the *arroyo*, washing our family's scarce clothes. My body was there, but my mind wandered in my troubles. I had offered to help out with the laundry, expecting to distract myself a bit; apparently it hadn't worked so well. Rosaura was crossing the running water of the small river from side to side; her skirt was already wet, but its cool wetness felt good when the air hit.

We were working under the mango trees. Mango season was on so we planned to take some of the yellowish fruit on the ground before going home that evening. Otilia kept putting water on her neck. But it was too hot to stand the heat no matter what you did. After finishing, Otilia asked Rosaura to take the basket back home while we finished the last batch. I couldn't take it any longer and walked to the middle of the running water to sit in it. Otilia cracked up with laughter, just looking at the scene. But it felt so good that for a moment I forgot everything and went back to being the old Maximiana Valdez.

I lay on my back. The water passed through my clothes, and my long hair waved itself with the rhythm of the moving water. I closed my eyes to hear the sounds around me and feel the fresh breeze going through my body. The birds in the distance sounded so free and powerful just from the fact that they could see so much from up there. I tried to open my eyes, but the midday sun blinded me instantly with its rays. My cheeks felt hot upon touching them, and I could imagine them looking red.

I was too much into the enjoyment of my aquatic adventure to hear the horse coming toward us. I felt a shadow on my face and, laughing, threw water from my mouth to who I thought was Otilia. Shocked in my error, I saw that the shadow belonged to Orlando Sarmiento, standing next to me in the water. I impulsively sat and turned my head to look at Otilia, who had frozen into a human rock, too embarrassed to say anything. As dignified as I could, I pulled down my skirts and crossed my arms on my chest. Then I realized my hair was hanging with the dripping water, and walking toward my sister, I made a knot of it. To the astonishment of the two of us, Orlando walked out of the water, following me.

His voice finally came out with a tone that betrayed preoccupation more than arrogance. "Can we talk?" he asked, looking at me.

Otilia's eyes widened, then she lowered them in a state of confusion. He was talking in a familiar way to me, too familiar and even supplicant. The scene made no sense. I stopped and turned around; looking directly into his eyes, I replied that, yes, we could talk. My sister continued staring at us in disbelief. Even though Otilia was older than I and had all the authority to say something, she kept quiet. We all knew nobody could contradict a member of the Sarmiento family. Orlando held my hand and began walking towards the horse. I followed without hesitation or looking back.

Oh God, I do not want to look back.

Never had I felt so happy and worried than I did at that moment. We got on his horse, and I sat behind him, holding him by the waist. We galloped through the forest of mango trees until we reached the sugar cane fields that covered acres and acres of the countryside. The men working in the fields followed the cloud of dust that the horse was leaving behind. We reached a point at the edge of the Sacanta Mountain and stopped.

"We need to talk," Orlando said when we were both standing face-to-face. "I don't want you to stop coming at night. I miss your visits and our talks. And why don't you talk to me anymore?"

"I talked to you today," I answered.

"You did, but it was as if you were saying good-bye to me, as if you don't want to be close to me anymore …"

"I want to be close to you but … I don't want to get in trouble."

"You haven't had any problems until now."

"No. But after what happened the night before yesterday, if it happens again and somebody sees me … I will get in trouble because people will not understand it. Moreover, your mamá doesn't want you to be close to the servants. I don't want to lose this job."

"Leonora? She is not my mother."

That statement took me by surprise.

"What do you mean? Señora Leonora Sarmiento is not your mamá?"

"No."

"Who's your mamá?"

"She's ... gone ..."

"But ... are Señorito Alejandro, Señorito Domingo, and the twin girls your siblings?"

"The twins are my half sisters."

Intrigue filled me. Like a true Roblenian, I jumped at the chance to delve into a mystery or solve a puzzle; I could not deny my heritage, my "Roble" curiosity. I walked towards some rocks and sat down. Orlando followed and sat in front of me cross-legged. Once he did that, I went down on the dirt and did the same.

"So, where is she?"

"My mother?"

"Yes. Where is your mother?"

Orlando lowered his eyes when he said, "I was eight when she passed away."

"I didn't know that. I'm very sorry," I told him, trying to imagine his pain. "But Señora Sarmiento is very nice."

Orlando didn't answer anything to that and just looked away.

"You see, Maximiana, you are the only person I can talk to this way."

Flattered by his statement, I said, "Look, we are not going to stop being friends. I just don't want to get involved in any other way."

"Why not?" he asked.

I gave him a look of exasperation. *How can you ask that?*

"I don't care that you are a servant in the house. I love you."

The phrase flew out of his mouth and eagerly jumped into my heart like a flamed arrow.

"I love you," Orlando repeated.

Why does he love me? I should've asked myself that day. *I am not exactly the beauty of the family; my clothes are all worn out, and I have sandals on my feet.* I didn't dare reply that I loved him, too, but when he asked, "Do you love me?" I replied with the honest truth.

"Yes."

His sudden embrace astonished me, and his kiss made me fall on my back. We kissed again, and my mind blanked out completely because I didn't want to remember Doña Luisa's words that morning about what happened to girls like me in this exact situation. It felt so genuine and sincere that I believed that moment was something real and true. I trusted him again, no matter what the world said.

We lay together, watching the sunset playing its game of colors in the faraway horizon; Orlando's chest held my head while his fingers played with my hand. Slowly, we got up and went to the horse; it was time to get back to town. He left me by the arroyo and waited until I entered the narrow streets at the edge of El Roble. Then I heard the horse's steps disappear in the distance while my feet felt heavier with the idea of confronting my parents, who, by now, were aware of my whereabouts.

My papá sat in the corner of our kitchen, looking out onto the stream that could be seen from our small house. He was smoking tobacco in his wooden pipe; my mamá did not look at me. My sisters turned their faces away when I entered the tiny door.

"Nothing happened," I firmly said.

"It makes no difference." Mamá turned around and looked at me; her words conveyed tiredness with her unjust life. "To everybody in town it did; you are one of the Sarmientos' 'pastimes.'"

"No … I am not. Orlando is my friend, and he wanted to talk to me about his dead mother. That is why he came looking for me and also because today I told him that …" Realizing I was about to uncover myself in my own lies, I corrected, "Señora Sarmiento did not want him to let me borrow books anymore, and he was worried about that, and … he told me today by the cane fields that he will let me use his books no matter what and that Señora Sarmiento is not his mother …," I recited without taking a breath.

Mamá ignored my words and walked towards Papá.

"Mamá … nothing happened … I swear to God," I stated. *God forgive me, but I do not have the strength to handle this on my own.*

"It makes no difference, I said; your reputation is on the floor, child." Mamá turned around and looked at me. "In our life, if that young man manages to help you out in some way, it might be the best thing that could happen to you. But whether good or ill comes from it, your papá and I can do nothing but watch and be quiet about it."

Her words hurt me more than if they had been physical blows that left me unconscious. That was our reality: We were peasants, ignorant cane field workers who labored our backs and wasted our lives away to have the Sarmientos living in the luxury and pompous richness that they did. Those words I learned from one of *their* books. A girl like me could not expect a Sarmiento boy to take her seriously. But why, then, deep inside my heart, did I feel Orlando was real to me? Why did I trust him so much? I trusted him because I knew him well; perhaps I, alone, understood his pain. He knew that, and for that reason, he trusted me as well. Yes, the world was right in its assertion of our relationship as "unequal," but it was wrong in its denial of our love for each other as true. I had to believe that Orlando was honest with me and he would never hurt me. Never.

From that day on, Papá avoided looking me in the eye. Mamá's proud attitude faded away so as not to attract any unnecessary attention and the harmful comments that the people of El Roble did not hesitate to direct towards her. Shamefully enough, I did not care. I did not think about it because the happiness of being in love with Orlando Sarmiento and his correspondence to me made every moment of the day magical. It did not matter if the world was wrong and unjust; it was not my fault nor was I in a position to fix it. I was only a fourteen-year-old girl in love with a sixteen-year-old boy who happened to be the most perfect human being living on earth. There was no point in questioning life's destiny, and neither had I the desire to do it.

Suspicious looks fell on my shoulders every time I walked in town. More harmful were the looks of the other workers at the Grand House. My trip to the cane fields with Orlando was of general public knowledge by now. However, oddly enough, Señora and Señor Sarmiento knew nothing about it. Apparently Orlando worked the situation of the book borrowing in a way that kept their suspicions at bay. Orlando and I still managed to exchange secret hugs and pinches when nobody was around us, and fortunately enough, I was able to continue reading his books. My visits to his balcony became more sporadic because I was afraid of going "too far" with him. *That,* I knew well, should not happen.

At night I read his letters over and over again. They were so beautiful that I learned to memorize the expressions I found dearest to my naïve heart. I remember my favorite one:

Dearest Maximiana of mine,

> *You are my girl that I love. You are mine. Forever. Nothing will ever keep us apart. I promise that I will always love you and take care of you, no matter what happens. You will always be mine.*

> *Yours forever,*
> *Orlando*

I remember reading the note and placing it on my chest with a sigh. My sisters had become accustomed to watching me reading those pages, papers with scribbles that meant nothing to them because they could simply not read them. They felt suspicious of Orlando, just as everybody else did. But I did not; I knew that we would be together forever, just as he said and declared in his notes to me.

Those days were filled with happiness and hopes. The world became a perfect place where nothing was out of place, not even my tired legs on the way back home after a hard day of work at the Grand House. I lived for the moments when Orlando would stand at a safe distance to look at me. And I just melted in my own feelings when he got closer and his brown eyes directly told me, without saying it, that he loved me.

Unforgettable, also, were the hours we spent in the balcony room, his head resting on my shoulder talking about things that meant so much to him.

"Mother was pretty," he said one day.

"How was she? Tell me …"

"Domingo looks a lot like her … big eyes, dark and tall … that is what I remember the most."

"She died young … right?" I asked, and he nodded.

"She killed herself," Orlando replied, turning his face towards me.

I had not expected that. Shocked, I kept silent.

"Alejandro found her in this room. That is why nobody else wants to sleep here but me. I am not afraid of Mother."

I had no words to offer, and I timidly looked around.

"She was good," he continued, "but I guess we were not too important for her if she left us like that, right?"

"But … why did she do it? Something must have happened for her to do it …," I tactfully declared.

"Nobody has ever explained that to us. I was eight when it happened, and I barely remember anything. Alejandro says that Father locked her in this room, and we were not allowed to see her. Domingo used to climb the balcony, and he would help me up to see her through the glass. When Father discovered that, he ordered Emilio to shut the windows with wood panels. Alejandro remembers hearing her cry. He would lie by the corridor's door to talk to her. But when Father was told, Alejandro was punished …"

Orlando did not blink when he narrated his sad story. I rested my head on his shoulder. It hurt my soul to listen to him.

"One day when Doña Luisa brought her food, she went out screaming for help. Alejandro ran in here, and that is when he found her on this bed. Mother used a broken glass to cut her wrists."

"How old was Alejandro?" I asked in a whisper.

"He was ten …"

He rested his head on mine again and in a low voice said to my ear the phrase that I cherished the most, "I love you."

I was intrigued by the death of Orlando's mother. The whole story was too horrific to even think about it. I wanted to know *why* Señor Sarmiento had put her in that locked room. Something terribly wrong must have happened for a woman to have been placed in such torture. She was young and had three little children. Orlando also said they were not allowed to see his maternal grandparents. My poor Orlando, how much he must have suffered because of that. And Alejandro, finding his mother in such a condition. I could picture Domingo climbing the balcony trying to reach his mother.

So many things happen in people's lives, and you are not aware of them, I thought. Who would have imagined such a tragic story lay hidden in the elegant walls of the Grand House? Those boys had everything, but they did not have their mother, and they had seen her suffer in such a horrible way. Tragedy seemed to get to everybody, sooner or later, I realized that day.

I felt I moved in a dream. Despite the hardness and discomfort of the outside seat of the carriage, just knowing my destination made it seem better than it actually was.

"Have you been to the port before?" I asked Raimunda. "The port" was the name people gave to the city of Mazatlán, twenty-six kilometers northwest of El Roble.

"Yes, I've been to the port twice," she answered, uninterested and looking the other way.

"How is it?" I asked enthusiastically.

"Noisy," she said, "and big."

I realized how unhappy Raimunda was to be in that carriage traveling towards Mazatlán. She was as discontented as Daniel felt when I told him Señora Sarmiento had chosen me to come to the city with them to help out with the twins. The girls liked me to read to them their beautiful books. I enjoyed those stories as much as they did, and to be honest, I liked Isabel and Lourdes as well. They were two sweet little girls, not contaminated yet by the social strains that would later separate my humanity from theirs.

We were going to stay in the port for two months before returning to El Roble in September. My parents quietly agreed to the trip, not that they had an option to say anything that went contrary to the Sarmientos' decision of taking me as their twins' nanny.

"I'm afraid for you, Maximiana," Daniel had told me. "I'm afraid you won't come back."

"Of course, I am coming back! It is only for two months, and besides, the twins are coming back to the Grand House in September. Who would I stay with in Mazatlán?" I asked Daniel, giggling.

He looked away from me, as he had been doing since my reputation had begun to fade away in the tongues of Roblenians. Daniel knew me well; he knew the talk consisted only of gossip, without basis, but still, those rumors seemed to haunt him.

"He may harm you," Daniel replied without saying Orlando's name.

"No, he won't," I reassured him.

Every human being on earth was sure of that specific fact. But I did not believe it. Orlando would never hurt me. He was noble, good hearted, and honest. I could trust him like no one else in the world.

However, I said to myself, *only he and I know that.*

My thoughts continued while the four horses pulling the carriage left behind the only physical world I had ever known. The Grand House could be seen in the distance like a nobleman's castle surrounded by its miserable shacks. The cane fields extended for so vast a distance that their expanse consumed all that my eyes could take in. The fields looked green and even, with the wind carving itself on the thin, velvety leaves. Raimunda and I sat with the drivers; I liked that better than sitting inside with Señora Sarmiento, her husband, and the girls. Besides, from outside I was able to enjoy the view of Orlando riding his horse. We were a group of three carriages, several mules, and many more riders.

When traveling to Mazatlán, the Sarmientos had to organize a party of several people, not only for their service but for security. It was a long trip to the port; people had to leave early morning in order to arrive by nightfall. The most dangerous part of the trip was getting the carriages across the Presidio River. People had to place them on wooden rafts pulled by ropes on each side of the river. I did not look forward to the experience of crossing it but had no choice.

By ten in the morning, we had reached the town of Villa Unión. I felt amazed to see a town different from mine. Villa Unión was bigger than El Roble; it was nestled next to the river. In the distance I could hear the sounds of the Presidio River in its forceful run towards the sea. The sea! In Mazatlán I was going to see the sea. Once, I had seen pictures of the beach in one of Orlando's books. He said seawater tasted salty.

My thoughts were interrupted by the sudden screams of "Stop!" and "Get off!" coming from the trip leaders. It was time to walk towards the river. They stood there for a while, discussing if we should cross it or not. Apparently several days of rain at the Sierra Madre Mountains had made the current stronger than usual.

I was secretly terrified of the idea of crossing. Discreetly I searched for Orlando's eyes; he painted a fainting smile on the corner of his lips that reassured me that everything was fine. Alejandro and Domingo rode towards the river, and Señor Sarmiento followed them. Alejandro was ready to go in, but his father stopped him with a scream.

"Where do you think you are going?"

Alejandro fiercely looked back at him.

"I'm not going back to El Roble."

"So you'd rather kill yourself? Are you an idiot?" Señor Sarmiento stated arrogantly. Alejandro looked at those present and gave everyone a cynical smile. He looked away from his father and entered the Presidio River, followed by Domingo. My heart sank, thinking that Orlando would follow them. My eyes looked for his, but he ignored me.

Look at me, Orlando! Please, look at me! Don't do it!

Domingo did not look back, nor did Alejandro. A tense air invaded those watching them cross the ferocious river. The current carried them down, but the horses fought back. Orlando stood there, watching his brothers without looking at his father. Señor Sarmiento barely controlled his anger at their defiance while Leonora Sarmiento exited the carriage to see the fate of her stepchildren; she seemed truly mortified.

They did it. They crossed the river and continued riding without looking back at the party that had expected the worst, left standing on the other side. Orlando's face tightened. He passed by my side but did not cross in front of me. His jaw looked tense, and his usual cheerless eyes, full of fury. My selfishness did not care about his pride; I just wanted him safe and sound on land.

After long deliberations, the guides decided it was safer to cross by the northern side of the river. We got in the canoes and started moving forward even though the current kept us going to the side. Once we touched land, a feeling of relief allowed me to breathe again. On the shore, we waited for the heavy carriages, riding on rafts that bounced dangerously back and forth. They, too, made the crossing safely, and we continued with the journey.

By midday, the sun's blistering heat attacked us with no mercy. I wore a straw hat, but my arms already showed purple from the exposure. It was summer, the worst possible time of the year to sit under its cruel rays. The wooden seat now really bothered me, and after several hours sitting there, the view did not interest me as before and failed to relieve the discomfort.

The water we carried for the trip had turned warm and void of its potential to satisfy thirst. I took a sip from the container anyway, but it felt as hot as the saliva in my mouth.

It made me uncomfortable to see the men carrying rifles and long guns. But, rumors of war circulated, some war that might liberate peasants from the *hacendados*. I had heard Papá talk secretly about this with Mamá; he had said a revolution was coming and the lands would be distributed to all poor people in México. It would take away the Grand Houses, or haciendas, and the hacendados would have to do some work themselves. As much as I understood the unfairness in which we lived and the need for change, I did not believe that would ever happen; I felt those were dreams people had to have in their hearts in order to survive their misery.

Evening had fallen upon us when we finally distinguished, in the distance, the faint illuminations that came from Mazatlán. I wanted to hear the sounds of the Pacific Ocean, but it was impossible even to see it. It had been a lonesome journey. Raimunda did not talk to me at all, and her posture showed her ill feelings. The other men on the trip kept quiet and looked around as if they feared being hunted by unseen eyes surrounding us. Orlando continued riding with the guides at front; he rarely looked back at my direction, but I understood his reasons. Poor Isabel and Lourdes, after several hours, began to whine about everything and wanted to ride outside with me, but their mother would not allow it. She said the sun would burn their beautiful light-colored bodies. They—the wealthy—wore their money on their skin; the lightness indicated they had the luxury to remain indoors, out of the sun, away from any outdoor labor. I had begun the trip with somewhat light skin … I erased those useless thoughts from my mind and concentrated on seeing as much as I could of the port of Mazatlán.

As we approached the town's streets, the bustle of the city became more obvious. People peeked through their doors and windows to see the procession as it entered Mazatlán. Movement and noises that I never experienced before surrounded me. Excitement filled me to see it all, and I wished only that it were daylight to enjoy it better.

"Look, Raimunda! We are almost here!" I exclaimed enthusiastically. Raimunda turned her face at me, and for the first time, I took notice that she was fighting tears.

She must miss her family, I thought.

"Don't cry … we will be back in El Roble soon …," I told her putting my arm around her arched back.

"It's not that," she replied.

"What it is then?" I asked in a smooth voice.

"I can't even talk about it."

"Yes, you can … tell me. Why are you crying?"

"Hush, Maximiana … somebody will hear us. Just hush."

I was a talkative parrot, yes, but I knew when I had to keep quiet. I grabbed her sweaty little hand and put it on my lap. Raimunda was pleased by it because, even though tears had reached her skinny neck, she made a struggling effort to smile at me. From that moment on, Raimunda and I started a friendship that would last a lifetime.

It was almost eleven at night when we reached the Sarmiento house in the port. I helped Señora Sarmiento carry Lourdes up to her room, and Raimunda took Isabel. The stairs inside were huge; I was out of breath by the time I reached the second floor. Señora Sarmiento was in a hurry to put them down and take a rest herself so she sent us down to our quarters right away.

My body felt in heaven when I lay on my back. Raimunda interrupted my idyllic moment by saying we had to help unload the carriages.

"You have got to be joking!" The expression came straight from my about-to-stop-beating tired heart.

"Do I look like I'm joking? Let's go," Raimunda replied.

I followed Raimunda, to my dismay, but Sebastián, the man in charge of the servants at the house, returned us to our room because he felt our help was not necessary. He even directed us with a lighted candle.

That was very nice of him.

Raimunda locked the door and went straight to her bed. I hesitated, wondering what to do about my sleeping garments, still in one of the carriages, and asked, "Raimunda, wha—?"

But she cut me off. "Sleep in your clothes, Maximiana. For God's sake, just go to sleep and let me sleep; I am too tired to think."

"But I'm thirsty."

"Why didn't you grab water when we crossed the kitchen? I really don't want to get up and go with you to get water," she scolded.

"I can go myself," I replied, very secure in my words. "I am not afraid of anything."

Without my sandals, I firmly stepped out of our room and walked into the kitchen. The water was fresh and felt good going down my throat. I heard movement outside as servants continued unloading the carriages and the mules. I couldn't resist my curiosity to look outside the street windows. The house across the street was as huge as the

Sarmiento's city house, even prettier. Inside, I moved to the next room. Paintings hung from all the walls, but the darkness kept me from distinguishing any of their fine details. I was dying to open one of the four doors surrounding that room; I bit my lip to restrain myself. But I couldn't. My feet took me straight to one of the doors, and slowly, I opened it. The door made a squeaking sound that almost sent me to the cemetery.

"Who's there?"

I recognized the deep voice of Alejandro Sarmiento, and I turned into an iron bench. Firm footsteps came towards the door. A hand pulled it open, and Alejandro stood before me in the doorway.

He recognized me and said, "Orlando's room is upstairs."

I do not know how many liters of blood the human body holds, but I honestly felt half of it jump to my head.

"I am not looking for Orlando."

He gasped, shocked at my answer.

"No? Who are you looking for then?"

"No one," I said as articulately as my nervousness allowed. "I was looking for water and saw this room, but since I am a little bit nosy, I came to see where this door would take me and …"

Alejandro laughed.

"You are honest, too," he said, "and, yes, you *are* nosy," he added with amusement

"I know," I replied in truth, but unsure whether he meant to compliment or chastise me.

"Did you get your water?"

"Oh, yes, I did … that was the first thing I got."

"Well, you are lucky you did not open that one," he pointed to the door on the opposite wall, "because that is one room *no one* wants to enter at night."

As an honest, nosy, young girl, I *had* to ask, "Why?"

"Because strange noises come from it, a woman crying for help …" He came closer to my face. "It is the ghost of a lost soul who was killed in that very room."

"I don't believe those stories are real," I answered, looking straight at his shadowed figure.

My statement obviously took him aback.

"No? Why don't you go and open it then?" he challenged me.

"I will," I replied bravely.

By this point, Alejandro was having the fun of his night. He stepped out of the room, but then he turned back and said, "Hold on; let me light a lamp."

I remained, staring at the door to the "haunted room," knowing that it was not true. I had grown up listening to ghost stories about apparitions at night of lost souls, even apparitions directing people to a "blaze coming from the earth" that guided them to pots filled with gold. But everything in my mind told me those stories were impossible. I obeyed my masters and the older servants, but my mind constantly questioned things that made no sense.

"Go ahead," Alejandro said, lamp in hand. I pointed my face up and moved forward, directly to the door. Heart pounding but outer body simulating serenity, I moved the doorknob to open the infamous "haunted door." Alejandro followed me, tiptoeing.

"Why are you walking like that?" I asked.

"Shhhh …"

I had no time to react as he pushed me inside and locked the door behind me. I did not scream, don't ask how I did it, but I held my horror inside and covered my eyes. Somebody was obviously in the room with me because I could hear him or her or … it … getting off … a bed? I slid down to the floor in hopes that no one would see me when I felt the "presence's" steps walking towards me. I had my nose touching the cold floor, and on the other side of the door I could hear Alejandro's muffled laughing. The "presence" tripped over my body, fell forward, and smashed into the door. Its knees went directly to my back, and a scream of pain came out of my throat. At this point, the "presence" and I could hear laughter on the other side of the door.

"What on earth!" the "presence" screamed.

Alejandro opened the door and placed the oil lamp down to allow his whole body to crack up at our expense. The "presence" and I gave quite a sight. I lay flattened on the floor with Domingo Sarmiento's legs on my back, and he hunched over me, holding his head in his hands. Slowly he got up, not amused at all. And I, feeling embarrassed, sat up on the floor and looked fiercely at Alejandro. He offered his hand in a token—and weak—apology and pulled me up to my feet.

Alejandro finally asked, "Do you believe me now?"

I started laughing because I had to admit, "You got me good."

"I know," he said, and he winked.

"What are you doing?" Domingo asked.

Alejandro related the tale of my night adventure, but a subtlety in his description caught my attention: He mentioned me by my name rather than by "the servant girl."

"Wait here. Don't go anywhere, Maximiana," Alejandro said while walking towards the kitchen.

"I won't move ... don't worry ... I am half paralyzed after Domingo's falling on my back," I replied.

Both of them laughed even though I had called Domingo by his first name. My boldness in addressing them matched Alejandro's toward me, and no one seemed to mind. Alejandro came back with a pitcher of water and three glasses. It felt so good to drink from a glass. He put the oil lamp on the floor and asked me to sit with them. They were obviously not sleepy after the prank Alejandro had played on me.

"So Maximiana was looking for water ...," Alejandro said suspiciously, trying to pinch my proud side.

"I was ... I told you already."

Alejandro looked at Domingo, and by the exchange of their looks, I knew exactly what they had on their minds.

"Believe it or not ... I was looking for water."

"I think you were looking for Orlando," Alejandro said, moving his eyebrows up and down. Domingo smiled.

"Why would I be looking for him?" I asked.

"Oh I don't know ... to ... read?" Alejandro said with a funny sarcasm.

Both of them exploded with laughter.

I put my hair behind my ears, and carefully thinking of a comeback, I said, "Do you want to hear a *real* ghost story?"

"Sure, go ahead," Alejandro said.

"Well, not long ago, the people of El Roble did not want to leave their houses at night because the soul of a woman in white was flying around town. People locked their doors and windows early because, if they did not do it, the woman in white might go inside their houses and … harm them."

Domingo's smile had disappeared; he probably thought I was as crazy as a goat. But Alejandro jovially listened to my story.

"So what happened?" Alejandro asked.

"My Uncle Nieves, who is very brave and was not afraid to go out at night, was coming back from a hunting trip. He heard the woman's screams right next to the cemetery …"

Their attention concentrated on my words.

"So was he really your uncle?" Domingo asked.

"Yes," I replied, "And then, the woman stood in front of him, waving her arms like a butterfly, the white cloth flying on the sides …"

"Could he see her face?" Alejandro asked.

"No, she wore a veil … so my Uncle Nieves said, 'STOP in the name of GOD!' but the woman continued waving her butterfly arms."

"She had butterfly wings?" Domingo asked, intrigued.

"No … I mean that she moved her arms *as if* they were wings."

"Oh, I see," Domingo replied.

Alejandro was seriously paying attention to my story. I continued my narration.

"My uncle Nieves told her again, 'STOP in the name of GOD or I will shoot you!' because he had his gun with him, ready to fire."

"I bet she didn't stop," Alejandro said.

"Shhhhhh," Domingo quieted him.

"The woman in white raised her arms one more time and got closer to my Uncle Nieves … and he shot his gun, aiming right at her head. BANG!"

Wide-eyed, Domingo and Alejandro looked shocked.

"The bullet went straight to her forehead … right between her eyes."

I kept quiet for a minute to allow them to imagine the whole scene, and then I said, "My Uncle Nieves ran to her side when he saw her fall to the ground floor on her back."

"She fell down?" Domingo asked.

Alejandro gave him a look.

"Then he cried out, 'Ihhh! Oh my God! Amelia! It is you!'"

"Who is Amelia?" both of them asked simultaneously.

"Nobody ... because none of this is true," I laughed and added, "I got *you* this time."

Alejandro looked at me and began to laugh, too, but Domingo held back, showing only a weak smile at the joke. However, they had to admit that I had gotten them good.

"Good night," I said as I stood up.

"Good night," Alejandro replied, still laughing. Domingo kept quiet and walked into his room. Alejandro walked with me to the kitchen, using the oil lamp to give me some light and waited until I entered the servant quarters. He silently said good-bye with a wave of his hand.

Hmm, I thought, *maybe they're not as stuck up as I had assumed.* I was glad; after all, my hopeful heart placed those two as my future brothers-in-law.

I entered the room carefully so I wouldn't wake Raimunda up, but I heard movement coming from her bed. In the dim light I could see she was sitting, curled up into a little crying human ball.

"What's wrong?" I asked with dismay as I ran to her.

"I-I-I can't tell you," she answered between sobs.

I hugged her, placed her head on my lap and passed my fingers through her hair, trying to calm her down.

"Why can't you tell me?" I asked.

"I just ... I just can't," she replied, drowning in her own tears. "But, if you hear someone coming, *please* hide quickly under your bed."

"What do you mean 'someone'? Who's going to come?"

"Don't ask. Just promise me that you will go under your bed when you hear someone coming and don't make any noise."

I answered that I would do that. More than intrigued, I felt heart-broken because I began to grasp the tragedy of the situation. At this instant, I wished to be safely at home. This was the first time away from my family. Now that it was past midnight, I started to sense the melancholy of being so far from my own house. I underwent an excruciating need to be close to Mamá.

Am I in danger? I asked myself. *Who am I supposed to tell if something goes wrong?*

It was a strange thought. I became aware of the fact that there wasn't much Orlando could do for me, and I began questioning how willingly he would defend me if something went wrong. Loneliness invaded my soul. I missed home, and my house seemed a world away.

5

Every morning, Señora Leonora Sarmiento liked to walk to the beach and take the twins with her. It was a blessing for me to be in charge of the little girls because I was able to leave the house, its chores, and the imprisonment of being a servant girl and experience the freedom of the beautiful Pacific Ocean. The two five-year-olds were always full of energy and enjoyed playing with the sand. Those were endless hours of fun for me because I liked it as much as they did. I held their hands, facing the rolling waters, and ran backwards every time the waves got closer. We played, stepping on the wet sand to see the water move away from the footprints. I always ended up completely wet, up to my waist, and tired from laughing so much.

Sometimes, I was lucky enough to be left alone because Señora Sarmiento would take the girls for a walk on her own. I would look for a shadow and take the weight off my feet and just stare at the waves and breathe the delicious salty air. It gave me the luxury of daydreaming with a gorgeous view.

Working in the city house was different from the Grand House in El Roble. We had, always, a little less work to do. And at night, I usually found enough time to read and relax a little bit. I was enjoying the book *Don Quixote de la Mancha*, and when I would read some funny parts to Raimunda, we would laugh together like a couple of little girls.

Orlando and I talked sometimes when nobody was around. Domingo would never even look at me, but Alejandro would always greet me, no matter who was around. Alejandro had a smile on his face all the time whenever he saw me; it was as if he never forgot the night of the "presence." Orlando pressured me to come to his room at night, but I never did. It was too risky, not only because someone might see us, but also because we might do something one of us would later regret.

Weeks passed by and a lot of people visited to have afternoon *tertulias* with the Sarmientos. The women dressed in ways that I had seen before only on Señora Leonora. Their hats looked too heavily ornamented to carry on their own heads. I kept asking myself what they did to keep them up there without falling. And their stomachs seemed unnaturally small in their tightly-waisted dresses. Even more perplexing was how in the world they breathed.

The young ladies seemed to be extremely attracted to Domingo, and he was well aware of it. Alejandro, on the other hand, showed no interest whatsoever in any of them. The younger girls giggled and exchanged looks amongst each other, looking at Orlando. He always behaved politely and engaged in sociable conversation, as I knew he had to. But, what bothered me was that he never acknowledged my presence when there were other people around. However, I justified his attitude as a preventive measure to avoid a bigger disaster. Despite his ignoring me in the company of "his" people, I deeply appreciated the fact that he continued bringing me books to read. Every time I finished one, he had another one ready for my hands. I knew that meant he often thought of me.

"Why don't you come up tonight?" Orlando asked me in a whisper when we were in the kitchen.

"I don't want to get caught. I told you already."

Other conversation in the room died, and the women in the kitchen started to get closer to hear what we were saying. Orlando grabbed my arm and led me to the backyard. A gigantic tree grew in the middle, and we walked to stand under its shadow.

"I'm getting tired of this. How am I going to see you if you don't come up to my room?" he said in an irritated voice. "It is not as if we haven't seen each other in a bedroom before."

I looked around to see if anyone had heard his demands.

"Why don't *you* come to *my* room? We can walk to the living room and talk there at night. Or in the kitchen," I said.

"I am not going to your room."

"Why not?" I asked, perplexed.

"It's the servants' quarters."

His answer left me puzzled.

"I didn't think that was a problem. After all, I have been going to *your* room for many months. But now you will not come to mine because it's the *servants' quarters?*"

Nervously, he replied, "You do not sleep alone. The other service girls might hear me come in."

Service girls? I thought. *Am I a service girl to him? And is that all I am to him?* But he had a point about Raimunda in the room with me. "Can't we meet somewhere else outside the house?"

"Where?" he asked me as if I should have any ideas.

"This is the first time I'm here. I don't know. The only place I know how to get to is the beach."

"Do you want us to meet by the beach? But, I cannot walk with you. I'll meet you there," he replied.

I looked at him trying to hide the pain that I felt from his words.

"It is not that I don't want to walk with you. It's just that if somebody sees us the gossip will spread very badly. And then they will send you back to El Roble before the end of the summer."

Yes, he was right. I felt relieved and asked, "Tonight then?"

"Yes. Meet me by the rocks."

"What time?"

"When all the lights are off. I will get out first and leave the door open for you. No wait! I have to tell Facundo about it, or he will not let you out."

My heart sank thinking that Facundo, the doorkeeper, was going to be aware of my escapades with Orlando. But then I didn't care; I truly felt that it was worth it. My goodness, yes. The idea of listening to the sound of those waves while resting in Orlando's arms made my stomach feel like a hurricane of flying owls at night.

Then Orlando did something that I was not expecting: He grabbed my face with his hands and planted a kiss on my lips, without caring that somebody might have been watching us, and turned and walked away. I turned my face down first, gathered the strength to raise it again, and then looked for witnesses. The spectators were there, unfortunately, crowding the windows with their jealous eyes. I walked to the pail of water, washed my face, dried myself with the bottom of my skirt, and went back to work as if nothing had happened.

I went through the rest of the day counting the seconds until the night would arrive to be with Orlando, the two of us alone again.

The sky was unusually dark, but I bravely followed the sound of the sea. A couple of men stood talking in a corner and made rude and disrespectful noises at me as I passed. But I continued my journey without looking to the sides. My steps had accelerated to the point where I found myself running until the breeze coming from the beach gently played with my hair. Carefully, I walked to the big dark rocks that the night waves hit mercilessly in the rising tide. Then a head full of soft curls rose above a dark figure. Orlando embraced me tightly for several seconds without any intention of letting me go. His chest felt warm against my body, his young arms stronger than mine. I buried my face on his torso, intensely smelling the sweet scent of his clothes, wishing to be lifted into the air by an invisible force that would raise us both, in that embrace, to the blinking stars above. I turned my eyes to his, asking without words, my desire to be kissed by his gentle lips.

"I miss you," he said in a hurtful voice, "I miss you very much."

"Oh, I miss you too, Orlando. I wish we could always be together," I replied, overwhelmed by feelings of trustful love.

"You are mine forever," he said in a whisper.

"I know," I replied, full of bliss. I was his forever; I had no doubt in my mind about it. My heart, mind, soul, body … all that I was belonged to Orlando Sarmiento.

"I have to tell you something about September," he said, finally breaking the silence.

"What?" I asked, intrigued.

"I am not going back to El Roble. I have to stay in Mazatlán and attend classes at the German School."

My heart shattered at the idea of separation from him.

"By yourself?" I asked, trying to suppress my pain.

"Domingo is staying, too. Alejandro is going back to help father in El Roble. So …"

"When are you going back to El Roble?"

"For Christmas."

Four months. Four months without seeing my Orlando. It was too much to bear.

"I have something for you." He pulled out of his pocket a seashell bracelet and put it in the palm of my hand. "So you will not forget me," he said sadly, smiling.

I wished his eyes would tell me more, but they did not. He had a mysterious and intriguing way of looking at you; his eyes would meet yours, but he kept hidden the deeper thoughts of his mind and the true feelings of his heart. He seemed to lack a connection between his eyes, his heart, and his mind. I could read his books, but I could not read Orlando, and that frustrated me profoundly.

"Let your hair down … I like your long hair."

Flattered, I untied my long braids. The wind made it fly. We both laughed about it. I passed my shy fingers through his brown curls; he closed his eyes at my caressing. Then Orlando asked me to sit on the sand, and as we walked away from the rocks, we held hands. The ocean, fresh and sharp against my skin, reached our feet. We sat away from the water, as far away as possible, but the tide kept coming at us.

"I have always wanted to hug you," he said, avoiding my face.

"You *have* hugged me," I replied, giggling.

"No, I mean … *really* hug you."

His words confused me. Nevertheless, I grabbed his arm and placed it gently around my shoulders. He continued facing the sea. Smiling, I looked for his eyes.

"Orlando … you *are* hugging me."

"Not like this," he replied sharply.

"How then?" I asked, still naïve about his meaning.

He turned around. One of his hands grasped my head and gently rested it on the soft sand while the other touched the side of my face. Then he placed his body over mine. I could feel the pulsation of my heart in my neck. Terror invaded me.

God … no.

"I love you," he murmured in my ear.

I closed my eyes and felt tears rolling down. I did not want this. I did not want it *like this.*

"I love you," he said again. He started kissing my cheeks, my nose, my chin, and my neck with a soft impetus. Images of the young ladies who constantly visited his house marched through my mind. I could not picture him treating any of those fine women in this way. I did not want this.

NO. Not like this.

"No …"

"W-what?"

"No. I do not want to do this," I said, shaking inside, with a proud voice.

"You don't want me to love you?"

"No … not … like … this … no." My words came out in broken pieces.

"Like what?"

"Sneaking … lying … on a beach …" I couldn't imagine a more perfect place, but that was not my point.

"Nobody is watching us."

"That is not the problem."

"What is the problem then?" His voice sounded irritated.

"The problem is what is going to happen tomorrow."

"Nothing … you will love me, and I will love you the same."

"Nobody knows that."

"Exactly," he said.

"Have you told somebody about us?"

"I can not tell Father."

"What about your friends?"

"Men don't talk about these things."

He retracted his body and moved away from me.

"Are you mad?" I asked, feeling disoriented.

"Go back to the house," he said and got up, shaking off the sand from his pants.

"But why are you mad? I do not want to do this … this way," I broke down. "We are not even … we are not even married!"

Flustered he turned his angry eyes at me. "Married? Are you crazy? We are what—sixteen?"

"You are sixteen; I am only fourteen."

"It's going to be years before I could ever get married. Besides, people do it all the time without being married," he stated with audacity.

"Really? Who?" Composure had returned to my mind.

"People like … who love each other."

"Or people who are just … people who have no other options?"

Orlando did not like my statement at all.

"So you think that you have no options? Am I forcing you? Am I forcing myself onto you?" He spat out each question with angry agitation.

"You are pressuring me," I said, my composure melting under his anger.

His annoyance grew stronger.

"You know what? Just go back to the house and leave me alone. GO!" He pointed his finger at the street. I looked around for my miserable sandals, and shedding tears, I walked away from him. I felt that I couldn't breathe. I bit my lip and went back to him. I tried to talk to Orlando again, but he pointed his arrogant finger at the air, ordering me to get away from him.

*What have I done? Did I make a mistake? Who am I after all …
just a peasant girl whose favors are solicited by the patron's son? Why
do I turn him away? Even Mamá said this could be the only good thing
that would ever happen to me. He does love me. I can feel it. He does.*
I debated with myself as I headed back to the house, and then I ran
back to the beach, but Orlando was already gone.

Wait a minute.

I stopped.

*What am I doing? I am Maximiana Valdez, and nobody owns my
body or my soul. If Orlando Sarmiento does not value who I am, then
he is not worthy of my affection.*

I took a deep breath and marched towards the ridiculously
immense, mango-colored house as fast as I could.

Nonetheless, once in my soft bed, a circle of salty water formed
on my pillow from the sorrow that had invaded my fourteen-year-old
heart, and only tears seemed to help wash it away.

I thought I was strong. However, nothing prepared me for what
came next.

The Sarmiento boys constantly organized evening gatherings with
their city friends. I never minded serving them; I even enjoyed listening to their conversations and secretly laughed at their silly jokes. The
young ladies usually sat in a separate parlor; they had been nice to me
more or less. I had no complaints as did the other servant girls in the
house that protested their rudeness.

At the next evening's event, I walked into the girls' parlor with
a pitcher of lemonade and glasses, placed them on the table, and
returned to the kitchen to get the pastries Señora Sarmiento had
ordered that morning. As I held the tray in my hands, I sensed somebody observing me. I looked in the other parlor and saw Orlando and
Domingo talking to each other. Domingo was looking at me, laughing. Orlando was not amused. I quickly looked away and entered the
girls' parlor room.

"Take a tray of pastries to the boys," Leonora Sarmiento said, "and
tell Raimunda to check on the twins." I nodded and rapidly moved

away. Without entering, I looked in the direction of the boys' parlor. Two of the young men turned their faces to me, laughing.

Please, God, don't let it be what I'm thinking.

I asked Josefina, another girl, if she could take the tray for me and pass Señora Leonora's order to Raimunda. To my good luck, she agreed. I sat on the kitchen table, waiting for more orders.

"Señorito Domingo wants you," Josefina stated at her return.

Earth devour me at this instant, please.

"What does he need?" I replied.

"I don't know, he just told me to tell you to go to him."

I threw my head back and closed my eyes. Sighing, I got up, all eyes in the kitchen on me. I took a deep breath before entering the parlor.

"Your order, Señorito?" I said, looking Domingo directly in his face.

"Well, nothing … it is just that my friends want to meet you," he said with a burlesque smile.

I did not turn around but rather stood there, looking at Domingo Sarmiento's perfectly beautiful face. I tried not to show any signs of distress, even though my insides were boiling in agony.

"How do you do?" one of them said.

"How do you do?" I responded in a clear voice.

"My name is Gustavo Inzunza."

"Maximiana Valdez," I answered and turned my face back to Domingo. He was becoming uncomfortable with my direct staring.

"We wanted to see how nice you are. Orlando says you are intelligent and like to read," another one named Teodoro de la Vega said with certain sympathy. But I could not mistake the joking tone of voice of the others.

"Thank you," I replied and looked back at Domingo, again. He turned his face away. "Anything else, Señorito?" I asked.

"Don't go yet, precious," the one named Gustavo declared while walking towards me. I did not move. He grabbed my arm and took me to a seat. I glanced at Orlando, who was standing next to the piano with a fake smile and mortified eyes.

"I don't think I should sit here, Señorito," I said, getting up from the mint-colored chair. "Anything else, Señorito?" I repeated to Domingo.

"Well, I don't know … anything else Orlando?" Domingo asked, mocking me. Everyone in the room exploded in laughter with the exception of Teodoro de la Vega. Then Alejandro walked in.

"Good evening, everyone. Hello, Maximiana," he greeted me as usual. Fighting tears, I responded:

"Hello, Señorito."

"'Alejandro,' please. Don't call me 'Señorito.'" He looked around and detected the undercurrents of the scene before him. He looked at Orlando, and then he looked at me and came towards the miserable space where I stood in my embarrassment.

"What is going on?" he asked me.

"Nothing," Domingo answered. "The guys wanted to meet *her*." He winked. But Alejandro's face tightened.

"Maximiana, you may go … please," Alejandro told me. The laughter in the room stopped. I walked out with my chin up, but inside, I dragged my spirit on the floor. I went straight to the backyard and walked away from the house. I walked and walked without thinking, trying to reach a place as far away as possible from that scene now engraved in my mind.

As the night approached, I had no remedy but to go back. I was glad some compassion remained for me in that kitchen. Nobody asked anything, and Raimunda greeted me with a warm touch on my arm. She was not very expressive, so it meant a lot to me.

"I will do your night chores. Why don't you go to bed now?" she said.

"It is fine, Raimunda; I can do it. Thank you, though," I responded, feeling grateful for her unselfish offer.

I was washing the gigantic dishes and pots when a sudden silence fell in the kitchen. I froze to death.

"Are you fine?" Alejandro asked behind me.

"Yes, thank you."

"Come with me. I want to talk to you."

I followed in silence, looking at his back.

"Sit, please," he said with a warm smile after arriving in the small living room next to the kitchen.

"Where?"

"On the sofa."

Timidly I sat, putting my hands on my lap but keeping my back very straight.

"I am very sorry for what you went through this afternoon."

Am I hearing right? Alejandro Sarmiento is apologizing to me?

"Thank you, Señorito."

"Call me 'Alejandro,' please. I told you before; I don't like people calling me 'Señorito.'"

"Why not?" As usual, I could not contain my questions.

"All people should be called by their names, not by titles that mark imaginary differences."

"The differences are not imaginary," I replied. He was taken aback.

"Do you really believe that? Because I don't ..."

"I don't know how to explain it."

"Try," he said, genuinely interested in my words.

"Well, I think we are all exactly the same … human beings … but some are born in positions or get in positions where those titles mark them as 'different.'"

"Better?"

"NO, not *better* but different." I regretted my words, but it was too late to reverse them.

"Do you think 'different' is good?"

"It depends."

"I agree," he said and smiled at me. "You like to read, right?"

"I do; I do love to read. All my life I wanted to learn, and when Orl … your brother let me borrow those books in order for me to learn, I was very happy. Ever since I learned, I can not stop reading; it is wonderful to read," I said cheerfully, completely forgetting my afternoon troubles. "It helps me live a world that I am not in, and I see things that I never imagined existed."

"What are you reading right now?"

"I am reading *Don Quixote de la Mancha*. It is so funny, oh my God! I like Sancho Panza; he is very sweet and naïve."

"Do you understand it? Because it is hard to read it. You know, Cervantes wrote it in old Spanish."

"At the beginning, it was hard to understand the words, but I am used to it now."

Alejandro laughed at my statement.

"I have very good books you could borrow, but they are written in English."

"Oh," I gasped. "Is it hard to learn English?"

"Mmmm … it takes time, but I think you can do it; you are very intelligent."

Nobody had ever called me intelligent before.

"I am glad you feel better," he told me in a friendly voice.

What kind of heart does Alejandro Sarmiento have?

That was the question for the ages. He walked to the kitchen with me and greeted everyone good night before waving good-bye with a warm smile.

6

Days passed in an imperceptible way, and my hope of talking to Orlando had faded away, when suddenly, out of nowhere, he approached me in the dining room.

"Good morning."

"Good morning," I replied, astonished.

"How are you?" he asked.

"Fine, and you?"

"Fine."

"Good," I responded with a faint smile while my heart tried to glue back together its shattered pieces. Unfortunately for me, since the beach encounter, I had lived the humiliation of Orlando completely ignoring my existence. Several times I had sought his inexpressive eyes without receiving a hint in return that I still meant something to him. The words of that morning weren't much, merely a couple of mundane phrases that people exchange informally every day. Yet, they filled my entire being with the one feeling I had so desperately grasped up to that moment: hope.

"We need to talk," he murmured in my ear.

Brilliance spread all over my face. "Yes, we should."

"Tonight?"

I nodded.

"I will knock on …"

Señora Sarmiento abruptly opened the door and directed her order to me.

"You … go get the parasols; we are going out."

I walked out of the room as quickly as possible and heard the door slam in the distance. Señora Leonora Sarmiento screamed at Orlando, but he walked out on her. On my way upstairs, Domingo was coming down. He disregarded me as usual, and I moved to the side to allow him to pass by me. I entered the twins' room, and then I heard someone's steps coming upstairs, echoing and reverberating in the old wooden staircase. Isabel grabbed my hands, excited about her upcoming excursion, but Lourdes began to cry. She wanted to stay inside, so as one girl pulled me to stay and the other pulled me to go, Orlando entered the room.

"Shut up, Lourdes!" he screamed. Lourdes hid behind my skirt and quieted in a flash.

"You shut up," Isabel spit back at Orlando. Orlando walked like a bull in a bullfighting ring and slapped Isabel's hand with force. Isabel screamed and started crying. That set Lourdes off onto her dramatic tantrum again while, desperately, I tried to calm them down.

"Don't hit her! Now they are *both* crying." With my eyes wide open, I shouted the words at Orlando.

"Go to your mother!" he ordered them out. I followed them, but he stopped me at the door, grasping me by the arm.

"I will come to your room tonight."

"Fine," I said and flew downstairs, following the twins. You could probably hear Lourdes's sobs all the way to the Pacific Ocean, and Isabel, without taking a breath, snitched on Orlando as soon as she saw her mother. When I arrived at the last step, I realized I had forgotten the parasols. Orlando handed them over, and I rushed to Señora Sarmiento's side, ready to go.

Señora Leonora Sarmiento was a gorgeous woman. She usually walked rapidly, as if she were running away from something or somebody. Often, I found it difficult to keep up with her, especially when I had to pull her twin girls by my side. Rarely could I detect her moods; her face always looked blank and empty to me. I suspected she was probably not a happy woman. Raimunda told me Señora Leonora had married Señor Sarmiento when she was sixteen and had the twins at seventeen. She was now no older than twenty-two. She belonged to one of the wealthiest families in Mazatlán—Elortegui de la Vega y Villareal; her father owned the biggest store in the city and had several others throughout the state.

I couldn't imagine being twenty-two years old and having three stepchildren almost my own age.

Her husband, Señor Joaquín Sarmiento, was ancient, around forty years old. His blood ran strong in Alejandro, at least in appearances. Both were tall and had light skin, a straight thin nose, and hazel eyes. And although they both had wavy, shiny, light brown hair, I could picture Alejandro as a little blonde boy. But they differed greatly in personality. Where Alejandro had a very gentle heart, his father kept a cold and distant attitude towards those around him. But, at the same time, Alejandro was brave and strong, maybe some would even say headstrong, as he showed the day we crossed the Presidio River.

Alejandro was as handsome as his father, but Domingo's features put him in the realm of gods, almost supernaturally good looking. He had flawlessly smooth, dark skin with deep, brown eyes, ones a girl could drown in. His nose, straight and of perfect proportion for his face, drew the eye to his mouth and its passionate crimson lips. Thick, straight, black hair created just the frame to set off his fine features. He was tall with broad shoulders and strong, tanned arms. Domingo looked different from his brothers, favoring his mother who had been known as the "Pearl of the Pacific." But, unfortunately, the differences extended beyond physical features. His manners were arrogant and rude. He always behaved as somebody who thought himself better than anyone on earth. With such beauty and strong self-opinion, Domingo found great popularity among the young ladies in Mazatlán, and he knew it. However, he favored one and regularly visited Catalina Barraza de la Torre, every bit his match in both beauty and presumptuousness. Those two certainly made a good couple.

Oh God. Not for one thousand pesos a day I would dare work as a nanny for their future children.

I could only imagine and when I did, goosebumps would cover my skin.

Señora Leonora liked to visit her parents' house often. Their mansion was located on the second floor of a colossal store. Evenly spaced windows lined the walls on all sides, and each window had a balcony of its own. The breeze coming from the sea reached every room in the house, and the inside air felt fresh all the time. The twins loved their grandparents, who allowed them to choose anything they wanted from the store and take it. They were lucky, I guess. I had fun watching the twins, especially Isabel. She would show her tongue to any child she encountered as a sign of a challenge. Lourdes was the reverse of her twin. Fearfulness surrounded her, and she cried about everything. But I had warm feelings for both of them because they reminded me of my younger sisters at home.

Each Sarmiento boy had a distinguishing treatment for the three females of the family. Alejandro was sweet with the girls, but he utterly ignored their mother. Domingo acted as if mother and children did not live under his same roof. And Orlando treated all three of them rudely; he could not stand Señora Leonora or his younger sisters. But the interesting part was that Orlando got along with his father better than his older brothers. Unfortunately, anybody could see Alejandro's resentment towards Señor Joaquín Sarmiento; no loving connection existed between father and son at all.

"The *tejuino* cart is coming!" Lourdes said to me full of excitement. They loved to drink tejuino, a corn-based beverage that, on occasions, sends you to the outhouse several times in an hour. I never learned to appreciate the taste—or the aftereffects.

"Tell your Mamá, and I will go get you some," I told her. She ran to the parlor where Señora Leonora was sitting with her mother and sister-in-law.

"Maximiana," Señora Leonora called, "get a pitcher from the kitchen and get us tejuino."

"Yes, ma'am." I went as fast as I could to follow her request. Secretly, I was terrified of her.

A boy named Jose Manuel filled the pitcher for me. He was a cute ten-year-old flirt with a head full of very dark bushy hair and the tip of his nose pointed up. He had the most intelligent eyes that I had ever seen in a boy that young, and even at such a tender age, he had all the markings of growing into one as dashingly handsome as Domingo Sarmiento.

"My name is Jose Manuel Diaz, what's your name, pretty one?" he asked.

"Angela," I answered.

"Angela what?"

"Peralta," I said when I took the container and went back in the house, leaving the young boy with a confused look in my giving the name of opera singer Angela Peralta.

That afternoon, on our way back to the Grand City House, as I called it then, Jose Manuel waved good-bye to me with a candid smile. He was still selling tejuino in his cart.

"You do look like an angel, Angela."

I smiled back, but Señora Leonora pierced me with her implacable glare.

"Why does he call you Angela?" María Isabel asked.

"Hush! Isabel. It doesn't look right for you to talk to the servants on the street!" the "she" version of Lucifer said. Isabel let go of my hand when her Mamá said that and walked in front of me with her mother; but Lourdes's hand reached mine with tenderness as if she understood that such a comment would certainly hurt my feelings.

I followed them in silence. Señora Leonora took a different route on the way back to her house. We crossed the Machado Square and took the sidewalk of the Rubio Theater. On the sidewalk, I could hear the singing melodies coming from inside. It sounded so beautiful. I desperately wished to go inside and see the faces that held such glorious voices.

In the square, some people sat on the white ornamented wood and iron benches while others talked inside the bandstand. The area had a circular sidewalk with the circular bandstand right in the middle of it, both of which, I thought, contrasted oddly with the name "square." People would stroll around it, holding arms, and stand under the trees planted along the street. Other times I had taken the twins to walk around the square; I enjoyed looking at the merchandise of the vendors that lined the sidewalk. However, I was saving every cent I was making during these two months to take back home. I wished so much to buy something; nonetheless, I restrained myself.

When we arrived at the Grand City House, I was ordered to go to the kitchen. Little did I know of the trouble that was cooking in the vicinity.

Sebastián called me, and I obeyed him right away. Señora Sarmiento had complained to Señor Sarmiento that I had talked to strangers on the street, and he had instructed Sebastián to set me straight. Out of fright, my heart almost stopped.

"I only talked to the tejuino vendor, and he was a little boy," I said to Sebastián in the middle of my confusion.

"When you walk with Señora Sarmiento, you cannot talk to anybody. You understand that?" he asked in an accusing voice.

"Yes," I replied.

"Go now," he said.

I didn't understand what the problem was. Honestly. But by this time, I knew firsthand how the water ran in the river. So, I just kept quiet and continued doing my chores, but my thoughts raced with indignation.

Is there no end to how I must deny my true self?

By dinnertime, the entire port of Mazatlán knew I had talked to a stranger in the street. When I helped Josefina and Raimunda serve the dinner course, I felt everyone's eyes accusing me of my horrible indiscretion. I wasn't surprised Orlando ignored me; he always did when others were around. But Domingo's mocking smile really got on my nerves. I tried to finish my chore as fast as I could, just to get away from that dining room.

Others had a different reaction to my unrestrained talking of the afternoon. Raimunda couldn't wait to go to bed and hear about my adventure with "the tejuino vendor." She was very disappointed when I told her he was no older than ten. There went the fun out of her day.

Raimunda liked to listen to my stories, so she said, "Tell me one of your stories, Maximiana."

"About today? And my dashingly handsome ten-year-old tejuino vendor?" I said, winking my eye.

"Ha, ha, ha … or make up one of those stories you imagine so well."

"Mmmm … not tonight. Orlando is coming tonight. We … he wants to talk."

In all these months, I had never talked to Raimunda about Orlando and my relationship with him. I could sense she wanted to say something, but she restrained herself.

"But tomorrow I will tell you a very good story that I have imagined about a mermaid who bewitched a sailor at sea and made him burn his boat."

"What?" she asked confused.

"Nothing, I am just making it up in a hurry."

I waited and waited for that knock to come, but nothing happened. Then just when I thought I couldn't hold my eyelids open one more second, I heard somebody coming. Raimunda turned and looked at the door.

"Go! Now! Get under the bed," Raimunda said to me with a frightening tone that alarmed me.

"It's Orlando," I replied, not understanding her reaction.

"No, go NOW."

I slid down like an earthworm and crawled under my bed. The door opened without anybody knocking on it. There was silence except for the steps entering the dark room. He was not Orlando; I could tell by the shoes. The man walked to Raimunda's bed, which was just like the body that inhibited it: still. I turned my face to the wall and covered my ears in terror and despair. I did not want to listen to what was happening; I bit my arm in desperation, suffocating the screams that tried to escape from my throat.

Otilia, I thought, *my sister Otilia has suffered this also.*

I could do nothing. Or could I …? I felt so helpless and terrified for myself and for Raimunda. It happened so fast, but at the same time, it felt eternal. My body filled with rage.

How can something like this happen without anybody doing something to stop it?

When it was safe, I came out of my hiding place and went to Raimunda's side. She pushed me away.

"You must tell Señor Sarmiento about this," I said from my bed.

"Shut up, Maximiana."

"Look, I can tell Alejandro; he is—"

"Shut up, Maximiana. Please, just shut up."

I debated my feelings of justice and duty to her. I could walk right that instant and tell Alejandro that somebody was abusing Raimunda against her will. I was certain Alejandro would do something about it. But Raimunda did not want me to do it. I didn't understand her. How could she allow someone to treat her like that? Did she think so little of herself?

"Please, Raimunda; I *know* Alejandro will do something about it."

"You really think it matters? It doesn't matter, Maximiana."

"Of course, it matters! *You* matter. Every single human being matters."

"Some do not," she responded in a whisper between her sobs.

"Don't believe that, Raimunda; don't put yourself down. Others might tell you that you are nobody or nothing, but if we *know* that is not true, it doesn't really matter what they say."

"But what can I do?" she asked in desperation

"Scream! Kick! Punch! Don't let him or anybody else do to you something that you don't want them to do!"

"They will kick me out in the street."

"But at least you will have your dignity."

"Dignity doesn't feed somebody such as me."

Raimunda's answer gave me a reality check that night.

I sighed when I told her, "You are right, but there are ways, there are always ways, and some day, things will change. There is going to be a time when people like you and me will not have to put up with all this sickening injustice. There is going to be a day that, if I wish to do something, I will be able to do it without having to ask permission of anybody."

"Maximiana, women always have to have permission from somebody, even if they are not servants."

"Why? No! *THAT* will also change. That is wrong."

"Maximiana, I swear to God you are a strange girl. Sometimes I think you are a little bit crazy."

"Why? Because I know I am worth as much as any other woman *or man* on earth?"

"You are making me forget my troubles. Thank you for making me laugh," Raimunda said in a low voice.

"Raimunda, I am not trying to make you laugh. I am serious about this. Look, I might not wear those heavy tight dresses or push my stomach in with wires, but I feel as beautiful as anybody else. You see? Those are only unnecessary adornments that people put on themselves. I don't need those to see the sun reflecting on the crashing waves and smell the salty wind filling my lungs. I don't need those silly hangings on my body to feel the warm ground under my feet or taste a sweet guava on a stormy night."

Raimunda exploded in laughter.

"You are something else. Did you get those words out of the books you read all the time? Ha, ha, ha!"

"Actually those lines, not just words, came out of a poem," I stated.

"A what?"

"A poem. A poem is like a song but without music or a piece of music without the words," I replied, pleased that I was making Raimunda forget her misfortune.

"That is confusing."

"I wish I had a book of poems to read one to you. They are very nice to the ear. I even wrote one once," I declared proudly.

"That is nice. You know? I never met anybody like you before. When you came that first day to work at the hacienda, I thought you were a silly whining little thing. But you are not silly at all. You have a lot of sense and a big heart."

"Thanks," I replied, flattered.

"No, thank *you*. For everything."

This time I knew I could reach her. I hugged Raimunda and then tucked her in her bed.

What a show I gave for Raimunda that night. Only I understood my internal feelings after witnessing such a horrendous scene. I was devastated, so devastated that I even ignored the fact that Orlando did not come as promised that night.

I kept asking myself if I should tell Alejandro of the situation. Even though Raimunda insisted that it shouldn't be done, something in my conscience told me I *should* tell him. On the first opportunity, I would, I promised myself before going to sleep.

Destiny was on my side the next day, giving me an opportunity to speak with Orlando alone when Josefina sent me to fix the Sarmiento boys' bedrooms. Alejandro was already up. Interestingly enough, Alejandro did his own bed here, just as he did in El Roble. His room was neat and in an perect order. I moved to "Sleeping Beauty's" room. Domingo was gone, so I did what I had to do quickly and took the stairs to the second floor. There I would find Orlando's bedroom.

My God, don't make them stop me before entering that room, I thought.

I knocked at the door softly. Nobody answered, so I entered. There he was, my beautiful curly haired boy, lying unconscious in the land of dreams. Cautiously, I moved towards him and, trying not to bother his sleep, took a seat on a chair. Orlando looked stunning in his slumber, like an angel fallen from the skies. He was twitching, and I wondered what he might have been dreaming and daydreamed myself that he was mine. Carefully, the back of my trembling hand touched his warm cheek. He felt my energy and turned his head away as a reflex. Then he opened his drowsy eyes to meet mine, so full of pure love for him.

"Good morning," I said.

"What are you doing here?"

"I was cleaning, but you were asleep." I felt embarrassed; my face turned red and hot.

"Oh, that is good. And after cleaning, you were going to get tejuino right?"

I stared at him, confused, even though I knew where "the joke" came from.

"Umm … I don't know, probably not unless Señora Sar—"

Abruptly, Orlando interrupted me, "You might even get it for free," he said while getting up and not looking in my direction.

"Why are you mad at me?" I asked, reaching for his arm. He pulled back just as he had done when he woke up to find me looking at him.

"I am not mad," he gasped, irritated. "I am fine; I have to go downstairs."

He moved away from me without looking back.

I followed him and said, "Wait, please … Orlando … wait. I haven't done anything bad. The tejuino boy was a little boy, no older than ten. I just don't understand. What is the big deal? I talked to a little boy who asked me for my name. I didn't even give him my real name! Look, I told him my name was Angela Peralta. On our way out, he said 'Angela like an angel' or something like that. But there is nothing wrong with that. *Believe me.*"

"I don't have to believe anything from you," he answered sharply.

"Yes, you do. You are mad at me for something unfair."

"HA! Why would I care about *that*? Tell me. Why would I care if you talk to a man on the street or if you flirt with any man you find on top of the *Sacanta*?"

"I would care if you did that to me," I said, injured by his words.

Throwing his arms unto the air, he rudely replied, "Well, guess what? I don't care!"

Everything in my logical mind told me that he cared more than he wished to admit to himself—or wanted me to know. Why else would he be so upset? But I didn't dare ask that.

"Fine. I understand," I whispered and turned my back at him to continue cleaning.

I understand that you are jealous, Orlando Sarmiento.

I didn't hear the door close behind me; I waited eternal seconds to pass but restrained myself from turning around.

What are you waiting for, Orlando? Leave then.

I did not know if his reaction should flatter or offend me. Sure, it felt good to realize that he had some kind of feelings for me, but at the same time he was so offensive when he screamed his lack of interest. I bit my lower lip to contain the sentiment of desolation that was settling inside. There was no way out. I had to turn back and do his bed next. He was standing there, looking at me. My heart filled with affection for that irresistible boy in front of me, and my first impulse was to run to his side, but I didn't. I started pulling the heavy covers when he walked towards me and grabbed my shaking hands.

"That is not true … what I said is not true."

"I know."

"Why do you act like this?" he asked.

"Like what?"

"As if you don't care … you said 'I understand' and kept doing what you were doing."

"I have to finish or I may get in trouble; you know that," I said with a broken voice, remembering my role in that room.

"Yes, I know."

"Why didn't you come last night? I waited for you."

I contained myself from telling him the horrible act I had witnessed the night before.

"I don't know."

"I'm sorry about what happened at the beach," I finally said, looking down. "I hope we can still be friends … even after that misunderstanding."

"Oh, yes."

I looked up at his eyes, waiting for an apology to what had happened in the parlor room the day after the beach encounter, but he said nothing.

"Why did you tell *them*?"

"Who?"

"Your friends at the parlor. Why did you tell them what happened at the beach … when I didn't agree to … *do it*?"

My question took him by surprise.

"I will come tonight to get you. Is that fine with you?" he replied, avoiding my inquiry.

"Yes, I have to go now."

He captured me on the way out and gave me a gentle kiss that erased my suspicions of betrayal, and throughout the rest of the day, I felt relief settled inside of me because Orlando and I had made up.

Alejandro had a smile carved on his face when he handed the little novel to me.

"Look what I have for you, Maximiana. I finished it yesterday and I know you will like it."

"Oh … thank you. *Maríanela*."

I passed my finger through the word.

"Leonardo brought it from Spain for his sister; do you know what Spain is?"

"Yes, the mother country."

"Yes."

"Thank you! I will start it as soon as I get a chance."

"Watch out for those tears because you are going to cry your heart out."

"Did you?" I asked, smiling.

"No, but I heard that people cry when they read about Nela."

I could swear my question embarrassed him.

"There is nothing more beautiful than a book that makes you cry," I said, "or a poem that makes you fly."

"Do you like poems?"

"Oh yes! I do! I love them. I haven't read many, but the ones I have, sent me up to the clouds."

My response truly amused Alejandro.

"Do you know who Ruben Dario is?"

"No, who is he?"

"An amazing poet from Nicaragua. He is the best."

"I would love to read his poems."

"I will look for a book by him and let you borrow it. Is that all right with you?"

"Oh my God, yes! Of course! Thank you." A broad smile spread on my mouth.

"You are funny," he said, grinning back.

"*I am?*"

"Ha, ha, ha, yes ... I mean it in a good way"

"Thank *you*, then," I said and walked away when Josefina called me from the kitchen.

Raimunda and Josefina couldn't contain themselves from teasing me.

"Somebody is popular with the Sarmiento boys," Josefina said, cracking up with laughter and putting her elbow in Raimunda's ribs.

"That book business is monkey business," Raimunda said, moving her eyebrows up and down.

"Ha, ha, ha!" I laughed at their humor.

"Perhaps we should learn to read and write, Raimunda."

The world opened up to me as soon as those words came out of Josefina's mouth.

"OH MY GOD! Would you like to learn? I could be your teacher! In my dreams I am a teacher; there is nothing in the world I would like to do more ... oh girls, and we are going to have so much fun! Wait! I have to ask Orlando for the reader I used when Beatriz taught me ..."

Josefina and Raimunda did not have time to react to my outburst of enthusiasm. I ran out of the kitchen looking for Orlando, forgetting for a moment that running was not allowed in the house. I froze when I saw Señor Joaquín Sarmiento standing in front of me. I slid to stop on time and not run over him. My heart fell to my feet when he gave me a look to send anybody to his or her tomb. I stood paralyzed with fear, my usual bravery disintegrated in an instant.

"Don't run in the house, girl," he told me with a hoarse sound coming out of his throat.

"I am sorry, Señor."

I turned back to the kitchen. Raimunda and Josefina noticed the perturbation of my face and, puzzled by my drastic change, asked me what had happened. With a silent sign I hushed them and pointed to the dining room.

"You look as white as paper," Raimunda whispered.

Señor Sarmiento never entered the kitchen, nor did he talk to the servants, except Sebastián and only to give him orders. Señora Sarmiento had charge of us.

Suddenly, we heard Señor Sarmiento knock on Alejandro's door and then a slam with such force that I was amazed the door wasn't broken. We jumped as summer toads when the screams reached the kitchen. Much tension existed between them, and we were all very much aware of it. However, we were smart enough to stay quiet and get away from such scenes.

"I will ask Orlando next time I see him," I finally said trying to think of something else. "He will say yes for sure; don't worry about it."

I crawled under my bed when we heard the knock, but nobody came in. The knocking continued, and I realized that it was for me this time. Orlando Sarmiento stood on the other side of the door, waiting. He held my hand and wrapped his fingers around mine while we walked towards the street. Facundo closed the door behind us with a blank expression on his face.

"Where are we going?" I asked Orlando.

"Don't you want to go to the beach again?"

"Can we go to the square instead?" I questioned back.

"Why?"

"I don't know. It might be safer."

"No, the beach is safer. Not a lot of people like to walk at night on the beach. Wouldn't *you* like to walk tonight on the beach?"

"Yes, I guess," I responded, hesitating because fresh in my memory was the last time we met in the beach.

We walked fast until we reached the warm and white sands that at night took on a dark purple color. How I loved the sounds and rhythms of the sea. I moved as in a dream, walking with Orlando, holding hands under the dark sky. The stars looked so distant yet so close when you saw them reflected on the mirror of the water.

"I wish you didn't have to go back to El Roble. I have never been apart from you for long," he said.

"Are you going to miss me?" I asked, hoping for an affirmative response.

"Oh yes. I like to have you around. I don't know why, but when you're not around, I feel that I am missing something."

"What are your feelings for me?" I timidly asked.

"Love."

"How do you know it is love?"

"I don't know. I just feel that it's something really big inside of me," he replied and then asked, "What do you feel for me?"

I stopped and turned my face towards him. I wanted to answer looking into his eyes for I knew our chances to be together as we were tonight were diminishing as my trip back to El Roble approached.

"I feel afraid of losing you."

"You're not going to lose me. I promise."

"I'm afraid that you will forget about me."

"I won't. I promise. I will never forget you."

"I'm terrified that you are going to stop loving me … or liking me or being my friend."

He hugged me and put his chin on my head.

"Don't be afraid of any of that. Trust me; it's not going to happen. I will never forget you, or stop loving you."

"But would you stop being my friend?"

"Never. I swear to God I will never stop being your friend."

"Because I know that I will never forget you. I know for a fact that you will always be in my heart, no matter what happens," I said.

"Nothing will ever happen because you are forever mine. I will never leave you. Do you understand that?"

"Will you always be loyal to me?" I asked.

"Yes," he said.

"How long are you going to stay in El Roble in December?" I needed to know that.

"Only for the school vacation time," he replied

"But, can't you go before December? At least once?"

"You know that is not possible. It is a long trip to go and come back. It doesn't make any sense. What are you afraid of, Maximiana?"

"I just told you: I'm afraid that you are going to forget me."

"You have to trust me. Do you trust me?" he asked in a firm voice.

My inner self told me to trust him. I wanted so badly to believe that all of this was a real love story and that I had found true love; I did not think of Orlando Sarmiento as a Sarmiento. I would've loved him just the same if he had been the tejuino vendor on the street. I loved him for who he was, for his beauty and his faults, all of which seemed so precious to me. I recognized his pain of losing his mother when he was eight, and I felt for him the resentment that invaded his soul when he saw his stepmother occupying his own mother's place. He was a difficult young man, yes ... and very hard to understand sometimes, but I knew he had a good heart. I knew he had noble feelings, feelings that he had to hide as a shield to the circumstances surrounding his existence.

"I do trust you," I said, expulsing from my thoughts any hints of doubts.

"How much do you trust me?"

"With all of my heart," I replied firmly.

"Be mine."

"I am yours."

"No. I want you to be mine ... completely."

"I am completely yours," I said, knowing exactly his intent.

"Do you understand what I'm trying to say?"

"I think I do ..."

"Then ...?" he replied with pleading eyes.

"I think it's too soon."

"We have been together for months."

"Only four months." It was my straight answer.

"Yes."

"I think it's too soon."

"I think it's time," he continued, arguing with me.

"But, you said it yourself: 'We are not going to get married until years from now.'"

"Exactly. That is why we can't wait so many years."

"Can we wait until I'm at least sixteen?" If my answer irritated him, he concealed his annoyance very well.

"You want me to wait two more years?"

"It is only one and a half."

"Fine."

"I'm sorry. But I don't want to find myself at fourteen with a child *and* without a husband."

His back immediately stiffened at my words. I don't think he had thought about the "child issue" up to that moment.

"You're right. We can wait until later."

He then looked at me with a very warm and sweet smile. His eyes lighted up. I had never seen them like that before.

We hugged and continued our night walk. I felt happy and special and proud because I had remained true to myself without losing Orlando's love. He respected me as much as I respected him, and he had proved that he had decent feelings for me. The parlor incident, I set behind me, determined to save this relationship no matter what.

How I wished for that night never to end. We talked on and on, and time slid away without us feeling it. We hugged, kissed, and held each other. The waves in their everlasting dance softened even more our words and caresses, and when the dawn's lights appeared along the horizon, we painfully said good-bye. No part of me wanted to let him go.

Raimunda allowed me to sleep late when she discovered my escapade had taken away any chance for rest for me. She told Josefina I was sick that morning and took over my chores. I don't recall dreaming anything, but powerful emotions shivered through me when I woke up and remembered the night before. Electric waves traveled throughout my body, and I hugged my knees, wishing they were Orlando and closed my eyes tightly. Sigh after sigh escaped from my chest, almost giving way to tears. No words could describe the immensity of my love for him; I would give my life for his without a second thought. He was so handsome and his voice … the memory of his voice sent waves of shivers down my stomach and directly to my legs. Even lying in bed, I felt a dizziness of loving and being loved and then numbness and finally a happiness that exploded in my soul with the energy of a million suns. I was in love with Orlando Sarmiento.

Domingo's steady girlfriend, Catalina María Fulgencia Barraza de la Torre had an attitude as impressive as her full name. And she wore her beauty arrogantly. She had soft, light skin and luxurious long hair and dressed in the latest fashion, as expected for a girl of her economic situation, and always kept her nose in the air.

Domingo often visited her house, and Señor Sarmiento proudly approved of his son's choice. I reached that conclusion because every time the girl and her family visited, he would act gentler than usual. Leonora Sarmiento apparently enjoyed the company of the Barraza de la Torre family; she would order the best pastries from the bakery every time they came.

Domingo and Catalina formed a good couple. They were both rich, beautiful … and rude. I wondered if they treated each other as inconsiderately as they did everyone else. Domingo acted like the perfect gentleman when they were together and seemed courteous to Catalina. She was in love with him—you could see it in the way she looked at him—which was understandable because Domingo was probably the most handsome young man in Mazatlán, if not the entire state.

Sometimes I brought refreshments to the family gatherings and heard their conversations. Lately, Catalina had started looking at me with scorn, as if I had inflicted some harm upon her. On the other hand, her mother never looked at the servants; she acted as if we had an infectious disease and she needed to keep us as far away as possible. Sometimes I asked myself how it would be to live like them, wear all those clothes and jewelry, and take tea sitting in a parlor room. I only wondered about it but did not wish it. Their conversations seemed meaningless and empty, just like that of the people from El Roble, mostly filled with gossip.

They seemed to put great effort in keeping up appearances. At least poor women did not have to hide their internal misery and pretend … The hacendados and their sons commonly had affairs with other women while the wives kept quiet at home, in their so-called place. But I thought that not all of them behaved this way; there had to be exceptions. For example, my mind couldn't picture Alejandro treating his wife or the woman he loved that way. Or certainly not Orlando. However, Domingo fit the stereotype well. I could just see his behavior in the future. Poor Catalina Barraza de la Torre, future de Sarmiento.

"Bring more lemonade," Señora Sarmiento ordered me, "and don't forget the ice." On my way out I heard her say: "This one doesn't know her place; I wanted to send her back to El Roble, but my husband did not agree …"

I stopped in the hallway, petrified, when I heard her words.

"Orlando is having his fun with her," she continued, "and my husband thinks it is good for him to have 'experience' here in the house."

"You don't say," Señora Barraza answered with an inquisitive tone of "*tell me more.*"

"You know how men are. He is proud of his son's male instincts," she continued. "I just hope she doesn't end up with a bastard."

"How old is she?" Señora Barraza asked.

"She's no older than fifteen, I think, but you know how *easy* these Indians are … and she is really brazen. You had to see her the other day on the street, the little witch was flirting with every man she encountered. You will see how this one will end up once Orlando is done with his fun."

"What about Alejandro? Is he playing around with the servants?" the woman asked, digging for more gossip.

"I don't know much about his affairs, but I have seen him too intimate with the same one."

"You don't say! She is a Jezebel!" Señora Barraza's venom rolled down the corners of her mouth. Catalina and her friend Dora Elena Mora approved of her mother's words, as did Señora Sarmiento.

I couldn't listen anymore and walked away, forgetting about the pitcher of lemonade. I took the hallway and hid in one of the rooms, seeking refuge under a dark wooden desk. I buried my face on my knees.

How can they be so cruel and heartless? They do not know anything about Orlando and me. And how can they even insinuate that I have something to do with Alejandro?

Spasmodic sobs jumped out of my chest. I didn't hear the door opening, nor did I realize someone had come in. Alejandro came down on his knees and looked at me.

Startled, I turned away, ashamed of my tears.

He stood up and walked out of the room. I hugged my knees with force, trying to shake all that pain out of my body. He could have gone to tell on me, but I didn't care. I stayed where I was, rocking myself back and forth in an attempt to suffocate my anger and embarrassment.

The door opened again, and someone gently pulled me out from under the desk. I looked up and, through my tears, recognized Orlando. We entwined ourselves in a hug.

"Alejandro told me where you were," he said as he began stroking my hair. "I don't know what they said to you, but I want you to know that whatever it is, it is not true. I love you. You mean more to me than anyone can imagine."

I leaned closer into his chest and caught the scent of his cologne.

"You know that, right?" he asked.

I nodded.

"Good." He pulled me away a bit and gave me a soft kiss on the lips. "Tell me what happened, Maximiana."

"Nothing."

"I know something happened for you to be hiding in here."

"How did Alejandro know I was in here?" I whispered.

"Leonora was looking for you, insulting you. Alejandro heard her and looked for you in every room until he found you and told me where you were. Don't listen to her. You know how she is."

"I think she is going to send me back to El Roble this time."

"She won't."

"She told them that she already wanted to send me back. This time she has a good excuse because I forgot to get the pitcher of lemonade."

"I won't let her," he replied, holding my face with his hands.

"I was too embarrassed to go into the kitchen crying. That's why I came in here to hide."

He hugged me tighter.

"What did she say? Please tell me."

"I'm too embarrassed even to repeat it."

"Please," he begged.

"She said that I was a Jezebel … No, *she* didn't. Domingo's girl-friend's mother said that. Señora Sarmiento told them that I was involved with you *and* Alejandro."

"What?" he exclaimed in consternation.

"Yes, that you were using me for fun and Alejandro was doing the same thing … and that I talked to every man that I found on the street."

He looked confused—and concerned.

"That you have something to do with Alejandro? Why would she say that?"

"I don't know."

He pulled himself away from me.

"There has to be a reason why she thinks there is something between you and Alejandro."

His words perplexed me.

"Do you believe that?"

"You are not answering my question. Why does she think that?"

"I don't know!"

"This is too bizarre."

"What does bizarre mean?"

"It means strange."

"Tell me something, Orlando … why did Alejandro tell you that I was crying in the room?"

He kept quiet.

"I cannot tell you that Alejandro is my friend. I do not dare to be that bigheaded. But I do know that he treats me with respect. He treats every servant in this house the same way. And I think he told you that I was crying because my crying worried him."

"Why would he worry about *you*?"

"Because he worries about people who suffer … How can you believe that I have something to do with your brother? That is silly," I told him, annoyed with his unfounded jealousy.

He smiled with relief. "You're right. I'm being silly. That woman is crazy."

I didn't reply to that statement.

He opened the door slowly while holding me. Once out of the room, I noticed, out of the corner of my eye, Catalina with her friend Dora Elena Mora, standing at the end of the hallway and looking at us with surprise. Their eyes clearly displayed indignation that sent fear to my very heart. I knew that Orlando hadn't seen them because he continued holding me with tenderness.

When we were almost at the kitchen, he asked, "Are you going to be fine?"

I nodded and said, "I think I will be."

"Good. And remember that, no matter what anyone says, you are the only one who knows the truth."

He gave me another kiss and walked away.

I wanted to disappear before Leonora Sarmiento found me, but how could I hide forever? She did find me, of course, and from that moment, my nightmare began. She hated me and made no secret of her opinion of me. She did not allow me to help with the twins anymore because, according to her, I was a bad influence. The rumors of my fallen reputation eventually reached even me. Raimunda informed me that I would help out in the kitchen only, until we returned to El Roble in two weeks.

Most of all, I missed taking the girls to the beach and walking in the square with them. But at least now I had more time to read; and sometimes during the evening, Sebastián would give us permission to get out of the house and take walks in the city.

Josefina was already twenty-three years old and could navigate the city with "closed eyes," as she used to say. She and Raimunda relaxed away from the house, and we had fun just having a long break from work. Everything Raimunda and I saw in the city amazed us. And strolling about Mazatlán and looking upon its beauty helped ease my sadness. Rows of two-story buildings with many adornments on the doors and windows lined the streets. I felt I walked in a different world. Sometimes we even dared to enter the huge stores and dream of having the money to buy some of the beautiful things sold there. Other times, Raimunda and Josefina bought candies and shared them with me.

Our return to El Roble was approaching, and I longed to see my family. But, at the same time, a deep sorrow invaded me when I thought about leaving Orlando behind.

One day while we were out, Josefina put her arm on my shoulders and said, "Don't be sad. You'll be back next summer. You'll see."

"I'm sure she's not only sad about that," Raimunda replied.

"I think I'm going to miss some of the things I do here," I answered, ignoring Raimunda's implication, "and I do not know if I'm going to have a job back in El Roble. Señora Leonora is really upset with me, and I don't quite understand why."

Josefina asked us to sit on a bench, and in a very mysterious way, she lowered her voice and confided, "Listen, I'm going to tell you something, but you have to promise to keep it a secret. Do you promise?"

"Yes," we both answered simultaneously.

"I think I know why Señora Leonora hates you, Maximiana."

"Why?" we both asked.

"She's jealous of you."

"No! I haven't even looked at her husband! I … but … oh, that is disgusting!" I exclaimed. Even Raimunda was shocked by Josefina's words.

"No! You don't understand. And lower your voices!"

"Please explain," I said.

Getting her face closer to ours, she said, "Señora Leonora is in love with Señorito Alejandro."

I was speechless.

Raimunda asked in astonishment, "How do you know that?"

"Just pay attention to the way she looks at him. And he's aware of that. That's why he completely ignores her."

Once I recovered from the shock, I could see Josefina's point. It seemed like a possibility.

"I have known her since we were little girls, and she used to come and play with the Sarmiento boys, right before they married her to Señor Joaquín."

Suddenly, I felt compassion for Señora Leonora's situation. It was outrageous; her entire condition was a tragedy.

"Oh, that is so sad …," Raimunda said.

"But Señor Joaquín … of course, he had to have a new wife … and with his wealth … but why didn't they marry her to Alejandro instead … do you think Alejandro has feelings for her?" I asked, intrigued and concerned.

"I don't think so," Josefina replied. "I heard he left a sweetheart in the United States."

"What?" I was excited for the news; someone as good-hearted as Alejandro deserved to have a sweetheart.

"Yes, he went to the United States after finishing his studies at the German School. He was there for two years. I heard he finished his studies before everybody else, and that's why he's back in El Roble. He is very smart. He even finished the German School two years before Señorito Domingo. "

"Oh … yes I heard about that," I sighed.

Raimunda kept listening in silence.

Josefina continued, "You should have seen Señora Leonora crying her heart out when he left the first time, and every time he returned, her face lit up with a mysterious glow."

"My goodness, this is really tragic," I responded. Those were my honest-to-God feelings.

"You see? She's—what?—twenty-two years old, and her stepson is Señorito Alejandro Sarmiento. She suffers a lot because of that."

"But she is wrong about Alejandro and me."

"I know, but she gets jealous like that. Before, there was a girl named María. She was a hard-working girl, but Señorito Alejandro paid way too much attention to her, and Señora Leonora found a reason to kick her out."

"Alejandro pays attention to everybody; he is very nice."

"True," Raimunda finally said. "He is strange sometimes, not in a bad way, though. He is very brave and strong. He fights with his father all the time, but also, he is very kind and gentle. I can't figure him out."

"We are not supposed to figure *them* out," Josefina replied.

"You know what I mean. For example, I figure Señorito Domingo out easily," Raimunda said.

"Oh, yes … me too. He is an arrogant, rude, and selfish young Sarmiento."

"Ha, ha, ha! Woman, leave some of him alive!" Josefina laughed. "Let's walk to the beach; it is so nice right now."

They had skipped Orlando.

"Mmmm … what do you think about Orlando?" I asked.

Silence.

"What do you think about Orlando?" I asked again.

"He … I don't know," Raimunda finally answered.

"He is too selfish," Josefina offered.

"Selfish? Why?"

"Something about the way he looks at people makes me not trust him," Raimunda declared. "I'm sorry to tell you this, Maximiana. I know you like him a lot."

"His eyes make me nervous." Josefina stated.

"Orlando has beautiful eyes," I defended, but deep inside I agreed with them.

"It is not the way his eyes look, but *how* he looks," Josefina corrected.

"He looks sad to me," I said in defense, again.

"Let's go for that walk, right?" Josefina said with a forced smile.

I felt tension in the air. Like everybody else, they probably thought he was just using me for fun and that he did not love me. But as Orlando had told me, only *I* knew the truth.

"Yes, let's go." I stood up and started walking, holding their hands.

Señora Leonora Sarmiento has feelings for Alejandro.

I did not expect that one coming. On the other hand, that might explain her disgust for me. A doubt entered my mind.

If, every time Alejandro has spoken to me, we were alone, how does she know he talked to me at all? Is she spying on him? Oh my God.

It was frightening.

My thoughts were interrupted by the question of a young man who approached us.

"Pardon me, ladies. Do you know where the Central Hotel is?"

"Yes, you have to walk two more blocks north. It is on a corner, right on Principal Avenue. You can't miss it because that is the only hotel on the block," Josefina explained.

He took off his hat and respectfully bowed to us. His gallant manners took us aback, and we simultaneously giggled.

"Thank you very much. Andrés Daniel Randal Rios, at your service," he stated with a smile and offered his hand. We shook hands with him, and I took notice of his face. His emerald eyes were concealed behind a pair of clear glasses, and he had wavy light brown hair.

"Josefina López Sánchez."

"Raimunda Lizárraga Osuna."

"Maximiana Valdez Amaya." We each recited our names with a curtsy.

"Nice meeting you all, and thank you, ladies," he said and walked away from us.

We giggled again. Young men usually did not treat us that way, offering a hand to us and calling peasant or servant girls "ladies," no, not in the city of Mazatlán at the beginning of the twentieth century.

"He was funny!" Josefina said.

"Yes! Imagine the idea! Calling us ladies as if we were women of high society," Raimunda added.

I felt a burning sensation in my stomach when Raimunda said that. Trying to control my temper, I said to them, "We *are* ladies; nobody should treat us otherwise." Both of them turned around at once. "You know, we shouldn't put ourselves down like that. People have imaginary titles that they give to themselves, but as Alejandro says, 'Those live only in their imagination.' We are as valuable as anybody else, and if they don't see us like that, that is their problem, not ours. So we should start by treating ourselves like ladies, and if somebody is as intelligent as that Señor Andrés who just greeted us as 'ladies,' we should thank him and move on. And *believe* his words!"

"For the Virgin of Guadalupe, Maximiana, breathe!" Josefina said, laughing, "You are going to give yourself a heart attack!"

I didn't feel like laughing because I meant what I said; I had spoken the truth of my heart. Raimunda gazed at me as if she clearly grasped the meaning of my words; she kept quiet and did not laugh. I smiled at both of them.

"Please believe my words."

"We do," Josefina said in a motherly tone of voice.

Raimunda kept quiet.

"But wasn't he dashingly handsome?" Josefina said, winking her right eye.

"Oh yes …," Raimunda replied, looking down. I just smirked.

"Don't tell me you didn't find him handsome, Maximiana," Josefina scolded.

"I didn't pay much attention to that," I said hiding that I had noticed the color of his eyes, so green and clear, and the eyelashes, impressively long and curled, and his hair, wavy and brown, but nothing else, I told myself. My eyes embraced only the image of Orlando Sarmiento, and looking at another boy in a different light felt, in my heart, as a betrayal to his dignity. I respected Orlando.

"You are lying! Oh my God!" Josefina pushed me forward, laughing. "I don't think you are blind, are you?"

"No, but I didn't look at him that way."

"We are here … I love the sea," Raimunda timidly said.

"Oh, I do too! I will never forget my walks on this beach …"

"Did you enjoy the walks with Señora Leonora? If I had been in your place, I don't think I would have," Josefina stated, putting her hand on her triangular chin.

"At the beginning, she was not evil to me; she just ignored me, as if I were invisible. Besides, I like the girls, especially Lourdes," I replied. Trying to invite Raimunda to the conversation, I asked, "Why do you like the sea so much, Raimunda?"

"I guess I would like to see what is on the other side ..."

"Oh it is called Baja California, and if you go farther you get to a country named Japan," I proudly replied.

"How do you know that?" Josefina wanted to know.

"Mmm ... Orlando told me that."

"I wish I could go there," Raimunda said in a dreamy voice.

"Go where? To Baja California or Japan?"

"Both," she said.

Josefina laughed and added, "I will be happy enough if one day I visit México City. I have heard many stories about how big and beautiful everything there is."

"I would rather visit Boston."

"What is that?" both of them asked.

"Boston is a city in the United States where Harvard University is, where Alejandro went to school."

"Why do you want to see Botson?" Josefina asked, intrigued.

"Boston," I corrected. "I don't want to visit ... I would like to go to school there."

They gasped, and with a pitiful sigh, Raimunda hugged me and said, "You are such a dreamer, Maximiana."

"But your dreams are kind of different, you know ...," Josefina finally said.

"Don't you dream of becoming somebody else? Don't you wish to have the freedom to express your thoughts and actually be heard?"

Now they were puzzled and heartbroken for me. I could sense it.

"Don't feel sorry for me ... it is wonderful to have dreams and wishes that may or may not come true ... but at least I dare to have them, right?"

"Yes, definitely," Josefina said, smiling at me.

"And you are trying to do something about it because you are always reading those books."

I was pleased to hear those words coming out of Raimunda.

I said, "That is why I want you to learn to read and write also. You will see how different everything is going to look once you start learning about so many things that are out there and you didn't know existed."

I had been teaching them from the book Orlando had lent me during the last weeks.

"Raimunda can continue her lessons because she is going with you, but what about me? Who's going to teach me?" Josefina asked in a concerned way.

"You may continue learning as much as you can on your own ... and ask Sebastián for simple little books, like the children's books from the Sarmiento's library. I am sure he will allow you to borrow them every once in a while," I encouraged her.

"Yes, I will. It is something I look forward to ... I like your lessons," Josefina said in a grateful tone.

"Thank you!"

Her words honestly flattered me. Raimunda and Josefina were great friends. Memories of my helping them to read and our discussions of the world live with me, as if they happened only yesterday. Those days marked the beginning of my inner self-transformation from a young woman into a challenger and a teacher.

8

The last two weeks in Mazatlán simultaneously moved in two directions. In one, the time went too slowly for my wanting to be with my family again. But in the other, it sped by too fast as the last days of seeing Orlando were coming to an end. Orlando managed to be close to me most of my free time, which gave a sweet irony to those unforgettable days. Once, he convinced me to swim in the ocean with him. We held hands, jumping with the waves; later, we let go and competed in the game. We laughed, and I, at least, drank tons of seawater. I loved feeling his strong hands on my waist, raising me as a feather when the waves came. I would also ride on his muscular back, going underwater and delighting in the feel of my breasts on his body. Other times, I embraced him with my legs and held him tight, so tight that he would pretend to faint from the lack of air.

We took many walks on the beach and talked continuously about everything that would come to our minds. I enjoyed telling him my thoughts about the world that surrounded us; he always listened and tried to relieve my concerns in the best possible way. Sometimes we wrote our names on the wet sand, messages that the coming waves would take away: "Orlando loves Maximiana," "Orlando and Maximiana together forever," or "Maximiana and Orlando = love."

Orlando had given me several books to take back with me to El Roble, but two days before departing, I informed him I had only three left to read. He didn't understand why I had such a passion for reading. Now I regret never telling him that reading allowed me to discover myself, a "me" beyond my girl's body or servant's position. Reading gave me the freedom to do and be whatever I wanted; books let me fly like an owl in the quiet of the night. I needed to learn so much, see so many places through those books. Although I never did tell him, I have never forgotten that I learned to read and write, thanks to him.

Señora Leonora Sarmiento continued giving me devilish looks and unfair treatment. I never even *looked* at Alejandro in her presence, just in case Josefina was correct about her assertions. He still said hello to me every time he saw me, though. Alejandro was so charming and sweet that, as time went by and I got to know him better, I realized he was simply an almost perfect human being. He had the sensibility to feel the pain of others but also the strength to fight for what he considered just, without regard to what other people might think. He had not a drop of selfishness in his heart. Yet, his eyes reflected a hidden suffering, due, I suspected, to the loss of his mother. And even though people were puzzled about his behavior of being so considerate towards others—after all Alejandro was Señor Sarmiento's son—I was not. I admired him profoundly, and secretly I held him very dear to my heart.

The day before our departure, chaos flew into the house. Everyone ran around getting ready for the long trip back to El Roble. Señora Sarmiento had four mules packed with her needs. Mixed feelings of joy and sorrow melted inside of me. I tried not to think about what—who— I would be leaving, but I could not avoid it. Orlando came up to me at the first opportunity to tell me that we needed to meet that night.

"Tonight in Domingo's room," he said.

"Yes, but why Domingo's room?" I asked.

"Because it is easier than getting out of the house with everyone running around … besides I already told him, and it is fine with him; we have traded rooms for tonight."

"Fine, I will meet you there at the first chance I get tonight," I said and walked away to continue my chores.

"I'll be waiting," he replied.

That night I crept out of the servants' quarters and, with a sinking heart, walked to our last meeting for four months.

Four months.

I opened the door to Domingo's bedroom cautiously. There he was, sitting at a desk, looking through some papers. I walked over and placed my chin on his shoulder.

"Hello …"

I gave him a soft kiss on the cheek, and he smiled. He stood up and gave me a strong hug.

Our last hug for four months.

"I wrote something for you," he said in a warm voice.

"Really? I did too … and …" I looked through my pockets but nothing was there. "I left it in the room. I will go and get it. Hold on."

He nodded and walked with me to the door, barely touching my back with his hand.

Once again, I opened the door to the small living room with caution. When I arrived in the kitchen, I saw the figure of a man entering the servants' quarters. I followed him on tiptoes, trying to make no noise and discovered he was heading to our room. Raimunda was already asleep when I left. My heart sank, thinking of what was coming to her. The stranger had not visited her since the day I had witnessed the atrocity. However, I knew something was still happening because the expression on her face didn't change. She looked scared and melancholic all the time. Raimunda refused to reveal his identity; fate presented me with the opportunity to discover the criminal myself.

In the darkness, I accidentally pushed a chair to the side, making a noise loud enough for the stranger to hear. Terrified and half dead,

I waited a few seconds to see if he had heard me when I perceived the sound of his steps close to the kitchen door. I immediately turned back to the little living room and made a run for it. I was not sure if he was following me, but I continued anyway. I was not going to take a risk. Then I realized that he, indeed, had followed me: I could hear the quick steps near me. In the middle of my terror, I opened Alejandro's bedroom door, which was closer to me than Domingo's, and immediately closed it. Without thinking, I ran inside and shook him up.

"Alejandro … help me … somebody is following me," I said, scared.

"Who?" he said, astounded by my sudden appearance in his room.

"I don't know … he was entering Raimunda's room and—"

I jumped when I heard the loud knocking on the door. Startled, Alejandro got up and told me, "Get under the covers."

Unable to see, I heard Alejandro rapidly tear off his shirt and throw it on the floor as he stepped to meet my pursuer.

"I'm coming!" he shouted and abruptly opened the door.

"Who walked into your room, Alejandro?" Señor Sarmiento asked in an angry voice.

Señor Sarmiento. God have mercy.

Coldly, Alejandro answered, "No one."

"I saw someone walk into this room. Someone was following me. Don't lie to me, boy!" the man screamed, losing his temper.

"Maximiana and I went into the kitchen to get water. You probably heard us when we closed the door behind us," he calmly replied.

"Maximiana is here?"

"Yes, she is here, but that is none of your business, so please get out." Alejandro started to close the door, but his father stopped him. Pushing Alejandro aside, the man marched into the room and violently pushed the covers away from the bed. I grabbed both of my knees in terror and closed my eyes.

"What do you think you are doing, Father? I thought it was your dream to see your son with women in his room!"

WHAT? What did he just say?

"Oh …," Señor Sarmiento exclaimed, his anger deflated.

Suddenly, I felt the covers back on me.

"Who did you think was in here, Father?" Alejandro asked, clearly concerned. His father tried to walk away, but Alejandro stopped him with, "Answer me! Why are you always so suspicious of me? Why?" Señor Sarmiento pulled away from Alejandro. "Answer me, Father!"

"I will leave now. Good night."

"Father! Don't leave me talking like this! Damn it! Father!" Alejandro followed Señor Sarmiento out of his room.

"How long have you been having this girl to your room, Alejandro?" Señor Sarmiento asked.

"That is none of your business, sir," Alejandro replied. My heart pounded with fear. Not only had I created this mess, now involving father and son, but I also had likely sealed my own fate. Señor Sarmiento would surely tell his wife, and she would have the perfect excuse to let me go. My days working for the Sarmientos would soon end. On the other hand, Orlando could probably hear the whole discussion between his brother and father, and he might even blame me for it. My goodness, I was a magnet for troubles.

"Why are you smiling, Father? Are you laughing at me?"

"No, I am not laughing at you. I just realized that I have been imagining things that do not exist, that is all," Señor Sarmiento said with a sudden happiness in his voice.

"What were you imagining?"

"Stupid things that are not worth mentioning … now go back to do your business … good night."

I had crept out of the bed when they had left the room, and now I stood behind the door, watching. Señor Sarmiento walked back towards the dining room, instead of the kitchen. I felt relieved he did not go to Raimunda. It was *he*. It was Joaquín Sarmiento who had abused my sweet friend Raimunda.

Alejandro walked back in.

"Tell me what happened."

"I can't." Now I understood why Raimunda wanted me to keep silent.

"Has Father been visiting Raimunda at night?"

I lowered my head.

Lifting up my chin, he asked, "Has he … done anything to you?"

"Oh God, no … no. But I heard when he …"

"*You* were in the room?"

 I nodded.

"But I hid under my bed … Raimunda told me that if I heard … that she would tell me when to hide …"

"My God … that is too sick … she is a very young girl."

"I know … only sixteen. And now he thinks you are doing the same thing with me … and Orlando … and he is pleased … that is really sick!"

"I know … but it is not true, so don't worry about it."

Alejandro comforted me. Then Orlando walked in.

"Maximiana hid in here. Father caught her in the kitchen."

"I heard …" Orlando replied, a little too unconcerned. "Are you coming?" he asked me without showing interest whatsoever in the situation.

I followed him out of the room, but on my way out I told Alejandro, "Thank you."

"Alejandro."

"Excuse me?"

"Say 'Thank you, Alejandro.' Call me by my name."

"Thank you, Alejandro."

 I smiled and ran after Orlando, who was already entering Domingo's room.

"May I ask you something?" Orlando asked while dropping himself down on the floor.

"Yes, of course," I replied, positioning myself next to him.

"Why did you run into Alejandro's room instead of coming here?"

"Because it was the closest door and I knew I would create a bigger mess if he had followed me here and found you instead of Domingo."

"And you had time to think about *all* of this?" he asked in disbelief.

"Actually I did."

"So, did you get the letter you wrote for me?"

"No … I was on my way to the room when everything happened," I replied.

"So … has Father gone into your room at night?" he asked, avoiding my eyes.

"Raimunda's room," I whispered.

"I think Leonora believes father visits *you* at night. That could explain why she dislikes you so much."

If you only knew, Orlando. My relationship with Alejandro she hates, not your father's visits to the servants' quarters.

My mind wandered away from Orlando before me and to Señor Sarmiento and his claims to Alejandro. He had been furious and intent on finding out who was in his son's room.

Can it be possible that he suspects his wife's affection towards his second son?

"What are you thinking?" Orlando interrupted my thoughts.

"Nothing … well … that I will not see you for four months."

Sadness came back to me; in the middle of all this confusion I had forgotten this was my last night in Mazatlán with Orlando.

"I am going to miss you so much, Orlando," I finally said.

"Me, too."

We hugged, and I rested my nose in between his ear and neck.

"I don't want to forget your scent, Orlando … please don't forget *me*." My heart cried out my biggest fear of all.

"I won't forget you, Maximiana. I promise."

"I will never forget you Orlando. No matter what happens you will always be within me."

"You will always be mine. You are mine forever, remember?"

He smiled and kissed my nose with tenderness. I began to cry. I ran my hand upon his chest. I touched his face, trying to trace every part of his features, as if my fingertips would engrave him into my mind for eternity. In the darkness of the room, I felt a drop of moisture and gently reached for its source. His eyes were wet with tears. I raised my lips to give him a small kiss on each one of them. I tasted the salty teardrops on my tongue and went down to his lips. A profound sigh escaped my chest. We kissed, falling into a fervor that did not want to end, for it was like making love, two souls drowning in a sea of forbidden passion.

My beloved Orlando, please do not forget me.

Those were my last words for him that night.

9

At daybreak, our journey to El Roble started. I said good-bye to Josefina with a sturdy hug; I could tell by the trembling of her lower lip that she felt our farewell deep in her heart. Orlando did not come down to see us go, and neither did Domingo. Perhaps it was too early for them to get out of bed on a Sunday. From the instant of our departure until the moment where everything became too minuscule to make out, I kept looking back. I stared hard at the second-floor window of Orlando's bedroom, expecting to see his head full of curls stick out and an arm wave good-bye to me, but he never appeared. Then I remembered that he was actually sleeping in Domingo's room.

I imagined him asleep like a cherub. My heart warmed, thinking of such a picture; he looked so peaceful when he slept. Once, at the beach, he had rested his head on me and had fallen asleep. I had held his head close to my chest and caressed his face and hair as if I were touching a soft rose petal. My soul had felt so close to him that I had wished he were a little boy who needed my protection. I had gently kissed his forehead, carefully, without waking up my sweet baby. And now, again, he slept. And as we drew farther and farther from the Grand City House and my Orlando, I hoped his dreams were memories about us.

Once on the road I could see the Sacanta Mountain, which was visible from Mazatlán. It is the tallest mountain in the region, and I was once told that when sailors come from the sea, the first land they distinguish is the enormous peak of the Sacanta. The Sacanta to me is synonymous with El Roble. I can't imagine separating one from the other since El Roble has a full frontal view of its beauty.

All day, its shadow from the sunlight plays tricks on the spectator. Depending on the time of the day, the Sacanta gives the impression of being either close enough that a quick jog would suffice to arrive at its foothills or so far away that it appears distant and mysterious. At midday, the Sacanta moves away; it becomes too plain and distant to distinguish its hills. By evening, the shadows become active, and it grows darker and creeps dangerously close to you.

But the Sacanta is most beautiful when clouds come down and dress it with their white soft skirts. Sometimes, the white fluffy clouds reach the lower hills and divide the mountain into different little pieces of ridges that make you wonder what hides between its edges. Children are told that the clouds came down to the Sacanta to drink water. I liked that story; it was my favorite pastime to imagine nature behaving like people. I could just picture the lady clouds, elegantly stepping down to the crevices of water and drinking with their delicate soft hands.

I liked walking to the Sacanta Mountain when I had the chance. One of my dreams was to reach the top just as my older brother, Augusto, had done several times. He told us that you could see Mazatlán and the Pacific Ocean from up there if you looked west, and if you looked east, El Rosario. On the other side you could see La Villa de San Sebastián, another town close to El Roble. Both El Rosario and La Villa de San Sebastián are older than Mazatlán and El Roble, although I have never been to either one.

I had a hiding place close to the Sacanta Mountain, an enormous roble tree—a roble is an oak tree—so big that I could sit against it and nobody would notice me. Only my sisters Otilia and Natalia knew about it because it was my little secret hideaway. Some days, when I got in trouble with Mamá and she was about to hit me, I would run to my oak tree and climb it as high as I could. No one could find me, up in the air, safe in my roble.

The jumping of the cart on the gravel road woke me from my daydreaming.

Even though it was already September, the summer heat of the tropics felt harsh upon our faces. The relentless sun did not bother Raimunda, who couldn't conceal her happiness in going back to El Roble. Now, I understood why. Alejandro rode his dark brown horse. Periodically, he would turn his face to us and smile. Raimunda thought he was looking only at me and not her, but once, as I talked to Roberto, one of the drivers, Alejandro smiled at her directly. Raimunda replied with a timid smile.

Señora and Señor Sarmiento traveled inside the carriage. The poor twins couldn't stop complaining about the trip, and I could feel their distress. We traveled tediously. The heat beat mercilessly. And the dust raised by the carts filled our nostrils and eyes. My hair had turned gray by ten in the morning. Alejandro came close to where I sat and asked me if I wanted to ride with him on his horse. I will not deny that his request surprised me.

"Oh! … well … would it be all right?" I asked, naïvely.

"Yes, come on!"

"Fine … but I get to ride up front … let me take the reins," I instructed boldly.

"Sure! Come on!" he said enthusiastically.

In my excitement, I forgot about those around us and realized only too late the piercing looks—and more—they gave me. Señora Leonora even stuck her head out the carriage window and saw me jump up on the horse. Alejandro pulled me up with one hand, and we headed towards the river.

I knew how to ride a horse very well. Father had taught me. We were one of the few families in El Roble that had a horse instead of a mule or donkey; Papá had inherited it from his Uncle Severo in Mesillas. I had always been the best horse rider in my family so when I took the reins, I dug in my heels, and we galloped off. The air hit my face and blew my single braid off my back. Did it hit Alejandro? I didn't care; I just relished the refreshing breeze. At least I had only one braid to blow behind me. Since living in Mazatlán, I had started wearing one instead of two; I thought it made me look older.

Once we slowed down, with the group barely distinguishable in the distance, Alejandro started talking to me.

"Did you get a chance to read *Maríanela*?" he asked.

"Yes! I did! I found some parts a little bit hard to understand, but the story is really beautiful."

"Did you cry like I warned you?" he asked in a light-hearted way.

"Mmm ... I did cry. I admit it."

"Ha, ha, ha! I knew it!"

"But ... do you think it was good that she died of sadness because of Pablo?" I asked.

"Well ... I think it is romantic for her to give her life away for love ..."

"But ... Pablo stopped loving her when he regained his eyesight because, once he finally saw her, he thought she was ugly and not as he had imagined her to be—as physically pretty as her soul."

"Yes ... but he fell in love with his cousin Florentina when he saw her for the first time. Remember? He even thought that Florentina was Nela," Alejandro said.

"Who was beautiful. But what about the beauty of Maríanela, her inner beauty?" I persisted while feeling touched by the romance in the whole story.

"Mmm ... but ... for love to exist there has to be physical attraction, too, and Pablo had been blind. He knew Nela only by her voice," he replied.

"And her soul ... they talked a lot, and she took care of him; she loved him dearly," I passionately declared.

"I see your point ... but don't you think it is beautiful that she died of love?" Alejandro asked.

"No."

"No?" his voice sounded surprised.

"No!" I shook my head.

"Don't you think there is nothing more wonderful than dying for love?"

"Mmm … yes … and no. It depends on the situation."

"I don't get you," Alejandro said.

"Well, if I love somebody and he is going to die, and I give my life so that he may live, then it is good to die for love—"

"Exactly," he interrupted.

"Let me finish … but to die for someone that rejected you after you gave him your entire self, just as Maríanela, then it is not wonderful; it is actually very stupid."

Alejandro started laughing.

"What? Do you think my idea is silly?" I asked with an indignant tone of voice.

"No! On the contrary … you have a way of seeing things that make a lot of sense. I hadn't thought of this book that way. Your point is very good, actually. So, since Pablo rejected her, he didn't deserve to have Maríanela's life."

"Yes, that is what I mean."

"Yes, you are right."

"I don't think that I would give my life for somebody that had rejected me like that. Would you?"

He took a while to answer.

"I don't know, Maximiana. I am awfully romantic," he said warmly, smiling.

So this is it. This is what makes him so different and interesting to everybody: He is very romantic.

"Maríanela was so good. Such a good-hearted person, full of beautiful qualities, and yet, she was not smart enough to get over Pablo's rejection."

"Only she knew what she felt … right?" Alejandro said.

"Yes, only the person that goes through something like that can possibly understand such sorrow."

"Sorrow is the best word to use in this case."

"Yes," I replied. "So, you are awfully romantic?"

"Ha, ha, ha! As I said, I am."

"Do you write poetry?"

"Mmm … no, I don't have that talent, but I like to read poems … *'What is poetry? You ask while nailing in my pupil your blue pupil? What is poetry? And you ask me? Poetry is **you**.'*"

"What a beautiful poem … you wrote it?"

"No, of course not; Gustavo Adolfo Becquer did."

"Tell me another one." I thrilled to listen to him, his melodious voice, and the perfect tone he gave to the words.

"Hmm … let me think … *'For a glance … a world, for a smile … a sky, for a kiss … I don't know what I would give you for a kiss!'*"

"So simple but yet so powerful"

"I know … that is why I like it."

"Ay! Alejandro, poetry is so stunning to the ear and to the heart …"

"You talk in poetic verses, you know that?" Alejandro said, putting his face next to mine.

"You notice? Yes, I do like to speak in poetic tones. Ever since I discovered reading and poetry, it sounds nicer to the ear."

"Yes, definitively. Oh … let me tell you another one of my favorites … *'Sighs are air and go to the air. Tears are water and go to the sea. Tell me woman, when love is forgotten, do you know where it leaves?'*"

I kept quiet after listening to that one.

"Do you know where it goes, Maximiana?"

"No. Do you?"

"No."

"Why do you like it so much?" I asked.

"It intrigues me."

"I can see why …" A shadowy feeling of intrigue fell upon me as well.

Is it possible for love to be forgotten? How could a feeling so strong and passionate be forgotten?

I didn't think that could to happen. Certainly not to me.

"Are you excited to go back to El Roble?" Alejandro finally said, breaking the silence and perhaps to change the subject that seemed to bother him as much as it bothered me.

"Oh yes! I miss my parents, my sisters, and my brother a lot … and my friends, especially Daniel."

"But, don't you feel sorry to leave my brother behind?" he asked, cautiously.

"Of course," I said in a low voice. "Imagine, I won't see him until December, for four months."

"Are you going to miss him?"

"What do you think?" I replied in a sarcastic tone.

"I think you will … and I have something for you from him."

His words lit up my mind with emotion.

"Yes, I have it in my bag. Hold on; I will get it for you."

He stopped the horse and helped me down. Out of his side leather bag he pulled out a little doll. She had porcelain face and hands, soft and wavy hair, and a purple dress with little shoes that matched. I was speechless.

"Thank you," I said at last.

"And this letter, he said, which, with all of the commotion last night, he had not been able to give to you."

"Thank you very much, Alejandro," I said, and I gave him a sincere hug.

"You are welcome," he said, smiling sweetly at me.

"What was your mother's name?" I asked.

His eyes turned away from mine as he replied, "Magdalena."

"I will name her Magdalena, just like your mamá."

Alejandro turned back at me and smiled again. He put his muscular hand on my right cheek and said, "Thank you." Then he raised me by the waist to the horse. "Now, *I* will take the reins," he said, and we started galloping again while I held tightly to my two treasures with hands wrapped round Alejandro.

The group had almost caught up with us. I asked Alejandro to put my doll back in his bag, and he agreed. For nothing in this world would I want to damage her. I placed the letter that I would read by myself later that night in the waistline of my skirt. I held Alejandro by the waist and rested the side of my face on his back. I closed my eyes to relax and remember Orlando. Alejandro didn't talk anymore, but his mere presence gave me a sense of security that I found hard to explain. Without a doubt, he seemed to be the one person in the world who understood me completely. From the outside, it didn't make any sense. He was Alejandro Sarmiento, the second son of Joaquín, one of the toughest and richest men in the state and—now that I knew him better, I could add—one of the meanest men in the world. Yet, his son Alejandro had completely different qualities—courage, a warm heart, and he acted as my sincere friend. He didn't seem aware of my status as a servant; for him I was just Maximiana Valdez—no, not "just" but Maximiana Valdez, a person as important as he, no more and no less. To this day, I thank him with all of my heart for recognizing me as an individual equal with all.

By three o'clock we had reached the Presidio River and prepared to cross. The current flowed decently, but the water level was higher than on our earlier trip.

"It is too deep for the mules, Señor Sarmiento!" Ramiro Montoya screamed.

"Get them on the rafts first, and then we will cross the carriage," Señor Joaquín ordered back.

"Señor … we should get the lady and the girls out of the carriage and cross them in the boat," Ramiro suggested.

Señora Leonora got out of the carriage and looked around her. She looked for Alejandro's face, which surveyed the whole scene.

"Maximiana, do you want to cross on my horse with me or would you rather take a canoe?" Alejandro asked.

"I will take the canoe," I said, "but give me my doll; I don't want her to get wet."

Alejandro walked to the horse and pulled Magdalena out of his leather bag, handing it to me. Señora Leonora glanced at us and turned around.

Then she exclaimed, "I am not taking the canoe; I will cross in the carriage!"

"Señora, that is dangerous. The raft may turn …," Ramiro said, staring down.

Shyly he looked for Señor Joaquín's intervention, but the crossing of the mules on the raft held his full attention.

Alejandro went to his father and said, "Father, don't let the girls cross in the carriage … they should go in the canoe."

"Yes … Leonora! Get the girls in the canoe; they are crossing next!"

"No, they are crossing with me in the carriage," she stubbornly replied.

"No woman! Are you mad? It may turn!" Señor Joaquín exclaimed, exasperated.

"There is no way I am taking the canoe with all those … people," she said.

Alejandro turned around violently, putting his back to the speakers, visually annoyed by her words. Next, he walked to the carriage and called the girls out. Lourdes followed him obediently, but Isabel stayed with her mamá. Señora Leonora stiffened when Alejandro advanced near her, but she kept quiet.

"Lourdes, sit with Maximiana … and you will wait for Mother on the other side, right?" he said, smiling at her.

She nodded. Lourdes held my hand with her sweet long fingers; little Lourdes had enormous hands, too big for the rest of her body. I smiled to reassure her that everything was going to be just fine. But Raimunda's attitude did not lend faith to my attempts at calming the girl.

Terror showed in Raimunda's eyes as we began to cross, and she nervously declared, "I don't know how to swim."

"This is not the moment to think about it, Raimunda; you can trust me on that one," I said with a wink.

The men holding the ropes on the other side struggled to pull the canoe to the shore, but the current kept moving it south.

"Do you know how to swim?" she asked, trying to distract herself with talk from the circumstances that clearly frightened her.

"Oh yes … Papá taught me," I replied. "You see … we are almost there."

I patted Lourdes' hand. And soon enough, we arrived on the other side and waited for the rest of them to cross. Raimunda sat under a tree because she was feeling dizzy. Lourdes sat next to her. I asked her to hold Magdalena for me, and she was delighted by it. I wanted to see how the others handled the crossing, so I went back to the edge of the river for a better view.

Señor Sarmiento did not convince Señora Leonora to cross the Presidio River in the boat. Her forcing little Isabel to remain inside the carriage with her visibly upset Alejandro, and he rode away, north of the river's edge. He said he would cross up the river, where the water was shallower.

All the remaining men got together to help pull the raft to the other side. I stood out of the way. Señor Sarmiento got out of the carriage and opened both doors. He stood on the raft, but stubborn Señora Leonora stayed inside with Isabel. They had made it half way across when the raft caught an eddy. All too quickly for anyone to react, it then tilted to one side and tipped over. Señor Sarmiento fell in the water, and you could hear Señora Leonora screaming for help as she felt the carriage lurching toward the edge of the raft. Men immediately jumped in the water, trying to help them out. In the chaos, the men failed to see what my vantage point showed: Isabel let go of her mother's hand, and she, too, slipped into the river. I jumped in the water in desperation and swam as fast as I could towards her. Fortunately, the current pushed me toward her, and I grabbed her by the hair and raised her face above the water. I floated with her and with my legs kicked toward the side where the journey had begun. I had not the energy to swim the greater distance to the other side, where Raimunda and Lourdes watched with terror. Down the river, my feet touched land, and I pulled her out with me. Poor Isabel, she hung on to me like a tick. We both coughed, and water came out of her nose.

"It's fine Isabel … we are safe," I told her. But the poor thing started to cry in terror. In the distance I saw the commotion, and on the other side of the river, I could hear the screams of the men who had followed us on land while we had traveled down the river.

"Maximiana! Walk back up! We will cross you by canoe up there!" one of them screamed.

I raised Isabel to my side on my hip and started my walk back. I stopped a couple of times to rest because little Isabel refused to walk.

"Isabel, listen … we will never get to your mamá if you don't walk."

She would merely sit and utterly refused to take a step on her own. We had almost reached the crossing spot when I saw Alejandro galloping towards us.

"Maximiana! Are you all right?" he shouted.

"Yes! But she doesn't want to walk, and I can't carry her anymore!"

He got off the horse.

"I knew this could happen. I told Father …"

"Is Señora Leonora all right? Did she cross?" I asked, avoiding inquiry into the fate of his father.

"Yes, Father swam across, but Roberto and Ramiro rescued Leonora … the carriage turned over into the river … there is no way to get it out."

I glanced back at the river and saw the beautiful black and gold carriage with its wheels upside.

"How are they going to get to El Roble then?"

"Ha, ha, ha! They will have to walk, I guess. I doubt that Leonora will want to ride on the cart with you and Raimunda, or get on a horse for at least three hours," he said.

I wanted to laugh, but God forbid I do it in front of Isabel, who was the miniature version of a gossipy lady. So I held my laughs to the inside.

When we had finally reached the crossing, I told Isabel to get on the canoe. But she would have none of it. She screamed in terror and wanted nothing to do with the water. Alejandro raised her and put her down on the canoe.

"Be quiet now … don't you want to go to your mother?" Alejandro asked.

She nodded.

"Then be quiet," he said softly.

Poor Isabel. She hugged my wet blouse and closed her eyes.

My wet blouse and skirt and …

I realized my letter was on the waistline of my skirt. Fearing the worst, I pulled the pieces of paper. The ink on the papers was gone; nothing remained but shadows of words penned for me. Carefully I held them on my hand. They would dry, and perhaps I could read at least some words on it. I bit my lip in dismay. How could I have jumped without taking it out first?

Señora Leonora walked towards us and grabbed Isabel by the hand, then moved away. Raimunda came to me and gave me a hug.

"That was very brave what you did."

"Thank you."

Applause exploded. I raised my head and looked around, searching for the reason of the applause, and then understood the applause was for me. My face turned crimson color, and embarrassed, I smiled. Lourdes came running towards me.

"Maximiana! Can I take care of your doll until we get to El Roble?" she asked.

"Sure," I responded, hoping she would not break it.

"What is her name?" she asked.

"Magdalena," I told her, going down on my knees, the better to speak to her face.

"Oh …," she said with emotion. "Look, Mother! Maximiana said I could take care of her doll. Her name is Magdalena!" she exclaimed, shouting all the way to her mamá.

To my alarm, it was too late for me to stop her. Señor Sarmiento turned around and looked at me when he heard the name of the doll. I swallowed and looked for Alejandro.

Earth devour me at once … again, please.

There was no way out of it; Señora Leonora and her girls had to ride in the cart with us. Raimunda and I walked for a while, and then Alejandro allowed us to take turns riding his horse. Other times Roberto would walk alongside and lead the mules so we could ride. With all the changes in position, time went faster; rather soon, Villa Unión appeared in the distance. By the time the sun was setting, we could see the soft lights of El Roble. My heart soared with emotion. I hadn't seen my family in two whole months. They were probably looking up the road of my house to see if we were coming. My house was located on the same street as the hacienda; and up the corner from the Grand

House, street oil lamps always illuminated the road. We enjoyed that little luxury of having lights so close to us at night.

Finally, we arrived at the entrance of El Roble. The tall *huana-caxtle* tree greeted us with its immensity. This final part, so very short, seemed never-ending; I just wanted to reach my house.

Then I saw Natalia and Otilia running towards me when they saw me coming down the street. I left the others and joined my sisters, and we entered my little house. I greeted Mamá and younger sisters. Papá stood up and gave me a hug. I turned around and pulled out of my blouse the little bag full of coins that I had saved for them. I handed the little package over to Mamá, who blushed proudly at my display of generosity and responsibility.

"I saved everything I earned, Mamá … every single cent is there. Where's Augusto?"

Mamá hugged me and replied, "He's still at work; he will be here soon … Daniel left a while ago. He waited for you, but Lorenza came to get him; he had to fetch water for his grandma."

"Oh, that is too bad. I missed him! I hope he comes tomorrow!" I said with sincere sorrow.

My younger sisters, Lucia and Rosaura, kept staring at my doll. Just as myself, they had never seen a doll as precious as Magdalena.

"It is a present, but you can take care of her for me during the day," I told them. "But at night, she will sleep with me."

They giggled and took her off my hands.

"You must be tired," Otilia said.

"And hungry!" replied Natalia.

"Yes, I am both. Let's eat and go to sleep. I don't know if I have to work tomorrow, though."

"I will tell Luisa you are sick from the trip. You will stay home tomorrow, my daughter," Mamá said and proceeded to warm up our dinner of beans with fresh cheese and newly made corn tortillas.

After our meal, my sisters desperately wanted to go to bed so they could hear all about my trip to the city, and they knew I would not spare a detail. We were getting ready to go to sleep when the tall figure of Daniel stood at our door. I ran to give him a big hug; he hugged me back and then started his usual teasing.

"Nope! You did not grow a centimeter!"

We all laughed when he said that, as if I would ever reach his height. The top of my head barely reached his shoulder. Fortunately, he had a heart as big as his stature. There was no one more honest and pure hearted than Daniel Gutierrez Tiznado. But his unmistakable sweetness most impressed all who met him. Daniel was my best friend, my true, loyal, and faithful friend. I knew I could count on him no matter what the circumstances, and for that reason, he always had a special place in my heart, just as I had my place in his.

"How was it?" Natalia asked, genuinely intrigued.

"The city has a lot of two-story buildings. The streets are not too wide, but carriages come and go all the time. There are at least two squares; one has an opera house next to it … girls, if you could see how beautiful it is … and its name is Rubio Theater. The decorations on the walls and the windows and doors take your breath away. There are stores so big that you can walk in them and look around and see … they sell everything in the same place from fabrics to sugar, all in the same store …"

"How interesting," Natalia said.

"How is the beach?" Otilia asked.

"Oh God, that is the best part of all! The sea is like a giant river, but waves keep coming at you and break on the beach like this," and I made the gesture with my hands. "They make a splashing sound but with rhythm, and the smell of seawater is delicious."

"Oh … I can just picture it," Natalia said, closing her beautiful sad eyes. "Did you hear the singers at the theater?"

"Sometimes when I took the girls to the Machado Square, I would sit close by and could hear them … oh Natalia … your voice is as beautiful as theirs. I bet you could sing in that opera house any time you want."

Natalia opened her mouth and gave one of those long, full, quavering sounds that only she could do.

We all laughed. My little sisters came to me with supplicant faces; they wanted to sleep with Magdalena tonight.

"Only tonight, Maxi, please."

"Fine, she can sleep with you tonight," I told them.

Then I remembered my wet letter. By the time we arrived at El Roble, the pieces of papers had dried into a knot. It broke my heart not being able to read Orlando's letter.

"Go to sleep now!" Otilia ordered them.

She and Natalia were dying to ask me about Orlando Sarmiento and anxious to get the little ones out of the way.

"Are you going to tell us about *him*?" Natalia asked in an undertone. "About Orlando?"

"Yes," both of them replied.

"He is so good to me that I feel I am living a dream."

"Why? What happened?" Natalia asked in her soft voice.

"Well … he says that he loves me and … he is very sweet to me … we took walks on the beach at night …"

Natalia closed her eyes again and heaved a profoundly deep sigh.

"Tell us more," she said.

"We kissed and hugged … we swam in the ocean …"

Otilia became uncomfortable and concerned.

"Nothing happened beyond that … I trust Orlando because he respects me."

"That is good news, Maxi," Otilia said.

"But making love lying on the sand, listening to those waves that you describe so beautifully must be too romantic, Max …," Natalia replied with her eyes still closed.

"I know," I sighed, "but I couldn't risk myself like that."

"Good thinking," Otilia confirmed.

"I don't know … love overwhelms you. I simply don't understand how you can stop yourself, Max," Natalia said then, noting our raised eyebrows, added, "I am serious."

Natalia had romance in her veins, and everyone knew it. She was so soft spoken and sweet with a beauty striking from any distance. She had a small frame, and her breasts were firm and round. Natalia's hair was light brown, wavy but short. She refused to let her hair grow; something that Mamá did not comprehend. Her eyes had a sad appearance and combined perfectly with a long and almost straight nose. Natalia had some freckles on her cheeks that gave her a childish look of innocence. Yet, when she sang, her voice came out so strong that you had to cover your ears or else become deaf. Natalia could sing in ways that nobody in town had heard before.

"You did good, Max," Otilia said again. "You have to be careful, especially with those people."

"No worries about it. Orlando is different, and so is Alejandro. Alejandro is the middle one."

"Yes, I know," Otilia replied.

"What about the oldest one?"

Natalia finally opened her eyes.

"Domingo is a pest. No man has more meanness and arrogance than Domingo Sarmiento; he takes after the father," I said, raising my voice at the memories of what gave proof to my statements.

"Hush, Maximiana … don't disrespect an older man," Otilia scolded me.

"Well, it is the truth!" I declared loudly.

"Shhh! Mamá will send us to sleep if you scream," Natalia intervened. "Tell us, what do they look like?"

"Alejandro and Orlando look a little bit alike, but Domingo is different. They say he looks like his dead mother. I think Orlando is the most handsome of all, but Alejandro is the sweetest and Domingo … as I said before … he is a complete nightmare of a person."

They both laughed at my last phrase.

"And his girlfriend, Catalina Barraza, is as bad as he is. Like him, she holds her nose in the air and has a group of girlfriends that scare me. They were too rude and egocentric."

"What, dear sister, is *egocentric*?" Otilia asked, barely containing her amusement.

"They only think of themselves and nobody else; that is what it means."

"Oy … Max knows so many new words since she's been to the city," Natalia joked.

"It was not the city, silly; it is my reading. By the way, I will teach all of you how to read and write." That statement took them by surprise.

"How?" Natalia asked.

"The same way I learned. Now I have more experience because I have been teaching Raimunda and Josefina, a girl who works in Mazatlán. Wouldn't you like to learn?"

"But how are we going to buy the paper tablets and pencils?" Otilia was concerned.

"I work; I could buy them. Besides, I brought some pencils the twins threw away. Look … we can start writing the letters on the dirt, with a stick, and then we will move on to paper tablets."

"It sounds like a good plan," Natalia said.

"Yes, it is. You have to start with the little ones," Otilia suggested.

"No! All of you together. I will be your teacher."

After proudly declaring these last words, exhaustion from the day's adventures fell upon me and tugged my eyelids closed.

"Let's go to sleep now … I am too tired."

"You are right," Otilia said as she kissed me good night. "We missed you, Maxi."

"Oh I missed you, too … a lot …," I responded in a fading, dreamy voice.

"Good night, Max," Natalia said in her angelic voice.

I couldn't answer that; my mind had already traveled to the land of dreams.

10

Two days later, Doña Luisa handed an envelope to me. Confused I took it from her hands.

"Señor Sarmiento asked me to give you this; it is a compensation for saving Isabel from drowning in the river," Doña Luisa said, visually pleased.

"Oh … but they don't have to pay me anything." *A thank you would've been enough.*

"Take it child and help your family with it," she reassured me.

When I opened the envelope, I saw fifty pesos inside. My mind raced, thinking about what this money meant.

"Thank you, Doña Luisa," I said, containing my impulse to jump with joy.

"Take that money home child. I don't want you to lose it … but come back as soon as possible; we have much to do."

I walked out fast; I didn't want to miss a second before telling Mamá.

"Mamá … guess what?" I said hugging her.

"What did you do? Why are you here so early?" Mamá replied, with hands on her waist.

"I have a surprise for you … Mamá you won't believe what I'm going to tell you!"

"Talk, daughter," she replied, losing her patience.

"Señor Sarmiento gave me a reward for rescuing little Isabel from the river! Mamá, he gave me fifty whole pesos!" I exclaimed full of enthusiasm. "Look!"

Mamá's face dropped. She took the coins from me as if in disbelief of having such an amount of money in her hands.

"Take it, Mamá. I have to go back to work."

Mamá was speechless.

But I had words. "Please go to the store at the corner, pay off all of our debts, and buy four paper tablets ... no! Buy five and five pencils. I want Daniel to learn as well ... we are starting our school today!" Then I gave her a loud kiss and ran out towards the hacienda.

Working at the Grand House was not the same without Orlando around. I missed him a lot, and thoughts of him constantly came to mind as I worked where he once had been. Cleaning his room once a week was a treat, giving me the chance to recall delightful memories and see some in a different light. For instance, I realized that jumping that balcony represented more than an adventure. It signified the liberation of my oppressed self as a girl: I didn't need a boy to come and see me; I could just go to the boy on my own and jump any height without fearing the fall. And at the same time, I learned to respect my inner self and control the situations around me. It also trained me to fulfill my desire to learn more than what was offered to me or expected of me; everything was possible. That was the most important lesson of all.

Alejandro allowed me to borrow more books; he liked to ask me about them and usually delighted in my answers. I avoided Señora Sarmiento, who continued looking at me with disgust.

One afternoon, while mopping the gigantic salon's black and white floor, Alejandro astonished me with an invitation.

"Maximiana, do you want to go to the arroyo today?"

"Mmm ... sure ... but is it fine with you if my sisters come along?" Apparently he was not very pleased with my suggestion.

"How old are they?"

"Oh … I meant my older sisters, not the young ones."

"Fine then, see you at around five?"

"I don't have a watch …," I said.

"Right … fine. I will see you after you leave the hacienda and after … let's see … later than that … I will see you by the arroyo, up towards the Twins' Well … yes?"

"Sure … I will see you then."

Otilia refused to go with us; she said she was too shy to sit at the arroyo with Alejandro Sarmiento. No human power in this world could convince her otherwise. Mamá was concerned, but she could not refuse to let us go; Alejandro was, as everyone knew, a Sarmiento, and his wishes were orders.

"Mamá, Alejandro is a sweetheart. You have nothing to worry about … just look at how nice he is to let me borrow books, and now that I am teaching, he is my biggest supporter."

When Alejandro found out about my teaching arrangements, he took it with a lot of pride. He showed as much excitement in my little school adventure as I felt making it. He provided colored pencils and more paper tablets for us and allowed me to borrow young reader's books for my students. After two weeks of lessons, little children in town started to come and see. In no time, I had a group gathered around my sidewalk every evening. Alejandro heard about it and came once on his horse to see us; my students were afraid of him, even though he greeted them with a big smile. After that, he promised to bring me a blackboard and a box of chalk from Mazatlán. His next trip would take place at the end of October, which was around the corner because it was the middle of the month already.

"Please Otis … come with us," I begged to no avail.

Natalia was more than ready. She put together a basket of pineapple *empanadas* and *coricos*. I loved the cinnamon taste of coricos.

We walked out of our little house through the back door. Natalia kept looking at me, smiling; she really wanted to meet Alejandro, and I think she idealized him through my tales of the fellow.

Alejandro was already waiting for us when we arrived. Evidently, he had walked to the arroyo because I saw no sign of his horse.

"Alejandro!" I screamed, waving my hand. Then to Natalia, I asked, "What's hanging on his back?"

"It looks like a guitar," she replied.

He waved back and walked towards us.

"Hello … this is my sister Natalia."

"Nice meeting you," he said, lowering his head while touching the tip of his hat.

"Nice meeting you, too," Natalia replied with a wide smile. Natalia had the same self-assurance I did; like me, she talked to people looking directly at their eyes.

"So you play guitar?" Natalia asked.

"I try," Alejandro responded. "Let's find some shade to sit in."

We followed him to a spot large enough for the three of us and sat after him.

"We brought empanadas. Do you want one?" I asked.

"Sure." He bit one and declared, "These are delicious. Did you bake them?"

"No, Mamá did," Natalia responded. "Please play the guitar for us, would you?"

"Fine, but don't run away trying to escape my horrible music!" he said, laughing.

Natalia closed her eyes when he started playing a very soft tune, and notes just naturally escaped her lips. Alejandro glanced at me in astonishment. The gorgeous sound, clear and beautiful, could not be ignored.

"Natalia, sing a song for us," I said.

She hesitated but a moment and then started to sing. Alejandro's eyes enlarged to their maximum. Natalia's voice threw anyone under a spell.

"Your voice is incredible!" Alejandro said.

"Thank you," Natalia replied with a smile.

"Yes, it is incredible … you should hear her when she screams! My goodness, your ears vibrate," I said proudly.

"Give me a high note …"

"A what?" we asked simultaneously.

"A high sound …"

"What is that?" I asked.

"Oh … right …" Alejandro understood our confusion and tried to explain. "It is a note, like … mmm … I don't think I can show you but it sounds … let me see … like 'thin' … like this," and he plucked the guitar's string.

"Like this?" Natalia asked and allowed a high note to escape from her chest. I quickly covered my ears.

"You are an Angela Peralta!" Alejandro exclaimed.

"Ha, ha, ha!" I laughed full of pride.

Natalia acted indifferent; that is the way she was.

"You know, Maximiana, you always surprise me, but this time you overdid it," Alejandro said, scolding me in a joking way. "I did *not* expect your sister to be a human nightingale."

Even Natalia laughed at his words.

"May I borrow your guitar?" Natalia asked.

Alejandro handed it over. Natalia began to pass her delicate fingers on the strings, which made very soft, harmonious music. She lost herself in the sounds. Alejandro sat there, looking at her in amazement.

"How old are you, Natalia?" Alejandro asked.

"Seventeen … and you?" she said without stopping her playing.

"Nineteen."

"I am almost fifteen," I said proudly, without being asked.

"Max … you just turned fourteen in May," Natalia said.

"Exactly, in a few months I will be fifteen."

Alejandro kept looking at both of us.

"So your nickname is 'Max'?" he asked, winking.

"Either 'Max' or 'Maxi,'" I replied.

"I like Max better," Natalia said.

"Why?" Alejandro wanted to know.

"Because Max is so different from everybody that she deserves a different name."

Alejandro became, beyond doubt, extremely interested in her words.

"How would her nickname play a part in that?" he asked.

"Well, Max is like a two-spirited person, you see? She is romantic like a girl but very strong and decisive like a boy."

"Yes," I interrupted, "but any girl can be strong and decisive like a boy, Natalia. There is no difference in what boys and girls can be."

Alejandro kept looking at both of us with wonder on his face.

"Two-spirited, huh?" he said.

"Yes, that is what I call her condition … two-spirited," Natalia said, laughing.

"And Max … why Max and not Maxi?"

"Because Max is a boy's name," Natalia replied.

"So you call me Max not because Maximiana is too long and Max would be shorter … but because you think I am like a boy?" I said, shocked.

"Yes," Natalia replied.

We all started to laugh.

"But … Natalia … don't think of me as a boy. Don't think that I am like a boy because I am strong; it is like saying that girls cannot be or do the same things as boys, and that is not true."

"Yes," Alejandro said, "but the way families raise girls *and* boys makes them act that way."

"And that needs to change. If I have daughters, I will teach them to be daring and strong, and if I have boys I will teach them to be romantic and delicate. All of it combined."

"Me too," Natalia said. "I will teach them to be both."

"I guess I should too, right?" Alejandro said with a smile.

"Yes!" we replied in chorus.

"There is no way for me to get bored in your company, Max," he said then added, "and now you, Nat."

"Same here, Aleh," I replied, and he burst into laughter with us.

"Yes, never bored with you two. Now, pass me another empanada," he said.

We had a wonderful time together that evening, and the most wonderful thing of all was that Alejandro and Natalia started a friendship of their own. That night Natalia couldn't stop talking about Alejandro Sarmiento and his way of behaving.

"I told you he was something else," I told her. "Any woman would fall in love with him, seriously!"

"I know," she replied, "he is so different from anybody I ever talked to … is Orlando like him?"

"No … Orlando is … he is perfect," I said, letting a sigh escape my bosom.

"I won't ask you about the other one because I know what you think of him," Natalia said to me in a teasing tone.

"Oh! God! Domingo … Natalia, if you *ever* meet him, he will send you running the other way. He is so very rude and arrogant. He looks at you as if you are an ant in his way. I talked to him once, and he actually laughed. I was shocked by it, but after that he never talked to me again, and when I encountered him in the house, he would turn his face away quickly to avoid me; he probably thought I was going to greet him …"

"Oh … he sounds awful."

"He *is*," I said. "He is too rude … I just keep my distance from him. To tell you the truth, I am a little bit afraid of him."

"He does sound scary."

"I know. Unless you start working in the Grand House, you will never see him; he doesn't get out of the hacienda when he is in town … he is probably afraid of the dust!" We both laughed.

Otilia sent us to sleep with one of her looks. I felt she was sorry she hadn't accompanied us to see Alejandro. Poor Otilia, her young soul carried so much pain; she needed all the understanding in the world.

I grabbed Magdalena and placed her next to me; I took the shell bracelet off my wrist and hid it very carefully under my pillow. My two treasures were safe with me. Then, I fell asleep.

11

November 10, 1907
Mazatlán, México

My dear Maximiana,

I am counting the days until I will see you again (35!) and one year and a half until you turn sixteen (don't forget your promise). Every night I dream of the times we had together. Then, I imagine the future, with you by my side. You love me, and I love you.

When I go to sleep, I see your beautiful face. Then I wake up, but you are not there. I miss you, my Maximiana, but the hope of seeing you soon helps me continue my days, forgetting my misery for your not being here with me.

I am glad that you liked the doll; she is pretty like you.

My brother told me what happened to the letter, by the way. Thank you for taking that brat out of the river.

I'm almost there, Maximiana. You are mine forever.

Love,

Orlando Sarmiento

I read the letter over and over in my mind, recording each word in my heart. I had to wait a few more days to see Orlando again, but it didn't matter because now it was sooner than later. When I first came back from Mazatlán, I thought I would have to wait for eternity to see December. But it was coming fast, bringing my Orlando along.

The upcoming Christmas seemed more special than any previous year. Yes, I looked forward to the holiday because Orlando would be home, but also, for the first time, my family had no debts at the corner store or the hacienda store. Also, Mamá had enough spare money to buy a new pot, some dishes to replace cracked ones, and our first set of glasses. She bought fabric and made new linens for all our cots, and we all had new skirts, blouses, and sandals. We secretly planned a big Christmas surprise for Rosaura and Lucia, my two little sisters; each would get a special Christmas present. For Rosaura, who was nine, Mamá wanted to buy a book of children's stories. I have to confess it was my idea. For Lucia, who was only seven, Mamá wanted to get a doll. She cherished my Magdalena, and we all knew she would love to have one of her own. Of course, we also talked about having a very nice dinner waiting for us after Rooster's Mass at church on Christmas Eve. It was less than a month away, but Mamá needed to order the book and the doll at the corner store. They promised to have them ready for us before Christmas. And candies, each one of us would get a bag of candies.

Natalia came up with the idea of decorating a Christmas tree. We would cut a short tree and take off the green leaves, then set it in a bucket with sand. We would cover each leafless branch with white cotton, to simulate snow. Then we would make our own ornaments and a star at the top. Mamá was not so sure she wanted to spend money on such frivolities, but we promised to save the ornaments and cotton for next year, and she agreed.

We couldn't wait for the holiday. This was going to be our first Christmas celebration with a nice dinner, a present for the little ones, and our very own Christmas tree.

Natalia had been practicing the song she was going to sing on December 12 at church for the celebration of the Virgin of Guadalupe. She had never sung in public before and felt very nervous about it, especially because the church would have an unusually large crowd, for everyone celebrated México's patron saint. Many flowers and colorful paper flags would decorate the church, turning it into a most beautiful setting. Everyone in town looked forward to the day for, in addition to the festivities, the Sarmientos would give them hot chocolate and sweet bread to take home.

Time flew and in an opening and closing of eyes, Orlando would arrive in three days, but the hours moved too slowly for my patience. Still, work at the Grand House helped the time pass. One day as I exited the hacienda, ready to go home, Alejandro said, "Maximiana, I have a suggestion. Perhaps Natalia could sing at the New Year's party celebration."

"She is going to sing tomorrow at the Virgin of Guadalupe mass … her first time in front of people … I don't know … but … sing where?" I answered.

"Sing at our party. I am sure Father will agree to pay her."

"I'll ask her today and see what she thinks, but … she doesn't sing the type of songs that all of you like." I honestly worried about that detail.

"But I could teach her … we still have almost three weeks left," he said.

"I will tell her," I replied and walked away.

As soon as I entered my house, I gave Natalia the news.

"Natalia. There you are. I have something to tell you. Alejandro asked me today if you would sing at the hacienda during the New Year's party."

Natalia looked at me in disbelief.

"Sing … in front of everybody … by myself?"

"Yes. He said they would pay you."

"I don't know … I don't even have a dress to wear for something like that, and I wouldn't know which songs to sing …"

"Alejandro said he could teach you the songs … you know how nice he is … he wants you to make money, I guess."

"Really? It does sound like a good idea. But, would Mamá and Papá agree?"

"I don't know … you tell them … I could even go with you that night. Yes, I think it is a great idea!" I exclaimed, thinking of having a chance to be near Orlando in the New Year's celebration.

"Yes … and I will be able to see the inside of the Grand House," Natalia said, her voice filled with enthusiasm.

"You will be disappointed, trust me on that one," I replied. "Talk to Mamá and Papá tonight; let's see what they say."

"Yes, I will."

The talk in town for the next year was Natalia's singing to the Virgin of Guadalupe on December 12. When she opened her mouth, magic filled the air. The church went dead silent, and only her clear, full notes penetrated the void, echoing off the walls and vibrating in every person's inner-self. No one would ever forget. Mamá beamed in pride, but Papá did not look up; he was too embarrassed to see her up at the podium singing. The Sarmientos sat in the front row. Alejandro could not hide his enthusiasm; he kept smiling and looking back at me during her entire performance.

When Natalia ended, she walked back to sit with us. I held her shaking and frozen hand while Otilia put her arm around her shoulder. I felt so proud to be her sister that, just like Alejandro, I couldn't stop smiling.

After church we went back home to enjoy our hot chocolate and sweet bread. Daniel stopped by our house on his way home.

"Natalia, I think you made the inside of my ears explode!" he said with a very proud expression on his face.

Natalia smiled at him.

"I could pull your ear for that … but I cannot reach it," she calmly retorted, and we all laughed at her idea.

The pounding of my heart woke me up on December 15. I was finally going to see Orlando today, so I hurried on my way to the hacienda first thing in the morning. I knew he would arrive in the afternoon. He was riding on horses with Domingo and the others, and by not taking a carriage, they advanced rapidly.

By now, I was very used to the routine at the Grand House. I did my chores accordingly and rarely got in trouble. I liked working with Raimunda; we had fun chatting about different silly things. Doña Luisa would hush us up as soon as she heard the giggling.

All the other servants in the house looked at me suspiciously. Apparently they all believed that I, in Orlando's absence, now had something to do with Alejandro Sarmiento, and knowing their way of *seeing*, at this point, they probably suspected Natalia as well because we would take walks at the arroyo with him sometimes.

On the other hand I was disappointed that none of the servants, save Raimunda, wanted to join our evening school. By now I had twenty-three students, children and teenagers; the blackboard Alejandro had brought me from Mazatlán helped me explain and demonstrate to such a large group. I wanted some adults to join, but they thought I was completely out of my senses. Mamá and Papá were the first ones to refuse. Doña Luisa looked at me when I asked her and literally started crying from laughter. Nonetheless, she hugged me when she finished expressing her amusement.

"Maximiana, I need you to help me in the library," Alejandro requested in front of Doña Luisa.

"Yes," I said. "What do I need to bring?"

"A rag to dust," he replied.

I grabbed one and followed him. Once inside the library, he told me the real reason for his requesting me.

"Maximiana, I have a dress for Natalia."

"Aha …"

"For her performance in the New Year's celebration."

"Oh …" I was stunned.

"You see ... she will be singing opera; she needs a dress like this one."

"But ... whose dress is this?" I asked. It was obviously not new; you could tell it had been used.

"It was my mother's," he said. "Is that all right with you?"

"That will be an honor," I replied, looking directly into his eyes. "But people might recognize the dress ... how ... they may think I stole it for Natalia to wear."

"Father will recognize it for sure ..." he said, satisfied, "and Doña Luisa, but I will explain to her that I gave it to you ..."

"What about your father?"

"I have nothing to explain to him."

"But ..."

"Listen; if there is a problem with him, I will explain the truth. Is that fine with you?" he asked in a tone that I had not heard him use before.

"Yes," I replied.

"Hey ... are you excited that Big Head is coming today?" he finally joked, noting my discomfort with the dress issue.

"Yes, I am!" I replied, forgetting for the moment Natalia and the dress.

"That is why I called you to the library, to allow time for him to arrive," he winked.

"Really? That was nice of you."

"Oh ... thank you ... why don't you sit down?"

I walked to the pink chair and sat. It felt so good to rest upon the feather-stuffed cushion.

"How many books do you have in here?" I asked, intrigued.

"Over five thousand ..."

"I wish I could read them all," I stated in complete sincerity.

Alejandro gasped at my spoken desire, and I smiled at his surprise—or was it disbelief?

"What time is it?" I asked.

Pulling out his pocket watch, he replied, "It is 4:55 ... they are almost here ..."

The sound of the gates opening interrupted his sentence. I ran to the window, and I saw him. Orlando had arrived. The dogs barked wildly as he and Domingo dismounted their horses and walked towards the house. I felt my body turn into a stone statue, just like the ones in the garden. Alejandro went out of the library and called Orlando. He looked tanner than when I had left him, his cheeks glowed pinker than usual, and his curls held evidence of the dusty ride. He walked into the library and saw me standing there. I was too nervous even to smile, but he came up to me and gave me a strong hug. I hugged him back.

"I missed you," I shyly said.

"I missed you, too," he replied. "But I have to go to Father … are you coming tonight?"

"Yes … I will," I said, and he walked out. I followed him up to the kitchen and saw him enter the house.

"Doña Luisa, can I go home now?"

"What is that?" she asked, looking at the box in my hands.

"It is a dress Alejandro gave to my sister … for the day she is going to sing here."

She looked at me puzzled.

"May I see it?"

"I guess …" I handed over the box. She walked into the storage room next to the kitchen and asked me to follow her. Doña Luisa placed the box on a table and opened it carefully.

"This is Señora Sarmiento's," she said in a whisper.

"Yes, Alejandro told me it was his mamá's."

"Wait here," she said and walked out of the room.

I examined the dress—gorgeous, dark red with black and old lace touches to it. I had no idea how to put it together. It came in three different pieces, but I thought we could figure that out. Then I folded it back into the box and closed the lid.

"Here …" she said at her return while handing me another box, but smaller, "she has to wear this under the dress. It is a corset. That will push her stomach and waist in so the dress will fit. Do you know how to use it?"

"No."

"Turn around; let me show you."

She put it on top of my blouse.

"Suck the air in," she said and started pulling the laces on my back. Slowly I began to feel the air cut off to my lungs.

"Doña Luisa … I can't breathe!"

"This is the way it works."

No wonder those girls are so frustrated! They are always out of air!

"Doña Luisa … I don't think … my sister … can … sing … wearing … this …," I said, unable to utter a complete sentence without gasping for breath.

"They do it the entire time, child; besides the dress will not fit her without a corset."

"Aye, Doña Luisa, this is torture. Are you done?" I asked in desperation.

"Almost." She seemed to be enjoying my encounter with high fashion. "There."

I placed my hands on my waist; the corset had reduced my middle to half its original size. Then Doña Luisa, showing a rare characteristic that I had no clue she possessed, called the girls working in the kitchen to come and see me. There I stood, the joke of the day. And what was the worst part? I couldn't grasp air to laugh with them.

"Fiuu! Fiuu! Maximiana!" They started whistling at me.

I twirled around and curtsied at them. They laughed even harder.

"Wait! Doña Luisa I want to know how it feels to sit when you are wearing this thing," I said.

Raimunda ran to get a chair from the kitchen and put it next to me. Now, *that* was mind-boggling. I felt my lungs crushing against each other, my heart moving up to my throat, and my bladder about to explode. I asked for Doña Luisa's hand to get up, and she came laughing.

"Please untie me from this torture!" I begged. She agreed while the others all went back to their work, still amused.

"Listen, Maximiana, your sister has to wear this underneath the dress. Tell her to practice singing with it, sitting down, and walking around with it …"

"Oh, I know Natalia; she will even sleep in it!"

"If she is a little bit like you, I don't doubt it," she said with a warm smile.

Then she explained to me how to put the dress together, and finally, out of her pocket, she pulled two golden hairpins. She placed them in my hand.

"Tell her these are from me as a thank you for her beautiful song to the Virgin of Guadalupe on her day."

I was touched. I felt my eyes getting watery.

"Oh … thank you, Doña Luisa," I said and gave her a hug.

She hugged me back. Next, she walked me to the gate, carrying the boxes herself. I took them and went back home, feeling the looks from people standing on the sidewalks and peering from the windows. Nonetheless, I greeted everyone, "Good evening." I was sure they thought the boxes were presents for *me* from Orlando Sarmiento, and they all would've given their lives to see what was inside.

Just as suspected, Natalia slept with the corset from that day on. I don't know if it was my imagination, but I could swear that her waist became smaller after weeks of such torture.

"Don't go, Maxi," Otilia begged me when she caught me about to sneak out of our house. "Everyone in town talks about you going into the hacienda at night."

"But nothing bad happens, Otilia … I swear to God for Mamá."

"I believe you, but it looks bad … please," she pleaded.

"I have to go, Otis … he is waiting."

I left her standing on our tiny sidewalk, and taking the longest strides I possibly could, I reached the hacienda's fence. Orlando was waiting. He helped me jump it, and then we climbed the balcony together.

"So … how are you?"

My "dizzy by love" mind could think of no better greeting. He bit his lower lip and went directly to my lips.

"Mmm … now I am better," he said.

How much did I love him? I don't know if a measurement exists that can say. Thoughts of him intoxicated my whole being, my mind, my body, my heart; I have no other logical way to describe my feelings for Orlando Sarmiento.

"Come here to me, Maximiana," he said after sitting on the floor. As I had done so many times before, I fixed my skirt to the side and sat on his lap. I placed my arms around his neck, and he hugged me tight.

"I missed you a lot!"

"Me, too!" I replied.

We both hugged, and I sighed profoundly.

"So … how was your school?" I finally asked.

"Boring and strict … at least I had Domingo and some friends there … and guess what?"

"What?"

"Domingo is going to Boston in the summer. He got accepted to Harvard University."

"Oh, that is great … your brother is lucky … so lucky," I said.

"When I am older, I will go, too," he said in a murmur.

My heart sank.

"Yes, you are lucky, too."

I fought my selfishness of not wanting to have him gone when I said those words.

"Really?"

"Yes … what I wouldn't give to attend a school … like the German School in Mazatlán …"

"Mmmm … that is impossible; the German School is for boys only," he said, smiling.

"Any school then … to have a teacher and learn so much … and then go to a university and become a medicine doctor or a teacher."

"Alejandro said you *are* a teacher."

"But I am not a *real* teacher."

"Well … that is true. But … women should not go to university; there is no point."

My face tightened when he said that, and he noticed.

"Right?" he asked.

"Mmm … why not?"

"Because they get married and have children, and they take care of their children."

"But the children also belong to the father, right? It is half and half."

"Yes, but the mother is the one that raises the children."

"Why? Why can't the father *also* raise the children … that way the mother can *also* go to university and do something else in life besides taking care of children."

"Because *that* is the way it is."

"But it could be changed, right?"

"I don't know, Maximiana; I don't make the rules," he said, irritated.

"I don't agree to that," I said, "and I think it can be changed."

"You talk too much," he said sharply.

I started tickling his ribs. He couldn't keep his seriousness for long and started defending himself from my tickling fingers. We landed on the floor, and I rested on his chest with a sigh.

"I love you, Orlando."

"I love you, Maximiana," he replied, crossing his fingers with mine.

"I wish you could stay the whole night and sleep like this …," he said.

"Me, too."

I closed my eyes at the thought, and he closed his.

"Guess what?"

"What?" I said in a low tone.

"Domingo is tired of Catalina Barraza."

I opened my eyes in a flash.

"They are not engaged anymore?"

"No … they were never engaged. Father wants him to get engaged to her because, as you know, her family is …" He cut himself short.

"Rich?"

"Yes," he said in a whisper.

"I thought Domingo liked her; they seemed perfect for each other."

"No, she is kind of silly … that is what he says."

"Mmm … she looked mean to me, but not silly," I replied.

"I don't know."

"So, they broke up?"

"Yes, Domingo broke up with her yesterday, the day right before we left."

"Ah … poor girl."

"No! She has a line of beaus waiting outside her window by now."

"Probably," I said, "but she looked absolutely in love with Domingo."

"Yes … I think Domingo likes somebody else already."

"Really?" I was intrigued. "Who?"

"I don't know … but she could be Olivia Villar or mmmh … Susana Williamson."

"Are they pretty?" I asked, feeling a sensation that I had never felt before.

"Oh yes, they are," he responded in a tone that affirmed his satisfaction on the subject.

I noted it and merely replied, "Oh," feeling my first tinges of jealously.

"Why are you so quiet?" he asked, sensing something had gone wrong.

"I don't know … I guess I hadn't thought about you around all those pretty, well-dressed girls in Mazatlán."

"Oh," he said and changed the subject, completely ignoring my statement.

"Is Alejandro seeing your sister?"

"How? What?" He took me by surprise.

"Is my brother going out with your sister, the one who sings?"

"No! They are just friends. What are you talking about?"

"I don't know … it is just that he … oh, never mind."

"Did he tell you that he likes Natalia?" I asked in amazement.

"Not with those words … but I suspect he does … you know how he is … he doesn't talk about such things."

"No? But he told me he left a sweetheart in Boston."

"He did?" he asked in astonishment.

"Yes. You didn't know?"

"No. He keeps those things to himself. Ahhh … perhaps that is why he wants to take Domingo to Boston himself."

My heart shrank when he said that Alejandro might leave.

"How long would he be gone?" I asked, preoccupied.

"Months."

I couldn't hide my disappointment.

"Orlando … I have to go now … it must be late, and I have to come to work tomorrow."

"Mmm … stay longer," he begged with a sweetheart face.

"I am tired, and you must be also."

"Yes … but I can sleep in late tomorrow …"

"I know … but *I* cannot; I have to be here at 6:30 in the morning."

He didn't listen to my words.

"Please … stay longer. You have hardly embraced me after … how long? Four months!"

He shut my mouth as I began to reply, and then as he turned over me, he placed his arms under my back and his hands under my head. His kisses overflowed with passion. Words left me, and I embraced him and kissed him back. He had a tremendous power over my emotions and sometimes over my will power, I have to admit it.

"I have to go now," I said when the situation started to get out of hand and his caressing began to turn into something more profound than my conscience allowed. He pulled away from me and raised himself up.

I kissed him good-bye. "I will see you tomorrow …"

He nodded and helped me jump the fence one more time.

Otilia was up when I tiptoed into the house through the side door.

"Maximiana … are you fine?"

"Yes," I said with a whisper and walked to my cot.

I took Magdalena and cuddled her in my arms. A sensation of despair entered my heart. I couldn't explain why, but I felt like crying. In the safety of my bed and the shadows of the night, I allowed my tears to slide down my face to my neck, silently so that nobody would hear me. I felt joyful that Orlando was back in town for two weeks, but I sensed that something was not right. I just couldn't grasp what it was. I told myself to stop filling my mind with nonexistent ideas, but the sensation of despair stayed, deeply carving itself into my heart.

12

Several guests arrived at the grand hacienda for the holidays, including the Barraza family. Señor Sarmiento wanted Domingo to reconsider his breakup with Catalina, and he was constantly arguing with him about it, but Domingo seemed oblivious to his demands. Alejandro was on Domingo's side, as expected. Orlando removed himself from the entire drama and kept his opinions to himself, if he had any at all regarding the infamous breakup.

Once the Barrazas arrived, the arguments stopped in consideration of the guests. As expected, Señora Leonora was very excited about the arrival of their guests; her parents were also joining them for the holidays. Lourdes and Isabel found no end talking about their coming Christmas presents from baby Jesus. And when Señora Leonora set up the Christmas tree in the grand salon, Lourdes and Isabel, in their enthusiasm for such a splendid sight, wanted to sleep under it at night. The colorful ornaments sparkled, even without any lights, and the nativity set looked more marvelous than any I had ever seen. For once, I wished I could stay later than I usually did to see how the Christmas tree looked when they lighted the candles.

Along with the Barrazas and Señora Leonora's parents, came two friends of Catalina, Dora Elena Mora, who I had met before in Mazatlán, and another one named Florentina Verdeño. Since the day of their arrival, they looked at me in a way that made me feel tremendously uncomfortable. But I kept out of their way as much as possible.

The young women were accommodated in Alejandro's room, and Señora Leonora's parents in Orlando's. The displaced Sarmiento brothers moved to Domingo's bedroom, across the path to the library. Catalina's parents were placed in the guests' quarters. I may add that our workload multiplied by ten when the guests arrived. And they had no reservations in giving us any type of orders that came to their minds, never once saying "Thank you," either.

Orlando and I kept exchanging looks at every opportunity. But returning to the balcony room was now an impossible task.

Meanwhile, Natalia memorized the song she was going to sing at the New Year's celebration, "Over the Sea" by Melesio Morales. According to Alejandro, she only needed to sing that one song, nothing else. I sensed something more going on with this requested performance and kept wondering what, but I trusted Alejandro; he would never do anything to harm my sister. Besides, I had received permission to accompany Natalia, and if anything would go wrong, in an instant, I would pull her away, and we would run out of there together. I felt very proud of Natalia; next to Alejandro, she was the bravest person I knew.

My family had a glorious Christmas celebration, unlike any ever before. Mamá prepared a turkey in the wood oven, fresh bread, delicious goat milk *cajeta*, pineapple, pumpkin, and sweet milk empanadas. She made *agua de horchata* to drink. The spindly Christmas tree actually looked very festive. We made the ornaments out of *papier-mâché* and little shiny crystals Mamá bought at the corner store. Fortunately, Lucia and Rosaura's presents arrived just in time, and Señorita Luz was nice enough to keep them hidden at her house.

Rooster's Mass started at midnight. We arrived early at church to get good seats; I felt the blood rush through my veins when I saw Orlando, looking dashingly handsome, entering the church. He sat next to his father in the front row; he looked back once and gave me half a smile. When Alejandro came to greet us and wish us Merry Christmas, Papá shook his hand softly. Mamá acted as her usual self, in complete control and seriousness. Otilia looked down when she saw Alejandro coming towards us. Through me, he had learned of the reason for her shyness.

"How are you, Otilia?" he asked her directly when her avoidance was too obvious to ignore.

"Fine, thank you," Otilia answered, staring at her hands.

"Merry Christmas," Alejandro said with one of his sweet smiles.

"Thank you, sir," Otilia replied with her cheeks as red as blood.

"'Alejandro,' please."

Otilia looked up and smiled. Then I realized that every single eye in that church was on us, except the Sarmientos'.

After wishing Merry Christmas to everyone present at church, Alejandro went back to sit with his family, right next to Domingo, who spent the entire mass looking directly at the altar and obviously avoiding Catalina Barraza, whose eyes fixed on him like lightning seeking the earth to strike on a stormy night.

After mass, we went home to eat our Christmas dinner. We talked and laughed until the first lights of dawn streamed forth in the sky. I loved listening to the stories from the time Mamá and Papá were little children. Mamá came from a small town called Mesillas; Mesillas is very close to La Villa de San Sebastián. She told us her grandparents had come from a small ranch called El Cuacoyol, which was located deep in the Sierra Mountains. They both remembered the cyclone that hit the area when they were children and hundreds of people died. They said the rivers overflowed and swept away everything within their reach. Mamá remembered that the waters reached the cemetery and dug out the tombs; caskets rose out, and to the horror of those watching, the current carried them off. I was more than glad that this story came up when little Rosaura and Lucia were already asleep. Even I found it too terrifying to think about it.

Neither one of my parents remembered celebrating Christmas as children, but they were glad that, for their own son and daughters, every year they had managed to do something a little bit special. They had known poverty and misery, they said, and unfortunately, each one of us understood.

"One day things will change," Papá said seriously.

"When?" Augusto asked.

"Soon."

Papá did not elaborate after Mamá gave him a look that said "no more."

"If there were a revolution, I would join it," Augusto said quietly.

"Revolution" had become a prohibited word among people living in poverty. The political system operated for the wealthy and held no tolerance for challenges. It kept wages low or non-existant, stole land from the peasants, and kept the poor ignorant and in debt. For the rich wished to hold onto their choice position as much as the poor wanted to have the opportunity to undo it. But any hint that workers could organize or even think about changing the oppressive system was a death sentence to their families. Everyone knew of peasants who had spoken out against the hacendados—and never would again. Yet brave souls continued to emerge from the oppressed lines; stories about the revolutionary seekers were multiplying by the day; the fact was that people would not take the abuse anymore. The difference between the few rich and the millions of poor was too great to ignore any longer.

"I would join it, too," I said.

They all looked at me, not surprised at all.

"Would you go against the fancy Sarmiento boys?" Augusto asked.

Would I go against Orlando and Alejandro?

"Not against *them* personally, but I would go against the system," I replied.

"They *are* the system, you idiot," Augusto declared, clenching his teeth.

"What kind of language is this?" Mamá said, jumping onto our words. "What a way of celebrating Christmas, you two, disrespecting each other like that."

Augusto turned his back to us.

But Otilia intervened, "Natalia, sing a Christmas song to us."

I didn't listen to the song. My thoughts got lost in my brother's words. Otilia came and sat next to me on the floor. She rested her head on mine and caressed my upper arm.

She whispered to me, "This is Christmas time … don't worry about any of that …," and kissed my cheek. I nodded with a distressed heart.

Too soon after I fell asleep, Rosaura and Lucia were up. Their screams woke me at once, and I made the sacrifice of getting up to share in their joy. Mamá placed their presents next to their cots, and when they realized they were gifts for them, they started jumping and screaming in excitement. It was a memorable scene. We all enjoyed their happiness as much as they did.

"Did baby Jesus bring it for me?" Rosaura asked, overcome by emotion.

"Yes," I replied, "he did."

"What did we do different this year, Rosaura?" Lucia asked, "Why did he remember us *this* time?"

"You are learning to read and write," Otilia replied, "and you have been trying very hard; that is why baby Jesus remembered you this time."

"So everyone in Maximiana's class got presents from baby Jesus!" Lucia exclaimed enthusiastically.

"Yes, they did!" I replied to the astonishment of everyone present.

In truth, Alejandro had purchased a little present for each child in my class, and their parents had hidden them, putting them by the child's cot for Christmas morning. They also received a bag of candies. Alejandro wanted to get something for my little sisters, but I refused because they already had presents; there was no need for an extra one that might spoil them. He thought that was a thoughtful statement on my part.

The hacienda gleamed with the holiday spirit. Almost every single day, the Sarmientos had gatherings with live music and drinks. Everyone seemed to enjoy him- or herself to the maximum. For us, it meant more work than ever. Orders came one after the other, nonstop. Cleaning up after their gatherings was absolutely tiresome. But we did what we had to do, especially because we all liked Doña Luisa, and she was responsible for all of our actions.

On one of these busy days a friend of Alejandro's stopped in El Roble on his way to La Villa de San Sebastián.

"Hello! Remember me?" he asked as I swept the back corridor.

Andrés Daniel Randal! The young man who had greeted Josefina, Raimunda, and me as ladies back at the Machado Square in Mazatlán. And here he had recognized me as soon as he had seen me.

"Yes, I do. How are you?" I replied, masking my utter surprise.

"Fine … I didn't know you work here," he said, "but then again, how was I supposed to know that, right?"

"Yes," I said smiling, "It makes sense that Alejandro is your friend, yes? He is as nice as you."

"Ha, ha, ha! Thanks! Actually, Alejandro is a friend of my brother Eduardo, but Eduardo asked me to stop by and bring him some documents."

"Oh … I see …"

Dora Elena Mora interrupted our conversation. "You …," she said, pointing her finger at me, "come along."

"Excuse me," I said and followed her to the great room where they were having morning coffee and treats. All of them were present, including Orlando and Domingo.

"My shoe got dirty … clean it," the girl named Florentina Verdeño stated.

I heard the giggling around me. Then I looked at Orlando, but he turned away from me. Next, a voice emerged that overwhelmingly shocked me.

"That is not her job here, Florentina," Domingo said.

I turned to look at his serious face. It had turned as red as a tomato, and his eyes expelled sparks of anger.

"That is fine …," I said and took the dust rag from my waist and knelt down.

"No," Domingo said and walked towards me. "Get up, Maximiana, and go to Doña Luisa."

With dignity, I stood up and walked out of the grand room. Andrés Randal was standing at the door and smiled at me on my way out. I had been only a few minutes behind the kitchen, still recovering from the shock, when Orlando arrived.

"Why is Domingo so mad and screaming at them right now? She only asked you to clean her shoe!" he stated, extremely irritated.

I wanted, at that precise moment, to punch him in the face and pull at each of his ridiculous brown curls.

"Why aren't YOU defending me, Orlando?" I replied, overcome with rage.

"What do you want me to say?!" the idiotic bigheaded boy replied.

"How about 'Leave her alone,' or what about 'That is not her job,' just as Domingo did?" With extreme effort, I tried to block out of my mind the words "She *only* asked you to clean her shoe."

"Florentina is very nice, she's my friend, and she deserves your respect."

His statement froze me.

"Maximiana," Domingo interrupted, "don't follow any of their requests … I already told Doña Luisa to keep you away from them … that bunch of rude vixens."

"Thank you, Domingo," I said sincerely and regretted every time I had unjustly misjudged him.

I walked away from both of them, deeply hurt by Orlando's attitude towards the situation and me.

Raimunda noticed the paleness of my face and anguish in my expression. But I didn't want to talk about it. I had no way of explaining what had happened without getting me sent as far away as possible from Orlando Sarmiento's side. And I wasn't ready to let him go or let me walk away from him. Every inch of my self refused to consider that possibility. Instead, I chose to keep quiet and go on, as if nothing had happened. And so did Orlando.

Fortunately, Doña Luisa did as Domingo had suggested and sent me "away from them" and to help Don Carlos, the gardener, on the lower gardens. They were divided into sections that went down the hillside in beautiful terraces. Stone stairs, lined by white Roman pillars, followed the terraced sections to the lowest level of the garden. There at the bottom on your right, you could find the tennis court, and to your left the stoned swimming pool, now empty during this cool time of the year.

Alejandro was showing Andrés the view of the Sacanta from the upper level of the hacienda. His voice sounded proud and excited. He waved at me, and I waved back. Don Carlos took his hat off to greet him. Andrés stepped down to the gardens, followed by Alejandro.

"You have done a beautiful job," Andrés told Don Carlos, who thanked him back shyly.

"He is an artist," Alejandro stated proudly and then continued showing Andrés the rest of the property.

"Señorito Alejandro is just like his mamá," Don Carlos said to me. "She always came to the workers and thanked us for the job. That woman was an angel fallen from heaven."

I was dying to ask Don Carlos why Señor Sarmiento had locked her in the room. But my respect for the memory of my friend's mother's kept me quiet.

In no time, New Year's Eve arrived, and we helped Natalia get ready to sing at the Grand House. Señor Sarmiento would pay her ten whole pesos for her performance, which was almost three times the money she made working for a week in the sugar cane fields. Beatriz was nice enough to come and help us get her ready with makeup and a nice hairstyle. When she had finished, we all stared at her, stunned by the transformation. My goodness, she looked like a goddess. And to match her attire, her personality manifested stronger than ever, carried with a natural elegance. Papá and Mamá looked upon her with pride, barely containing their emotions.

Then it hit me that I had always been right about my assertion that the only difference between people like the Sarmientos or the Barrazas and people like us is their fashionable clothes and the mannerisms that anyone can easily learn. Then *why* did we live so strikingly different from them? Pure luck, a matter of birth into a family with power or into one with none, determined our fate. Such injustice! Why did the rich require such excess when the rest of us lived in such extreme need? Everything was so unequally divided that the only way for a beautiful girl, like my sister Natalia, to wear a dress like this was if a Sarmiento gave it to her.

Then I looked down at my own outfit for the evening—a simple plain blue skirt, a white blouse, and my brown sandals. For the first time, I became aware of the striking difference. Shamefully, I felt embarrassed to go dressed this way. Even though I understood what I wore did not matter in who I was, my heart still felt the disgrace of being poor and different from those girls that were going to be at that party. I would stand at a distance, hiding. And by then, I knew for a fact that Orlando would not even look at me during the night.

But I couldn't go back on my word and stay home. Everyone would know that I felt ashamed. I couldn't do that to my parents, who were not responsible for my insecurities. I took a deep breath and told Natalia to get ready to leave. It was good that the dress was really long; otherwise her brown sandals would have shown. As we were about to leave, we heard a knock on our door.

"Maximiana!" Raimunda exclaimed, "Doña Luisa sent you this dress to wear tonight. Alejandro got it for you!" and she handed me a box.

My sisters gathered around her. Then everybody gasped when she opened the box and revealed a beautiful purple dress. My favorite color! And more—she had even included the torturous corset to go with it.

"Come on! Get ready, or we are going to be late!" Natalia exclaimed.

"I don't need a costume. Let's go," I said and walked towards the door, leaving everyone behind me stunned. Natalia did not move.

"So … am I wearing a costume then?" she asked, visibly hurt.

"Yes, you are. This is your performance costume, Natalia. I don't need one because I am not going to sing nor am I a guest at that party," I replied.

Proudly, Augusto came to me and put his hand on my shoulder. I walked out, and Natalia followed.

"Raise your face, Natalia! You are the most beautiful girl in México!" someone yelled behind us. It was Daniel, who as usual, came to give his support.

"May I walk you ladies to the entrance of the hacienda?" he asked and offered each one of us an arm.

We took his offer and proudly walked with our dear friend. As we passed along, people came to their doors, astonished by her beauty, and watched Natalia walk towards the Grand House. My heart exploded with pride, but at the same time, it was filled with an inexplicable sadness, a sadness that would settle in my eyes for a very long time. I had begun to realize the impact of "differences" in people's lives.

We waited in the kitchen for Natalia to be called to sing. She was very nervous. We could hear the laughter in the great room while the piano played nonstop. Alejandro came to greet us and asked me why I didn't wear the dress he had sent me.

"There is no point to wear such a dress to come and sit in the kitchen," I said.

Annoyed he replied, "I was going to ask you both to stay for the party after the performance."

"Why don't you take us now, Aleh?" I asked.

He stared at me, answering with a deep sigh, then bit his lip.

"Don't worry about it … we understand. Go back to your party now."

He stood there, motionless.

"Please, Alejandro, don't worry about us." I gave him a reassuring smile.

He sighed and left the kitchen.

"Alejandro!" I called, "Wait!" and he returned. "May I stand in the Venetian-floor hallway to see Natalia's performance?"

"Of course!" he said with a big smile.

Natalia remained lost in her thoughts, too nervous even to smile. But when the time arrived and Doña Luisa came to get her, she transformed herself into a diva. She rose and walked towards the great room with a posture that any dancer in the world would be envious about. I followed her but stayed behind in the hallway. Alejandro came to get her at the great room's door and pompously walked with her, taking her by the arm.

"Everyone," he started, "I introduce to you Señorita Natalia Valdez, a soprano singer with a voice that I am sure will astonish you as much as it astonishes me every time I have the privilege of listening to her. Señorita Natalia Valdez will sing for us the song 'Over the Sea' by the great Mexican composer Señor Melesio Morales."

Then he proceeded to sit at the grand piano. Natalia stood next to him, and delicately placed her right hand on the shiny top. She looked into the distance, and the notes arose in a melodious expression of beauty and pure magic.

> *Come with me, silent beautiful girl, over the sea.*
> *Come to be my partner when the solemn sun rules*
> *Or when a horrifying tempest covers us with a gloom.*
>
> *Why do I care to be captive*
> *If here I live with your love,*
> *If tied is my life with your death?*
> *Always attached goes my fate to your existence*
> *And your absence is my pain.*
>
> *Why do I care to be captive*
> *If here I live with your love?*
> *Come with me, silent beautiful girl, over the sea.*
>
> *Come with me without fears,*
> *That through the misty winds towards the port, and*
> *Always soft, our ship will be taken over the sea.*

Silence fell over the great room when she had finished. Then Alejandro rose and began to clap. Everyone followed in disbelief. I looked at everyone present, and they were clearly surprised by Natalia's beautiful performance. Then I noticed that Domingo Sarmiento neither clapped nor smiled; he looked intensely at my sister, who shyly smiled at everyone. Señor Joaquín Sarmiento had an expression of fear on his face and abruptly walked out of the room. Señora Leonora did not follow him; she stayed behind, staring at my sister, who continued standing next to Alejandro, an action that clearly bothered her. Orlando looked in my direction and smiled at me. I smiled back. Catalina kept her guard up for Domingo, and her friends apparently did not know how to react to this beautiful, well-dressed girl, who sang in a way that left everyone present speechless. Next, Natalia whispered something in Alejandro's ear, and Alejandro looked in my direction. Both started walking towards me.

"You sang wonderfully!" I told my sister, full of pride and hugged her.

"Hold on," Alejandro said and moved back into the great room, "I will catch up."

We walked towards the path out, the one on the side of the house. Natalia couldn't wait to start asking questions.

"Who was the man wearing the burgundy tie?" she asked with intrigue in her eyes.

"Oh … that is Domingo," I replied.

"Maximiana … *that* is Domingo Sarmiento?"

"Shhhh! Natalia, don't scream … yes … *that* was Domingo Sarmiento, and the one standing next to him, the one with the brown curly hair, is Orlando," I said proudly.

"*That* is Orlando?" she asked surprised.

"Yes, isn't he dreamy?" I questioned.

She burst into a laughter that forced her to sit on the library's sidewalk.

"What is so funny, you idiot?" I asked, both puzzled and bothered by her obvious burlesque laughing.

"I don't know … I just expected him to look a little bit different … you always said that he was 'perfect' and 'beautiful' and 'sooo handsome' that I thought he would look at least a little bit like Aleh," she said without any consideration for my blindness to Orlando's true physical appearance.

"Shut up! He is gorgeous," I claimed, but my statement only made her laugh harder.

"Oh, I'm sorry, Max … it is just … that … well … it must be that he was standing next to Domingo."

She winked, but I was not amused.

"Wait!" Alejandro screamed, running towards us, "here is your payment, little nightingale."

Natalia took the envelope and gave it to me.

"Why are you sitting here?" he asked, intrigued.

"Mmm, Natalia had to sit, but we are leaving," I replied.

"You don't have to go. Why don't you stay for dinner?" he asked, as gentlemanly as always.

"No, that is fine," I replied, "but thank you, just the same."

Alejandro ordered the gatekeeper to open the door for us, but Orlando stopped us.

"Alejandro!" he shouted.

We all waited by the gate.

"What?" Alejandro replied.

"Hold on."

I stopped abruptly and turned around.

Natalia, well mannered as always, slowly turned his way and, smiling, said in her low voice, "We are leaving."

Orlando ignored her and turned to me.

"Happy New Year," he said in my ear and gave me a passionate hug.

I held him and whispered the words, "Happy 1908."

Alejandro and Natalia walked away from us. Orlando took my hand, led me into the library, and without turning on the light, he kissed me.

"I'm sorry about the other day," he said to my astonishment. I honestly had thought I would never hear those words leave his lips.

I buried my face on his chest and gently replied, "I am more afraid than ever of losing you, Orlando."

"No … don't be afraid; you will never lose me … I will always love you, and you will always be my girl, the one I love … you are mine forever … remember?"

"But you are leaving the day after tomorrow …"

"But I will be back for Holy Week …"

"Three more months …," I said with disappointment.

"Are you going to wait for me?" he asked jokingly.

"No … I am going to leave," I replied, trying to be funny in the middle of my anguish.

He softly took my face in his hands and kissed my nose.

"I swear to God, Maximiana, that I will never forget you, that … I will be back in Holy Week and everything is going to be the same … nothing will ever come between us …"

"Nothing or *no one*?" I had the courage to ask.

"Nothing and … or no one," he said and crushed my body upon his chest. "I swear on my mother that nothing bad will ever happen between us. Trust me."

"I believe you, Orlando, and I trust you," I said from the very depth of my soul.

He did love me. I believed in him and felt that he didn't care that I dressed in rags or wore sandals, that my hair hung unstylishly in a braid, or that I had learned to read and write only less than a year ago. It meant nothing that I was a servant girl at his house or that my parents were peasants and lived in a little two-room house. I wanted to believe that he loved me for who I was. I said good-bye in tears; he was leaving on the second day of January with the singing of the roosters. This time, he showed no sadness as he had in Mazatlán at my departure.

13

In bittersweetness began the year for my inexperienced heart. Before Orlando even left town, I felt his absence. I woke up earlier than normal the second day of the new year to see the horses galloping west towards Mazatlán. A strange sensation shook me.

Oh God ... take him safely to the Grand City House.

I offered those prayers throughout the next days until I heard the group that had taken him and Domingo to Mazatlán had returned to El Roble.

Alejandro told me that his father had walked out in anger after Natalia's performance because she had worn his dead wife's dress and the song had been her favorite. But Alejandro was more than satisfied with his reaction. Apparently, that had been his intention since the start.

Mystery and intrigue surrounded Señora Magdalena. She had had a tragic death, a suicide; that much I knew. But Doña Luisa and Don Carlos secretly talked about her as if she were a living angel. But then, again, the people in town called her a lunatic. My common sense told me that they did not know that she was not a lunatic. A lunatic would not talk to her children through the crevice of the door. The biggest conundrum in the whole story was that her sons were not allowed to see her family. That, for me, held the key to the mystery and the fact that her own family had abandoned her to die in that room.

Why did no one in her family come to her rescue?

This intrigued me.

"Aleh, we need to bring the dress back to you, but Mamá doesn't know how to wash a dress like that one …"

"Natalia can keep it. It is a present from me," Alejandro said in his usual cordial voice.

"Mmm … but when could she use it again? It is not as if she can wear it for El Roble's celebrations," I said laughing.

"Ha, ha, ha! Or for church …"

"Yes, so true."

"Look … you never know … any of you may need it at some point, unless you don't want it because Mother is dead," the light in his eyes turned off.

"God no, Alejandro, please do not think that. Please," I said, mortified. "It is just that … it is so beautiful and elegant and we … you know."

"Move to the next plant; this one is drowning already," he said.

"Oh … yes."

I had given so much attention to the conversation while gardening one of the terraces that I had forgotten to move and the water was already overflowing the pot.

"Hey … do you want to meet tonight?" he asked.

"Where?"

"By the arroyo … we can lie down and look at the stars and talk …"

"Ahhh, that sounds nice …," I sighed. "Bring one of your books of poems and a lamp to light so we can read …"

"So, you will come?" Alejandro asked in a hopeful voice.

"Mmmm … is it going to be late?"

"No … as soon as the stars start to come out …"

"Fine, I don't think that will be a problem …," I replied, smiling.

"Come alone," he said, surprising me.

"Why?"

"Because I want to talk to you about something …"

My heart felt a rush of palpitations.

"About what? Is … everything fine? Is Orlando doing well in Mazatlán?"

"He is fine … trust me on that."

"But—"

"It is not about Orlando, even though I wish I could talk to you about him."

"Then please do talk to me about him!" I begged.

"No …," he replied and looked away.

"Aleh," I sought his beautiful face, "what is wrong?"

"Nothing … look I want to talk to you about something else; it is not about Orlando."

"If there is something I need to know about him or anything that is happening that I should know, please tell me."

"No."

Exasperation clouded my mind and frustrated my attempts to learn more. I continued to try to open Alejandro. "But you are my friend …"

"And he is my brother."

"If … if … there is something going on and you know it … but will not tell me … Alejandro … I don't know if I could forgive you …"

Tears rested on the edge, ready to roll out of my eyes. Then Alejandro surprised me again, this time by hugging me.

"No, Maximiana … look … don't think about something that is not there. I will see you tonight … are you still coming or are you mad at me?"

"No … I am fine. I will see you then." I tried to smile at Alejandro, but my eyes contradicted my lips.

"Maximiana …"

"What?" I replied, distracted.

"Move to the next pot; the water is reaching the tennis court by now," Alejandro told me with a smile on his face.

"Yes! Sorry!"

I moved to the next pot and welcomed the smell of gardenias.

Memories returned to me of my earliest days at the Grand House, when the aroma of gardenias had hit my senses for the first time. It felt as if it had happened a very long time ago.

"This place frightens me at night," I said to Alejandro while lying on a blanket next to the arroyo.

"But the view is glorious. Come now, don't tell me you don't see it," he joked.

Indeed, the clear sky and crisp air showed a full canvas of stars.

"Look, the clouds are coming down to the Sacanta," and I pointed to the shadow of the majestic mountain standing in front of us.

"It is fog, not clouds."

"You are right ... but it looks scary."

"Like London. London is a city in England, and its winter nights are foggy."

"Inspiring, fog inspires me," I said with a sigh.

"To do what?" he asked without looking at me.

"To think and to dream about mysteries and intriguing stories."

"True ... fog plays with the mysterious."

"Do you remember the story of the Twins' Well?"

Alejandro rested on his elbows. "I haven't thought about that tragic murder in a long time."

"The well is not far from here," I muttered to Alejandro, who looked in the well's direction.

"I know. It is so sad, though."

He looked towards the well with a worrisome expression on his face.

"Do you think it is true that the spirits of the twins wander through the arroyo at night?" I asked.

"Do you think that if I thought that was true I would invite you to come here at night?" he asked, trying not to laugh.

"Ha, ha, ha! Yes ... you're right."

"I remember when Doña Luisa told us the story. I couldn't sleep, thinking about it," he said.

"Same here," I agreed.

"But the part about the tree that cried affected me the most."

The story of the twins happened years ago. According to the people of El Roble, a peasant family owned several parcels of land around town. The couple had twin boys, but when they were six years old, both of their parents died of the yellow fever that came to the area in 1883. Both boys had to move to live with their uncle, their father's brother. One afternoon, when the twins were seven years old, people working in the fields saw the uncle walking towards the well; the twins were riding his donkey behind him. Days passed, and people began to smell a bad odor coming from the well, and nobody dared to fetch water from it. Finally, suspecting an animal had fallen in it, people sent a young man down to investigate what was rotting inside. The man started screaming to pull him up when he found the decomposing twins' bodies at the bottom of the well. The uncle denied he had had anything to do with it, and suggested that the twins had probably fallen in the waterhole while playing around it.

The man inherited the twins' lands, and the suspicion that he had killed his twin nephews to inherit the lands stayed forever in El Roble because the uncle claimed to have not noticed they were missing. After the children's death, people said the tree next to the well cried tears of sorrow for them. By the time I was old enough to visit the site, the tree was gone; somebody had cut it down, fearing it was not tears of sorrow but a curse on the town.

I wished I had seen it at least once to prove on my own if it was true or not. However, Mamá and Papá told us they saw it with their own eyes, and every evening, drops of water would roll down the leaves of the sad tree without anyone understanding the reason. Most people called it a miracle. For me, I still think about it as an interesting subject of investigation.

"Margarita told me she saw a little boy in white underwear running around the arroyo the other night and that she thought he was one of the twins," I said.

"Strange."

"I know," I replied, "but how terrible that story is."

"Just think about how those two boys felt when they were falling in the well," Alejandro reflected, "and if they were alive inside for days … just thinking about it gives me goosebumps."

"I don't think they were alive for days because if they had survived any person fetching water would've heard their screams."

"True," Alejandro agreed.

"I think the evil uncle killed them before throwing them in the well," I said.

"Probably … to avoid anybody hearing them ask for help," Alejandro replied, pensive.

"He planned the murder very thoroughly. He could've killed the boys and buried them, but then, somebody would have to have killed them and buried them. But by throwing them in the well, he could argue it was just an accident," I stated.

"You could easily be an investigator of crimes," Alejandro said with a serious look.

"Are women allowed to be investigators of crimes?"

He glanced back at me. "I never heard of one."

"I should be the first one then," I responded, believing in my words.

"You could be anything you want, Maximiana; you are very smart."

"But I am not allowed because I am a woman, right?"

"Unfortunately."

"And a *poor* woman, too; that guarantees I cannot," I said unhappily. "Things need to change."

"Do you dream of getting married and having children?" he asked.

"Mmm … before I learned to read and write, I thought about that as my only destiny. Now, it is something that I see as part of my life but not everything."

"Really?"

"And you?"

"I don't know."

"You don't dream of getting married and having children?"

"'Dream'? No, not really. Ha, ha, ha," he laughed. "Look, Ursa Minor; it doesn't look much like a bear, more like a scorpion."

"Aleh … may I ask you something personal?"

"You may ask, but I may not answer."

"Fair enough. Are you in love with someone?"

"Yes. But let's not talk about it," he said without looking at me.

"Why not? We are friends."

"Some things I'd rather keep private," he said but seemed far away and lost in his thoughts.

"How old are you—if that information is not private, of course," I asked, clearly hurt by his lack of trust in me.

"Eighteen … almost nineteen. Most men my age are already married; some have children."

"Yes … and many girls my age are also already married and some also have children."

"Tragic," he said.

"I just can't imagine myself dealing with a child of my own at this age—or even older. I want to bear my first child when I am at least twenty-seven years old!"

"Ha, ha, ha! Me, too!"

"Alejandro … you cannot bear children," I teased.

"You know what I meant Max … don't be silly," he said and gave me a little push on the shoulder.

"So … what did you want to talk about? You said you needed to talk to me about something."

"Nah! I changed my mind; we are having fun as it is."

"You know how nosy I am … you cannot leave me with the intrigue of not knowing what you wanted to talk about!" I cried out.

"I will tell you another day. Look … what do you think is up there?"

"In the sky? Heaven? Or what?"

"Sky."

"Air … lots of air?" I had no idea what could be up there. "Are there books that talk about the sky but without mentioning God and heaven?" I wanted to know.

"Yes, but I haven't read much about it."

"What do *you* think is up there?" I asked.

"Stars are suns … did you know that?"

"No … what do you mean?"

"Stars are really suns, and they look so small and not like our sun because they are so far away."

"I didn't know that … do you know how many suns are up there?"

"Millions," he replied, moving his eyebrows up and down.

How I relished talking about different concepts such as the sky and stars being suns. There were so many things I wanted to know and find out that I felt my life wouldn't be long enough to discover them. The Sarmiento brothers were really lucky to learn all those things through their books and teachers. I realized that I needed to talk to my students about different topics and not just what we already knew, not just stories about ourselves or our town. We needed to start *thinking* about what happens around us.

Alejandro was an easy person to talk to, but in my mind, he was as mysterious as his mother. He seemed always to be thinking about profound ideas that I could not completely comprehend. Orlando was different from him; he had no interest in the issues Alejandro cared about. However, unlike Alejandro, he did talk with me about private issues. As for the third Sarmiento brother, since Domingo's visit in December, my thoughts about him had changed somewhat. I still felt he was obnoxious and rude, but at the same time, he had a heart that cried for justice, in his very own particular and discreet way.

14

March 21 came sooner than expected. The hacienda's gardens were blossoming in an explosion of colors and aromas that left you in an inexplicably delicious state of wonder. My observations on the beauty of spring were sharper than ever because today Orlando would return to El Roble for his Holy Week vacation. He wrote to me once through Alejandro, but apparently he had done so in a rush because the letter did not make sense. Nonetheless, I received it happily, just as I did every time I heard news from him.

Raimunda had been sick since the beginning of the month so we all took over her chores. Doña Luisa thought of replacing her, but I begged her not to do it. Raimunda's family depended on her salary at the Grand House to eat. I visited a couple of times, and she gave me the impression of being really sick. She looked pale, and her eyes were lifeless. Doña Luisa was thinking of asking Señor Joaquín Sarmiento to send a doctor to see Raimunda. I just hoped Doña Luisa would hurry before she died. I missed having Raimunda around while working; nobody made the work pass as quickly or sent me into peals of laughter as much as she did. Even though I got along with everyone in a very good way, she was the one I trusted the most.

My thoughts were interrupted when I heard the doormen opening the gates to let the carriages into the hacienda. I pushed my hair back and walked around the water tower to look at them coming in. This time only Domingo rode a horse; Orlando was nowhere to be seen. My heart accelerated.

Where is he?

They closed the gates and the carriages' doors opened. I breathed in relief when I saw him coming out of one. He held the door and offered his hand to a young woman getting out after him. Then an older woman and two more young ones followed. The first one stood next to him, holding his arm.

Domingo approached the other carriage to help three more young women out. The first one to get out was Catalina Barraza; the second was her friend Dora Elena Mora with yet another girl that I had never seen before. They seemed excited to be there and walked towards the view of the Sacanta Mountain. Immediately, I hid behind the water tower when I heard their talking and giggling, but I could still peer around to watch the arrivals. Orlando strolled with the women, explaining about the gardens on the terraces. Domingo walked away, apparently annoyed by their laughs, and a frown on his face failed to hide his irritation. Something about Domingo seemed different

I followed them with my eyes until they finally entered the Grand House. Then I realized there were other young men with them. Some were the ones I had met at the parlor room in the Grand City House during the summer. I hid behind the tower again; a feeling of sickness entered my stomach.

"Maximiana … we are not done yet," Margarita intervened to get me out of my traumatic trance. I followed her voice back to the washing stones. Time to go home had almost arrived, but without knowing the sleeping arrangements, I could not risk visiting Orlando at the balcony room. I just hoped he would come up to me and tell me the plans to meet. I was very excited to see him; he looked as handsome as ever, only his curls were shorter than before but precious, as always.

I went home smiling in happiness because my Orlando was in the same town as I. It was a strange feeling of completeness to know he was close to me. Natalia couldn't hide her enthusiasm when she heard they had arrived back in town. Even though she never said a word about it, I suspected that she had a secret infatuation with Domingo Sarmiento. My poor Natalia. I didn't dare tell her she had an impossible love. But I knew the joy in dreaming and her romantic nature, so I didn't dare remove her from her fantasy.

"Did you see him?" she asked discreetly.

"Domingo?"

She blushed. "No … Orlando."

"Oh yes, not for long, though. But I did see him. I also saw Domingo, frowning about something that bothered him," I said with a teasing smile.

"Oh …," she sighed, moving her flirty eyes to the side.

I hugged her, pushing my cheek to hers, because I couldn't contain my excitement any longer, "Natalia … he is back! He is back!"

"I am happy for you," she said in her melodious voice, and we raced to the shower quarters, giggling to see who would reach the water bucket first.

I should've read it on Alejandro's face. But I didn't. I was too naïve to see beyond the obvious and walked into Orlando's room, looking for him to greet him. And then my world of illusions and made-up fantasies collapsed under my leather sandaled feet.

"Orlando!"

He turned and kept his arms down when I hugged him.

"How are you?" I asked, confused by his reaction.

He moved away from me without answering.

"What's wrong? Why don't you greet me?"

"Mmm … I don't think it is a good idea for you to be here with me."

"Why not? When can I see you?" I replied still refusing to see the truth.

"I brought my steady girlfriend from Mazatlán, and I don't want her to find out about you," he replied in a cold tone, looking directly into my eyes.

Numbness surrounded my entire being—soul, mind, and heart—and the blood in my veins turned into stone.

He then added, "Sorry, but I don't want to mess things up with her."

I had to turn my back on him. My eyes moved directly to the floor. He said something … I don't know what because the pain in my soul stabbed so sharply that I could hear my own tears splashing on the floor.

"You don't love me as before?" I asked with a broken voice without turning back at him.

"No," he replied firmly.

I grasped the last strength left in my heart and asked again, "Not even a little bit?"

"No … Good-bye, Maximiana," he said and walked away without waiting for my reply.

"Good-bye, Orlando." The automatic response came out of my mouth as he shut the door behind me.

I did not collapse on the floor but within myself. I stood there stone cold, gazing at the mango tree outside the balcony. The spring air was traveling through the same room where I had once filled myself with hopes that had seemed so true to me. And it blew on, carrying away those shattered memories of lies, leaving only fragments as mocking representations of my stupidity.

I allowed the tears to roll down, to dampen my blouse, skirt, and feet. I wanted them to kill themselves on the floor and leave the traces of sourness that only tears that come from betrayal leave behind. I closed my eyes to let the sobs finally escape my tightening chest. Resting my face on my arms on the edge of the balcony's window, I knelt and cried my sorrow and pain without stopping to think about anything but my own betrayed self. Vaguely, I heard the piano playing; it was *he* playing it for *her*. I heard their laughter, their animated chat far away in the distance yet so close to my despair. It burned inside of me. Then the door behind my back opened, and Domingo Sarmiento walked towards me. Without moving a centimeter, I looked at him and cleaned my face off with my dirty hands.

"I thought I heard mother crying," he said in a low voice.

I ignored him as he had done with me so many times and hugged my trembling knees, then buried my face between them and continued my sobbing unabashed.

He knelt and rested his big hand on my shoulder, but I pushed it away with a sudden force that sent it flying against the wall.

"Don't touch me!" I screamed at him. "Go away!"

My swollen face confronted him with rage, but his expression showed only sadness. I couldn't contain myself anymore. I needed somebody to hold me; I crushed myself against him and exploded in painful and miserable loud sobs. Domingo Sarmiento held me tightly against himself.

"Mother used to cry like this in here," he said and began to accompany me in my grief. My pains commenced to fade away when the long contained sobs for his mother came out of him. Suddenly, his feelings seemed so much more devastating than mine that I grabbed his head and rested it on my chest, kissing it through his soft hair several times until the straight hairs were lying on my lips, wet from my own tears.

"I'm sorry about your mamá," I murmured. "I am so sorry you could only hear her voice through the door ..."

Domingo looked up at me, his beautiful face hurting. He closed his eyes, and I kissed each of them with gentleness, just as I had done once to his younger brother to console him.

He straightened his legs on the floor and embraced my waist with his arms. I held him and closed my eyes with him. Sighs filled with tears of pain started escaping both of our chests, releasing all the energy that was left in our bodies. I could feel the wind entering through the balcony window and the aromas of the gardenias traveling in the distance. I wanted to fall asleep there and let time pass and take with it the pain of not having Orlando by my side. I wished for years to go by so I could look back at the moment that I had just lived and see it in a distance so far away that it could not touch me anymore.

Now I understood how Marianela felt when Pablo stopped loving her. And now I also knew, finally, how you can die of sorrow even if the traitor to your feelings doesn't deserve your life.

❦   ❦   ❦

There is no way to describe how I experienced the following days, but lying on a branch of my tree, far away from El Roble and the hacienda allowed me to breathe in peace. My eyes kept staring at the green leaves enclosing me; there, I was finally free to ask myself what had gone wrong and what had happened to Orlando Sarmiento and me. I found it impossible to believe he had lied all this time and that his only intention was to have fun with my person, as everyone believed from the beginning but I had refused to recognize. I could continue to ask endless questions and guess at all sorts of answers, but reality rested upon one simple fact: He had told me to stay away from him, and he meant it.

Domingo continued living inside my thoughts. The way he had reacted to my pain still shocked me because, even if I had reminded him of Señora Magdalena when he had heard me crying in the balcony room, it was heartwarming that he felt some kind of compassion to what had just happened between his brother and me. His reaction did not make sense. All this time I believed he was indifferent to others and coldly distant to me.

I felt lonely and lost and too embarrassed to talk about Orlando's rejection with anybody, even my sisters or Raimunda. How much I needed my dear Alejandro with me, but consistent with my bad luck, he had left for Mazatlán two days before his brothers arrived in El Roble. So I let Domingo fill up the spot left empty by Alejandro.

I forced myself to return to the hacienda the next day, knowing I would see *him* with *her*. Some of the guests at the house did not help my situation as they constantly challenged my dignity, trying to make me feel worthless with cruel remarks. Fortunately, Doña Luisa was sensitive enough to keep me away from them as much as possible while Margarita and the others kept a distance and respected my quietness.

Orlando did not make eye contact with me again; neither did I look for it. He avoided me, and I avoided him, as if neither knew of the other's existence, as if we had never been together in the balcony room, had never touched each other, had never promised to God to love each other forever.

I closed my eyes to listen to the sounds coming from the Sacanta Mountain, and Domingo came back to my mind. It was *he* now who walked to me and smiled. It was *he* who offered a book that morning and touched my elbow with a tenderness that scared me.

I had the right to fear. And I told Domingo to stay away from me; I screamed at him not to think that I was going to be a toy in his hands, just as I had been to his brother. I claimed my dignity, looking straight into his eyes. I declared the purity of my body and soul, my loyalty and respect towards others. He grabbed my shoulders with both of his hands and seriously replied that he would never treat somebody that way and that I was worth more than all the young frivolous ladies staying at El Roble's hacienda. Domingo said I had earned his admiration. I was too hurt to believe him and pulled his hands away from me before walking away. Catalina Barraza was standing at the corridor looking at us, but I could care less. I passed by her, and she muttered something that I had no interest in knowing. She called to Domingo, but he ignored her and walked after me. He told me Alejandro would arrive today. I stopped. The world spun, sending nonsense to me and uprooting what had grounded me and, worst of all, destroying any sense of myself in the process. I was so numb in confusion that I didn't know who I was anymore.

But for now, I just wanted to be alone, lying in the roble tree at the edge of the Sacanta Mountain. It had been only one week, but it felt like an eternity since Orlando had left me standing in the balcony room of my naïve illusions. Two tears rolled again down my cheeks just as the sun was setting and a few last rays, like myself, struggled to shine some light.

> *Sighs are air and go to the air.*
> *Tears are water and go to the sea.*
> *Tell me woman, when love is forgotten,*
> *Do you know to where it leaves?*

I recited the poem softly.

Where did it go? Where is the love that I felt to be so real and eternal? Is it possible for it to have completely left his heart?

I was trying to hang on to a hope that he might regret our separation and return to me. Oh naïve me.

"Max ..."

I heard Natalia's voice coming from under my branch.

"Leave me alone Natalia ... I want to be by myself ... can't anybody understand that?"

"Please ... may I go up there with you?" she begged in her childish voice.

"No."

"Alejandro and Domingo are here with me."

I opened my eyes.

"Listen, I *really* want to be on my own ... leave me alone, *please*."

"Maximiana," Alejandro said, "Domingo told me what happened and—"

"You knew, Alejandro; all this time you knew and did not tell me," I interrupted.

"Max ... please get down from there. How can I talk to you if you don't come down?"

"There is nothing to talk about."

"Yes, there is. Please come down, or I will go up there," Alejandro threatened.

"Be my guest."

I didn't move.

"Fine."

He climbed up my tree and sat at my feet. Domingo and Natalia stayed down.

"Max ... how do you feel?"

"Numb."

He chuckled. "I mean how you feel inside."

"I feel numb."

"I understand," he replied in a sincere tone of voice. "I don't know if you will believe me, but I think Orlando is just going through a moment of craziness and he will recover from it any second ... because I know he has feelings for you, Max ... I know my brother."

I sat on the branch and let my legs hang on the sides. "*Feelings for me*? Are you mocking me?" I said, trying to contain myself from smacking him.

"No, I would never mock you, Maximiana … I honestly think that."

"I don't agree with you, Alejandro," I replied, "but thank you for trying to make me feel better." Pride spoke for me.

He extended his hand, "Come on, Max, I want to hug you … come close to me."

I pushed myself towards him, and as soon as I leaned my face on his chest, I started crying in silence. He knew it right away and placed the palm of his hand on the back of my head.

"I don't think you understand, Maximiana Valdez, how much you are worth," he whispered to my ear. "You are a girl who touches the heart of every person that is lucky enough to meet you … you have a charisma that makes you irresistibly adorable to those around you … I never met anyone like you … you are smart and beautiful … you are sensitive and caring, straight-forward and loyal like no one I have ever met in my life … you pay attention to the little details that others see as superficial and take the time to go deep into them … don't cry, Max … don't cry anymore for this."

"If I am a person like the one you are describing, Aleh … then explain to me why am I suffering this sadness? Why did Orlando make a fool of me that way? Tell me why … and I will believe you," I replied in a low voice desperately trying to keep my feelings a secret.

"Because he is not smart enough to see you the way we do," he answered.

"Will I ever forget him, Alejandro? Will the sorrow go away?"

"Oh yes … the hurting goes away … remember, it just happened. And you know he is leaving in two weeks; that will help you forget all of this sooner."

"I don't think I will ever forget it," I murmured.

"You will. You will fall in love with somebody who will appreciate you, and your heart will explode with a passion never before known to you; you will see."

"I already know that passion, Alejandro; it is not unknown to me."

"You are a passionate girl, I know that. That is why you can feel poetry the way you do … but I want you to trust my words. You haven't fallen in love yet with the man that will make you feel real love, the love that makes you … feel like you never felt before."

I thought for a moment.

"I wish I didn't have to see him anymore, but I have to work ... there is no way out."

"Don't hide, Max ... you didn't do anything wrong. It is *his* mistake, not yours."

"But it breaks my heart to see him with *her*, Alejandro." I broke again.

"I know ... I can only imagine how you feel."

"And the way they make comments in my presence, the way they try to hurt my feelings in the worst possible way is unbearable to me right now. It breaks my heart when he smiles at their rudeness."

"Oh Maximiana," he hugged me tightly. "Maxi ... you are stronger than that. And smarter than all of them. I will be very careful to be around you these days, and Domingo will help out as well. We will not let anybody hurt you anymore. I will talk to Orlando about it; he has no right to be acting that way."

"Aleh ... Domingo is acting awfully nice with me ... do you know why?"

"You earned his respect, Max."

"How? I don't remember even trying ..." I twisted my lips, feeling embarrassment.

"You don't see the things that you do, do you? For example jumping in a river to pull out a five-year-old girl or keeping your chin up high when a group of vicious males try to mock you in a parlor room ... all of them older than you, may I add?"

"Oh that ... I thought he hated me for that."

"On the contrary, you made Domingo *think*. He told me so."

"Do you think there is somebody out there in the world that will love me ... but really love me, not in a fake way as Orlando did ...?"

"Max ... listen to me ... there's more than one out there who already has a special liking for you; don't tell me you don't notice it ..."

"No ... I don't."

"Because you were always paying attention to Orlando and nobody else. Do you remember Eduardo Randal's brother? His name is Andrés."

I raised my face to look at him; he looked down, raising both eyebrows.

"Yes, I met him once in the Machado Square in Mazatlán, and then he came during Christmas on his way to La Villa de San Sebastián."

"That day at the gardens, he asked me about you … he said your eyes were expressive and your smile was a killer."

I chuckled, "Is that good?"

"I think tall-prince-look-alike Andrés Randal has special feelings for you."

"You are mocking me again, Alejandro Sarmiento!" I said laughing.

"Hey! You are back! You are laughing!" he said, squishing me in his strong arms. I loved Alejandro with all of my heart.

"But … I don't know if I will trust somebody again."

"I love you … do you believe me?"

"I know you love me. I mean the other way. Orlando seemed so real to me and honest. I trusted him."

"He … he has other interests now that go more according to Father …"

"And what the world expects of him?"

"Yes … you see … I am a rebel to all of that and since seeing Natalia, Domingo has moved to our side."

I instantly composed myself when he said that.

"Domingo likes Natalia?" The question came out naturally.

"When I went to see him and Orlando in February, he asked me about her. He told me that since the night of New Year's Eve he couldn't stop thinking about her."

"Aleh … ask him to stay away from my sister. I don't want another Sarmiento to break—"

"Domingo is not Orlando, Max … don't be unfair."

He could be worse, I thought, but prudently replied, "Just think how your father will react to it. He still is angry about Domingo and Catalina Barraza's breakup."

"Domingo doesn't care, and I support him … besides he is nineteen, almost twenty, now and we have our own money, Mother's money. We have been seeing our grandparents, now that he can't control it."

"When you talked about 'our side' what are you referring to?"

"You see, we are a group of people who think that all this misery around us is not right; things have to change."

Revolution!

I kept quiet. Augusto's words came to my mind: "They *are* the system."

"Are there many of *you* ... who think like that?"

"No. But there are many who live like *you* who think this way, and we agree with them."

"I see." I didn't mention my brother and father's exact ideas.

"I brought you some nice books from Mazatlán, for your school. I have been talking to some friends about you and your sisters. Eduardo Randal sent several materials you may use."

"Really? Thank you!"

"You see ... there is much more to the world than a first-love heartbreak ..."

I looked down.

"But I understand you. Every single tear you have shed because of this, I understand because I have been there."

"I can't imagine a girl leaving you, Alejandro ... no."

"It is true, Silly Face; I ... was heartbroken just as you are right now and for similar reasons."

"What? She left you for a millionaire? She thought you were not worth as much as another one because you didn't have as much money, class, position, and education?"

"Something like that ... but using different words."

"When did it happen?"

"Some time ago ... and believe me ... the pain slowly but surely starts to go away. And speaking of pain, my buttocks may never recover from this ... do come down from this tree with me now ...," he said, pulling my nose and wisely changing the subject.

"Sure ... let's go now."

When we landed on the ground, I saw Domingo and Natalia talking in the distance. She was resting her back on a nearby tree as they chatted, and she smiled at him in the way only Natalia knew how, a way that kept an army of boys passing our street day and night.

They looked beautiful together, not just because of their physical features but also because the good feelings flowing back and forth between them made them literally glow. I was trying to stay optimistic about Domingo's intentions towards my sister, but living what I was living at that moment made it an almost impossible task. Nevertheless, I talked to Natalia that night, and Otilia agreed with me that she should be extremely careful with Domingo Sarmiento.

My sisters continued keeping silent with respect to Orlando's breakup with me; I still didn't want to talk about it. Daniel, on the other hand, was not taking "no" for an answer. He came to see me that same evening and tried to make me laugh with his silly jokes. Eventually, he got around to his investigation and, upon hearing the truth, shyly said he'd known all along this would happen, but I hadn't wanted to listen to anybody. I agreed and asked him to change the subject; after all, as Alejandro had said, there was more to the world than Orlando Sarmiento.

The idea of having new materials for my school filled me with joy. I wished we had a special room for our classes and not just a sidewalk, even though it was nice to be in the outside fresh air. Teaching outdoors also let passersby get a taste of school. I liked it when spectators would come and sit to watch because I knew they were learning, too. I felt secretly swollen with pride when the children called me "Señorita Maximiana" or "Teacher Maximiana." I was almost fifteen so the title "señorita" sounded grown up and even a bit pompous. And the title "teacher" made me feel fulfilled by identifying me as somebody making a positive change in the world. My goodness, how much I wished to be a *real* teacher.

The breakup made me mature ten years in a few days. I wanted Orlando and his friends to go back to Mazatlán and, hopefully, never to see them again. After talking to Alejandro on my tree, I realized that the little hope still hanging in my heart of reconciliation was just a silly dream. I couldn't compete with those girls or with the way Orlando was raised to be. Neither, I eventually realized, did I want to compete for somebody who had rejected me in such an insensitive way, who had not thought about my feelings even for an instant. Orlando could have prepared me for it, at least by sending me a letter ahead of time or not bringing his steady girlfriend along with him. I deserved that respect as the girl who had trusted his words for such a long time.

But he didn't do it because I was nobody to him, a mere servant with no status. He would never have acted this way to a girl of his class. That is a fact, and for that reason, I had to erase him from my heart and my mind forever. *That* is what a self-respecting young woman has to do when betrayal reaches her. It was not going to be easy. But I could do it, I kept repeating to myself.

"Why are you so sad?" Lourdes asked me in her babyish voice.

I tried to smile when I replied, "I am not sad; I don't feel good … that's all."

"Do you want a candy?" She offered a hard mint to me.

"Thank you." I took it from her hand and put it in my mouth. "Mmm … it is very good."

"I am going to help you clean my room today," little Lourdes said while picking up her toys from the floor. "I want you to be happy like before."

Despite my resolve, the sorrow of my broken heart was obvious to others. Even when I fought it with all the strength within me, I could not conceal it.

"Alejandro is back," she unexpectedly said. "I want him to be with us. I missed him too much."

"Oh, I missed him, too," I replied to her politely.

Margarita entered the room looking for me; Doña Luisa needed me to clean one of the guests' rooms.

"I am coming," I replied.

"Don't worry, Maximiana; I will clean my room completely," Lourdes said on my way out.

I walked towards the guest room, feeling a weight of ten tons on each foot. The burden increased when I discovered the young women clustered in the room I needed to clean. Apparently, they wished to relieve their boredom at my expense.

"So … are you from this town?" Catalina asked.

Immediately I sensed the intentions coming after the question.

"Yes," I replied and hurried to make up the beds.

"Is it true that you used to walk on the beach with Orlando?" Dora Elena asked.

Silence fell in the room.

"I walked with Señora Leonora and the girls." I didn't see why I had to tell them my personal life.

"Ooo, she answers back," Catalina said, laughing.

I raised my face to her and said, "I only answered your question."

"You are rude! Get out of here! NOW!" she screamed at me.

Clearly, her intention was to humiliate me. I looked her in the eyes and walked out. How silly they were; they needed to scream and ask me out of their presence because I made *them* feel uncomfortable.

Or did they need to humiliate others in order to feel better about themselves?

I didn't know, but their stupidity was more than clear.

"Wait!" the one named Dora Elena yelled at me.

I continued walking as fast as I could, pretending not to hear her screams. I crossed the parlor room and hallway and reached the back corridor. Through the window, Catalina Barraza called Orlando, who was at the corridor; I hurried ever more to get out of his way.

"They are calling you; go and see want they want," he coldly said without looking at me. I felt a bucket of freezing water falling on my head, but I gathered the strength to turn around and go back to the corner room.

"Who do you think you are? Why did you walk out on us like this, you stupid servant girl?" Dora Elena stated to my blank stare, as soon as I walked into the room.

Through the corner of my eye I saw Orlando standing at the window and Virginia Del Rincon smiling at the scene.

"I am done, Maximiana!" Lourdes said when she entered the room running.

She grabbed my hand and pulled me to her room, which was next to the one we were standing in.

"You did a very good job! Thank you!" I gasped in pretended admiration. "You are very good at organizing your toys."

She smiled at me, proud of her accomplishment. I debated for a second if I should go back to the corner room or not and decided to do it. Not returning gave them power over me. Orlando was holding the iron bars of the window, smiling at everyone inside.

"You see ... you are thinking wrong about us; in reality we want to make you our 'pet,'" Dora Elena said with a sarcastic tone in her voice. "I would love to fix your hair and give you one of my dresses; you would look like a doll in them."

I kept quiet.

"Don't you say, 'Thank you'?" Catalina asked.

"Thank you for offering it to me, but I don't need it, thank you."

"So you are proud ... the little thing is proud!" Dora Elena exclaimed to the enjoyment of everyone present, including Orlando Sarmiento. The girl named Angelina walked out of the room, and then I realized she had not been laughing with them.

"May I go now?" I asked, looking into Catalina Barraza's eyes.

"Well ... I don't know ... do you need something, Virginia?"

"Yes, I need her to get out of my face."

My pleasure.

I walked away. I could not deny the effect that such humiliations had over my emotions when I remembered Orlando's attitude towards the girls' words. His behavior made no sense at all. I continued asking myself what wrong had I inflicted upon him that made Orlando treat me this way? But how clever of *them* to show me his real self, even though they were not aware of it and were obviously doing it for the wrong reasons. But regardless of my questions and the reasons behind their intentions, Orlando's behavior hurt me just the same; it hurt me in a way that there were no more secret tears left in me to shed at night.

15

Domingo and Alejandro noticed the specific request for "Maxi-miana" to serve the refreshments at the picnic. The gathering had been arranged to celebrate Dora Elena Mora's birthday before they returned to Mazatlán the next morning. Domingo and Orlando were going to leave three days later. I was glad it was almost over. I just wanted them all to go and keep a distance from me forever. Alejandro and Domingo had been very helpful during these weeks by trying to keep those women away from my presence. But with Señora Leonora on the girls' side, their mission was almost impossible.

New yellow linens decorated the garden tables on the upper terrace. Upon them lay the finest china cups and saucers, waiting for the delicate hands of the ladies; Señora Leonora had ordered the most elegant pastries. Only the best would do. She relished showing her sophistication in the parties she gave.

Alejandro could not hide his annoyance at the gathering. Apparently he did not find the jokes very amusing, and he could interest no one in a more intellectual conversation. Domingo sat amid the group with his face turned away, ignoring everything and everybody. Señor Joaquín Sarmiento left the picnic, and Domingo tried to follow him out of the party, but his father ordered him to go back and sit at the same table as Catalina Barraza. Even more irritated, he returned and fixed his gaze upon the Sacanta Mountain.

In contrast, the excitement of the other men was evident, especially Teodoro de la Vega and Gustavo Inzunza, who seemed to be very interested in the ladies' presence.

I stood next to the refreshment table, waiting for their orders. I was to hand out drinks to whoever wanted them and replenish the pastry and snack plates. I kept looking at the Sacanta to avoid the malicious stares.

Dora Elena Mora rose from her seat and walked towards me. Alejandro's guard went up and followed her with his glare. She walked around me, and Señora Leonora smiled, satisfied. Alejandro turned and looked at Señora Leonora with a disapproving look. At that moment, Margarita came looking for Alejandro; Señor Joaquín needed him, and mortified, he left the picnic, looking back at me. I smiled to reassure him that I was fine; I could handle the situation. He gave an accusing look to Orlando before walking away. Domingo then took over, watching out for me.

"What are you doing?" he asked Dora Elena. "Why are you walking around Maximiana?"

Señora Aurora Garrido, the older woman who had chaperoned the women to El Roble, dropped her jaw at his words.

"I am walking around her to see how bad she smells," she said with a malevolent smile.

You don't "see" how a person smells, you idiot.

Laughter burst out among the party, including Orlando. However, neither Teodoro de la Vega nor Angelina Castro joined in. They became stiff with the comment, and seriousness settled on their young faces. Domingo rose and took "smiling Dora Elena" to her seat. I observed the entire scene with a better understanding of how the world works, hiding my discomfort in the best way I could. I bit my lip and continued looking intently at the Sacanta.

Silence fell again when Domingo approached me and took me by the hand to the other extreme of the garden. He stood behind me and looked at the picnic gathering.

Then, secretly into my ear he whispered, "Tell Natalia to meet me tonight by the sugar cane fields by your roble tree."

I smiled and looked at him knowing his intentions to confuse the people who observed us with indignation. They were imagining the worse.

"I will … what time?"

"Any time she can. I will be waiting patiently … you are my favorite 'almost-sister-in-law,' you know that, right?" he said and kissed me on the cheek.

"I know that," I said with a wink.

He grabbed my hand again and walked with me to the refreshment table. Before he left, he bowed to everyone with a grin. Then I noticed that Orlando's smile had faded away, and Virginia observed him with puzzlement. You could tell how uncomfortable she became after that; no one could ignore her obvious bewilderment, not even Señora Leonora.

"You, go and tell Luisa to take your place serving," she said.

I nodded and headed towards the kitchen. Satisfaction overwhelmed me. I knew she had displaced me because they could not destroy me. They could not humiliate me. And they could not keep me from turning their worst intentions around into my favor. They had even helped me understand my inner strength. The outside doesn't matter—the clothes you wear, the style of your hair, the color of your eyes or skin, or your last name; your essence is *you*. They let me know that I was who I was due to my personality and behavior.

The next morning I arrived at the hacienda when the carriages were being loaded with passengers and luggage. I witnessed when Orlando grabbed Virginia's hand, kissed it, and led her up to her carriage.

"Happy birthday, Dora Elena. I love you very much," he said as his friend took the first step up the carriage. Domingo was nowhere to be seen, and Señor Joaquín Sarmiento sent Alejandro to bring him back to see everyone off.

Señora Leonora looked sad to see her parents go back to Mazatlán; they kept telling her that summer was around the corner. Little

Lourdes and María Isabel were more indifferent than concerned about their grandparents' departure. I saw Doña Luisa in the distance and went towards her, my chores were waiting.

On my way to the kitchen, I bumped into Alejandro, who greeted me with his usual "Good morning." Then he told me that Domingo didn't want to get up from bed and that there had been nothing that Alejandro could do to force him to go and say good-bye to Catalina Barraza and the whole departing party.

"Is he still asleep?" I asked.

"Profoundly …," he replied.

My sister Natalia's refusal to get up and go to the fields this morning became a parallel scene to Domingo's sleepiness. I was truly concerned about Natalia's attitude towards her relationship with Domingo Sarmiento. No human power could convince her to take things really easy; she simply didn't grasp a lesson from my experience with the younger Sarmiento brother. As much as I appreciated Domingo's brotherly protection and care of me, I lacked complete trust in his relationship with Natalia.

Can he have the capacity to see her as a human being without any social prejudices? I highly doubt it.

Doña Luisa asked Margarita (who was now taking over Raimunda's chores) and me to start cleaning the balcony room. We took the brooms, mops, and buckets from the storage and marched to our morning work. Even when I tried with all of my will, my feelings of desolation were not yet fading away, and the pain from Orlando's betrayal was still settled in my heart. However, I managed to dismiss the hurting feelings as soon as they began to harm me again.

We took the covers off the bed. I offered to take them to the washing area, but Margarita wanted to do it herself. I agreed and started sweeping the floor in a hurry. I had a feeling that Orlando was near me. I rushed to finish the balcony room when he appeared through the garden door and walked into the bedroom. I dismissed his presence and picked up the bucket of water to walk out with it. I do not know if he looked at me for I passed by his side as if he did not exist.

On my way back to Doña Luisa, I heard the clash between Domingo and his father, who screamed in exasperation about his son's attitude towards the Barraza family and the other guests. Apparently Domingo was not willing to take his father's onslaught and screamed back at him that he was free to do whatever he wanted. Then Alejandro joined in and tried to intervene in favor of his brother, but Señor Joaquín yelled back that Domingo's behavior was Alejandro's doing.

"Blame it on me as always, Father!" Alejandro screamed and shut the door behind him.

"As soon as you arrive in Mazatlán, I want you to pay a visit and apologize to the Barrazas! Do you hear me, Domingo?" Señor Joaquín kept repeating to no avail because Domingo continued answering that he would do "no such thing." I moved as fast as a flash when Señor Joaquín marched out and crossed in front of me, giving me a piercing look.

"Doña Luisa … when is Raimunda coming back?" I asked, concerned. It had been almost a month since she had stopped coming to the hacienda.

"Next week … she said she is coming back next week."

"Is she better? What happened to her?"

"Look … come here," she said in a low voice. "Raimunda is with child and almost lost her baby. That is why she hasn't come to work."

"Oh! Doña Luisa …"

My heart fell to the floor. It had been months since we had left Mazatlán.

"But how many months is she?"

"I don't know, Maximiana, and that is none of our business."

"Oh, Doña Luisa," I whispered in her ear, "I know who did this to her."

"Who?" Doña Luisa replied with intrigue.

"Come in here," I pulled her to the kitchen storage. "The man who abused her is Señor Sarmiento."

"Which one?" Doña Luisa asked, perplexed.

"Señor Joaquín."

"For the Virgin of Guadalupe, child, don't repeat that."

"But it is the truth."

"Shhh! Where did you get this from? Tell me ..."

"When we were in Mazatlán, he would walk in the room at night and—"

"Are you sure?"

"Yes ... Señorito Alejandro knows and Señorito Orlando."

"My God ... does Señora Leonora know?"

"I don't think so, but Doña Luisa ... he continued doing it here," I said in shock. "I thought she would be free of that once we were in El Roble."

"No child, that is not the way things work," Doña Luisa said with sadness. "Poor Raimunda, she is not the first one or the last one to pass through that man's hands."

Lupita walked in to ask for Domingo's breakfast.

"Señorito Domingo said that he wants Maximiana to take his breakfast."

Doña Luisa gave me a disapproving look.

"What is this business of yours with Domingo now?" she asked, clearly bothered. "And Alejandro who jumps around you as a flea?"

"Nothing, Doña Luisa, I promise. There is nothing going on," I reassured her.

"I don't like the way things are going, Maximiana. First it was Orlando following you around the hacienda, don't think that I never noticed, and then when you came back from Mazatlán, Alejandro started following your steps and now Domingo ... what is going on here?"

"Nothing ... Señorito Orlando is not my friend; he never was," I replied flippantly. "Señorito Alejandro is excited about my school, and Señorito Domingo ... I don't know ... he just liked to bother Señorita Catalina Barraza through me, I guess ...," I replied indifferently.

"Ahhh ... so that is what is going on ... are you proud of that?"

OH YES! I thought, but instead said, "I am very proud of my school—"

"Don't try to outsmart me, Maximiana; I am four times your age."

"Doña Luisa, Domingo is going to get mad if I don't hurry up with his breakfast."

"Señorito Domingo," she scolded.

"Yes, sorry … Señorito Domingo."

I smiled and walked away with Raimunda's image inside my head. I needed to tell Alejandro about Raimunda; after all she was carrying his brother or sister, and if he didn't help her, who would?

"Here is your breakfast, Domingo."

"Maximiana, we are leaving in two days," he replied with sadness.

"I know … you must be excited to go back to school and all that," I said, resting my arms on a chair, trying to forget that Orlando was leaving with him.

"I am not excited at all," he said. "How is Natalia?"

"She is fine. You saw her yesterday."

"Yes."

He looked away from me. Instinctively, I felt that his question had something to do with last night.

I gathered the strength to tell him, "I hope you are not taking for granted her feelings."

He turned his face to me again. "No, I wouldn't do that."

Our conversation was interrupted by Orlando, who walked in the dining room and sat to have his breakfast.

"I will bring your breakfast," I said and got out of the dining room. Upon my return, Alejandro was sitting with them, drinking coffee.

"Aleh … do you want me to bring you your breakfast?" I asked casually.

"This is fine, thank you, Max," he replied.

I left as fast as I could. I was turning around the long corridor when I heard my name pronounced on the lips of Alejandro but not directed toward me. I stopped.

"Is that what you are thinking then?" he said.

"No," Orlando replied to him in a low voice.

"Don't you have any feelings for her, any feelings at all? You did before," Alejandro continued.

"No, I don't. Never really did."

Orlando's words made my respiration cut short.

"I love Virginia; she is better for me. And … she is just a servant … I would never take somebody like Maximiana seriously … there is no comparison next to Virginia."

This time, the tears coming down my face felt like burning fire. I closed my eyes, trying to disappear from the face of the earth.

"Don't say that," Domingo replied.

"You may regret it later, Orlando … don't say that," Alejandro scolded.

"No, I won't," Orlando answered firmly.

Doña Luisa made my presence known to them by calling my name and asking me what I was doing standing in the corridor by myself. Alejandro came out and walked towards my spot with a sorrowful look for he knew I had heard everything.

"Max …," he said with a sympathetic tone of voice.

I looked down on the floor, trying to hide my tears, *one more time*. Domingo came after him.

"Just forget about him," Domingo said. "He doesn't know what he is saying."

"He does," I replied, "and I understand. I just wish I hadn't heard that because it is very humiliating."

Both of them looked down.

"I don't think I will ever forget his words …"

"You are more than what he says …," Alejandro replied.

"I know that." I raised my face to him. "I know I am."

But you don't erase feelings for a person in a matter of weeks, no matter what that person thinks of you or how that person mistreats you.

"I have to go now … don't worry about me. I am fine."

"Max," Alejandro called, "I know your birthday is coming on May fifteen, right?"

"Yes," I replied, heading to the parlor, dust rag in hand, to start pushing away the memories however hard to do.

My poor Natalia was heartbroken when daylight broke over the horizon and her beloved Domingo Sarmiento prepared to leave. It was her turn to weep this time and my turn to console her and say, "He will be back soon," even when deep inside my heart, I didn't believe it. She walked to the street corner and looked at him in the distance when they left. Domingo kept turning back and waving. Orlando never did.

It was a strange feeling to walk into the hacienda knowing that, at one time, the reason for my happiness in that house had been Orlando Sarmiento and, now, he was gone from my life forever. As I walked into the side entrance, Aleh approached me and put his arm around my shoulder. Señor Joaquín and his wife stood some distance off by the back corridor with their backs to us. They must have heard the sounds of our footsteps for Señor Sarmiento turned and looked back at us, frowning. Señora Sarmiento said something to her husband that made him turn around again and stop. I moved away from Alejandro because I sensed danger coming my way.

"She has to go; Catalina has been very upset with her presence!" Señora Leonora finally claimed, full of anger.

"She is not going anywhere," Alejandro replied. "Domingo has no interest in Maximiana. What are you talking about?"

"Don't disrespect Leonora, Alejandro!" Señor Joaquín scolded.

"She is always around you and Domingo, and she thinks she is some kind of guest in my own house," she replied clearly upset.

"Guest? Since when do *guests* work like mules for miserable cents in the place they are visiting!" Alejandro screamed back, with eyes blazing. "Father, she doesn't know what she is saying!"

"Shut up, Alejandro; don't talk to Leonora that way."

"Maximiana is not going anywhere, sir."

My legs were shaking listening to the discussion. I couldn't afford to lose this job, no matter what. I moved away, but Alejandro held me by the arm.

"Don't you appreciate the fact that Maximiana Valdez saved your child, Leonora?" Alejandro asked, and her face tightened.

Then Señor Joaquín pronounced an unbelievable sentence in *my presence* as if I were an invisible, insensitive *thing*.

"Look, you can put up a house for her. I will pay for everything."

I wished to strike the rude, lecherous man to the floor.

"What are you saying?" Alejandro asked, fuming.

"You know what I am saying …"

Leonora Sarmiento's world collapsed under her expensive satin shoes. She looked at me with a hatred that could have cut me to pieces in a second.

"Ha, ha, ha! I truly admire your Catholicism, Father! I really do!" Alejandro replied in a defiant and sarcastic way.

"I don't think that would be proper," Señora Leonora intervened immediately, but I knew Alejandro Sarmiento was the only reason behind her pronouncement and the salvation of my soul mattered not a bit to her.

"Then stop bothering me about this Maximiana Valdez, for God's sake, woman!" Señor Joaquín exclaimed, exasperated.

"Or I could marry her," Alejandro suddenly said and turned his face to Señora Leonora, who couldn't hide her distress.

Soon, Alejandro's attitude calmed down, and he looked at me. By now, I think he realized that he was the reason for this argument and not I. Fortunately, Señor Joaquín remained oblivious to the reality in front of him and simply walked away, irritated by Alejandro's proposal of marriage to me. Señora Leonora followed Señor Joaquín, and I walked directly to Alejandro to slap his arm.

"Are you out of your mind?" I chided. "If you say such a thing, Señor Joaquín will kick me out on the street, Alejandro. What would I do without this salary? Think about my school."

"I stopped her, didn't I?" he said, but he seemed distracted with some other thought, no doubt his stepmother's attitude towards him. He looked at me, wanting to say something, but he restrained himself.

"There is always something, Alejandro. I can never be at peace."

"That's life, I guess," he replied and hugged me while we walked to the kitchen.

❧

By now all the workers at the hacienda were used to my relation-ship with Alejandro, and everyone knew he equally respected each one of them. Alejandro Sarmiento had no concerns in the rumors about his clear affection for the servant girl, who was also the town's enthusiastic school teacher.

For days I thought about Raimunda and her tremendously unfair situation. She had had no say in the decision to have that child; her family was very poor and lived in a misery far worse than mine. I asked myself if Señor Joaquín would help her out. After all, he knew the child was his baby. My thoughts were interrupted by the sounds of the bells from church. That was strange; it was no later than mid-day, and I wondered why Father Felipe was calling the people in town for mass.

I took a look outside the kitchen window and noticed dark grey clouds filling the sky. A storm was coming, so I walked to Margarita to ask if she knew something about the church calling, but she was as confused as I was. I hurried up to finish my chores and go home; the fresh air coming into the windows was starting to feel a little bit too strong. After a while, Doña Luisa came in asking us all to help get the chickens in the hen house and go home; Father Felipe had announced a storm was coming. Some people who had just arrived from Villa Unión told him to announce it; the wire had come from Mazatlán this morning, and nobody was crossing the Presidio River.

I placed my hand on my chest. Domingo and Orlando had left this same morning. I wondered if they had crossed the Presidio River on time. But even if they had, they would never make it to Mazatlán before the storm hit.

"Hurry! Hurry! Help us shut the windows and doors! Quickly!" Doña Luisa screamed at all of us.

"But Doña Luisa, this is not the time for storms." Nobody had caught that detail. "Storm season starts in May, and we are in April."

"God knows what is going on, child; just do what you are told and quickly go home. People are taking refuge in church," she replied and walked away from me in a hurry.

I left after attending to my "storm duties" and crossed the gate out of the hacienda when I spotted Daniel coming with his family and mine. Rain started to sprinkle, and the time of day felt more like seven at night instead of midday. The sky became dark, and the clouds were rapidly covering every inch of blue sky in the distance. I took my younger sisters by their hands, and feeling the strength of the wind, we quickly marched to church. The Sarmientos did not need to seek refuge anywhere. The Grand House had walls thick enough to withstand anything; nothing would move them or the heavy roofs. I kept wondering if Domingo and Orlando, their two friends Gustavo and Teodoro, as well as the others had made it back in time to El Roble.

People gathered in church and talked about this strange event. By now everyone was aware of the fact that this was not storm season. Some proclaimed the end of the world, others that the sea might enter land, and a few more realistic (or sadistic) started to guess that the Presidio River might overflow and reach El Roble. Up to this day, I don't understand why adults talk about these horrible events in the presence of children, as if children did not already have over-active imaginations. I grouped the children around me and told them that I would tell them a story. All the children got excited and sat down. Natalia and Otilia, as well as other young women, decided to sit and listen to me instead of the tragic predictions coming from the adults.

The wind started to blow with force. The bell resonated from the push of the storm, and the sound inside the church was unbearable. Papá proposed to move some benches to the two side doors because they were shaking from the blasts of the winds. We could hear the branches of trees scratching and hitting against the walls and windows of our sanctuary. Some of the children started to cry in fear of the noise; it felt and sounded as if the gale would tear off the very walls and send them flying away, like scraps of paper.

Father Felipe asked us all to pray with him. Putting my mind to prayer made me feel some peace, and I asked God to keep Domingo, Orlando, and the others safe, wherever they were. I dearly hoped they had made it to the hacienda, even though by the time I left they were nowhere to be seen.

After almost two hours of forceful winds, calmness came.

"It seems like the eye in the storm," Papá said.

Father Felipe opened one door, and some of us walked outside. Branches and roof tiles littered the streets and grounds everywhere. Otilia pointed towards the huanacaxtle tree at the entrance of El Roble, and panic descended on us all. The river water had already reached the edge of town. Raimunda held on to me, her belly already showing even when she shamefully tried to conceal it.

"The river has never reached the church," Father Felipe told us all. "Calm down and walk back in. Everything is going to be fine; trust yourselves to God."

I looked in the direction of the hacienda and saw Alejandro coming out of the front entrance. He walked to church to check on everyone. He said Domingo and the others had returned before the storm had struck and were safe in the Grand House. Father Felipe ordered him to go back to the hacienda because the wind was starting again, and we all walked back in.

"Father Felipe, the roof is moving," Daniel's father said. "We need to open the doors and windows, or the roof will blow off."

We all moved away from the windows and doors as the men released them, and the air entered the church with such force that it smashed the doors against the walls.

Time passed slowly, but finally the storm winds calmed down sometime in the night, even though the rain didn't stop. Some people decided to spend the night in the church, too afraid to go back to their houses. Papá and Augusto went to check on our house. Only part of the kitchen roof had been blown off, but nothing major had happened. Other people had had greater losses; the wind had blown away their houses, along with animals, vegetable gardens, and trees.

When morning came, we saw the desolation left by the strange storm. Fortunately, nobody from El Roble had perished in the storm; but people in other towns had not been as lucky. El Guayabo, a town close to El Roble by the edge of the Presidio River, was completely flooded. Some people had not escaped in time to El Bajio or Lomas Del Guayabo, the two closest towns that are located, like El Roble, in the upper hills. Horror stories of death and survival started to flood our imaginations; the devastation of the storm was the main topic of discussion for many weeks to come.

16

Crossing the Presidio River after the storm proved an impossible mission. Domingo and his group had to stay in El Roble until news came that the waters had retreated sufficiently for them to safely get to Mazatlán. Señora Leonora was worried about her family in the city. No communication made it through for days between towns because trees and debris left behind by the river's high waters blocked some of the roads and the winds had knocked out everything in its path.

The sight of so many dead animals that couldn't escape the storm saddened me. And my heart broke when I picked up from the water tower three little owlets in their nest; apparently they were left orphaned by the winds.

I walked to the upper terrace from where I could see the countryside almost in its entirety. What a sight! Before me I saw the sugar cane fields completely flattened down; such a great loss would affect everyone. The Sarmientos had resources to get through this with no problem, but the rest of us were not as fortunate.

The work at the Grand House the day after the storm challenged our stamina. Many of the rooms had been inundated by water that had entered through windows and doors, and we spent hours drying them. The rain had also entered the storage rooms and the warehouses, ruining the grains kept for the family's consumption as well as for the next planting season. Chaos ruled, and no one could pay much attention to anything but the task at hand. So, when Doña Luisa sent me to bring corn for the chickens out of one of the warehouses, I followed her orders even though I was afraid to go into the huge empty building alone.

As I headed to the storehouse, Orlando's friend Gustavo Inzunza came walking in my direction.

"I have never gone in the warehouse," he said. "Is it flooded?"

"The rain got in, but already somebody is taking the water out and pulling out the corn sacks," I replied.

He followed me into the building. Rapidly, I walked to the open sack in the corner and started filling my wood bucket. All of a sudden, the room became dark. I turned around and saw the shadow of Gustavo Inzunza putting the wooden bar on the door to shut it. Shivers ran down my body and hit my fingertips in panic.

"Open the door," I said with a strong voice.

He kept silent and came near me.

"Don't touch me because you don't know what I'm capable of!" I screamed.

"Don't be afraid. I am better than Orlando, Alejandro, *and* Domingo ... you will see," he replied while reaching for my face.

I pulled his hands off me and tried to run to the door. He grabbed me by the waist and pushed me with force to the floor. I tried to scream, but he covered my mouth with his disgusting hand, and I bit him with all the force of my jaw, marking his hand with my teeth. He let go as an impulse, and I put both of my hands together to serve a blow to his head, then ran for the bucket and threw the corn at him.

He got up, seething, and punched me in the chin, but my knee simultaneously went directly into his groin. He buckled under, and I hit him with the bucket and ran towards the door. He grabbed my foot, but using my free leg, I kicked as hard as I could, sending blows to his face, neck, and shoulders.

"Let go of me! LET GO OF ME!" I continued screaming and threw the bucket to the door, hoping that somebody on the other side might hear the commotion.

I turned around, and with my free foot, I stepped on the filthy hands that held my foot. Still he wouldn't let go, so I went for a bite on his arm. He recited a song of insults and bad words that are not worth repeating but applied to him perfectly.

"YOU are *that* and more! YOU ARE ALL *THAT* … YOU DIRTY PIG!" I screamed and continued my fight. He finally let go, and I crawled to the door. I removed the wooden barricade, opened the door, and struggled with myself not to go back and hit him with the bar a couple of times. He got up, and I ran out of the room. Don Carlos was walking in my direction when I got out of the warehouse, and by the expression on his face, I could tell that I didn't look good at all.

Once outside, I felt a sharp pain in my lower lip. When I touched it, it burned, and fresh blood made a puddle on the tips of my fingers. I stood for a moment speechless, and then, once I had put a safe distance from the place where I had been cowardly attacked, terror struck me. I felt the wet soil under my right foot and realized I had lost my sandal in the struggle and my blouse was out of the waistline of my skirt.

"Don Carlos," I said with a shaken voice, "Gustavo Inzunza attacked me in the warehouse."

"Aye, child, why did you go in there by yourself?" he said with a mortified look. Margarita came walking in our direction.

"What happened?" she asked, concerned, her eyes wild with terror.

"Gustavo Inzunza attacked me in the warehouse," I said, still numb by the fright that was finally settling inside me, "but I fought back."

The warehouse door opened, and Gustavo Inzunza stared at us, angry and confused. At that moment, the hacienda gates unlocked, and Señor Joaquín Sarmiento rode in on his horse, followed by Domingo, Orlando, Alejandro, and Teodoro de la Vega. Don Carlos looked down, not daring to say anything. Margarita sought Alejandro's face and turned to me, in an attempt to indicate what had just happened. Alejandro saw my face and jumped from his horse at once.

"Why do you have blood on your mouth, Maximiana?" he asked, and then looked down at my feet and outfit. "What happened here?"

I glanced at the warehouse door where Gustavo Inzunza stood. The truth was more than obvious; Gustavo Inzunza had a cut on his eyebrow as a result of my hitting him with the wood bucket. Domingo got down from the horse, followed by Señor Joaquín, Orlando, and Teodoro de la Vega.

"What happened, Carlos?" Señor Joaquín asked.

"The Señorito attacked Maximiana in the warehouse, Señor," he replied.

Señor Joaquín shook his head while placing both hands on his waist.

"What do you mean 'attacked'?" Domingo asked.

Gustavo Inzunza walked towards us, with his right hand on his eyebrow, trying to hold the blood from gushing through his face.

"He raped her," Margarita said bluntly.

"NO! He did NOT! I didn't let him!" I exclaimed while Alejandro marched to Gustavo Inzunza like a bull and started punching him. I covered my eyes in panic; I didn't want Alejandro to get hurt. But in a matter of seconds, Domingo was by his side, pushing Gustavo away from Alejandro, who was relentless in his attack on the dirty pig.

Señor Joaquín stood there, watching the whole scene with pride, a most strange reaction, I thought, to the situation. I glanced at Orlando, who was staring at me in an apparently confused state of mind. Teodoro de la Vega was speechless, especially by the violent reaction on Alejandro's part. The commotion reached everyone in the hacienda, and by now, almost every person, with the exception of the twins, had gathered at the scene.

Teodoro de la Vega asked Gustavo Inzunza to apologize, but Señor Joaquín said there was no need for it. Alejandro's face hardened with rage at his father's words.

"Luisa, take this girl to wash and continue with chores; nothing happened here," he said and walked away.

Señora Leonora stood petrified, looking at Alejandro who seemed ready to turn his violent reaction against his own father.

"If you ever try to harm *any* of the girls that work here, or *any* *woman* I know … I will kill you … do you hear me?" Alejandro said, grinding his teeth in anger while holding Gustavo by the shirt. He reacted with a sardonic smile. Domingo walked to him and said something to his ear that I couldn't hear; however, by the reaction of Gustavo's face I could tell it was not agreeable at all.

The crowd dispersed. Doña Luisa placed her warm arm around my shoulders.

"How are you doing, child?" she asked in a maternal voice.

My mouth started to tremble with indignation as I answered, "I lost my sandal … it ripped to pieces when he was pulling my foot."

Domingo shook his head, and Alejandro came near me.

"I am sorry, Maximiana; I'm sorry this happened to you," he said.

"I know, Aleh. Thank you for defending me. Thank you," I said, breaking into sobs.

My dear friend Alejandro hugged me with tenderness while Margarita marched into the warehouse looking for my sandal. Señora Leonora left the scene at once without looking back, but Orlando stayed with his brothers. He never said a word, but he did not move away from them either. Teodoro de la Vega accompanied Gustavo Inzunza inside the house. Gustavo seemed more consternated than embarrassed by the whole situation because the mocking smile had faded away.

"He will pay for your sandals," Alejandro said.

"No, I don't want anything from that dirty pig, and I don't mean to offend the poor pigs … it is just an expression," I replied. "I would rather go barefoot for the rest of my life than take anything from him."

Doña Luisa approved my response with a nod. Then Domingo said he would buy me new sandals. I was too proud to accept it and said thank you, but I could fix the ripped one. Margarita came back to us with a glass of sugared water in her hand.

"For the fright," she said.

"Thank you."

I took it from her hand. I drank it and walked away to continue my chores.

Cowardice your name is Orlando Sarmiento.

Throughout the day I felt an uneasiness of what had happened to me. Somebody had tried to harm me merely because I was a woman and, as such, perceived as a usable object.

News of what had happened reached my house before I arrived. My parents felt gratitude towards Alejandro for what he had done. I felt the same way but didn't want to talk about it anymore. It was an episode that I wanted to erase from my memory as soon as possible. That night, Otilia slept, hugging me. She understood how I felt.

After the storm, an unbearable heat wave hit us. All the storm's heavy rainfall and floodwaters swallowed by the earth's soil had begun to evaporate. The stifling, hot air held so much humidity that you could almost taste it with your tongue. In one of those extremely stuffy, warm nights, when everyone had fallen asleep, Natalia and I went outside to sit on the sidewalk of our house in an attempt to escape the suffocating heat inside.

"There is something that I have wanted to tell you for days, but I haven't had the chance because Otilia or someone else is always around …" Natalia said once we were seated.

I kept waving air at my face with a dry palm leaf.

"What is it?" I asked, feeling sweaty wetness on my neck.

"The other night when I met Domingo at the sugar cane fields …" she paused, sighed, and continued, "something happened between us."

My heart knew what she was about to say next. I had told her so many times not to do it; lamentably, she had not considered my advice.

"Natalia … I am younger than you, but … how could you do such a thing?"

"I love him, Max …," she said in her melodious voice.

And I believed her. Of course I believed her, but her loving him was not the point at all. I wished she had understood that.

"He is leaving again soon, Natalia, and during the summer he will travel to the United States. He is going to attend university there for at least three years. Did you know that?"

"Yes," she whispered, "and he will take me with him."

Oh God, my poor Natalia is so naïve.

"Nat … do you believe him?" I asked as tactfully as my rising anger would allow it. One thing was for Domingo to play his game of conquest with Natalia; another was to tell such a lie to her.

How can he even dare to say that he is going to take her with him to the United States?

"I believe him, Max; he loves me for real," she replied, closing her eyes and placing her delicate hands on her chest.

"I believed Orlando also, Nat, and he was lying to me."

"But Domingo is different; he truly is."

That is what I believed also.

"Natalia, you could be left with a child … what are you going to do?"

"Oh no … I won't … he said he knew a way to avoid it," she said casually to my surprise. "He said that if he—"

"Please don't tell me the details," I interrupted, "I really don't want to know too much about *that* between you and him."

"Oh Max … no … don't say that … it was beautiful … he was very—"

"No, no, no," I covered my ears, "Natalia, please don't tell me the details … you are my sister."

And I don't trust Domingo Sarmiento with your heart or body.

"Promise, Natalia, that you will not do it again … don't risk yourself like this."

"But love is the most beautiful thing in the world, Max. How can you say that?"

"Because he is leaving, that is why …"

"He will take me with him, he promised," she insisted.

"Look, his trip to the United States is two or three months away … so many things can happen in between. For example, he is leaving for Mazatlán one of these days; he could forget about you." I had to say it, even when these words hurt me more than her.

"Oh no, Max … Domingo will not forget me; he loves me, and for real … why don't you believe me? He is not Orlando. You do not know the things that he says to me, how he talks to me, how he kisses me and hugs me."

I know word for word, Natalia; trust me. I have been there before, with his brother.

I fanned her with my dry leaf.

"I just don't want you to get hurt; that is all."

And be left behind with a broken heart, just like me, or worse, a baby.

I knew firsthand what was to come as a consequence of her eager and amorous heart.

"Natalia, try to be smart about this and don't do it with him again. If you are lucky enough that he has not left you with a child already, *that* is a blessing. Don't risk it anymore. For Mamá and Papá, stop doing it, for yourself … for the child."

"There will be no child, silly," she said, giggling. "I told you he knows how to avoid it."

"But—"

"And I love doing it with him …," she said while a sigh escaped her chest.

"By God, Natalia … you have no shame?" I asked, blushing.

"There is nothing to be ashamed of Max … love is beautiful, and I love being his lover. Do you know what a lover is? A lover is somebody who truly loves … otherwise the word wouldn't exist."

She left me speechless.

"Did Domingo tell you that?"

"Of course not, silly. I have always felt that way, ever since I fell in love for the first time at age seven …," she laughed.

"You are silly … and not," I reasoned. "I understand what you mean, and it is true that there is nothing more beautiful than being *a lover* when you are truly loved back by the one you love."

"Yes …," Natalia sighed.

"But what would happen if he is lying to you …?"

"It doesn't matter to me because I have enjoyed each moment as much as he has," she winked at me. "Didn't *you* enjoy your moments with Orlando?"

"I did … but I now regret each one of them," I said in a low voice. "The pain that comes after is unbearable, Natalia, when you discover that you were living a fantasy."

"I know Domingo is not lying; I can feel it."

I did too. I felt Orlando's love each time he touched me with his words, hands, or lips, but in the end it was all make-believe.

The strumming of guitars was playing at our door step. This was not the first time that men had serenaded our house. Before Otilia's abuse, she had had a beau who used to bring the guitars to play for her. And for Natalia, it was a normal event in her life. Several young men, not only in El Roble but from other towns as well, aspired for my beautiful sister.

My brother Augusto complained about the guitars all the time. He felt they signified a lack of respect to bring music serenades to a house where the girls were not steady with a boyfriend. I had no hopes for receiving a serenade anytime soon; after all, to the young men in El Roble, I was the "Jezebel of the Sarmiento brothers." But I enjoyed listening to them just the same; it was awfully romantic.

"Natalia … serenade for you," Otilia said.

"Mmm … I am too sleepy," Natalia replied in dreamland.

I got up and looked through the door's eye hole. There is no way to deny the astonishment I felt when I saw gorgeous Domingo Sarmiento standing outside like a prince from one of his twin sisters' fairy-tale books.

"Natalia, Domingo is outside," I whispered in her ear.

She jumped off her cot like a deer and ran to the door. Yes, Domingo Sarmiento was serenading Natalia Valdez, and he didn't care that all the neighbors and probably the entire El Roble town were witnesses to the event.

"Oh my God, it is Domingo!" she said full of happiness.

Otilia and I smiled at her enthusiasm. Mamá came to us, listening to the commotion. When she saw it was Domingo Sarmiento, she put her hand on her mouth. Papá and Augusto did not bother getting up; they were probably covering their ears.

"Maximiana, why is this young man serenading you when the one taking you horse-riding is his brother?" Mamá asked.

Silence took hold in our small room.

"It isn't for her, Mamá; it is for me," Natalia said shyly.

Mamá frowned at her answer but kept quiet, then returned to Papá, clearly uncomfortable.

Custom dictated that the young lady stay inside while the guitars played for her, but Natalia wanted to break the tradition and go out to thank Domingo. It took a lot of persuasion to convince her that she should not do it, although her enthusiasm was understandable.

After three songs, the guitarists left, but Domingo remained on our sidewalk. Natalia walked out, ignoring Otilia, who continued trying to convince her to stay inside. She was with him for a couple of minutes, then came back inside, and went to her cot. I heard Domingo's footsteps walk away from our house, but I suspected they had planned an encounter (I am sure I would've done the same thing in their place), and he was waiting for Natalia to sneak out.

There was no point in trying to stop her. She would do it just the same, and she did; her will was as strong as her vocal chords. As soon as Otilia gave signs of being asleep, Natalia put her sandals on and carefully opened the door to the street. I followed her out and saw her running down towards the arroyo where Domingo awaited her. I saw the pair disappear into the sugar cane fields.

I fought with all of my being not to feel jealous of my sister's happiness and to expel from my mind the disappointment of knowing that Orlando would never reconsider what had happened between us. During that night, restless with insomnia, I realized that I still hung on to a thread of hope of my first love coming back to me, even when from his very lips had come the words that revealed his attitude and true intentions towards me, *I never had feelings for her. She is not good enough for somebody like me; she is nothing like Virginia Del Rincon.*

How stubborn we girls tend to be when it comes to love, just like Maríanela. She died from her refusal to see the senselessness of loving one who had rejected her, not from a lack of intelligence or from sorrow. I needed to stop thinking about this somehow. I planned to ask my dear Alejandro for a good book that had nothing to do with love or romance. And he did; he gave me his secret copy of Karl Marx's *Communist Manifesto*.

From that day on, the words "bourgeois" and "proletariat" entered my vocabulary with an ardent passion. At almost fifteen, I finally started grasping the realities of my life, and the pieces began to fall into the right places. I belonged to the proletariat, and it was time once and for all to move on with my life.

Noticeably pregnant, Raimunda returned to work at the Grand House during the first days of May. We all tried to help her with her chores as much as possible, but the sadness in her face never left; not even my best stories made her smile. Alejandro was very upset when he saw Raimunda in her delicate state; he probably complained to his father about it. However, he never mentioned his feelings about the matter to me.

Alejandro's nineteeth birthday was coming right after mine on May 15, but he refused to have a celebration. Señora Leonora had been in charge of making a birthday gathering for her favorite stepson each year since her marriage to Señor Joaquín, and given the fact that organizing picnics and parties was her favorite task, she was probably disappointed about Alejandro's refusal to have a birthday party. Señora Leonora's attitude was easy to understand for more than one reason; after all, there wasn't much for her to do in El Roble.

I had no idea if I was going to spend the summer with the Sarmientos as the twins' nanny again, but I was not betting on it. Secretly, I dreamed of going back to Mazatlán. I wanted to be close to the sea, but for various reasons, the idea of staying in the Grand City House had no appeal to me at all. So I lost no sleep over thoughts about whether I would travel to the port again or not.

We were doing laundry when the racket began. Raimunda stood behind Doña Luisa who kept her usual calmness as she tried to explain to Señora Leonora that Raimunda's chores were done as usual. Señora Leonora did not want Raimunda to work at the hacienda while expecting a child, and Doña Luisa replied that she had hired expecting girls before and they did their chores as required. Señora Leonora walked back into the main house through the back corridor extremely upset. Raimunda started to cry, but Doña Luisa told her to calm herself down and assured her that everything was going to be fine.

Indignation built up inside of me, not only because it was unbelievably unfair to fire a girl who desperately needed a job, but also because Raimunda was a victim of horrible circumstances outside of her control.

I was very sorry that Alejandro was not in the house when the exchange took place because I knew he would have defended Raimunda. Señora Leonora returned angrier than when she had left and was ready to burst all of her frustrations out on Doña Luisa and Raimunda. Doña Luisa kept looking down quietly while this younger woman, who could have been her daughter, screamed at her. Poor Raimunda buried herself behind Doña Luisa.

"I am the lady of this house; do you hear me!?" Señora Leonora screamed at the ever embarrassed Doña Luisa.

"Yes, ma'am. I understand that clearly. Please do not misunderstand me. This girl works very hard, and her family, as well as she, need the money very much, ma'am"

Innocent Doña Luisa kept trying to reason with the self-centered woman, but how could she? Señora Leonora was full of arrogance, the kind that only those with infinite money and resources dared to flaunt and use as ammunition against those without the same.

"This is going to set a bad example for the rest of *them*," she said, pointing at the miserable laundresses working under the blistering sun, "thinking that they can get pregnant and return to do half their work and get paid the same!"

A disgusting bourgeois woman she is.

"Señora Leonora, with all due respect, I have never had such a problem with expecting girls—"

"Look, Luisa, you are not listening to me! I do NOT want pregnant servants in the house. Are you grasping my words?"

"Yes, ma'am, but this girl does not have a husband to support her, putting her in the street would be a sin …," Doña Luisa replied, lowering her voice even more. Fire was flowing through my veins.

"But the child has a father, doesn't it?"

Good question. Tell her Raimunda; tell her who did this to you! my inner voice was screaming, but poor embarrassed Raimunda limited herself to crying in silence, hiding behind Doña Luisa's person.

"The father does not take responsibility for the child, ma'am," Doña Luisa answered.

"Then this is a regular Jezebel! This is what you get for hanging out with that Maximiana Valdez. I hope you are satisfied," she scolded Raimunda to the astonishment of Doña Luisa. "I want you out of my house. I don't care what you say Luisa; she is out!"

"Señorito Alejandro will not agree to it," Doña Luisa finally said. "He told me to bring her back."

Señora Leonora exploded in irritation, "How dare you defy one of my orders! Rude woman! I can put you in the street as fast as the snap of my fingers!"

Señora Leonora Sarmiento's frustrations ran deep that she felt compelled to take out such wrath on these two poor women who could not defend themselves from her superior authority. Margarita and Lupe continued washing the heavy linens shaking their heads in disapproval.

"This is unbelievable," Margarita said. "What can that poor girl do if she is kicked out of here?"

Lupe shook her head with her, "This is the life of poor people in the hands of the rich, and what can we do?"

"Alejandro will not allow it," I said positively. "He would never allow such an injustice." Both of them turned to me and, with a smile both sarcastic and full of indignation, said, "*He* is the father."

"The father of whom?" I asked intrigued.

They can't mean Raimunda's baby!

"Raimunda's child," Margarita replied very sure of her words. "I think that is why Señora Leonora wants to kick her out of here. Señor Joaquín does not want a grandchild around the house coming from one of the servants."

"That is not true," I said. "Alejandro did not do this to Raimunda; that is a lie!"

My goodness! What confusion, I thought and turned to the kitchen's corridor scene.

Doña Luisa was still trying to convince stubborn Señora Leonora of her mistake, and miserable Raimunda continued her blank stare to the floor, tears streaming from her eyes.

Shortly after, Señor Joaquín and Alejandro entered the hacienda through the back gate. They took the stairs up through the garden terraces. Señor Joaquín was giving Alejandro instructions about the transportation of mangoes to Mazatlán in the coming days. Once they reached the upper terrace, Alejandro greeted us all.

Señora Leonora hurriedly walked towards them, telling Señor Joaquín she wanted pregnant Raimunda out of the house and the girl would set a bad example for the other servants. The girls working in the water tower ironing came out when they heard the commotion. Doña Luisa kept looking at Señor Joaquín without blinking her dark brown eyes. Alejandro raised the usual guard whenever he saw injustice coming his way.

"You cannot ask Raimunda to leave. She has to stay here and eat breakfast, lunch, and dinner before going home, and I want her to take a basket of groceries for her weekend—" Alejandro was cut short of his words.

"Are you crazy?" Señora Leonora replied. "You—"

"And she needs medical attention …," Alejandro continued without looking at Señora Leonora, who desperately looked for her husband's support.

Señor Joaquín was indifferent to the whole scene and replied to Doña Luisa that his wife was in charge of the servants, to follow her instructions. Alejandro exploded in rage and walked inside the house. Raimunda broke in tears of desperation while Doña Luisa was stunned but kept silent. But I could not.

"How can you be so heartless? How can you throw on the street to die of hunger a girl that has been abused repeatedly in body and soul?" I said this as I stood in front of Señora Leonora Sarmiento, my eyes spitting fire at her and her abusive husband.

She became white as a cloud and laid a quick and heavy slap to my face.

I didn't care.

"Don't you see she is a *victim*? Don't you see that she is a poor girl who has no option but to agree to the abuse?" I screamed. "Do you think she can say no to an attacker that has all the power in the universe over her because she is a woman and poor? Do you think she can fight back?! DON'T YOU SEE SHE IS THE VICTIM OF A MAN JUST AS YOU ARE?!"

"Maximiana!" Doña Luisa screamed, "Be quiet, Maximiana!"

"Why do I have to keep quiet to this horrendous act of abuse? Why?"

Señor Joaquín Sarmiento grabbed my arm and tried to pull me out of their sight, but I fought back with all of my strength.

"Alejandro! Alejandro!" I screamed. Alejandro came out and, shocked by the scene of his father dragging me, ran to my rescue.

"Let go of her, Father! What are you doing?" Alejandro exclaimed full of indignation.

"You!" the rapist said, pointing to Raimunda, "OUT of my house, OUT!" His mouth was frothing with rage.

Terrified by the turmoil building around them and by Alejandro's involvement, Señora Leonora abruptly changed her mind about Raimunda and said, "No, Joaquín, don't pull her, she is expecting!"

"It is *your* child, Father! How can you be so cruel!" Alejandro finally said to the shock of everyone and the horror of Señora Leonora Sarmiento, who put her hand to her mouth in a sign of disbelief.

Señor Joaquín turned to me and screamed that he didn't want to see me around the hacienda ever again and to get out, right that instant. He approached us, but Alejandro stood in front of me and Raimunda.

"Don't you dare touch them," he challenged his father.

I took Raimunda's hand and told her to walk with me out of there because her dignity was worth just as much as everyone else's. Doña Luisa was crying while Alejandro stood tall; Señora Leonora lowered her head in apparent shame while Señor Joaquín Sarmiento left the scene like the coward that he was. Raimunda walked with me sobbing, her big belly jumping at each step. Alejandro followed us to the front gate.

"Wait … Raimunda, don't worry about anything … I know that child you are carrying is my blood. I will look after him and you throughout this time." He pulled coins from his pocket. "Take this money and go home; I will send you a basket of food with Doña Luisa every third day, and she will also give you a weekly allowance."

"Thank you, Señorito Alejandro," Raimunda tried to kiss his hand, but he stopped her.

"No, please don't do that, and call me 'Alejandro.'" He gave her his angelical smile. Alejandro was a living angel on earth, and I was lucky enough to have him in my life.

Up to that point, I was only thinking about Raimunda and forgot about my own sudden jobless situation. This time I had really done it. I had placed myself on a golden platter to be fired from my job at the Grand House. Still, I felt it had been worth it.

"You … Silly Face," Alejandro said, smiling at me with worried tenderness, "don't worry about it; I will find a job for you …"

"I will work in the fields; that is fine with me, Aleh … I don't want to work at your house anymore," I said, forcing myself to smile. "I tell you that I don't want to work at your house as if the choice were mine," I concluded jokingly.

"Go home, and I will stop by this evening. I want to talk to your parents about something that I have been thinking about," he suddenly said to the surprise of Raimunda and me.

"What do you mean? What do you want to talk about with my parents?" I asked, genuinely intrigued.

"I will tell you tonight," he said, "when I see you."

Raimunda remained quiet all the way to her house. Her mother was worried she had fallen sick and had had to return home. But Raimunda quickly replied that Alejandro had sent her home with money and that he promised to support her for as long as necessary. Raimunda said no more, but she only delayed the news of the afternoon scandal to her mother because in just a few hours the gossip would reach the entire town.

For years to come, people speculated that Raimunda's daughter was in reality Alejandro Sarmiento's child. Raimunda did not confirm it or deny it, and I could understand why. However, the little girl was named María Magdalena, in honor of her protector's mother and future godfather, Alejandro Sarmiento. I advised Raimunda that not having to go to that place was better for her. Besides, she had to take care of herself and that baby, who was a victim as much as she was. She promised to start attending my classes again, and my happiness at that decision made me hug her so tight that she exhaled a gasp of satisfaction.

"I will always be your friend, Raimunda, and will do everything within my power to help you be happy again," I said.

"There have not been many moments when I have been happy, Maximiana; don't you know that?"

"Then, we will find a way for you to find more happiness. I promise."

"I believe you, girl ... you are the bravest person I know ... the way you screamed at *them*."

"Oh, there is nothing to them but the clothes they are wearing. Inside they are just like you and me, only with a million tons of arrogance and rudeness."

"Not Señorito Alejandro," she said with a sigh.

"Of course not. Alejandro is the nicest person in the world ... I have to go now; I need to beat the gossip before it reaches Mamá and Papá. I will come to see you tomorrow," I said and walked away.

Papá and Mamá were proud of my defense for Raimunda. Augusto's eyes filled with anger when I told them the entire story, but with my parents, he agreed that I had done the right thing by telling my mind, even if my words were completely dismissed by them. Augusto had to admit that he couldn't figure out Alejandro Sarmiento; he thought his attitude was out of the ordinary. I could no longer hold my secret; I let them know what Alejandro had discussed with me—about the "Cactus," a group that thought such treatment of the poor was unjust. I told them about the *Communist Manifesto* and read some parts of it to them, and I said that Alejandro wanted to change the way things were.

Papá took the *Communist Manifesto* from my hands and looked at me concerned, and then Augusto tried to read it.

"Do you see why it is so important that you learn to read and write, Augusto? There are so many things out there that could help us if we could just read them!" I scolded my brother who was not as interested as my sisters to learn to read and write.

"Keep your voice down, child," Papá said, his voice sounding distressed. "These words on paper could send us to the cemetery … When did Señorito Alejandro give you this? I don't think we should have it in the house."

"A few days ago. He said it was his secret copy because his father wouldn't allow such readings in the Grand House," I said while hiding the booklet in the bottom of my trunk again but feeling a little bit nervous after Papá's proclamation of danger.

"I still have some money left from Maximiana's reward and Natalia's payment in December, even though I just took three pesos for the roof materials," Mamá said in an effort to change the subject that was making everyone nervous.

"I will work in the fields with Natalia and Otilia, Mamá … don't worry about it, and we will figure it out," I said with optimism, even though the idea of working in the fields was killing my back before even starting. "Oh," I said casually, "Alejandro is coming this evening to talk to you two."

Dead silence fell in our kitchen.

"What does he have to say?" Mamá asked in shock.

"He wouldn't tell me, but by the sound of his voice, it seems to me that he has very good news," I replied with another optimistic smile.

Otilia and Natalia looked at each other with a curious look. But I raised my shoulders as a sign of having no idea what Alejandro wanted to talk about.

In the middle of my lesson, Alejandro Sarmiento came to pay his visit. He sat and patiently waited for class to be over; the young girls present were fascinated by his presence while the children, again, showed fear.

"Pay attention, everyone. Señorita Otilia will be in charge of class because I have to talk to Señorito Alejandro Sarmiento. I will see you all tomorrow."

"Yes, Teacher Maximiana," the children repeated in chorus.

Shyly, Otilia rose to take the piece of chalk from my hand. I gave her the reader and pointed out what she had to write on the board. Then I instructed Natalia to practice a song with the students after they were done copying the lesson, before sending them home. I walked into my house with Alejandro and directed him to our kitchen; he had to lower his head when he crossed the threshold. Papá rose from his chair at once, too embarrassed about the visitor, while Mamá timidly lowered her head.

"Please sit," I told him, and he pulled a chair. "What do you have to tell my parents?" I asked, desperate to hear the news Alejandro had with him.

"Señor and Señora Valdez, I have been thinking for a while … since I realized how smart and outgoing Maximiana is," he started with diplomacy, "that she should be working as a teacher, not as a servant in a house."

"I already work as a teacher, Aleh," I replied to the surprise of my parents who had never heard me talk to a Sarmiento with such familiarity and openness.

"But I mean to be a paid teacher, Max," he replied with equal familiarity. "Look, you could work as a private teacher in Mazatlán; I have friends whose families would be willing to hire you as a nanny and teacher for their children. You would have room, board, and a salary, weekends and afternoons off. What do you say?" he asked, looking at all of us, and without waiting for a reply, he continued, "Maximiana is a very intelligent girl. She should try to open up her future beyond El Roble."

My mind was racing with the idea. It would mean that I could live in the city and perhaps attend a school; the possibilities were endless. I just had to find them.

"Papá, Mamá … that would be wonderful! I could learn so many new things in Mazatlán, and I would send you my money with Alejandro or people who would be coming to El Roble, and I will visit every single time I could … oh please, say yes … I don't want to work in the fields; I want to be a *real* teacher."

"You are a real teacher, Max; the point now is for you to have a salary," Alejandro responded. "Think about it, Señor and Señora Valdez. Maximiana will have her afternoons and evenings free; she could take classes with the nuns because they teach several practical subjects that will only help Maximiana in life and would eventually help her make money. They teach ceramics, dress making, cooking, and pastry making—"

"But I want to learn about literature, poetry, science, and the law …," I interrupted to the astonishment, once again, of my parents.

"You must learn that on your own, Max; those types of schools are … restricted."

Mamá and Papá kept staring during our heated discussion, realizing that I had made up my mind without their say on the subject. But how could they stop me? The world had become small to me since I started reading and thinking on my own. I had to leave, and they knew it. They also knew, I hoped, I was going to take good care of myself just as I had at the Grand House.

"Please agree to it. I want to work as a paid teacher. Please agree to it," I begged.

"Who is this family that will hire Maximiana?" Mamá asked.

"I am thinking of the Pattersons. They have three children of learning age; their private teacher is moving to México City in June. He is a friend of mine, and he has heard about Maximiana's school here in El Roble. He thought she could work as a salaried teacher in Mazatlán. They are very good people, decent folks. She would be fine with them."

"But you haven't told them yet, right?" Mamá asked, concerned.

"No, but this is my idea: Maximiana can travel to the city with me, and she can stay at a pension while I make the arrangements … I will take care of the expenses."

"She cannot travel alone with you," Papá finally spoke, "but her brother, Augusto, may accompany you as well."

Am I hearing right? They are actually making the arrangements for me to move to live in Mazatlán and work as a teacher!

The joy I was feeling inside was overwhelming.

"Yes, and we can return together to El Roble after Maximiana is settled in the right place; he can even decide if he agrees to the place or not—"

"Excuse me?" I interrupted again. "I will decide, not my brother."

"Aye, Maximiana. Stop interfering. Augusto is older than you, and he can make better choices," Mamá scolded.

"So is Otilia; she should come instead of Augusto."

I was trying to make a point, but to my disappointment, no one grasped it.

"The road is too dangerous, Max; you know how it is. It is safer for men to travel than women," Alejandro responded in an attempt to save me from my "about to ruin everything" exposure of women's limited role in society in front of my parents.

"When can we leave?" I asked in an eager mood.

"Whenever your parents agree to it," Alejandro replied. "I have to travel to Mazatlán for business in a week or two. Father wants me to negotiate some dealings; then you and your brother may travel with me."

"Do you know how much money they need to take with them, for their board in the city and Augusto's return?" Papá asked.

"I said I will take care of everything, Señor Valdez," Alejandro replied.

Papá looked down and humbly said, "Thank you, sir."

"'Alejandro' please; just call me Alejandro."

Papá and Mamá turned their faces to each other in wonder, just as did every person who heard that statement from Alejandro.

Daniel waited until Alejandro left to talk to me. He was one of the best students in my class and the most enthusiastic. Children loved Daniel for his understanding and patience with them but, more, he knew how to make them feel an important part of our group. I kept telling him he would be the perfect teacher, and he agreed, even though he admitted that his dream would be to become a medicine doctor, just like Dr. Marcus Andrade, El Roble's physician, who tended his patients and received a basket of eggs or other food as payment. But it was an almost impossible dream for a young man of his economic condition.

When I told him about my departure, Daniel Gutierrez was very sad. I felt sad too; after all, I was starting a new part of my life without my family and friends close by. Until Daniel brought it up, I hadn't thought in detail about the fact that I would be staying in a completely new house, in a place where I didn't know anybody. But at least Josefina would be nearby, and Alejandro would visit sometimes. And I would make new friends soon enough.

"Oh! And that Gustavo man, he will never bother you again," Daniel unexpectedly said.

"Why do you say that?" I frowned.

"I heard what he tried to do to you, and you can trust me when I tell you that he will never bother you again," he said, smiling with his eyes.

"Why? He is afraid I will kill him or something like that?"

"Yes, something like that," he winked at me, "Maximiana! I'm going to miss you a lot! A LOT!"

"Me, too! But I will write to you every single time somebody travels to El Roble, I promise," I said, meaning every word of it. "Otilia and Natalia will stay in charge of the school. Are you going to help them?"

"Yes, of course, I will. The school is important, Maxi; we have to keep it going."

"Definitely." I nodded. "Alejandro will continue helping with the materials, and I will send what I can from the port."

"You know … I was thinking that perhaps we could build a school … all of us could do it," Daniel said, full of enthusiasm.

"Yes … I have thought about it, too, but you know how difficult it is for everyone around here, especially after the hurricane. Who has the money to buy materials?"

"But we could make it out of wood from the fields and just be creative about it."

"That would be a great thing to do … imagine if we could get a bell!"

"Yes!" Daniel answered with his usual excitement.

"Perhaps Alejandro could get the bell for us, but I would be shy to ask him."

"You? Shy? Don't make me laugh, Shorty!" he teased me.

"Believe it or not, I am shy!" I replied just to defend myself. But his marvelous ideas had me thinking.

My goodness! Imagine building a schoolhouse for El Roble! A classroom with a bell to call the children in.

I couldn't wait to tell Alejandro about it and Otilia and Natalia.

During the next two weeks I worked very hard at home, preparing for my trip. Mamá decided that I needed at least two skirts and blouses more appropriate for a teacher. She bought the fabric at the corner store, and Señorita Luz let her borrow a skirt and blouse pattern. Mamá also bought me a pair of shoes and socks to wear. Otilia and Natalia approved of my two new outfits. One skirt was dark blue with tiny white stripes on it, and the other was brown and yellow. Mamá made them long enough that they would cover my ankles because, according to Señorita Luz, that was the correct length for young ladies. Both blouses were white with long sleeves. I explained to Mamá that I would die in the heat, but she said I had to get used to it. I helped Mamá sew both outfits, and she made sure they fit me correctly when I was wearing the famous corset Doña Luisa had given me in December. Natalia insisted that I take her dress and mine, the ones we got for New Year's Eve. I thought it was crazy.

For what do I need such pompous outfits?

But even Mamá said it was true.

"You never know if you may need them," she concluded firmly.

I just felt awkward putting those beautiful clothes in my bundle. To my delight, Doña Luisa came to give me an old suitcase of hers. She was very pleased with the news of my departure to work as a teacher in Mazatlán and wanted to wish me good luck. She also suggested that I should cut my hair a little bit and hold it up in a bun. Natalia ran to get Mamá's hairpins and her own beautiful pins that Doña Luisa had given her to wear for her performance; she wanted me to take them. The generosity of the women around made me realize how much appreciated and loved I was by so many in my life. Orlando Sarmiento crossed my mind for an instant, but I needed to be strong and keep his memory out for good.

The night before my departure, Mamá organized a little farewell party. My students were very sad to see me go, and their affection and some of the little ones' tears of genuine sorrow touched me. I explained to them that their new teacher was Señorita Otilia and her assistants were Señorita Natalia and Señorito Daniel. I told them that I was proud of them and that I would never forget them because they were my first students. I felt very emotional about leaving behind my life in El Roble, but I knew I had to take the step in order to go forward and advance and learn.

Doña Luisa came to wish me the best of luck and secretly put a beautiful tiny satin purse in my skirt pocket. She had placed five pesos in it and a handkerchief with an "M" embroidered on it. Daniel's grandmother had knitted a beautiful white shawl for me with yarn purchased by all of my friends. He told me that he was afraid I might die of a heat stroke if I wore it in the summer, so I promised not to wear it until winter time. I loved my shawl, a perfect reminder of my many friends and my home.

I felt strange with all these new beautiful things for myself and even stranger to dress with my new clothes and hairstyle. But Mamá was right: I was a salaried teacher, and I had to look accordingly. However, I convinced her that I was going to travel in my own clothes, but that as soon as I was established in the pension in the port, I would wash and dress up with my new outfits. It was a real sin to ride a horse in one of those beautiful clothes. My entire plan fell apart when Alejandro arrived and told us that he was taking the carriage to the city and I was going to travel in it. The carriage would pick me up by the huanacaxtle tree—apparently, Señor Joaquín had no knowledge of the arrangement—and Augusto would ride one of the Sarmiento's horses. We didn't understand the reasons for Alejandro's decisions, but we intended to follow his orders. And I had no way out; I would have to dress up as a teacher. My sisters and Mamá were truly excited for me to dress up that way. Secretly, I was too.

After many jokes, sweets, horchata, and tejuino drinks, my guests started to go home. Our long journey at the beginning of June would start the next day at five in the morning, and I needed my sleep.

I rose before the roosters' singing and started to dress myself with my new clothes. The shoes felt incredibly tight and painfully uncomfortable, but Señorita Luz had explained to us that I would get used to them. I just had to wear them everyday, and the leather would expand. Mamá was the next one to rise; she put on the firewood to start cooking the food we would take for the trip. She was quiet. I took a deep breath and went to her, stood behind my beloved Mamá, and hugged her tight.

"Mamá … this is a wonderful opportunity … thank you, Mamá, for letting me go and trusting me this way. I will not disappoint you or Papá. I give you my word." My voice was shaking with the sentiment of leaving the woman I loved the most in the world.

"I know, child … I have always known that there is something different about you … you have to go, Maximiana, and fill yourself with all the things that you are looking for and that I still don't understand … but I am willing to try to comprehend."

"Mamá …," I hugged my mamá with all of my heart, "Mamá … I will make life better for all of us, and I promise you … please support Otilia more than anybody else; she needs you the most. Now that she is a teacher, please praise her for it. She is wonderful, Mamá, and needs all of our understanding."

I would have loved to tell Mamá that my plan was to take Otilia one day with me, but such a plan would mortify her. Letting go of one daughter this way was more than enough for the moment.

"I wish you were leaving because you had gotten married …," Mamá shyly said.

"No, Mamá, I want more in life. There is so much more in life."

"Aye! Child, I don't understand such things," she said, hugging me to her bosom.

"Soon you will, Mamá, and you will see everything very differently. I promise."

Mamá gasped and said, "You and your promises! Let's get you ready now, or you are going to miss your ride to the port. Go and wake up Augusto."

When Alejandro reached the huanacaxtle tree, we were waiting. Papá helped put my baggage on the roof of the carriage, and Alejandro offered his hand to help me enter it. I sat and took a deep breath. This was it. I looked through the window and waved good-bye to Mamá, Papá, and my sisters. They raised their faces and nodded to me as their way of telling me they supported my decision and to go with God. Alejandro asked if I was comfortable and commented that my food basket smelled delicious. He smiled at me and started galloping towards the road to Villa Unión. Augusto and the others followed. I looked back again, and I saw my family walk away as we moved forward. Soon the huanacaxtle tree was lost in the distance. I placed my white shawl as a pillow on the carriage seat and laid my head down; soon the sound from the wheels and rhythm of the carriage going over the dirt road rocked me to sleep.

18

Mazatlán mesmerized Augusto. This was his first visit to the port, at age twenty-one, and a good time for him. Alejandro took us to a pension across from the central market. The lady in charge was very nice to us, especially because Alejandro asked Señora Estela Ruiz to take good care of us. I was dying to walk to the beach on the very same evening of our arrival, but Augusto was too tired to go for a walk and, instead, washed and went to bed. He suggested I do the same, but he spoke without any bossiness.

I noticed the change. My brother did not treat me as authoritatively as he had before. His expectation of being in charge solely because he was a man had given way to a more respectful attitude toward me, and I took pride in his transformation and in his thinking that had to have precipitated it. As Mamá once said, "The world starts changing at home." I don't think she was thinking of a revolution, but it made a lot of sense to me for any kind of change.

"Augusto, we should get up early tomorrow morning and see the sunrise at the beach," I told my brother when he was half asleep.

"Sure, we can do that … is it far from here?" he asked with a tired voice.

"Mmm ... a couple of blocks away, but we can do it and be back in time to get ready and wait for Alejandro."

"Did he say what time he's coming?" Augusto asked with his eyes already closed.

"Mid-morning," I replied from my bed, "and he means it; Alejandro is the first one to rise in that house ... Aye! Augusto I hope I get the job as a teacher soon. I cannot wait to start working. Besides I want to look into those classes with the nuns Alejandro talked about, even though I am more interested in other subjects, but everything helps, don't you think?"

Augusto's tired snores cut my chattering short.

I hope the family I work for has a library as big as the Sarmientos'. I want to learn about science and so many other things. Wouldn't it be wonderful if the city had a library for everybody in town? A place where you could go and sit to read, even borrow books! Oh! If I had the money, I would do that in a flash.

I fell asleep with hope, filled with ideas that in my heart I felt were needed in order to change the world I lived in.

"I will take my sandals because I want to get my feet wet in the water," I declared to Augusto, who was probably beginning to notice my constant excuses to avoid wearing the shoes. Oh, my poor feet, unaccustomed to such constraints, rebelled and gave me much pain whenever I slipped them on. He nodded, and we walked out towards the sea. Augusto kept looking at everything around him. It was early and still quiet, but the fishermen were already working. My brother couldn't believe the immensity of the Pacific Ocean; the way the waves rolled and jumped made him look in wonder.

"If you go straight in a boat, you hit Baja California, and beyond that there is a country named Japan," I said while feeling the salty water up to my knees. "You cannot swim in the ocean as you would at the river; here the waves move you up and down and sometimes there are undercurrents that may take you into the sea ... some people have been pulled by those and never come out."

"I wouldn't go in," my brother replied without looking at me.

"Oh Augusto ... do you see those rocks over there? By that hill ..."

"Yes, I see them."

"Sometimes when the tide goes up or the current moves that way, the boats or men who are swimming are pulled in that direction, and I heard that if the wind gets harder, you may crash against the rocks, and ... well ... when that happens, a person doesn't survive."

Augusto turned his face towards me, frowning. "Why do they go in, then?"

"It doesn't happen all the time; it just has happened before ... that is what I heard."

"Have you gone? Have you swum in there?" he asked concerned. "Do women go swimming in the sea?"

"I used to accompany Señora Leonora Sarmiento every morning to this beach, and the twins liked to get wet," I replied, avoiding his question as best I could.

"But did you go in?" he persisted.

"Yes, sometimes ... but I never got deep in, just a few meters in."

"Ah Maximiana ... I don't know how you didn't drown," he said, shaking his head. "Besides, I don't imagine other girls would do the same thing."

"Well, I think those girls would miss out on a lot of fun," I replied, giggling.

He shook his head again, smiling, and pushed me away.

"Why do you want to be a boy, Maximiana?" he suddenly asked.

"I don't want to be a boy ... I want to be a girl with *all* the rights and all the opportunities boys have; that is what I want," I replied firmly. "Are you going to tell me that 'girls are girls and boys are boys' and that we are 'different'?"

"Women and men *are* different."

"Different, yes, but *not* inferior, Augusto. *That* is my problem with the meaning of your words, brother."

Augusto frowned again but not in an angry way. I smiled at him and gave him a sweet punch on his arm. He was reflecting on my words, I was sure, because he was not trying to argue with me.

In fact, he kept quiet the whole way back to the pension until he said, "Maximiana, promise me that if you go into the ocean, you will only do it if there is somebody out there ready to rescue you if you start drowning or the undercurrent pulls you towards the rocks."

I hugged my brother's arm. His sweet heart was concerned about my safety. How much I appreciated that he was letting *me* decide what to do with my life, instead of ordering me how to act.

"I will; I promise on Mamá and Papá. Don't worry about it," I said. "Thank you, Augusto."

He shook his head again, smiling, and placed his long arm on my shoulder. We hurried back to the pension because Alejandro would be coming to get me soon.

The Pattersons' house held a choice spot on a corner, not far from the sea. It was a two-story white mansion with an impressive entrance at the corner of the house. A long corridor ran the length of the second floor, decorated with stone carvings that depicted an underwater scene of mermaids and seashells.

Señor George Patterson, a citizen of the United States, had come from San Francisco several years before, but his wife, Señora Enriqueta "Queta" Patterson was a native of Mazatlán. The young couple owned transportation ships in the port, but they did not flaunt their wealth or act superior because of it. On the contrary, Señor Patterson was a gentleman in the full extent of the word. He had an even temperament and a mellow voice. Señora Patterson looked like a happy woman, always smiling and very well liked by all the people working at the house. I gathered the same about her husband, who greeted everybody respectfully. They seemed very happy with each other, and I sensed their five children, all under the age of ten, would show equally good dispositions.

Alejandro gave high recommendations for me as a teacher. He explained to them that I had been working as a teacher for a year in El Roble and that I was a personal friend of his, someone he trusted and appreciated very much.

Señora Patterson offered lemonade and cookies; I followed her manners by placing my napkin on my lap and biting the cookie on the side. I sat very straight and answered their questions with a clear voice.

In the middle of our meeting, Señor Patterson stood up and apologized; he had to leave for a business appointment. Alejandro walked with him to the entrance door.

"I think we are going to get along very nicely, Maximiana," Señora Patterson said to me smiling, "and my little devils will do just fine under your tutelage. They are fond of teacher Alberto even though they complain a lot about his mathematics lessons!"

Oh no! I have to teach mathematics!

"Yes, Señora Patterson, and I would like to start preparing for my classes as soon as possible. If you approve, I want to sit in Teacher Alberto's last classes to see how your children are learning with him."

"That is an excellent idea! Would you like to start tomorrow?" she asked.

"Yes, ma'am," I answered, trying to hide my worries about the mathematics lessons. "Also, when do I start working for you? I am living in the pension, and my brother is staying with me but must return to our town soon."

"Let's see. Today is Wednesday. I think that your room will be arranged by next Monday. Alberto leaves for México City on Monday morning. Is that fine with you?"

"Yes, ma'am."

"And you will have some afternoons and evenings off, as well as the weekends. The children have school from Monday to Friday from eight in the morning to midday. After that, I will need your help some afternoons to stay with them while I run errands or go visiting. Saturdays and Sundays are off for you, but I might need your help sometimes; that is extra pay."

I couldn't believe my ears.

"My husband has liberal ideas about schedules; he thinks that Saturdays and Sundays should be rest days for workers, and I agree. Now, the workers at the house take turns getting the weekends off because, as you can see, we have too much work to do around here, and I couldn't manage myself."

"Yes, Señora Patterson, I understand."

"Good." Señora Patterson turned to Alejandro, who was entering the room with a pleasant smile. "Alejandro Sarmiento, I truly appreciate your help in finding us a new teacher for the children. Oh and another thing," she said, turning back to me, "the children have music and painting lesson once a week; you are in charge of making sure they attend their classes."

"Yes, ma'am, I will," I replied, satisfied with my responsibilities.

Alejandro rose from the burgundy seat, also pleased with the arrangement. On our way back to the pension, he told me I had made a good impression and I had showed initiative and wisdom in suggesting I attend teacher Alberto's lessons on Thursday and Friday.

"But, Aleh, what am I going to do about the mathematics lesson?" I asked, concerned.

"I will talk to Eduardo Randal; his brother Andrés, the one you met already, might be willing to start teaching you today. He is a volunteer teacher at the German School. Don't worry about it; it is simple arithmetic, and you know much of it already, even though no one has formally taught you. Remember, the children are still very young; they will not need higher mathematics for some time. You will manage just fine."

"As you say. I think Augusto can go back to El Roble tomorrow; he has to work in the fields."

"Yes, I agree."

"Aleh … could you do me a favor?"

"Certainly, just ask."

"Please tell Josefina I am in town. She is one of the cooks at your house."

"I will tell her … should I tell Orlando you are in town?" he asked seriously.

"No, of course not." I meant it. "Thank you for all your help, Aleh."

"There is nothing to thank me about," he replied and left as soon as we reached the pension.

I greeted Señora Estela Ruiz and told the news to Augusto, who was lying on the soft bed, enjoying every second of it just as I had the first time my body had rested on a mattress. He was happy for me, but I could see he did not look forward to returning to El Roble.

"Do you think I might find a job here in the port?" he asked.

"I think so. You can see people all around working different jobs."

"Perhaps I will be back later on; I like it here."

"I will keep my eyes open for you, Augusto, and if anything comes up, I will send you word with Alejandro."

"Yes, that would be good," he said, still fancying the idea.

Alejandro returned that afternoon to let me know Andrés Randal was more than happy to instruct me in mathematics. He agreed to come to the pension that evening to start my instruction; we would use Señora Ruiz's dining table. She readily agreed to it, which I think had a lot to do with the fact that Alejandro Sarmiento and Andrés Randal made the arrangements with her. As soon as I heard, I went to the store to buy a paper tablet and pencils, thanks to the five pesos Doña Luisa, God bless her, had put in my silk purse.

The finer points of Andrés Daniel Randal's unique personality revealed itself under my closer scrutiny. He approached people in a direct way, with penetrating eyes. And although he was serious, his smile, whether given to you or someone else, made everyone feel happy. It was as if he was so truthful to himself that he would never smile unless he really meant it. A thick shawl of long lashes protected his shy emerald eyes, and his nose, long and thin, looked perfectly straight. The well-defined lines of his chin and jaw made him look strong even though his body lacked much muscularity. His medium-length, brown hair had gentle waves, and he wore sideburns. He was a very interesting young man. I calculated his age to be around eighteen, and I was right.

The first time he saw me at the pension, he said my appearance surprised him, and he hardly recognized me with my hair up. He did not mention the clothes, but I knew they had contributed to his reaction.

Andrés proved a very good teacher; he explained mathematics in a direct way, not trying to impress or confuse me just to make himself look more important.

He came to the pension throughout the rest of the week, and we made arrangements to meet at the Machado Square during the evenings once I started working at the Pattersons' house. Filling my free time with his lessons—he had me memorize the time tables, and I studied his arithmetic book—worked well for me, especially in the beginning. I felt really lonely when Augusto's time to return to El Roble arrived and Alejandro was too busy running errands for his father's businesses. But when the weekend came and Andrés asked me if I wanted to attend a dance at the City Club on Saturday evening, I rejected the invitation; I wasn't ready for those adventures yet, I said.

"But at least you will go with me to take a walk on the beach on Sunday, yes?" he said with his direct tone.

"I go every day … I enjoy the sunrise and the sunset," I replied.

"May I join you, then?" he said, inching his face closer to mine.

"Yes, if you wish." I felt a hint of shyness inside.

"Afterwards … would you like to have a sweet ice cream bowl with me?"

"What is that?" I asked, confused even though the name made some sense.

"You will see when you try it," he replied, looking intently into my eyes.

I have to admit it; he intimidated me a little bit.

"Fine."

"I will see you right before sunrise, then? I will pick you up," he said on his way out of the pension's dining room. I agreed and walked with him to the door. He kissed my hand good-bye, as he did every day before leaving. He bowed to Señora Ruiz, and she nodded with her hands placed on her round belly.

"What a nice gentleman, Massimiana." Señora Ruiz did not pronounce the "X" in my name. But I thought her mistake was cute, so I never tried to correct her. "He is very handsome, also."

I didn't respond to that. But seriously thinking about it, I had to agree: Andrés was handsome. And from his lips came a strong manly voice. I shook those thoughts from my mind right away; my heart was in no condition to fall for another deception. Although almost three months had passed since my heart had been pulverized and the memories were becoming somewhat distant, I still felt the pain sharp in my soul.

❦

"Would you like to sit down?" Andrés asked me while holding the ice cream bowls in his hands. I nodded. "Try it; you are going to like it."

I took the ice cream from his hand, and we sat on the sand.

"It is fine to lick it," Andrés said smiling, "or you may use the wooden spoon, it is up to you."

I used the spoon. My goodness! I had never tried anything like it before. The taste was delicious, smooth and creamy with a sweet vanilla flavor.

"Are you ready to move in with the Pattersons tomorrow?" he asked, licking his ice cream.

"Yes, even though I think I like living in the pension. I feel free."

"Why don't you stay there over the weekends? Perhaps Señora Ruiz will allow you."

"No, I cannot afford it. My family needs the money back home."

"Oh, I see," he replied, looking at the waves. "So, do you like the ice cream?"

"I do! It is delicious!"

We talked of the ice cream, but my eyes couldn't stop looking at his lips; I felt blood go up to my cheeks and quickly looked in the direction of the dark rocks in the distance.

"Hold this for me, please," he said, passing the ice cream to my hand, "I have to unbutton this shirt; I am cooking in it."

"You are lucky to be able to do that—" I said and then regretted it.

"I know!" he said and burst into laughter.

My face went red.

"I know what you mean," he tried again, still failing to alleviate my embarrassment.

"Would you like to swim in the ocean?" he asked.

"I can't with these clothes, they are too uncomfortable," I said and pointed to my shoes.

"Yes … but up north there are beaches where you can swim freely in any clothes you want and nobody is around to see you in case you are embarrassed by it; you can bring your other clothes and then go in … or do you have a bathing suit?"

"No …"

"You should get one. The bloomers under the short skirt make swimming so much easier for women."

"Yes, that sounds much more practical … when I used to go in, my skirt was a problem … the waves kept pulling it up."

"Do you like Mazatlán better than El Roble?"

"In some respects, yes … I do. Do you live here or in La Villa de San Sebastián?" I asked.

"I live mostly here in Mazatlán because I attend and teach at the German School, but I spend my vacations in my old town. My family works for the Panuco Mines' owners, up in the Sierra Madre Mountains. So we come and go as needed," he replied casually, without a hint of snobbishness.

"Are you going to attend university in the United States?" I asked, excited.

"No, I want to attend the National University of México in México City. I want to study law."

"You are very lucky, very *very* lucky," I sincerely replied.

"What would you like to study if you were to attend university?"

No one had ever asked me that, what *I* wanted.

"I would like to be a teacher and medicine doctor."

"Impressive …," he said without being surprised by my unlimited ambition. "You could attend the Normal School for Young Ladies in México City. They train teachers there. The first Mexican women dentist, medicine doctor, and lawyer graduated from the University of México around 1889, not long ago. Since then, others have graduated … I am sure you could, too."

My mind went crazy with the idea. It *was* possible then; I just had to find a way to get to México City and attend university there.

"Is it expensive?" I asked.

"It is, but you could find a sponsor ... and, unfortunately, you will also need a connection to get you in, somebody of influence. If you are interested, I could lend you the entrance exam preparation materials; I have them all."

"Thank you ... so ... when are you going to start?"

"I was supposed to start this year in September, but my parents decided I should stay a year here and help out with the business. In the meantime, I will continue classes at the German School and teaching."

I felt glad he was not leaving yet; Andrés was a nice person to be around and a good mathematics teacher. That is what I kept telling myself.

"I am glad you are not leaving soon."

"Oh? Why is that?"

"Because you act as my friend ... and I have no one else since my brother left."

"I am a friend. Besides, Alejandro asked us to take good care of you and to keep his youngest brother away from you."

I glanced at him and then looked down. I was very sorry he knew about that; I had been living the fantasy that in Mazatlán nobody knew my history and that that part of my life had never happened.

"What did he tell you?"

"He only said that we—that is Domingo, Eduardo, and I—should not let Orlando bother you. That is all he said."

"I don't think he will bother me, and if he does, I know how to take care of myself."

"Yes, I heard the beating you gave to Gustavo Inzunza."

"My goodness! Who told you about *that*?!" I exclaimed, mortified.

"Domingo ... and Gustavo will never go back to your town because on the way back somebody shot at him, missing his head by a couple of centimeters but hitting his right ear."

Daniel.

"I hope he doesn't know about my presence in the city. In reality, I am afraid of him and his ill intentions," I said.

"He won't dare, but if he bothers you, just let me know," he replied with firmness. "Now I am thirsty; this is too sweet."

He rose and offered his hand to help me up from the sand, and together we walked back to the street.

"Do you attend Sunday mass?" I asked, hoping he would say yes so I wouldn't have to attend alone.

"No, but I will go with you if you wish," he replied with an indifferent tone of voice.

Gratefully—and somewhat reluctantly—I accepted his offer, and we walked to the Cathedral of the Immaculate Conception. Afterwards, Andrés accompanied me to the pension. Señora Ruiz looked at me as if I were an accomplice to something secret but pleasant to her heart.

"Best of luck tomorrow, Maximiana," he said to me.

"Thank you … and I will see you on Wednesday then? At the plaza … is five o'clock fine with you?"

"Yes, I will be there." Andrés kissed my hand and shortly disappeared into the narrow streets of Mazatlán, enveloped by the summer heat and busy movement of people. I went straight to my room to prepare my luggage and get ready for the following day. It was June 8, 1908, and my first day as a salaried teacher started on the ninth.

Señora Ruiz saw me off at her door when Alejandro came. He wanted to take me to the Pattersons' house himself because he was leaving for El Roble the next day. I would miss my dear friend, but Alejandro's departure marked a point in my life where I would start to practice a higher level of self-reliance; I liked the idea of total independence, but still, slight melancholy settled inside me. He told me he would be back in August because he was going to accompany Domingo to Boston, which reminded me of Natalia, who was still awaiting Domingo Sarmiento in El Roble. I asked Alejandro if Domingo had plans of traveling to El Roble soon. He said, yes, Domingo intended to spend a month in El Roble before embarking for Boston. Their father was not pleased with the idea because he still had hopes his son would reconcile with Catalina Barraza.

"Alejandro, as my friend who I trust with all of my heart … please talk to Domingo about Natalia. I don't want him to hurt her anymore; tell him to leave her alone."

"He won't harm her, Max," he replied. "Domingo is not as bad as he looks."

"Oh, he does not *look* bad; don't misunderstand me," I replied, smiling but talking with sincerity. "As a matter of fact, he is too good looking to be real."

Alejandro laughed at my words and still repeated that Domingo had no intentions of harming Natalia.

"He said he is coming to see you this week. Your friend Josefina also said she would look for you; you will not be lonely … and Andrés? How do you like him?"

"He is very nice; I like him."

"Good," he said, smiling.

When we reached the Pattersons' house, Alejandro got out of the carriage and offered his hand to help me down. He took my suitcase and walked me to the front porch. A woman named Ursula opened the enormous gate and asked us in; Señora Patterson thanked Alejandro again and instructed Ursula to direct me to my bedroom while Alejandro waited by the entrance.

Upon my return, I had to say good-bye to my dearest Alejandro. I saw him off at the front door where he gave me a heart-felt, drawn-out hug and kissed my cheek. I fought tears of sudden despair; suddenly I didn't want to see him go away and back to El Roble. He said he would return soon and that if I needed anything to tell Domingo, Andrés, or his brother Eduardo, and that he had made arrangements with Señora Ruiz to take me in if necessary. My sweet Alejandro had thought of everything. How I would miss him. Tears rolled from my eyes, and Alejandro dried them with his thumbs. I held his face in my hands and kissed his cheeks twice; then he smiled sadly and walked away.

I took a deep breath and went back in; my new life would start right away.

Carolina, George Jr., and Elizabeth were nine, seven, and five years old, respectively. Their younger siblings were Ismael, who was three, and baby Martha. They were very sweet children, especially Carolina. She enjoyed her schooling more than any of them, and to my good luck, she really liked poetry. George Jr. and Elizabeth were still young, but they were well behaved.

Since my first day as their teacher, they treated me with respect, and they called me Señorita Maximiana. I felt flattered that they used the formal form of "you" when they talked to me. Señor and Señora Patterson also used the formal form of "you" to address me, and they called me teacher. An invisible empowerment came into my consciousness; I stood tall and tried my best to live up to the trust they had placed in me.

Their library met all my expectations—and more; they had so many books on all subjects, but I most appreciated their beautiful atlas. The children enjoyed looking at it as much as I did, and I usually based our classes around it. I came up with the idea of connecting knowledge among all subjects of learning. If we were doing math, we would count how many countries were in America or measure the distance from France to Japan using our ruler. If we did history, we looked at the map and searched for pictures in the encyclopedia, then wrote poems, and went to the garden to organize a stick war that represented the countries in dispute.

Sometimes, I asked permission from Señora Patterson to teach the children about constellations at night; Señor Patterson was so enthusiastic about my idea that he ordered a telescope for my students to use. How much I enjoyed passing my little knowledge to children! On my free time, I read and researched in the library, and on my free days, I would walk to the beach just to sit on the sand, savoring every inch of my new freedom.

Andrés continued teaching me mathematics until I was able to work on it on my own and consulted with him only when I encountered a problem I could not solve. He would come to my door and wait for me on the porch, and then we would walk to a soda shop and talk for long periods of time. Andrés was very articulate and sharp on many topics; he had an opinion about each. And he read a lot about everything, but politics most stirred his passion.

So did it with others in the city; almost all the conversations I overheard concerned national affairs. The Mexican president Porfirio Diaz had been in power for decades, and most agreed, the country was heading down a hole faster and deeper than ever.

"Are you part of the Cactus?" I whispered into Andrés's ear. He became rigid, and I added, "Alejandro talked to me about it."

Andrés looked at me out of the corner of his eye and kept quiet.

"Are there women in the Cactus?" I asked in an even lower voice.

"There are. Would you like to join?"

I felt his breath on my ear and the throbbing of my heart accelerated. My eyes widened, but I wasn't sure if it was in reaction to his nearness to my face or the invitation to join the Cactus.

"Yes, I would … what do I need to do to join it?" I asked, speaking in whispers.

"I will take you to our next meeting," he replied, pensive. Then, to change the subject, he asked, "What did Domingo say yesterday?" After all we were in the middle of a soda shop, and the Mazatlán natives indulged in gossip as freely as those in El Roble.

"Domingo visited me the day before yesterday. He didn't stay long because he was on his way to the German School, but it was nice of him to stop by," I explained to Andrés Randal.

What an odd scene his visit had presented—a Sarmiento stopping by and greeting a former servant. Domingo had asked me if Orlando had passed by to say hello, and I replied no. *Of course, he had not! What an idea!* He shook his head in disbelief of his younger brother's attitude towards me.

His lips touched the quivering skin of my neck; I closed my eyes while raising my hand to feel his soft wavy hair in my palm and fingers. I turned and passed my warm lips over his throat and then on his earlobe, softly tasting it with the tip of my tongue. He seized me by the waist and raised my body to my tiptoes while his moist lips met mine in a passionate flurry of infatuation. An electric shock traveled throughout my body and landed on my young bosom. Andrés's lips reached my chin; his eyes opened and penetrated mine, and I lost all sense and gave way to unrestrained desire. My breathing rushed as I felt his soft fingers touch my naked virgin thigh.

I jumped as a reaction to his touch and found myself on my own bed in the Pattersons' house. I sat trying to normalize my breathing because the dream perturbed me and dried my mouth in a second. I had never had a dream so vivid to all my senses. The moment he had opened his eyes, I had recognized Andrés Randal, and I could still feel his embrace on my body.

I got out of bed to drink a glass of water from my nightstand and walked to the window to open it. The breeze coming from the sea brushed upon my face and swept through my hair. Still shaken by my dream, I held onto the iron bars of the window and closed my eyes to feel the fresh air flow over me. When I was about to close the window, I glanced across the street and saw the lean figure of Andrés Randal looking in my direction. My heart stopped and fell to my stomach, and I immediately closed the window and curtains.

What is he doing there?

I took my hand to my throat, still feeling the contact that had felt so real in my dream. Not being able to control myself, I opened the corner of one curtain to peek outside and see if he was still there, but he was not.

Am I still asleep?

I opened the window to take a better look, wishing those iron bars were not there so I could stick my head out when I felt his hand touch mine on the iron bar. Fear grasped my throat, and only my extreme shock kept me from screaming out.

"Did I scare you?" he whispered.

The fading light on the post hid the obvious; his appearance had robbed my face of all color.

"Yes … what are you doing here?" I asked, disturbed by his hand still over mine.

"I just had a dream about you," he said, looking directly into my averted eyes, "and I had to see you."

"It is midnight; you cannot come in …," I replied

"I know … I was walking towards your window to knock on it … when you opened it," he said, reaching to my other hand on the bar.

"What did you dream?" I asked looking down.

Andrés let go of my hands to extend his arms through the bars and reached for my waist. I felt the bars on my breasts and his chest crushed against them.

"I dreamed of you and me … together … like I have you right now … but without the bars."

His breath hit mine as he spoke those words, just as Orlando's breath had penetrated me not long before. Still shaken and embarrassed, I gently took his hands off my waist. Andrés pulled away without taking his eyes off mine. I held his hands and asked him to leave; Señor and Señora Patterson might not approve of their children's teacher meeting young men at the bedroom's window in the middle of the night.

"I am in love with you, Maximiana … I wanted you to know that tonight," Andrés said while pulling my right hand out from between the bars. He then kissed it, without taking his eyes off mine.

I didn't know what to say.

Is he mocking me as Orlando did?

"Good night," he whispered, lowering his eyelids.

"Good night, I replied.

A strange mixture of sensations ran wildly through me—reluctance and excitement, dread and anticipation, shock and bemusement. I doubted his words, but those same words kept me fighting sighs for hours after his departure. My one decision to teach was bringing me all sorts of changes, to all areas of my life.

19

Sunday evening at the Machado Square was a treat for children and young people in Mazatlán. They would dress with their nicest clothes and walk around the bandstand, buy sweets, and talk to friends, sitting on the beautifully ornamented white iron benches. Señora and Señor Patterson liked to take the children to the square for this weekly entertainment, and I gladly accompanied them. And I could dress appropriately for it. Now that I had been working for almost two months, even after sending much of my earnings to my parents, I had enough left over to buy more articles of clothing for myself. I felt so independent and accomplished and, yes, proud and joyful when I bought a couple of short-sleeve blouses and a pair of dress sandals.

Summer in Mazatlán was relentlessly hot and humid; people had to take a bath mornings and evenings, and not having enough clothing and appropriate shoes was a nightmare. However, the short-sleeve blouses were a blessing because they helped keep the heat bearable. I relished having enough money to buy personal necessities that I hadn't had access to before moving to the city. Powder was a blessing for the rash that sometimes broke out from the heat. As soon as I could afford it, I bought myself a bottle of scented powder. I could just imagine Natalia and Otilia enjoying it as much as I did, and I made sure to send a bottle as a present when Domingo traveled to El Roble. He was more than happy to take my savings and such gifts to my family. I secretly hoped Mamá would send back to me some of her fabulous pineapple and pumpkin empanadas; but she would probably be too shy to ask Domingo for the favor.

I was sitting on a bench, looking at everyone strolling around the square when I heard a familiar voice on my side. My heart jumped.

"How are you?" Orlando Sarmiento said seriously.

"Fine, thank you," I replied and slightly curtsied to his companion, a young man about Orlando's age who, bowed back at my greeting with a pleasant smile.

"This is Francisco Reveles."

"How do you do?" I replied politely.

Orlando Sarmiento had never introduced anybody to me before and, of course, had ignored me altogether for months.

Francisco Reveles kissed my hand and replied the same.

"And your name is?" he finally asked, realizing Orlando had no intention of introducing *me* to him.

"Maximiana Valdez," I said

Orlando became clearly uncomfortable when I said my name, especially because his friend turned to look at him, surprised by my answer. With mortification, I realized that Orlando has spoken of me to his friends in less than adoring terms. The awkwardness of the moment made me get up from the bench and excuse myself to leave. Orlando held my arm abruptly, and I stopped, having no intention of creating a scene, especially for Señor and Señora Patterson.

"Please let go of my arm; I have to leave now," I said cautiously, without looking at Orlando while his friend became clearly perturbed by the scene.

Apparently, Orlando Sarmiento could not see me as Francisco did. For his friend, I was an attractive young woman, dressed in a fashionable outfit and hairstyle that placed me above the status of servant girl. To pull a girl's arm in public that way and to try to restrain her was a public insult, though not to a girl of a lower social and economic status. But again, Orlando Sarmiento could not see me beyond that.

Francisco Reveles spoke into Orlando's ear and asked him to let go of me. But Orlando ignored him, frowning back at me with anger.

"I want to talk to you," he ordered.

"I work as a teacher at the Pattersons' house. If you need to speak to me about something, you may find me there. Now, let go of my arm. Please."

He let go after some hesitation. I hurriedly walked to Señora Patterson's side, who fortunately, had been occupied with two lady friends and had not witnessed the embarrassing scene.

Moments later, I looked back at Orlando, who was still standing with his friend at the bench, without smiling. His eyes denoted frustration, as if I had ruined the moment by disobeying the command of remaining by his side. I took Elizabeth's hand and baby Martha from Señora Patterson's arms as an excuse to walk away from his eyeful reach.

I found another place to sit with the baby while Elizabeth played with her doll. Trying to forget the incident with Orlando, I started paying attention to the musicians playing in the bandstand. Elizabeth's doll was dancing in her hands while baby Martha danced on my knees. A girl no older than eight kept staring at us. I smiled back at her, but her eyes shied away from mine. She was sitting on the ground next to her mother, who was selling homemade coconut candies. A flashback of memories came to me of my own childhood in El Roble. The clothes she was wearing were sparkling clean, but rags, and she had no shoes on her little feet. Then I realized she was staring at Elizabeth's doll, not at us, just as I used to stare at Anita Flores's doll in the distance, when I was around the same age. The extreme contrast between the two children was painfully real, but nobody seemed bothered by it, at least not those on the comfortable side of the balance. On the other end, I imagined that little girl's mother wished her daughter to have a pair of good sandals and a complete dress and that little angel wished to have a doll just like Elizabeth's in her hands to love and cherish. I remembered Magdalena sitting on my bed back at the Pattersons' house.

I took the children back to Señora Patterson and asked her if I could go back to the house, that it was an emergency. She agreed and asked her eldest, Carolina, to go with me. We rushed to the house and retrieved Magdalena. Carolina was excited when I told her Magdalena had been a present and now she would be a present *again*, but for another girl.

Back in the Machado Square I introduced myself to the mother, and she told me her little girl's name was Filomena López, eight years old, and she had seven more children at home, "all boys," she said. I asked Filomena to take good care of Magdalena and suggested that if she changed her name, to leave Magdalena as her second one. She nodded and smiled, without ever saying a word.

"Say 'Thank you' to the lady, Filo," her mamá scolded; "say 'Thank you.'"

Filomena wouldn't do it with words, but by the sudden glittering of her look, I knew she was very grateful to have the beautiful doll in the purple dress for her own. I told her mother not to worry about it and went back to Señora Patterson, who had observed the scene in the distance with her friends.

"That was very kind of you, Maximiana," Señora Patterson said, patting my arm.

"There is no point in having that doll just sitting on a bed when she can be giving so much happiness to a little girl," I said, meaning every word from the bottom of my heart.

She agreed and so did her friends. Inside of me, I wished they would do the same one of these days and share some of their wealth at least with the poor young children living so close to them.

On the way back to the Pattersons' House, I saw Orlando Sarmiento talking and laughing with his friends. His steady girlfriend, Virginia, and friends had joined his party; however, none of them recognized me when I passed by their side. Orlando took his usual attitude towards me when those people were around: He dismissed my existence.

Our earlier exchange was the first time that I had seen him since he had left El Roble. I had dreaded meeting him in Mazatlán, but I knew I would have to do so at some moment in my life and was glad it was finally over. His betrayal and insensitive mockery still touched me sometimes, but I continued to look forward: I had a new life now and felt fulfilled.

Andrés Randal stopped by the Pattersons' house on Wednesday afternoon; I hadn't seen him since our midnight meeting at the window. He apologized for his absence and explained he had been in bed, suffering from the influenza. I mentioned that I hoped he hadn't caught it from that night in the fresh air. No, he said; some workers that had just arrived from the Sierra Madre Mountains came sick with the symptoms, they stopped by his family's business, and he caught the flu from them. I was glad to hear he had recovered—and to hear the truth. I had feared he had been avoiding me.

He invited me to go for a walk, but instead of an amorous stroll, he wanted to tell me about the next meeting of the Cactus. This was my chance to enter. I agreed to attend that evening; he would pick me up at six thirty.

During our walk, Andrés lightly held my arm, something he had never done before. I felt a strange sensation to feel his hand on my elbow, but it did not make me feel uncomfortable. As a matter of fact, I liked it.

At about six fifteen, Doña Ursula called me. I thought Andrés had come early to pick me up, but when I arrived at the foyer of the house, it was empty. Doña Ursula then said the young man refused to enter the house and he was waiting in the side garden. I became suspicious and quickly moved towards the side garden to discover Orlando Sarmiento standing next to the garden bench. My hopes of having a pleasant evening of adventure suddenly had vanished. He must have felt equally ill at ease because he stiffened when he saw me cross the French-style garden gate.

"What are you doing here?" I asked, trying to hide my evident perturbation.

"I want to talk to you; I told you at the square on Sunday," he replied.

"Tell me whatever you need to tell me because I have to go out at six thirty."

"I cannot talk about it right here. Can we meet somewhere else?" he asked, getting closer to me as the words escaped his mouth.

I stepped back.

"Whatever it is, you can tell me here …," I said; "I don't sneak out anymore."

"It has to be in private," he replied. "Besides, who is going to recognize you dressed *that* way?"

His question annoyed me.

"I don't want to risk—"

"We could meet at night at the beach, as before," he abruptly interrupted me, "or at Francisco's apartment. He lives alone, and once school starts, the apartment is empty most of the time."

"That is not possible," I said, hurting inside by the intention behind his proposal. "I have to go now; it is after six, and I am not ready yet."

Orlando tried to contain his exasperation, "Maximiana, I *really* need to talk to you. *Please* meet with me somewhere where we can be alone."

"I cannot meet with you at night or in secret. I have nothing to hide. If you need to talk to me, you can do it in a public place, but not today because I have to go."

"Where are you going?" he asked.

"For a walk with Andrés Randal, and he is almost here."

Orlando's face involuntarily tightened with my response. Doña Ursula stood at the door and said Señorito Andrés Randal was waiting for me in the parlor.

"Thank you, Doña Ursula, I am on my way," I replied, trying to control the trembling of my voice. "It will only be a minute."

I turned to Orlando, and before I could say a word to him, he walked out on me, bumping into my shoulder.

"I'm sorry," he apologized without stopping and left the house through the side garden's gate, smashing it open on his way out.

I knew I had to put myself together before seeing Andrés Randal or he would notice my sudden anxiety. Orlando Sarmiento still managed to disturb my peace of mind.

I walked to the parlor room and asked Andrés for a minute to get ready; he stood up and agreed pleasantly. Once inside my room, my lips started to shake in profound misery. I had dreamed so many times of the moment that Orlando would look for me, but *never* had I dreamed of this way, with an arrogant attitude and ill-intended proposals of secrecy. On the other hand, I had a young man sitting in the parlor room, waiting patiently for me. He was gorgeous and a sweetheart to me.

What sign do I have that he is being honest with his intentions?

I shook my thoughts away, and in an instant, I was ready to see Andrés. I couldn't allow myself to ruin my chances of a real friendship because of Orlando Sarmiento.

Andrés's perfect white teeth broke into a smile when he saw me. He brought down his reading glasses from his forehead and asked me if I was ready to go. I nodded and left the Pattersons' house holding his arm. We greeted Señor Patterson at the entrance, and gladly, he shook hands with Andrés and sent salutations to his father.

"Today we are walking, if you don't mind," he said, winking; then to my car he whispered, "Nobody should see our carriage parked outside the Cactus meeting place."

I was already enthusiastic with the mystery surrounding such a meeting. I nodded and smiled, but I didn't fool him. He stopped and placed himself in front of me, right in the middle of the sidewalk around the corner of the Pattersons' house.

"You are smiling, but your eyes are not … what is wrong?"

"Nothing!" I replied. "I just have a little headache; that is all."

"Are you sure?" he asked, placing his forehead on mine.

"Yes, but I don't want to miss this opportunity, so let's go."

That was the honest truth; I had waited a long time for this meeting, ever since Alejandro had talked to me about it in El Roble. For me it was the ultimate chance to learn from people like Alejandro Sarmiento and his idealistic friends.

"My sister, Paula, is anxious to meet you," he said when we renewed our walk.

"You have a sister?" I asked, shocked that I had not known that.

"Yes, she is the oldest in the family," he continued, "and the smartest, too."

"How old is she?" I asked, intrigued with the news of a sister.

"She is twenty-three; then Eduardo, who is twenty, and I, the youngest."

By the time we reached the apartment where the meetings took place, the soles of my feet were burning. It was several blocks away, in a beautiful two-story building very close to the sea. A family lived in half of the first level; a hardware store occupied the other. The second floor was divided into apartments; one of them was rented by Señorita Agatha Santos, a woman so different that my imagination immediately placed her as the protagonist in an exotic and radical book. She was a painter and spoke five languages fluently. As one of the leaders of the Cactus, she had secured the apartment next to hers for the secret meetings. She shook my hand with force before lighting a cigarette.

"Have they explained to you what this is all about?" Agatha asked, blowing smoke through the side of her mouth.

"I have an idea ...," I replied.

"Comrades, this is Maximiana Valdez, a friend of Andrés Randal and Alejandro Sarmiento."

Everyone greeted me. I looked around and discovered Teodoro de la Vega sitting in a corner. Andrés introduced me to his brother, Eduardo, and his sister, Paula, as well as each one of the other members.

"Not everyone is present today; eventually you will meet them all."

I nodded and took a seat. Agatha instructed Andrés to explain to me the function of their group. He told me it was secretly organizing people to fight and bring social justice to everyone in México.

"A revolution is coming," Eduardo Randal said, "and we need to have as many people as possible ready for the changes with a new order when it comes."

"Only through education can effective change come," Paula said. "We have to mobilize teachers in the area of Mazatlán to train peasants in reading, writing, mathematics, business … they have to be ready for the time when this is all over … Porfirio Diaz's days are counted … this system will die, and the new México will emerge."

"Yes," Agatha continued, "a México where everyone has access to education, good health, and a dignified life."

My heart was pounding with emotion. My sisters, the teachers in El Roble, without knowing it, were helping out in this project of the Cactus. Andrés raised his hand and talked about that very consequence; he said that I was the teacher Alejandro Sarmiento had talked about and the recipient of their educational materials.

It is they who have been sending those books and paper tablets with Alejandro!

I didn't understand why such a wonderful project had to be kept a secret. I asked Andrés in a low voice, and he explained to me that people who tried to mobilize the poor through any type of project were accused of being traitors to the republic and that, even though education was obligatory in the country, in reality the educational system was nonexistent or just a mediocre imitation of it.

Shyly, I raised my hand to ask a question, "Why does our government want the people to be ignorant?"

A man, short of stature and with the most intelligent eyes, responded, "There is no system of oppression more perfect than one that controls millions of people by keeping them hungry, unarmed, and uneducated." His name was Ernesto Hernandez, and every time he spoke, stillness took hold in the room.

"The *Afternoon Mail* will publish an article on the election next week," Paula Randal announced. The *Afternoon Mail* was Mazatlán's daily newspaper. "Even though Diaz will surely remain as president and 're-election' better describes this, still, it is very important that as many people as possible read it and talk about it. I say we organize a few gatherings to discuss the election."

Eduardo Randal spoke, "Let's spread ourselves out, meeting in different times and places, so we can reach as many people as possible … but keep your guard up and keep it low-key."

Everyone agreed. I couldn't believe I was actually sitting in that room full of so many good ideas. Later, Andrés explained to me that ours was a "progressive movement" with "socialist roots" from the *Communist Manifesto*. At the beginning, those words sounded like a foreign language, but as time passed and my understanding of their meaning grew, the subject of social justice became a normal topic of my conversations with those in the movement.

On the way back, Andrés asked my thoughts about the meeting, and I shared my enthusiasm with him. He also said he had been thinking about me; his words shied my eyes away. It was very easy for my young heart to get caught up in emotions that I wanted so much to have again. Andrés held my hand and entwined his fingers in mine, hiding them on the side of my skirt. People passing by us would notice our closeness but could probably not guess that we were holding hands in public.

The way back to the Pattersons' house felt shorter. Right before arriving at the front gate, Andrés asked me to accompany him to Saturday's dance at the German Club, across the street from Machado Square. Initially, I hesitated; after all, I had never been to a dance. On the other hand, this was an opportunity to go to my *first* one. He explained that his family was invited and that he and Eduardo could take a guest. I had no reason to reject his invitation; Andrés Daniel Randal was my friend and treated me with the utmost respect and consideration. I agreed under the condition that Señora Patterson allowed me to return to the house late.

Fortunately, Señora Patterson not only agreed to my late return from the dance with Andrés but also suggested she help me get ready.

Her offer to me proved once more that Señora Enriqueta Patterson was a woman of a great heart.

Señora Queta and Doña Ursula made sure I was ready when Andrés Randal's carriage stopped outside the house. They put colored powder on my cheeks and colored oil on my lips and charcoal on the lower line of my eyelids and on my eyelashes. However, plucking my eyebrows was the worst part. Fortunately, they did that before applying the makeup; otherwise, my tears would have ruined it. Next they helped fix the corset, another painful preparation, and made my waist unnaturally small and my posture completely straight. After I stepped into my long purple and white dress Alejandro had given me in December, they wrapped me in gardenia perfume, a little bit exaggerated to my own taste, but according to Señora Queta and Doña Ursula, that was the "fashion of the day."

I felt proud of the way I looked. Even though I did not consider myself vain, I took great pleasure in looking like a woman instead of a young girl. I only wished I wore glasses as Andrés Randal did; they made him look absolutely intriguing.

The sound of the wheels rolling on the cobbled road reached the Pattersons' house soon enough. Andrés Daniel wore a gray suit, and on our way out, he plucked a purple lilac from a bush and put it in the button hole of his lapel. In that moment, I wished aloud that Mamá and my sisters could see how I looked. Andrés said I could have my wish: He promised me that he would have a photographer at the dance take our picture. I had never had a photograph taken of me—one more first for me that evening.

In no time, we arrived at the German Club. I felt overwhelmed by all the people present and the loud music, and feeling so many eyes on Andrés and me frightened me slightly. We walked to the table where Paula and Eduardo Randal were sitting with their parents, and Andrés introduced me to them. They greeted me with politeness. Once I overcame my initial shyness, I started looking more closely at the people present. In the distance, I recognized Dora Elena Mora with her friends; next to them was Orlando Sarmiento with Virginia

Del Rincon. They all seemed to be having a very good time, chatting and laughing. None of them recognized me, and I was glad for it.

"Do you want to dance?" Andrés asked, rising from his seat.

"Yes, but I have never danced to this kind of music … so just be patient," I replied, taking a deep breath while placing my gloved hand on his.

"I will … and you … just relax and follow my lead," he whispered to me.

We walked to the dance floor; Andrés placed his arm around my waist and, with the other, held my hand. I did as he had suggested and found the waltz was actually simple to follow. Andrés smiled at me, noticing my obvious enjoyment of the dancing.

"You smell very good," he said, winking one eye at me, "and you look beautiful."

"Thank you … you look very handsome, too," I replied with sincerity.

"It is very warm tonight … would you like to stand at the window to catch some fresh air?"

"Oh yes, let's go."

We crossed the dance floor and went directly to the nearest window. Andrés offered to get us a drink and momentarily left me. I pulled out the Spaniard fan Señora Patterson had let me borrow and started fanning myself, thinking about what a good time Andrés and I were having together. I was too distracted in my thoughts to notice Orlando Sarmiento approaching me, but his familiar scent woke me from my reverie. He seemed about to say something but apparently changed his mind at the last minute because, once in front of me, he walked away as if he did not know me. My heart pounded with force as he approached, but I quickly controlled my tenseness this time.

"Alejandro's stepmother asked me if you were Maximiana Valdez," Andrés said as soon as he returned. My heart sank, thinking that not only Orlando was there but his father and Señora Leonora as well.

"What did you tell her?" I naïvely asked.

"Mmm … yes?" he started laughing. "Of course, I said yes; that is your name … right?" he joked, not understanding the situation.

"I think I should go home now," I said mortified.

"Why?" he asked, consternated.

"It is a very long story ..."

And I'd rather not talk about it.

"Please don't go. We will just stay away from the Sarmientos ... nobody will bother you, I promise, and if you become too uncomfortable, we will go ... is that fine with you?"

"And Orlando Sarmiento's friends, I don't think they have recognized me yet."

"What is wrong with *them*?"

"They spent some time in the hacienda when I worked there and ... they were very rude with me. They don't like me, especially Dora Elena, Catalina, and Virginia."

"I see ... but now you are here with me and my family; nobody will bother you again," he reassured me with the directness I admired in him.

Once we finished our fresh lemonade, Andrés asked me to dance with him again. Hesitating a bit, I held his arm and walked to the dance floor. This time Andrés looking intently into my eyes as we danced, as if he wanted to make sure I would not preoccupy myself by noticing anybody else.

"Would you like to go to the beach with our group tomorrow? We are having a picnic in the evening."

"Oh, very much! Yes, I would like to go," I replied enthusiastically.

At that moment, I noticed that Catalina Barraza stood next to me, and by the expression on her face, I could tell she had recognized me. She walked away to her group, and from the corner of my eye, I saw their surprise and emerging comments.

"They recognized me," I told Andrés who discreetly turned to their direction and looked back at me with seriousness.

"It is fine; don't worry about it. What can they possibly do?"

"Ridicule me," I replied with certainty and uneasiness in my heart.

"There is nothing to make fun of, Maximiana. Look at me."

My eyes started to moisten in my distress. Andrés stopped dancing and, delicately holding my arm, directed me to the salon's terrace. We passed by Orlando and his group, but I avoided their staring.

"I am very proud to be here with you … but I want you to tell me the truth," he stated in a low voice without blinking his penetrating emerald eyes. "Are you distressed because of those girls or because Orlando Sarmiento is with *them*?"

I stared at him and responded, "I am afraid they will start insulting me as they always did at the hacienda or that they will find a way to hurt my feelings."

"What about Orlando?"

"He ignores me, and I ignore him … there is nothing about him, unless he decides to laugh at me along with them, as he used to do in El Roble."

Andrés frowned in disbelief. "Why did he do that?"

"I don't know; up to this day, I don't understand."

Andrés looked in the direction of Orlando, who was still standing next to Virginia. Orlando returned the look at Andrés, and Virginia faced us in a sudden turn. I turned my face to the Machado Square, and Andrés moved his entire body closer to me. He softly brushed my cheek with his nose and whispered that he would take me home if I wanted to go now. I nodded.

We walked back to his family's table and greeted them good night. They were very polite, and Eduardo rose from his table to walk us to the door. On our way out, we passed by Dora Elena Mora and her group and heard their mocking giggles and fragments of snide remarks. In that instant, Andrés smiled at me and whispered into my ear, "I love you."

I lifted my face and walked out of my first dance with all the pride that my humble heart allowed. I knew that if I took the same attitude as those young women and played their games, I was as worthless as they were. But I was better than that; I was a teacher; I wanted to change the world I lived in. And I would begin by refusing to waste time with such frivolous and hurtful antics.

"Thank you very much for this evening, Andrés," I said at the door of the Pattersons' house while pulling the key out of my borrowed purse.

"Thank you for accepting the invitation," he replied, kissing my hand. "I wished we had stayed longer, but I understand why you wanted to leave."

"Yes … are you going back to the dance?" Suddenly I felt a hint of jealousy for the lucky girls that might dance with Andrés Daniel Randal at the party.

"I will; all of my family is there … but without you, it won't be the same."

I gasped, "Good night."

"Good night, sweet gardenia," he replied, half smiling.

I turned around and hugged him, feeling his strong body against mine. He crossed his arms around me and held me tightly. Lightning illuminated the sky, followed by a roar of thunder. We both jumped and laughed.

"I am terrified of thunder," I said, "especially when there is a lot of wind."

"I wish I could stay by your side until it goes away, holding you like this," Andrés whispered. His delightful voice tickled my ears when he spoke to me in whispers.

And I wish to kiss those lips of yours, Andrés Randal.

He caught my eyes looking at his lips and, without asking, brought them to mine in a kiss so full of fervor that he took my breath away. As we kissed, we simultaneously leaned into each other for support so that it seemed we were one. I didn't want any of it to end—the kissing, the sensations, the night. The intensity of the moment overwhelmed me and shunted from my consciousness the flashes of lightning and sounds of thunder; only when the heavy drops of summer rain fell on our faces did we move apart, childishly giggling.

"I am in love with you," Andrés said, holding my wet face.

"Even with the charcoal running down my eyes?" I asked in a useless effort to make a joke of my ruined makeup.

He kissed me again.

"I don't want you to catch a cold … you should go inside," he said. "But … I will pick you up tomorrow for the picnic, right?"

"Right," I replied, smiling.

He took the steps to the front door and waited for me to go in. When I entered my room, I turned on the light to wash my face and find my sleeping gown, and then I turned it off to change. The lightning kept illuminating my bedroom, but I didn't feel scared.

I pulled the covers over my face to hide my own silly smile for I admitted I had feelings for Andrés Daniel Randal, good, deep, loving feelings. And I realized the wonderful reality that he did not mind my condition as a peasant or my family's poverty. He did not care if others saw us together in public; he introduced me to his family and to his friends; he naturally walked the streets of Mazatlán by my side. He was *not* Orlando Sarmiento, and it was time for me to stop thinking of Andrés as such.

However, that night I had a dream that shamed me for days to come. In it, Orlando Sarmiento held me once more in his arms, and he made love to me as he had wanted all the time we had been together. His voice sounded real and kept repeating the phrase, "You are mine forever."

I was on my way back from picking up telegraph messages for Señora Patterson when I spotted Alejandro Sarmiento walking towards me. He greeted me with eagerness and told me they had arrived from El Roble the night before. It was the middle of August, and the trip to Boston was around the corner.

"How's everybody in El Roble?" I asked, happy to hear news from my family.

"They are all fine. As a matter of fact, your mother sent some treats for you and letters from different people. But Domingo has them; I think he will bring them to you this evening."

Domingo? That is a little bit odd. I am still not used to the idea of having Domingo Sarmiento as one of my friends.

"How is Natalia? Did you talk to her?" I prepared myself to hear of her broken heart; hopefully she was doing fine with Domingo's departure to the United States.

"She is fine; don't worry about it," he replied, smiling his usual sympathetic smile.

"Oh, Alejandro, it is so good to see you!" I exclaimed, giving him a hug.

Despite the criticism of this type of public demonstration for single women, I refused to deny such an innocuous expression of welcome to my dear friend. Alejandro was one of my best friends, and I could not hide my affection for him.

"I missed you so much!"

Alejandro hugged me back with the same affection. People skirted around us, shaking their heads in disapproval.

"I missed you too, Max. How is it going here? What's new?"

"I love teaching the Patterson children; they are well-behaved and eager to learn. And the family is more than I could have asked for. The parents treat everyone working in that house with consideration and respect. Señora Patterson's heart is as beautiful as her looks. You have no idea, Alejandro, how helpful she has been to me … and their library! My goodness!" I gasped for air to continue. "I also attended a dance last Saturday."

Alejandro was surprised, "Great … who did you go with?"

"Andrés Randal," I replied feeling a hint of embarrassment. "He also invited me to join the Cactus," I said in a secretive voice.

"Good, good, good," Alejandro nodded. "We have a lot to talk about, then."

"I have to go now, Aleh. Señora Patterson is waiting for these messages. When can I see you?"

"I will come to invite you for a walk at the square today. Are you allowed to go out evenings?"

"Oh yes, but I return no later than eight. I will be ready then. It is so good to have you close by, Aleh!" I said with utmost sincerity.

"Thank you, Silly Face," he replied as we parted.

I hoped Domingo would send me my letters with Alejandro this afternoon because I couldn't wait to read the news from my family and town for too long.

Upon my return to the house, I handed the telegrams to Señora Patterson. She was very excited to read the news and told me that she and Señor Patterson were finally going to take the trip to Europe that he had promised her since their marriage. Evidently, they would take the same ship to San Francisco and train to the east coast of the United States that Domingo and Alejandro would. She explained that her parents were going to stay with the children and be in charge of the house. I felt a little bit of melancholy, thinking of the household without them, but also gladness for them. Señora Patterson's parents were a conservative, serious couple, but so far they had always been nice to everyone working in the house, so I wasn't concerned at all.

Señora Queta Patterson also told me that Señora Leonora Sarmiento had sent an invitation for tea that afternoon at her house. I became pale as a cloud when she pronounced those words.

"What is wrong, Maximiana?" she asked.

"I used to work at their house in El Roble, as a servant girl."

"Oh we know that. Alejandro explained everything to us when Alberto brought him over to discuss the possibility of your becoming the new teacher for the children."

Everything? What exactly did he explain to you? my mind screamed to ask.

"Don't worry about it, Maximiana; by now we know you," she said as if reading my mortified mind.

"Thank you, Señora Patterson," I sincerely replied and walked to the kitchen to ask Doña Ursula if she needed help with anything. Once I finished helping her and the cooks, I retired to my room to continue reading Vicente Blasco Ibanez's *The Black Spider*. I needed a good book to get my mind off Señora Queta's tea engagement with Señora Leonora Sarmiento.

After ten pages, I placed the book on my lap and closed my eyes to rest. The stifling heat of the afternoon did not allow me to concentrate on my reading. I grabbed my cardboard fan to try to alleviate the suffocation in the room, but it was useless. August's heat denied any means of comfort. Even though my bedroom, located in the corner of the first floor and closest to the sea's breeze, tended to be cooler than any other room in the house, when the wind stopped blowing, even it became an oven too hot to do anything, including think.

Except about Andrés Randal. I could think about him under any circumstance.

I hadn't seen Andrés since the picnic on Sunday when we met at the beach. Some members of the Cactus, including Agatha and Paula, brought picnic baskets to share. We took our shoes off and walked north on the sand until we reached places that were completely untouched by humans. It was beautiful and peaceful. On our return, we took the beach's boardwalk as soon as it began because walking on the sand tired our feet. However after a few steps on the hot boards, we ran back to the sand freshly wet by the waves.

Agatha always came up with the most outrageous ideas, and she did hilarious imitations. For México's first lady, Señora Diaz, she would light a cigarette and start giving a speech on how it felt to be first lady and having to entertain at all those parties where you could drown in French champagne and expensive liqueurs. In closing the speech, she would proudly announce the donation of Christmas toys to the "little people's children." Her humor had a touch of political unrest sprinkled throughout.

Agatha looked very much the artist. Small framed, she wore her hair very short and colored it bright red with henna, contrasting sharply with her pale skin. Enormous, sparkling green eyes peered over a couple of shy freckles scattered over her cheeks. A painter, she often depicted scenes with fishermen of the sea, but she always represented them as skeletons. Actually, all of her paintings had people as skeletons, living an everyday life. Once you entered her apartment, you couldn't take your eyes off her fascinating paintings. I also had the impression that she had a very special relationship with Eduardo Randal, too peculiar to describe and unlike any other I knew, but they seemed to be connected as one.

Once the sun indicated the approach of late afternoon, I washed myself to get ready for Alejandro. Perhaps Andrés would call on me again today, but since he didn't mention it on Sunday, I had no intention to wait, even though I really wanted to see him.

Señora Patterson left for her tea invitation at the Sarmientos, and I walked out of the house with Alejandro. Something about his manner made me suspicious—of what, I had no clue.

"Where are we going?" I asked with curiosity.

"To Agatha's apartment."

"Is there going to be a meeting today? I didn't know; Andrés didn't tell me."

"There's no meeting today, but I have to give you the treats your mother sent and the letters; Domingo has them there."

I felt there was no point in asking why. But nothing prepared me for the surprise that awaited me when Domingo opened the door of the Cactus apartment.

"Maximiana!" Natalia screamed and ran to my side to hug me and dance with my stiff body from side to side. "Max! I am so happy to see you, little sister! Mamá sent you pineapple, cajeta and pumpkin empanadas and sweet *natillas*." She walked towards a suitcase and pulled out a package of letters. "Each one of the children in our school wrote a letter for you, and Otilia and Daniel … oh, and Mamá dictated one that I wrote for you—"

"Natalia … what are you doing here?" I interrupted, still confused with her presence.

"I am going to the United States with Domingo," she said to my surprise.

"Do Mamá and Papá know you are here? What …? Explain to me what is going on …"

She walked to Domingo's side and hugged him from behind, placing her beautiful face on his shoulder.

"We got married," she said. My jaw dropped, and my eyes sought Alejandro's reaction to her words.

Alejandro nodded and Domingo spoke, "We got married in Villa Unión yesterday morning, in a secret ceremony in church. Alejandro was our witness."

"Do Mamá and Papá know about it? Or … you eloped?"

"They do know, Maximiana. Domingo spoke to them before we made the decision … and I am hiding in here until the boat leaves for the United States," she replied.

"I don't want Father to know because we need to make it to Boston and I want to finish school; then I will be on my own," Domingo added.

"I will accompany them and leave them settled, Max. If Father finds out, he will cut his financial support to Domingo, and we don't want to use Mother's money yet. So … Natalia will stay in this apartment until we leave. Agatha will take her to the boat before us; that way nobody will see her board it," Alejandro said.

My mind raced at the speed of his words but overtook them and ran circles around them. What confusion! But I had to react to the news.

"Congratulations, then …," I said and gave them a hug. I was truly shocked with the news. Domingo Sarmiento *did* love my sister Natalia and they were now embarking on an adventure of traveling to another country and living in Boston to attend Harvard University.

"Oh, Natalia … please find a school and take classes there; you must learn English and everything you can!" I said, realizing the tremendous opportunity in front of my sister.

"I want to study music and singing, Max … Alejandro says that I could be an opera singer if a teacher trains me …"

"Oh yes! Yes, of course!" I hugged her again. "You are so lucky, Nat." Then a cloudy feeling descended upon me when I thought of my sister being so far away from all of us. "I am going to miss you," I said, "but I know you are going to be fine with Domingo because he loves you … *for real.*" I looked down hiding tears of emotion and sadness.

"Max … I am going to miss you, too … ever since you left, you have no idea how quiet our house is."

"Natalia, I am going to the store with Alejandro and bring you both something to drink and eat … we will be right back," Domingo said. We saw them off.

"Natalia, I cannot believe you got married!" I exclaimed once we were alone.

"Yes … I know we are not that old, but Maxi … I just couldn't see him go away again; I would've died without Domingo; I love him so much," she said full of emotion "And I know he loves me as much as I love him, Max … please don't doubt it anymore."

"I don't … he married you, and you two are traveling together to Boston. How can I doubt him, Nat?" I smiled while holding her soft hands.

"Did you make up with Orlando?"

"No … of course not." I looked away to hide my perturbation.

"Do you still love him?" Natalia asked, seeking my eyes.

"No."

"I am sure that you are going to find somebody as wonderful as Domingo or Alejandro, and you will fall in love with him, and every single trace left of that Orlando Sarmiento will be gone forever from your mind."

"I am seeing somebody already."

Her eyes widened and an enormous butterfly outlined her smile, "Really? Tell me … who is he?"

"His name is Andrés Randal. He is a friend of Alejandro and well … I attended a dance with him last Saturday," I said, giggling.

"Is he handsome? Oh, please don't answer! You have the weirdest tastes in boys!"

We both laughed.

"Actually he is not that handsome … but his personality is overwhelming."

"Oh … overwhelming," she said moving her questioning eyebrows up and down.

"I cannot even explain it … he is very sure of himself, and when he looks at you, his eyes penetrate you as if he knows what you are thinking all along. He wears glasses sometimes, and he doesn't care about what others think."

"He sounds very interesting … I hope to meet him before leaving to Boston."

"Oh, yes. I will make sure that you do, and please don't make fun of my taste in boys! Next to Domingo Sarmiento, *any* boy looks ugly."

We both laughed again.

"Are Mamá and Papá happy about your marriage to Domingo?"

"They were happy that I married him but very sad that we had to leave this way. Augusto thought it was wrong to hide our marriage, but we are adults; we know what we are doing."

"True," I responded, "and I hope that everything goes as planned."

Our conversation was interrupted by Domingo and Alejandro who walked into the apartment with Andrés Randal by their side. My face turned crimson red when I saw him standing in front of me smiling. I rose to introduce him to my sister, who immediately offered to take the food to the kitchen to have it ready.

"Max … oh my God … *that* is Andrés Randal?" she asked with her mouth opened wide.

Here we go again.

"Yes, and I told you he is not a Domingo Sarmiento."

She peeked through the door to take another look.

"He is gorgeous, Max … what are you talking about?" she said in a murmur. "He looks very … interesting. His face is fascinating."

"I know."

"Does he like you? I mean … is he interested in you?"

"That is what he says," I answered casually, trying not to give too much hint of my real feelings for Andrés.

"How old is he?"

"Eighteen."

"He looks older … it must be his personality. He looks like somebody that knows exactly what he wants. He is tall, too … my goodness, Max … he is *very* handsome."

"Yes … he is."

"Do you love him?" she giggled, pinching my rib.

"No."

"You are lying."

"I like him, but I don't love him … I don't want to get too much into that yet." I replied, trying to hide as much as possible my interest in Andrés.

"You will; I know you will because I cannot imagine a girl not falling in love with somebody like *him* … I bet the girls at the party you attended on Saturday where jealous of you."

"To tell you the truth, I didn't pay too much attention to it. I was more concerned with Señora Leonora Sarmiento's presence there as well as other people that you don't know about."

I had never told my sisters about my terrible experiences of humiliation and mockery from the girls in El Roble, but this was not the best time to do it. I wanted Natalia to stay as happy as she looked.

"Was Orlando there? At the party?" she asked enthusiastically.

"He was, but he ignored me as he always does when somebody is around."

"He is such an idiot. Oh, I wish I had seen you, little sister."

"Actually there is a way … Andrés and I took a picture; I will bring it tomorrow."

"Oh, yes, do! But now we should join the others and take in the pastries … help me with the lemonade," she said, and we walked out of the kitchen and into the living room.

Andrés walked me home that evening. He was very sweet and gen-tlemanly with me. I told him of my concern for Señora Leonora and Señora Queta's meeting, but he said I shouldn't worry about it. After all, if anything happened, I could move to the Cactus apartment, and they would help me find another job. His words gave me tremendous peace of mind, but still, I didn't want to leave the Pattersons; they had been the support that allowed me to turn my life around in Mazatlán. Besides, I had secret hopes that they would eventually sponsor me as they had sponsored Alberto, to go to México City and attend the National University of México.

"Thank you for bringing me down, Andrés … it was good to see you," I said, opening the front gate. His face became serious. I sensed he wanted to say something but took a step back and walked away. I followed and stopped him by his arm.

"What's wrong?" I asked, fearing he was mad at me for some reason.

"I don't understand you," he said, grinding his teeth. "Sometimes you treat me as someone you care about, and other times, you dismiss me as a stranger … what is it *this* time? You saw Orlando's brothers and that troubled you?"

I felt my body freeze with embarrassment. "I am worried about Señora Queta's meeting with Señora Leonora … I don't mean to hurt your feelings … I am sorry; please don't go like that, Andrés."

"I just don't understand what kind of relationship you and I have, that's all."

"Why don't we talk about it … somewhere else, another time … nobody should hear our conversation on the street," I said, hanging on to his arm. "Please, don't go away like this."

"Pardon me," Andrés replied, sighing. "I'm sorry for my childish behavior; I just get frustrated when you act this way."

I knew he was right, but I honestly did not know what to do about it. "I'm sorry, Andrés," I said from my sincere heart.

He half smiled and walked away from me. When he left, emptiness filled my heart. I didn't care about Señora Leonora or what she had to say to Señora Enriqueta; what I cared about was that Andrés Randal was walking on Principal Street, in Mazatlán, disappointed in me. He didn't deserve that kind of treatment; he had been a true friend to me. I raised my skirt with both of my hands to run faster and took off like a hare to catch up with him.

"Andrés!" I screamed, and he turned around. "Andrés, please forgive my attitude; nobody has ever treated me the way you do—"

"I don't need your gratitude, Max. I am fine. Really, don't worry about it. I have to go now."

"No! Andrés that is not what I mean …" I held his hand in a desperate attempt to stop him. "Nobody has ever made me *feel* the way *you* do."

Andrés' intent to run away from me ceased when I said that. He turned around.

"How do I make you feel, Maximiana?" he asked, giving me an intense look that denoted suspicion in my words.

"I would give my life for you …"

He was taken aback by my open and explicit response. We stood in silence for several seconds, looking into each other's eyes.

"I mean it."

"Me, too, I would give my life for you …," he replied and, closing his eyes, rested his forehead on mine. He walked with me back to the front door and waited for me to go in. I touched his hand until the door was closed behind my back.

For an instant, I had almost lost Andrés's trust in me. I could never let that happen; even the idea of losing it, I realized, I could not bear.

Everything seemed normal at the Patterson household, but I still held some reservation about my former employer talking with my current one. Nevertheless, my fears completely vanished when Señora Queta, holding my hand, told me there was nothing to worry about and, even though Señora Leonora Sarmiento had a serious attitude problem towards me, she had her own way of seeing things, and she disagreed with Señora Leonora's prejudices. I thanked her for her trust in me and told her not to worry about anything during her trip, that I would help out with the children as much as needed. She gave me a pat on my shoulder as a sign of gratitude, but my heart felt it as a caring gesture from a family member.

That night, I lay on my bed thinking about Andrés and my feelings for him. I also thought of Natalia, married to the dashingly handsome Domingo Sarmiento, the young man every girl in town, if not the entire state, wanted but had crossed off as "unattainable" after he broke up with *the* Catalina Barraza. I would give a finger to see her face when she found out Domingo had married my sister. More than anything, I wanted to see if her arrogance and egotism would come down a little bit after that.

The following two weeks were full of excitement everywhere I turned. At the Pattersons' house, we were all preparing for Señor and Señora Patterson's trip to Europe. Señora Queta's parents would come the last week before the departure to get organized. I was also helping Natalia get ready for her own trip with Domingo. Agatha and I, and sometimes Paula, went shopping for her needs—everything from petticoats to gloves, hats, and shoes. She quickly tired of hiding in that apartment, but the risk was too big to go out. Domingo came to see her every day, and Alejandro also visited to keep her company every once in a while. Domingo did not tell Orlando about his marriage to Natalia; he was afraid Orlando might tell their father. Fortunately, nobody suspected anything.

Due to the comings and goings, I didn't have much time available to see Andrés Daniel Randal. He understood, though, and helped out with Natalia's preparation for the long trip as well. We were concerned she might get seasick; after all Natalia had never been on a boat, other than the little one crossing the Presidio, so Andrés offered to find the right remedies for it. She also needed a permit to leave México and enter the United States. Discreetly Eduardo, Teodoro, and Andrés made the arrangements for that.

Domingo and Natalia were extremely happy together; theirs was a passion that could not keep them apart. They were always next to each other, or Natalia would sit on Domingo's lap, not caring about others' opinions of their effusive demonstrations of love. Andrés would discreetly touch my hand when we were in the Cactus apartment visiting them; I knew he wanted me to sit on his lap, as well, but I was not that daring in public. I gave my affections in private, away from other people's eyes.

❦

In no time, September came, and the boat was ready to set sail. The night before their departure, I talked to Natalia for a long time, and we cried together for Mamá, Papá, our brother, and our sisters. We cried for the separation of thousands of miles between us, even though our minds would continue together. She promised to write as soon as she arrived to let me know where to find her. I told her that when I heard she was safe and sound in Boston, I would go personally to El Roble to inform our parents.

I begged her to visit Harvard University and have Domingo take her picture in front of its buildings; Alejandro would bring them back upon his return. I just needed to see a member of my family standing in Harvard, as Alejandro called it. Alejandro had told me so many stories about the place that I pictured it as a paradise of learning and freedom of thought, and I wondered if there was a school for women as Harvard was for men. I kept asking myself if the National University of México would be the same; Andrés would have to tell me once he studied there.

How lucky my sister Natalia is!

I kept telling myself to fight the evil feelings of jealousy that would suddenly enter my heart.

I said good-bye in the apartment to Natalia early on the morning of her trip; the boat was leaving at eight. I planned to be at the dock at the time of departure, but I couldn't risk being seen with my sister by the Sarmientos. Señor and Señora Patterson were very sad to leave their children behind, but Señora Queta's parents assured them that everything was going to be fine. We all wished them *bon voyage* when they went aboard the enormous ship, and I waved baby Martha's hand good-bye to her parents. Señora Patterson was crying, and I had to hold my own tears back when I thought about my Natalia boarding the same boat at that moment to go so far away from us.

I glanced at the Sarmientos, seeing off Alejandro and Domingo. Señora Leonora was visually heartbroken with at least one of her step-sons' departure, Orlando seemed very distressed by both his brothers' leaving, and Domingo was utterly upset with Catalina Barraza and her family's presence.

As soon as Alejandro saw me in the distance, he came to tell me good-bye. Señora Lorenza Villanueva smiled when she saw Alejandro kiss my hand good-bye; I had already given him an enormous hug that morning, unknown to her. Then Domingo came to do the same. Both of them promised to write to me, and Señora Lorenza smiled with approval. As I watched them return to their party before boarding, Señora Leonora sent darts of severe hatred in my direction. Orlando, as usual, ignored me and looked down when he saw me to avoid giving a smile or greeting or some other acknowledgment of my presence. I turned to Domingo and Alejandro to wave good-bye, and they returned my greeting from the ship's gangplank.

Tears rolled down my cheeks; I couldn't contain myself any longer. Señora Lorenza saw me crying and asked if one of them was my beau. I answered they were very dear friends of mine.

And my sister is on that boat as well.

She took the baby from my arms and asked me if I wanted to go closer. I agreed and ran towards the ship. Alejandro and Domingo came to the rail and waved their hands at me, but I desperately was seeking for the familiar beautiful face of Natalia. Alejandro signed to me with his eyes to look up deck, and then I saw her. She was standing like an owl princess—stately, serene, and ready to take flight on a wonderful new adventure. The light of the day made her look more beautiful than when I had seen her that morning at sunrise at the Cactus apartment. She blew a kiss at me and smiled, waving good-bye.

The breeze from the sea kept moving her short curls to her face, and coquettishly, she kept putting them away; then the familiar scent hit me … I knew Orlando was standing next to me. He waved to his brothers a good-bye, and then he saw Natalia on the upper deck of the boat.

He got closer and whispered in my ear, "Natalia is traveling with them."

I didn't answer because I had no way of knowing if he was asking or affirming the statement. I couldn't control my tears; it hurt too much to see Natalia going away and not knowing for how long. Alejandro was also leaving me; without him close by, I felt like the tiny owls in the nest the day after the April hurricane: abandoned.

I didn't notice it when Orlando placed his arm around my shoulders, but by the expression on Natalia's, Alejandro's, and Domingo's faces, I felt something was wrong and that perhaps Señor or Señora Sarmiento had seen Natalia on deck. I turned around to see their party, but they were talking to the Barrazas; only Catalina was looking in my direction with astonishment. I signaled them with my face, "*What is going on?*" But Alejandro only smiled at me while Domingo winked. Natalia was stunned; I signaled her, but she didn't respond. I looked the other way, but Señor and Señora Villanueva were busy overseeing their grandchildren and paying attention to their beloved daughter's departure. Meanwhile, Doña Ursula was looking in my direction with severe seriousness.

The ship's horn announced the departure, and my heart shrank with melancholy at the loss of so many people dear to me. I bit my lip to suppress my sobs because I didn't want Natalia to see me crying.

"Don't worry … Domingo will take good care of her," Orlando said in a low voice.

"But I am going to miss her a lot," I replied drowning in my desolation. "I don't even know when I will see her again."

It was when he placed his head on mine that I became conscious that Orlando Sarmiento was holding me in public. My back became stiff in an instant, and then I looked at the party of three aboard that boat; they were pleased by the scene, and Natalia was smiling in a rascally way. My eyes widened in disbelief and nervousness and confusion.

"I miss you, Maximiana," he said in a murmur; "I miss you a lot."

"Please take your arm off my shoulder; everyone is looking—"

"I don't care," Orlando replied sharply.

"But I do. I don't want any more problems with Señora Leonora, Catalina, your steady girlfriend, and the rest of your friends. Seriously, put a distance between us."

"Virginia is not my steady girlfriend anymore. I broke up with her on the day of the dance … I miss you … I have come by the house where you live several times, but I don't dare call on you."

I kept silent when I felt the warm air of his words on my ear, "*Secretly they meet at night, like owls in disguise* … forgive me, Maximiana."

I hadn't thought of that poem in a long time. I turned, and his face came the closest it had been to mine in months. His eyes were still as quiet and empty as before; he had not changed … no he had not changed at all. I said nothing.

What can I say to the person who has harmed me the most in life and who took almost six months to realize my value as a person deserving respect in public and before others?

Natalia would've given her finger to know what he was saying to my ear. Alejandro looked pleased, Domingo excited. Perhaps it had been their idea to convince Orlando to talk to me about this. Apparently, I knew their youngest brother better than they did; I knew I could not trust him; I had seen how he would change his mind in an instant and smile at those who took pleasure in hurting me if he considered their approval necessary for his *own* benefit. He could display signs of deep affection to those who humiliated me; and he would never bother to explain his actions to me, let alone apologize.

The ship started to move, and as an excuse to move away from Orlando's embrace, I walked with it as it moved on the water as far as I could and then stood at the edge of the pier, following with my eyes as it took my sister away until it appeared to me like a tiny cigar in the distance. When I turned to look at Señora Villanueva, they were getting ready to leave. Orlando stood motionless where I had left him.

"I am going home now, Orlando. Good-bye," I said, and accelerating my steps to avoid any response, I reached the Villanuevas. I took baby Martha in my arms and climbed into the carriage to return to the Pattersons' house.

"You must dearly love your friends to cry for them this way," Doña Ursula said in a tone of voice that made me feel uncomfortable.

"Yes, especially Alejandro; he is like a brother to me," I replied, taking a deep breath to conceal my distress for Natalia's departure, Alejandro's going away for almost six months, and Orlando Sarmiento's sudden demonstration of public affection. All of a sudden, I was glad Andrés had not come to the pier that morning; I could not have taken another stroke of distress, explaining the presence of a former boyfriend to my current one.

That evening I read my letters from El Roble over and over again. I wanted to feel close to home somehow, and I didn't have any other way. Andrés came to my window; it became his custom to avoid calling on the front door for me too often. He saw my sadness and gave me space to be in private. I told him everything had gone well, and Natalia had sailed off with Domingo and Alejandro without any incident. But I was too sad to talk about it; he said he would call on me later in the week and passed me a coconut candy through the iron bars.

"She will be back in no time; you will see," he said with nonchalance. "Time flies."

"I know, but still …"

"Yes, I know …" Andrés let go of the bars and passed his hand between them to reach mine. He pulled it out and kissed it.

"I will see you on Friday."

I nodded and he left. I walked to my drawer to retrieve the letters. I lay on my stomach on the soft bed to reread Otilia's because it was my favorite one of all.

13 August 1908
El Roble Sinaloa

Dear Maximiana

By the time you read this letter the news of Natalia's marriage will have reached you I am very happy for my sister but heartbroken as you because she is going so far away we don't even understand where it is we just know it is in the United States many kilometers away and that they will take a boat and then a train to get to that place Natalia is very happy and for that reason I am happy for her

How are you little sister Alejandro told us all about your job as a teacher in that house he said you are very good at your job and that the Señor and Señora talk wonders about you everywhere and that the children love you I am not surprised about it everybody loves you Maxi

I miss you A LOT we all miss you A LOT Raimunda had a baby girl she named her María Magdalena you have to see that precious little baby Maxi she is incredibly cute and her head is full of brown curls and has a button little nose like Alejandro Raimunda has been coming to class everyday and we all including me fight over who is going to hold Marimag that is the nickname we gave her I don't know if Natalia remembered to tell you but Raimunda chose me as the godmother and Alejandro as the godfather before I forget I have to tell you that Daniel Gutierrez has fallen madly in love with Tomasa Valencia! She started coming to our school when they started dating I never thought I would see the day of seeing Daniel acting serious you have to see him Maxi he is very sweet and considerate with Tomasa he walks her home from class everyday and decided to learn to play the guitar

  Now that Natalia is gone I am the only teacher in the school but Daniel helps me out and Raimunda you have no idea how much I enjoy my work as a teacher Maxi I look forward the time when our class will start but I have to give you the greatest news of all about the school Alejandro convinced his father to build us a classroom! We will have our very own classroom soon and Alejandro promised to send us the bell before leaving on the trip ay Maxi I hope that when you come to visit our classroom is finished we call it school though not a classroom because that is what it will be we even thought of a name for it BENITO JUAREZ PRIMARY SCHOOL what do you think

  I like it

I put the letter down for a second to rest my eyes and made a note to myself to send a book on punctuation to Otilia because reading without commas, periods, and question marks gave me headaches. I continued reading.

  I like it and hopefully as time goes by we will be able to build another classroom to separate children by ages when are you coming Maximiana did you like the treats Mamá made just for you Lucia and Rosaura send you kisses and hugs but they will also write a letter for you do you see how good everyone is writing now please write back to us at the first chance and hug Natalia very hard before she leaves

  I love you little sister and I miss you don't forget that I am very very very proud of you

truly yours

Otilia Valdez Amaya

21

It had been too good to last. When I saw Señora Leonora Sarmiento, Señora Barraza, and Señora Del Rincon Valle sitting in the Pattersons' parlor room drinking tea with Señora Lorenza Villanueva, I knew my days at the Patterson house were coming to an end, especially when Señora Lorenza frowned when she saw me walk by on my way to the house's library. Quietly I went into the library and tried to read, but my hands were shaking in fear. I prayed that Señora Villanueva would not listen to the women and their ill intentions towards me, but I was not that fortunate. When her guests left, Señora Lorenza called Doña Ursula, who told me to go into the parlor.

"I want you to collect your belongings, bring them over to have them checked to make sure you are not taking anything that doesn't belong to you, and then leave. I don't want you in my daughter's house," Señora Lorenza said in an angry voice. "And don't say a word because I don't want to hear you."

I turned to Doña Ursula, who ignored my begging eyes.

Carolina encountered me on my way out and asked where I was going. I told her that I needed to go to El Roble, and she hugged me, asking when I was coming back. I was too heartbroken to answer. I brought my suitcase and a bundle with my things in it to the parlor and Señora Villanueva checked everything with Doña Ursula. Then she paid me for the days of the month I had worked since Señor and Señora Patterson had left and pointed me to the street. Night was falling, but I walked rapidly to Agatha's apartment. She wasn't there, so I sat on her doorstep inside the building.

Andrés' house was too far away to walk at this time of the night, and there was no way I would knock on the Sarmientos' door looking for Josefina, who was the only other person I knew with family in the city. As the hours passed and Agatha didn't show up at her door, I started debating if I should go to Señora Ruiz's pension, but it was too dark and dangerous to walk carrying my suitcase and bundle. At least I was inside a building and not on the street. I checked to see if the Cactus apartment was open, but the door was locked.

My heart throbbed with misery at finding myself empty-handed, sitting on a doorstep. I had daydreamed for a long time to complete my year working as a teacher for the Pattersons and then take the admissions exam for the National University of México, hoping that a sponsorship might be offered to me. On the other hand, I could never escape the harassment of those women throughout Mazatlán. My mind raced, trying to find a solution, but nothing came. Oh, how I missed Alejandro, too far away to do anything to help me.

Still the hours were fading, and I needed to use the washroom. I debated if I should knock on the door of one of the apartments on the floor below, but it was probably midnight by now. I put my bundle as a pillow, wrapped myself in my white shawl, and curled on the floor, trying not to think of my physical needs and, after much struggle, fell asleep.

It was probably the way I was dressed that convinced the woman who lived at the end of the hall to wake me up in the early hours of the morning. She asked if I was waiting for Señorita Agatha, and I said that I had tried to surprise her but I was the one surprised by her absence. She offered her help, and I happily took it, eagerly because my bladder was about to explode. I asked if I could leave my things at her apartment while I looked for a place to stay until Agatha's return, and she agreed, not without offering a cup of coffee and sweet bread.

Her name was Bernardina Solorzano, a childless widow who had lived in that building for years and supported herself as a seamstress. Later I found out she had sewn some of Natalia's pieces to go to Boston, so when I informed her that Natalia was, in fact, my sister she was more than pleased and felt good in having come to my aid.

As soon as I freshened up, I took the street to find Andrés's house. His family owned a very nice building across the street from the second square in the city. They used the first floor for the family business and lived on the second. It was around nine o'clock when I arrived and asked to speak with Andrés. Eduardo Randal was at the front office and called Andrés from the back; he was getting ready to go to the German School.

"Good morning, Maximiana." He greeted me with surprise and asked me to come into Eduardo's office.

"I need to speak to you in private," I replied discreetly. "It is very important, Andrés."

He told Eduardo he needed to go out for a minute, and we crossed the street to the Hidalgo Square.

"What's wrong?" Andrés asked me, concerned, for he could tell by the expression on my face that something very bad had happened.

I hid my dismay and replied, "Señora Villanueva asked me to leave the Pattersons' house. Señora Leonora and her lady friends visited her yesterday."

Andrés shook his head. "Where did you sleep?" he asked with a long look of concern.

"I walked to Agatha's apartment, but she wasn't there—"

"No, she is in Escuinapa right now, visiting her family; she will be back next week … but where did you sleep?"

"On her doorstep," I answered in the lowest possible voice. "I wanted to look for you, but my suitcase and bundle of things were too heavy, and the night was already falling when she asked me to leave the house … Agatha's apartment was the closest one."

"And where are your things now?"

"Señora Bernardina Solorzano, who rents at the end of the hall, saw me this morning sleeping on the floor, woke me, and offered her help."

"I'm glad to hear that she helped you out," Andrés said holding my hands. "I have the keys to the Cactus apartment. Go back there, take your things in, and at the first opportunity, I will come over ... have you eaten?"

"Yes, Señora Bernardina gave me breakfast, and I have money saved ... don't worry about it. I will stop at the Pino Suarez Market to buy some food. Thank you."

"Hey ... how are you?" he asked, holding my chin.

"Just imagine ...," My eyes filled with tears. He placed his forehead on mine as he usually did when he wanted to let me know he was *with me*.

"We will fix it." He looked around and in a flash planted a sweet kiss on my lips. "I have to go back to work now, but I will see you later today ..." I nodded and crossed the street with him. He entered his house to get the keys, and I walked east towards the Pino Suarez Market with the saving key in my side pocket.

When Andrés knocked at the apartment door, I was already getting ready to eat dinner. I was glad Señora Bernardina had given me wood and matches to light the wood stove in the kitchen. The autumn winds were arriving in Mazatlán by the middle of September, so preparing a warm vegetable soup sounded like a good idea.

"Come on in and have a bowl of soup with me," I said to Andrés, flooded with happiness to see him. He sat at the table and started to talk.

"We thought of an idea for you. Paula can find you a place at the newspaper."

"In the *Afternoon Mail*?" I asked, surprised and not able to guess what my job duties could be in a newspaper office.

"Yes, Paula can get you a job at the front desk, receiving people who walk into the office, run errands, and do odd jobs like that, and eventually, you could start publishing those stories that you write so well."

"My stories? Don't be silly," I said with a flattered laughter. "Those stories are just for fun among us."

"They are actually very good, Maximiana; you just need to polish them a bit. Paula is a very good editor, and she is willing to help you."

"What is an editor?"

"Someone who revises your work and helps you make it better."

"Oh … that sounds good … but can she get me the job as a receptionist at the newspaper for sure?"

"She talked to them this afternoon; the director is a very good friend of hers … and a secret member of the Cactus. You will start tomorrow at eight; you will work from eight to one, and you must return from three to five. Teodoro is looking into finding you also a part-time job as an evening tutor with another family, once a week. That way your teaching will not stop."

I couldn't believe my ears. "Thank you so much, Andrés. You have no idea how much I appreciate your help and your sister's and well … also Teodoro's."

"We will also see among members if you can stay here permanently."

"I will pay rent, Andrés," I replied. "I would like to stay here, especially because Agatha is next door and the lady at the end of the hall is really sweet. If not, I will try to find a place of my own … even if it is only a room with a kitchen; I don't want to board in a house anymore."

"Paying rent is not the problem; we are more concerned that our meetings could be blamed on you at *your* place."

"I don't mind the risk … really."

"But I do," he said with a look of concern.

"How long do you think it will take you all to decide? I need to find a place to live if I am not going to stay here."

"Soon, it won't take long. But in the meantime, don't worry about it. We won't throw you out on the street as certain devoted *Catholic* ladies have done to you," he said, shaking his head in amused sarcasm. "I don't mean to make a joke … but those attitudes are exactly what we need to change around here, Max … all those appearances that keep this country in the hole it is right now."

"It was very humiliating when Señora Lorenza and Doña Ursula went through my belongings … as if I were a thief … and the way she did not allow me to defend myself … She listened to those women because they are rich and disregarded me because I am poor," I said with disappointment. "I don't understand Doña Ursula; she kept quiet and did not explain to Señora Villanueva that those women had talked to Señora Patterson before and she had ignored them completely. All this time I felt Doña Ursula was honest and sincere with me."

"She probably didn't want to risk her job."

"If Doña Ursula thought that by telling the truth she was risking her job, she thought wrong. Señora Patterson acted different, though. But … enough … I'd rather not talk about it anymore …," I said pensively. "I'd rather look to the future and the new opportunity in front of me."

"The soup is good; I like it," Andrés said, smiling.

"Do you want me to brew some coffee? I bought sweet bread at the market this morning."

Andrés accepted, and we sat on the sofa to enjoy the warm drink.

"Do I go to the newspaper office tomorrow then?"

"No, go to my house, and Paula will take you along with her."

"I will do that … it is chilly at night now. Señora Bernardina offered me a blanket and pillow …"

"But where are you going to sleep? There is no bed here …" He looked around.

"I'll figure it out; trust me … after spending the night on a doorstep, everything is possible!" I replied, trying to keep positive.

"I'm sorry this happened to you, Maximiana; it is very unfair."

Andrés held my hands.

"You know? Mamá always says that a thing happens for a reason, so there has to be a good reason for this to be happening … do you have a library at home because my access to books has been cut now."

"We don't have a Sarmiento or Patterson library, but we have some books … and members of the Cactus have access to them so don't even worry about being able to borrow them."

"Good."

"I should get going now; you have to get up early," Andrés said, rising from his seat. "I will be back tomorrow, and hopefully, we will know by then if you can stay here … and I will bring you a book to read."

"Great! At what time are you coming?" I asked, embracing his waist.

He smiled, "At any time you want me to come."

"You know my schedule; come on the first opportunity … and thank you, Andrés."

"Don't thank me … more than anything … I am your friend."

"Yes and I thank you for that with all of my heart." I hugged his waist tighter, pressing the side of my face to his chest. He hugged me back with a quiet tenderness, but the beating of his heart accelerated.

"Do you have feelings for me?" he asked.

"Yes," I assented without explaining more.

My experience with romance had been a disaster so far, and risking my friendship with Andrés Randal was out of the question. And even though I had intimate moments with him—instances of kisses and hugs—and I knew that he was attracted to me and I to him, I firmly believed our relationship should go no farther than that.

"But … I think we should continue being friends and not risk losing our friendship with … something else …," I said, hesitating.

His arms loosened up.

"You do not think being with me is worth the risk?" he unexpectedly asked.

"You are worth it … of course you are worth the risk, Andrés, but … things can suddenly turn around in a very bad way, and it wasn't long ago when something really bad happened to me … I will tell you about it … but not today—"

"You're right … I better go now because you must be tired from last night and today," he said, letting go of my body and moving towards the door.

"Can we talk about this tomorrow? Tomorrow evening …"

"Yes … we can do that. Good night," he said, kissing my hand.

"Thank you, Andrés, a thousand times *thank you*," I said, holding his face in my hands. His lips that had become so familiar to me drew a tiny smile, but his eyes penetrated mine, telling me that he was not happy and my attitude towards him bothered him. And that worried me.

"I will be counting the hours to see you again tomorrow," I said and, risking it all, pulled his face to mine and gave him a kiss.

He took my hands from his face and crossed them behind my back in an embrace that left me open and exposed in his arms. He planted an ardent kiss on my mouth to finally whisper again, "Good night." Andrés closed the door behind him, leaving me in a state of awe because I realized I had still many new emotions to feel and enjoy that I had never experienced with Orlando Sarmiento, just as Alejandro had told me that day at my roble tree. I took my hand to my bosom to feel the throbbing of my heart, pumping with an emotion both familiar yet very different from anything I had felt before.

The *Afternoon Mail*'s office was a pleasant place to work. My first day as receptionist went smoothly; I ran a couple of errands and was introduced, for the first time in my life, to a machine called a typewriter. Paula explained how to use it, and to be honest, punching those buttons entertained me like a child with a new toy. The company that ran the newspaper was an editorial house and bookstore; it also printed books, magazines, and pamphlets. I couldn't believe my good fortune when I saw the quantity of books they had at the bookstore and realized I could read the newspaper for free everyday if I wanted to. I, thus, began learning about the daily events happening around the world, made possible through reading the *Afternoon Mail* newspaper.

The members of the Cactus agreed that I could stay at the apartment. It was a one-bedroom flat with a tiny cooking area and a washroom. It contained several chairs and a table but nothing else. They thought my renting the room would give them better cover because their meetings could be justified as visits also to Maximiana Valdez and not only to Agatha Santos. Members of the Cactus sympathized with my situation and brought pieces of furniture and pots and dishes for the kitchen. I bought fabric to make myself a pillow and linens, and Señora Bernardina stitched them for me. I also bought two blankets, for the fall winds were turning colder as the days went by.

Teodoro de la Vega found me a job as a tutor to a fourteen-year-old girl named Adriana Peraza. I met with her twice a week to help her out with her studies, but she surpassed me in her knowledge; she was very smart and articulate, funny and utterly original. I think she liked my company more than anything, and she enjoyed teaching *me* instead of my teaching *her*. She concealed that detail from her parents, and eventually our meetings became times for exchanging ideas and dreams.

Adriana liked to write short stories, but those she kept secret from others. Her stories described the crude realities of life and criticized the conservative people around her. She knew they would be too disturbing among her circle of family friends, so she hoped to grow up and move away in order to publish them.

"I will move to México City, and my stories will be published under a pseudonym," she announced to me.

"That is a good idea," I told her. "Your stories are very realistic …"

"Yes … do you want to see my drawings?"

"Oh, yes …"

She was an amazing artist. She went beyond depicting just physical features of people and let the inner feelings show in their faces. Even though she and I had flipped the tutoring arrangement, her parents were pleased with my work. They sensed that I liked Adriana and she enjoyed me; no other tutor had been able to keep up with her before. Her teachers had been intimidated by her questions and inquiries where I met her challenges. Whenever she had a question, I invited her to find the answer together. She really liked that; she refused to call me "teacher" and asked me to call her by her first name, no "Señorita" attached to it. I definitely agreed.

22

Josefina was very happy to know I now had a place of my own. It took a lot of creativity to make her aware of where to find me after I moved out of the Pattersons' house. Fortunately, Jose Manuel, the flirty tejuino vendor, agreed to take her a note from me to the Sarmiento house. She was very excited to visit me and endlessly talked about all the pieces of gossip going on in the Sarmiento house and surroundings during the last year. She asked me if she could travel with me to El Roble on my next trip because she really wanted to meet Raimunda's baby.

"Are you going to El Roble for the Day of the Dead?" she asked, dunking the sweet bread in the coffee I served her.

"No, because I want to spend Christmas with my family, and if I go on November 2, then I cannot also travel the following month. It is expensive, and I don't want to miss days of work. I would rather wait. Besides, they have received news from me because I sent them word when I heard Natalia arrived safe and sound in Boston, right after you told me," I replied.

"It is a good thing the Sarmientos spend the Christmas holiday in El Roble because then we get a chance to take some time off …"

"Well then make the arrangements to go with me. I can hardly wait to go back; it will be six months in December since I left. I am more than ready; it is so cold here!" I shivered, wrapping myself in my warm white shawl.

"Maximiana … I have to tell you something."

"Tell me then," I giggled.

"Señorito Orlando asked me about you … he wants to know where you live."

"Don't tell him," I replied sharply.

"I didn't but … you know something? He is now courting Maricela Inzunza."

"Gustavo Inzunza's sister?" I asked, attempting to hide my shock.

"Yes … he is—*or was*—one of Señorito Domingo's friends, but now he is always at the house because he hangs out with Señorito Orlando … they go to the German School together."

"Gustavo Inzunza tried to abuse me in El Roble … the day after the April hurricane …"

Josefina took her hand to her mouth. "Maximiana … what did he do to you?"

"Nothing … he couldn't do anything because I defended myself … and Alejandro beat him up with Domingo's help," I replied with a mixture of pride and sadness.

"Does Señorito Orlando know about it?" she asked, frowning.

"Of course he does. He was there when it happened … well … he was not present at the time of the attack, but he saw my bleeding mouth, pulled out hair, lost sandal, and ripped blouse and skirt … he saw me right after it happened, and I was shaking in fear."

"He didn't do anything?" she asked, still upset by my description of his attitude.

"No … of course not … you said it yourself that day at the square … remember? You said that there was something about him that you didn't trust … well … you were right." I lowered my eyes. "He never took me seriously, and his only intention towards me was … you know *what* … and apparently he continues pursuing the same idea. That is why he wants to know where I live … he still hopes to get his way. That is the only thing he cares about—*to get his way*."

"Maximiana ... Raimunda and I worried about you when you were visiting him at night ..."

"Nothing beyond kisses and hugs happened. I swear to God," I replied.

"Really?"

"I swear to God," I confirmed.

"And we thought that for a Sarmiento boy or any other rich boy to take a servant girl for anything other than his pleasure was impossible," she sighed.

"I used to think the same way, too. But then I discovered people like Alejandro and Domingo who don't think like that ..."

"Alejandro, yes. Domingo? Don't make me laugh!" she exclaimed.

"He is not as bad as he acts sometimes ... I really like him now."

Her eyes expanded because she had heard me insult Domingo Sarmiento several times in a row without taking a break to breathe.

"You know what would kill Señor Joaquín? If Domingo likes a girl poorer than Señorita Catalina! You had to hear the arguments about it when Señorito Domingo refused to go steady with her again. The man wanted to tie his son and drag him up to the Barraza mansion, but Domingo wouldn't go for it."

Well ... Señor Joaquín is in trouble then.

"Have you seen Señorito Orlando lately?"

"No, not lately ... fortunately," I answered.

"Perhaps he wants to know where you live to tell Señorito Gustavo."

"I don't know, but it could be. He does whatever it takes to be well liked by his friends ... but I am glad you told me; I will ask Eduardo and Andrés to help me put a bar on my door."

"Yes ... you should, just to be on the safe side."

That evening, I explained to Andrés that I needed a bar for my door. He wanted to know if something had happened for me to be so nervous, and I replied that Josefina had visited and told me Orlando was trying to find where I lived. His face hardened with the news. I also explained that he was now very good friends with Gustavo Inzunza and that I feared he was searching that information for his friend.

"I am afraid of Gustavo … that day at the warehouse, I was lucky that I had the bucket, but here … I am more vulnerable."

Andrés stood up and walked to the window.

"It is true; I have seen them together at the German School. Orlando is now visiting Gustavo's sister."

"Yes, Josefina told me that also."

"Did you ask her?" Andrés questioned with an irritated tone.

"Of course not. She told me without asking."

Without turning from the window, he said, "Tell me what happened between you and Orlando Sarmiento."

I hesitated for a moment, "I first met him in the hacienda's library days after I began working for his family; he offered me a book to learn to read and write … he became my friend first and invited me to come into his bedroom at night to teach me about different things in books …" Andrés held the iron bars on the window. "I fell in love with him when I was fourteen and believed that he loved me, too. I believed that he was my true friend and that we would be together forever. How silly I was, yes?"

"And then what happened?" he asked in a murmur.

"I came here for the summer, still working for his family, and he wanted me to be with him *the other way*, but I was smart enough not to accept it, even when he stopped talking to me for weeks or his treatment became cold and distant and hurt my feelings deeply … in December he visited El Roble and … he was more or less fine with me, but he had an attitude that hurt me. However, I didn't want to let him go … I … I was willing to put up with everything for him."

"Did it happen in December?"

"What? The breakup?"

He nodded.

"No. He returned to El Roble during Holy Week and told me to stay away from him because Virginia was there and he didn't want to ruin his relationship with her because of me." I started to cry in silence. "Then Virginia, Catalina, and their friends began using me as their entertainment … and he laughed with them and helped them out."

"How did he help them out?" he asked, visibly bothered by my narration.

"Just to give you an example … once I walked out of their room because they were insulting me, and I encountered him in the back hallway … he ordered me to go back to the bedroom where they were … and he stood at the window as they continued to mock me … I remember he was laughing with them."

Andrés left the window and knelt in front of me, cleaning the tears off my face with his fingers.

"Everything they did was very stupid, Maximiana … don't even take it seriously."

"It is easy for you to say it … but you must live it in order to understand how it feels."

"Yes …" Andrés shook his head. "Those women have nothing else in their heads but hypocrisy, gossip, and schemes to get a beau and marry him … they are empty-headed … don't take any of their actions seriously."

"Their actions bothered me Andrés, but *his* actions *hurt* me."

"Does it hurt you that he is now visiting Gustavo's sister?" He sat on the floor looking directly at me.

"It hurt me that he is friends with Gustavo Inzunza after what he did to me … it hurts me that he is trying to find my address to give it to Gustavo."

"Why?"

It took me a moment of reflection to answer. "Perhaps … in order to love again without being afraid of betrayal, I hoped Orlando would recognize one day that my feelings counted as much as his … and that all those feeling inside of me for *him* were worth something."

"Do you still love him?" he asked.

"No. But thinking about that part of my life still hurts, and I cannot avoid it," I sighed, the red in my eyes clearing up.

"Do you love *me*?"

"I do."

"But do you *trust* me?"

"I don't know," I spoke softly while trembling inside from fear that my sincerity would push him away from me.

"The first time I saw you at the Machado Square, I knew I had to talk to you and came up with the silly question of looking for the Central Hotel … do you remember that?"

"Yes," I gasped, remembering the scene.

"Then I saw you at the hacienda in El Roble. You looked very different from anybody I had ever met; you were quiet yet when I talked to you … you looked directly into my eyes, not afraid of anything. Then Alejandro told me to stay away from you because Orlando liked you … and I could understand why."

He continued, "Once here, when I started teaching you mathematics, I realized that I wanted to be close to you all the time … and when Orlando Sarmiento gets close to you—indirectly—I wish to push him away from you … he acts in a strange way, yes? He tries to be my friend, as if to show me that he doesn't care I take you out on Sundays or we go together to dances. I cannot ignore such obvious intrusions."

"He is not pretending … he *doesn't* care, his only interest towards me is to get his way. That is all."

"Has he ever looked for you?"

"Yes … he did once at the square, then he came to the house and wanted me to meet secretly with him, but I refused. Then on the day Natalia, Alejandro, and Domingo left, he came to stand next to me and told me that he missed me … and that he had broken up with Virginia, but I dismissed him and moved away from him. That was the last time I saw or heard from Orlando until today, when Josefina told me about his inquiries."

"He has been visiting Maricela Inzunza since the beginning of September … it has been over a month," he replied.

"I am not surprised. But now … I need a bar put on my door. I don't want Gustavo Inzunza to come and visit."

"Or Orlando Sarmiento, yes?"

"*Or* Orlando Sarmiento. Can you do it tomorrow, perhaps?"

"I can. Tonight you should place a chair against the door as an extra support ... and tell Agatha and Señora Solorzano about the situation."

"I will ... even though I don't like to talk about it. But, Andrés, I am glad I talked to you about this."

"Yes, thank you, Maximiana. I can see you still hurt," he replied, touched by my revelations. "I understand you, and although I can't imagine ever hurting you, I may sometime do so without knowing. But I want you to believe that your feelings mean a lot to me, your feelings *for me* mean the world to me."

I rested my head on the chair and closed my eyes. Andrés Randal's words sounded sincere, and I needed so much to believe him.

"Maximiana ... do you want to go and see a movie with me tomorrow night? They are showing a film at the Rubio Theater."

I turned to him, smiling. "I would love to! Of course I do! At what time shall I be ready?"

"We will go from here after I install the bar on your door."

"Oh, what fun! I have never seen a film before."

"That is what I thought ..."

He rose from the floor, and I followed him to the door. He kissed me on the cheek and smiled with tenderness.

"I love you, Maximiana."

"I love you, too," I replied without thinking and forgetting that I had promised myself never to tell a boy those words again.

Andrés' beautiful smile spread on his face, showing his perfect white teeth, and he gave me one of his hugs that raised me from the floor. He bit his lower lip and with eyes half opened whispered to my ear, "Since I met you, I haven't stopped thinking about you for a minute, Maximiana Valdez. Your confident quietness has me crazy for you."

A profound sigh escaped my chest, and a sweet illusion settled in my heart once again. Then I realized that I, indeed, was a quiet person now and that my days of non-stop talking were fading away along with my interest in getting an apology from Orlando Sarmiento.

❦   ❦   ❦

The first telegraph arrived from the city of Los Mochis, and then a second one from the state capital city of Caliacán: An unusually powerful hurricane was heading to Mazatlán and the surrounding region. I was fortunate enough to work at the newspaper when the news came and the corner announcers took to the streets, screaming to let the people know a hurricane would hit us within hours. My heart went out to El Roble, thinking about my family, but I knew they would seek refuge at church. I just hoped they would get the news in time.

Our employer dismissed us early from work, and on my way home, I stopped by the grocery store to buy food; there was no way of knowing if there was going to be anything left the next day.

As soon as I got home, I informed Señora Solorzano of the news; I could find Agatha nowhere. Señora Solorzano said that she was waiting for her nephew to come and get her as they always did when a storm hit the city; she was going to spend the next few days at the edge of town with her family. She was worried about me because, apparently, I would be the only one left on the entire floor, but I assured her that Agatha would be coming at any moment now. I helped her out to the street when the wind was blowing and the sky was turning a horrible gray. I looked at both sides of the sidewalk, hoping to see Agatha's familiar face, but she was not there. Once Señora Solorzano took off, I went back upstairs to prepare as best I could.

I moved my bed away from the window, afraid that the wind might blow it open and the rain would drench my bed. I put everything on top of chairs and the table to keep them off the floor in case the rain poured in. Then I made sure the oil lamp had enough oil. Even though we had electricity in the building, it would be a miracle if it still worked the next morning. I placed the wood on top of the stove and the matches away from any risk of getting wet. Finally, I stored all of the food safely in the cupboard.

Agatha, where are you?

It was a blessing that my apartment was on the second floor because I had heard stories of the winds getting so strong that the waves jumped the jetty and the sea entered the city. Mazatlán lies several feet below sea level, so if the waters entered the city, they would remain for some time. I looked down from my window, but the street stretched out, deserted, as the wind started to pick up. Around five o'clock, the edge of the hurricane entered Mazatlán. I said a prayer to God to protect everyone that the storm might reach. Then I closed the windows in the bedroom but left one window on the side of the living room open, remembering the April storm and the "air needs to circulate" or the "roof might blow off."

I jumped when I heard the knocking on the door. I ran to the eye-hole and saw Agatha on the other side. I opened the door quickly to let her in. She was soaking wet because she had been painting on the north side of the beach, and by the time she knew to get home, there was no carriage to bring her back so she had had to run. Her lips were purple from the cold. I helped her out of her clothes and covered her with my blanket while I put fire on the stove to heat water for coffee.

"Max … go to my apartment and bring me dry clothes; I am freezing," Agatha said with chattering teeth. I reached the key from her dress pocket and took her wet clothes with me to hang them in her living room to dry. I grabbed more blankets and pillows from Agatha's apartment and took them with me; it was going to be a long night.

"Perhaps we should go to your apartment, Agatha," I said when I returned.

"There is more room here, Max; my paintings are all over the place …"

"All the windows are closed, but you should leave at least one open," I suggested.

Once she finished dressing and had put on warm socks, we walked to her apartment to open the little kitchen window. As we undid the latch, the wind smashed the window against the wall, and the glass broke into tiny pieces. Forcing it against the wind, we closed the frame again. With the hole in the window, air was going to circulate, no matter what.

Back at my place, we listened to the fury outside. The sound of the ferocious wind invoked images of the storm clearing everything in its path. Very soon the electricity went off, and we were left in the dark. The glass on my windows vibrated, and I felt they would fly at us at any minute; we decided to stay away from them as far as possible, but curiosity was too strong. I walked to the window and saw the dark gray clouds swirling away in the sky and the rain falling in torrents. The trees outside the apartment complex had lost a lot of branches. Earth seemed engaged in a struggle with the storm, fighting to keep hold of her trees. The lamp post that had stood on our corner was not so lucky. However, nothing terrorized me more than to see the seawater passing through the street, as a river in its bed.

"Agatha … the sea is entering the city," I told her in disbelief.

"Those are waves jumping the jetty because of the wind but nothing more … don't worry about it," she replied calmly. "Do you mind if I smoke a cigarette?"

"Just open the door and exhale the smoke out of it." Smoke bothered me a lot.

Agatha opened the door and realized the window at the end of the hall had a tree through it and the wind was blowing with strength. Already, a pool of water had formed in the hallway and was expanding to the stairs. She threw away the cigarette and asked me to quickly put towels at the doorstep to prevent the water from coming in.

"Señora Solorzano's flat is going to flood … when did that tree smash the window … I didn't hear it, did you?" I asked, consternated.

"There is so much noise outside that it is hard to say … let's put some towels under her door as well …," she replied while grabbing all the clothes she could to stop the water from coming into the apartments. My feet were already wet.

"We are going to catch a cold from this; the water is freezing," I said, shivering.

"I know … I hope my family is all right in Escuinapa," Agatha said.

"In El Roble, people take refuge in church, but to tell you the truth, I have never heard the wind blow with such force."

"Neither have I … it has been two hours already, and there is no sign of the eye yet."

"What is that noise?" I asked when I heard a sound of scraping.

"It is the roof! The roof is moving!" Agatha screamed.

The roof was constructed of tiles and wood trunks, and it was making a screeching sound as if fingers of the wind were scratching at the sides, trying to tear it off. Up and down, up and down, it moved with each gust of wind.

"Quick! Help me open all the windows and the door, the air must circulate more, or the roof is going to blow off!" I replied.

"We need to find a way to keep them open … tie them with something! Come and hold them. I have a rope at my place!" Agatha said.

She ran to bring the rope while the storm pelted me, hitting my skin like tiny knives. We tied the windows open, holding one to another, but the remedy was getting us wetter and colder.

"There is no one downstairs. If the roof blows off, Maximiana … we need to think what to do," Agatha said with her eyes wide open. "And the water is probably up to our knees in the street by now …"

"We cannot take to the street. We have to stay here, and if the roof blows off, we will go downstairs … to the hallway downstairs …"

"But the water is coming in, I tell you!"

We got out of the apartment, and from the top of the stairs, we saw the water already reaching the third step.

"Damn it!" Agatha screamed.

"Let's keep calm … the roof will not blow off … it is not making the noise anymore, you see?"

"Where is Eduardo when I need him the most!?" Agatha exclaimed, losing her patience.

"What can *he* possibly do that we can't, Agatha? We just have to keep calm … look … I am going to drink more coffee before the fire dies off … do you want some bread?"

"Yes and a cigarette … no problem with the circulation of air now!"

Stuck in such dilemma, we laughed through our clattering teeth. And then, calmness outside settled upon us.

"It is the eye," Agatha said.

We walked to the window and saw the sad desolation outside. We signaled to our neighbors in front so they knew we were fine.

"We should go downstairs to the street to see what's going on," Agatha suggested.

The water on the first floor reached up to our knees and was freezing. We were only able to get out onto the sidewalk because the cold water reached mid-thigh. Many people looked through the windows; some men stood at the doors. Everyone seemed as if he or she did not know what to do, debating whether to leave or go back inside.

Some trees had fallen and lay across the street, a carriage was turned over, and in the distance, I could see roofs dotted with gaps where the tiles had been blown away.

"We should go inside before it starts again," Agatha said, chattering her teeth.

"Yes. The wind is starting," I answered, shaking from the coldness.

The apartment was freezing, and the open windows had completely blown out the fire in the stove. I took out all of the blankets I had, and we wrapped ourselves in them like tamales and thought that perhaps we should go to Agatha's place, but Agatha refused to step in the water again.

"Maximiana! Agatha!" We heard Eduardo Randal's familiar voice outside the door.

"Come on in!" I screamed. "It is open!"

"Are you girls okay? I came as soon as Father allowed. I tried to get here earlier, but the storm started, and I had to return home … the seawater is in," he said once he was inside, after hugging us both.

"We are fine … but the roof was jumping, and we feared it was going to blow off," I answered.

"You look cold," Eduardo said to both of us. "Let's close the windows, and I will get the stove started …"

Guiding himself with an oil lamp, Eduardo made a fire in the stove while Agatha and I tried to warm ourselves on the bed. He brought us hot coffee, but after only three sips, Agatha set her cup down and immediately fell asleep. Outside the sound of the wind's appetite could be heard. Helplessly confined to the apartment, we could only hope for the best and that the roof would sustain the force of the gale. Eduardo sat next to Agatha and wrapped himself with part of her blanket. I was glad that he had come.

"Mother didn't want me to come, but they couldn't stop me …," he said, trying to make conversation.

"Ah, your poor mother, Eduardo … I am glad you came, but your family must be worried … how did you get here?"

"I came on a horse … then I let it go. But we are safe …"

"But the horse is out there in the hurricane right now …"

"No … it probably went back to its corral already … now … don't worry about it."

"The roof is moving," I said, looking up. "It may fall on us."

"It won't happen …," he sighed.

"This has lasted too long …"

"Yes … Agatha is completely asleep," Eduardo said, smiling.

"Lucky Agatha, nothing disturbs her …" I started feeling shivers in my body.

"Are you still cold?"

"I feel shivers … but I can't drink anymore coffee, and I have to use the washroom." I had to tell Eduardo of my needs because I couldn't hold it anymore.

Eduardo got up and raised me on his arms, "Don't step on the wet floor anymore … you are going to get sick."

"Thank you," I replied, shying away my embarrassment when I closed the washroom door.

Morning finally came. I woke up feeling a headache, but my appearance was not as bad as Agatha's. She said her head and body hurt badly; I touched her, and she felt as if she were running a fever. Eduardo needed to go back home, but he promised to send a remedy for Agatha with Andrés.

Outside, the people of Mazatlán looked upon the hurricane's destruction. An eerie quiet lay over the city—no raging storm, but no bustling of people and carriages and horses either.

I proceeded to clean up the mess as soon as Eduardo left, not without thanking him from the bottom of my heart for coming to check on us the night before. I was worried about Agatha; she didn't look good at all.

"Take this tea, Agatha; it is cinnamon." I brought the teacup to her mouth.

"How is everything outside?" Agatha asked in a low voice.

"It looks gray, and it is still raining, but the water on the street is almost gone …"

"I hope nobody got hurt, Max …"

"Me, too."

Agatha tried to get up.

"No, don't get up yet; just rest and try to sleep … you don't look good."

"I don't feel good!" She tried to laugh but couldn't let out more than a sorry cough. "My throat hurts."

"Try to sleep; I am going to clean up your apartment …"

"Oh no, Maximiana, I will do it myself as soon as I can get out of this bed."

"Look … I have to dry everything somehow … don't worry about it, just go to sleep."

She didn't respond because she was already asleep when I said those last words.

My young heart cried for the unfortunate ones after the tremendous devastation and tragedy of the hurricane. Several people died, and many others lost their houses and everything they owned, as did Josefina's family; but fortunately, everyone in her family survived. After a couple of days, Agatha's cold went away, and things slowly started to get back to normal. I received a letter from Otilia, telling me our papaya tree was left uprooted the day after the hurricane, and that in the middle of the storm, Mamá remembered our parrot Diego was hanging in its cage in the guava tree behind our house. Papá went out and got him, luckily, before the wind had blown Diego away. She also told me everyone in Mesillas and Cuacoyol was fine; our grandparents, uncles, aunts, and cousins had sought refuge in the brick house.

The newspaper office suffered some damage to its roof, but within a week I was able to go back to work.

The mailman whistled outside, and rapidly I went to get Agatha's or Señora Solorzano's mail. And then I was jumping up and down inside when I read my name on the envelopes from Natalia and Alejandro in Boston. I pressed them to my bosom and ran upstairs to read them. My midday break from work gave me the luxury of leisurely reading through them. I lay on my bed to read Natalia's letter first; it had many pages, to my heart's joy.

4 October 1908
Boston, Massachusetts

My dear sister Maximiana,

I hope that when you receive this letter you are doing well, as well as everyone in our family and friends. I am good, thanks to God.

Max, the boat trip was unbelievable! You have no idea how much fun I had once I stopped crying at leaving you all behind. Poor Domingo, he didn't know how to console me from my sadness. Alejandro kept a distance from us; he says honeymooners should be alone … but after a couple of days, we missed him. Oh Maxi … we had our first fight when we finally arrived in Boston. Everything is different here, very very VERY cold and the houses are big and look nothing like the houses in Mazatlán, but it is beautiful, Max. Everything reminds me of the pictures in the storybooks you used to bring home. We live in a house-apartment close to Harvard University; Domingo's family owns it. It is very nice, actually. It has beautiful stairs that take you to the second floor, and Alejandro is staying with us, but he is bothered by our discussions. Domingo wants to go out and do things with his friends, but I am too cold to get out of the house. I rather stay inside in front of the fireplace. I never felt cold like this before, I promise, Max, and it gets into your bones. I miss the warm sun of El Roble and my family; everything feels too far away. I don't understand a word of what people say, and Alejandro said I had

*to take a class to learn but with a private tutor because there is
NO WAY I will go in the cold to take a class in a school.*

*Maxi, I feel very lonely here. Domingo started school the day
after we arrived, and he is at school all day, and then he comes
home and has homework to do. On the weekend he wants to go
out and have fun, but I am too cold to go out. And Alejandro
is gone most of the time, but he looks happier than ever. I think
he is seeing somebody, but you know how Aleh is; he is secretive
about the women he likes.*

*Last Saturday, I went out with Domingo to a party of his
friends. Nobody knows I am his wife; Domingo said it had to
be kept a secret just in case his father came one day to Boston.
I could tell they were talking about me, but Domingo looked
happy that I was there with him. Alejandro and Domingo told
everyone that I am their cousin from México. The girls here are
beautiful; their eyes look different from ours, and it is not only
the color; it is something else that I cannot explain.*

They *read*, dear Natalia. That is the difference of their eyes from
ours. Not only do they know how to read, but they also actually do
read books.

*The girls look at Domingo and Alejandro with curiosity,
but I can tell they find them very attractive. My husband especially. But Max, it was terrible that I couldn't understand a
word they were saying, and Domingo tried to translate everything for me but after a while he forgot or got tired, and I just
stood there listening to a ;lkgsglfgklc;jgjalgutulgk a;lfjlfj!! Hah-
hah!! Lfjalfjlfjfffjjsfj out of their mouths and smiling politely as
many times as I could. When Alejandro left the party, I felt
lonelier than ever. Domingo noticed, and he came to sit next
to me, but Max, I could tell he was very bored and wanted to
join everyone else. I told him to go back and talk to his friends,
but he stayed with me instead. When we arrived home, he
asked if I had fun, and I lied; it isn't his fault. I just hope that
by the time you receive this letter you and Orlando are already*

planning your trip together to Boston. With you here, this would be different, Max. Please convince Orlando to travel to Boston and bring you with him.

My sweet Natalia, the last image she had of Orlando and me was the one at the dock where his arm wrapped around my shoulders. How mistaken she was.

Oh Max! The food here tastes different from the food in México. It took me a long time to get used to it (I still am adjusting), but now it tastes a little bit more appetizing.

Alejandro told me that it was going to get even colder! He said it was even colder in the winter than in the fall because it snows and freezes. Can you imagine that? I don't know how I will be able to survive it. But I know that next to Domingo, I will be able to do anything because I love him and he loves me. That part of our life continues being the same.

Please write back to me. I love you, Max. I miss you a lot. I will be anxiously waiting for your letter. Please tell Mamá and Papá, Augusto, Otilia, Rosaura, Lucia, and friends that I am fine and give them a big kiss and hug for me. Don't forget to write to me; try to write to me every day. I feel very lonely. I love you very much, my little sister.

Truly yours,

Natalia Sarmiento

A strange sensation crept in my mind when I read her signature and became conscious of the fact that Natalia was now a Sarmiento.

It was pleasant to receive a letter from Natalia. I hoped that she would learn to adapt to life in Boston because by the sound of her letter she was struggling too much with the change.

I decided to answer back that same day, right after reading Alejandro's letter.

4 October 1908
Boston, Massachusetts

My dear Silly Face,

How are you? As always I wish you the best. It is good to be back in Boston, Max, but I fear Natalia and Domingo are not feeling the same way. They started arguing as soon as we arrived in Boston and haven't stopped ever since. I am afraid of leaving them this way, and what is coming towards them is even worse. Maxi, Father telegraphed us to explain that Catalina Barraza and her family want to spend the Christmas season in Boston. By the time you receive this letter, they will probably be on their way to the U.S. Domingo hasn't told Natalia yet because the reality is she will have to move to a hotel while the Barrazas are in town; they will board at our townhouse. Just picture the mess. You see? This is one of the many reasons why I tried to stop Domingo from marrying Natalia and bringing her all the way over here. I knew it was not going to be as easy as they had pictured it, but there was no way of convincing him otherwise.

I feel sorry for Natalia, Maximiana. She will have to spend the holidays alone. We will find ways to keep her company; our friends do not speak Spanish, nor does she speak English, so we will not get help from that side. Do not tell your family about this; they will only worry about it, and there is nothing anybody can do. We will figure things out somehow.

I put the letter down, feeling frustrated and sad at my powerlessness.

How are things with the Pattersons? Are you happy teaching for them? Please write back soon and tell me all about it and about the "Big C." How is Big Head behaving? We had a serious talk with him before leaving México, and from what I saw the day we left, it seemed to me that he finally understood his mistake with you and was ready to fix his mess.

I miss you, Maximiana; I miss you very much. I love you dearly.

Yours truly,

Alejandro R. Sarmiento
Valladares y Lastra

I took a deep breath before getting up and returning to work. I needed to answer those letters the same day, so I planned to write them down at night. It broke my heart to think of how miserable sensitive Natalia was going to feel in that strange hotel room, in wintertime, and alone during the holidays. Things were not going well for her, and I just hoped she was intelligent enough to overcome whatever came her way and be strong to deal with it.

10 November 1908
Mazatlán, Sin., México

Dear Natalia,

I was very happy to receive your letter; I hope you are well when you receive mine. Everything is fine here except a hurricane blew through almost three weeks ago. It caused many deaths and much damage in the city and many towns in the countryside, but fortunately, the whole family is fine.

I continue seeing Andrés, and I have started to prepare for the admissions exams at the National University of México. I do not even know if I will be able to take the exam because I am not registered in a school, but I will try.

The people in El Roble think you are working here in Mazatlán with me. You can just imagine the gossip going around: By now you are "about to give birth" to a little Sarmiento, and as usual, they are charging the child to Alejandro. In their minds, Raimunda's little MaryMag is about to have a half sister or brother! Poor Alejandro, he has "fathered" more children that he can handle. By the way, according to Roblenians, Aleh set up a house for me in the city; that is the place where I live. Amusing, isn't it?

Nati … I am worried about you being so cold and sad in Boston, but you know what? It will pass. You just have to get used to it. And Alejandro is right: You MUST LEARN THE ENGLISH LANGUAGE because you will be living there for years to come, Nat, and how can it possibly harm you to learn another language? Besides, studying it will give you something to do, and you will not be bored anymore.

Natalia, you have to be strong and do what you have to do to be happy. Don't think so much about El Roble and the sun; think about the beautiful place you are in, the romantic gray days, the fireplace … oh sister! You are so lucky to have that opportunity! Imagine! You will see SNOW. You will have a white Christmas like the ones we used to see in Anita's Christmas cards. Do you remember, when we were children, you used to dream of being able to see snow? And we played it was soooo cold, and we covered ourselves up to our heads, pretending snow was coming? And we had a fireplace? Imagine Natalia, you will SEE it for real. Please don't forget to take pictures and send them to me with Alejandro. I am very happy to hear that Domingo and you are still in love with each other. I am not surprised. You are very lucky to be in such a place with a young man as nice as Domingo, who loves you so much and cares about you.

Natalia, I am now working in a newspaper office. I am a receptionist and also a tutor for a teenage girl. I am living on my own in the apartment you stayed in, in Mazatlán. You have no idea how happy I am to be independent. My new job is very nice.

Nati, I will write to you every week. Do the same, please; we have to keep in touch as much as possible. Write to Mamá and Papá and Otilia to this address.

I love you very much, Nat. Take care of yourself, and give a big hug to Domingo and Alejandro for me. Listen to Alejandro and Domingo's decision on what to do now that the Barrazas will visit Boston. You must trust them and be patient with the whole situation.

Your sister who never forgets you for a second,

Maximiana Valdez

I also wrote a letter to Alejandro and asked him with tears in my eyes to take good care of Natalia. She was a sensitive girl and a passionate dreamer. Natalia was as delicate as a nightingale, not as strong as an owl like me. My heart went out to all three of them, dealing with so many changes and challenges and disruptions to their plans.

23

The Cactus meeting had gone smoothly the evening before, and I was pleasantly working at the front desk of the *Afternoon Mail* when Orlando Sarmiento walked in, looking for me. He said he needed to talk and that it was an emergency.

"Is Natalia fine?" I asked, concerned.

"I think so," he replied.

"What do you need to talk about, then?" I asked, confused.

"We need to talk somewhere else."

Here we go again.

"I told you: I am not meeting you anywhere in secret or at night; if you have something to say, say it here. Who told you I work here?"

"Paula Randal, and fine … good-bye." He walked out with his usual childish behavior, not allowing me to answer back.

During my one o'clock break I took the public carriage home, and at the top of the stairs, the familiar figure of Orlando Sarmiento stood in front of me.

"What are you doing here?" I asked, visibly irritated.

"I'm waiting for you … we need to talk."

Bothered, I walked by Orlando. He followed me, and without asking if he could go in, he entered my apartment. He closed the door, but I walked back to open it again.

"Why do you open it?"

"I don't want the neighbors to think things that are not true. Say what you need to tell me—I have to eat, freshen up, and go back to work."

"I … tried to find you since last time I saw you, at the pier, when my brothers left. I looked for you at the Pattersons' house, but I was told you didn't live there anymore. Then I asked your friend who works at my house, but she wouldn't tell me where to find you …"

"I asked Josefina—she *does* have a name—not to tell anybody … I don't want to have any more problems with certain people."

"You don't have a problem with me … do you?"

I cannot believe what I am hearing coming out of his mouth!

"The only reason I don't beat you up Orlando Sarmiento, as I beat up your friend Gustavo Inzunza, is because you are Alejandro's brother …"

"Do you hate me?"

"I don't hate you, but I don't like to have you close by."

"So … you don't love me anymore?"

You've got to be kidding me!

"How can you even ask that? My God, Orlando … what is this all about? *Seriously!*" I exclaimed, losing my patience once and for all.

"I never forgot you … and I don't think I will ever forget you …," he replied in a whisper.

"Nor I you! You can trust me on that. I will *never* forget you."

He raised his eyes to meet mine, "Are you being sarcastic?"

"What do you think?" I replied. "No, I am not. I will never forget what you have made me go through … that is for sure, but there is no point in even talking about this … is that all you wanted to say?"

He turned his back on me and said in a voice struggling to come out:

"That night, when Domingo brought your sister the serenade, I was there … and after she ran after him and you came out of the house, I saw you from the distance, when you stood on the hill look-ing at them go into the fields … but I didn't dare talk to you …" He paused. "When Domingo talked to you at Dora Elena's picnic, I was dying of jealousy when he kissed you and I … wanted to kill Gustavo when he tried to harm you that day in the warehouse …"

"*Tried?* He *did* harm me, Orlando, or do you think that bloodied lips and unwanted hands grappling my body and a woman's dignity don't hurt when she is treated that way?"

"That is not what I meant and you know it …"

"And to make up for being such a coward, Gustavo Inzunza is now your best friend? And you are steady with his sister Maricela …," I stated, fighting tears of anger to see that he could never be honest with me.

"Who told you that?" he asked without turning around to face me.

"Did they lie?" I replied with yet another question.

"No," he said and walked out, slapping the door behind him. I took a deep breath to calm down and started warming up my lunch. A knock on my door shook me out of my thoughts. It was Andrés Ran-dal who had seen Orlando walking out of my building.

"What did he want?" he asked, frowning and obviously upset.

"He came by the office this morning; Paula told him where I work and live. He was already here when I came at one."

"Is Natalia well?" he replied, concerned.

"That is what I thought at the beginning, that he needed to talk to me about Natalia, but no …," I sighed in frustration, "Orlando Sarmiento still thinks that I am a little doll in his hands and that he can just appear out of nowhere and I will run after him …"

Andrés' face tightened. "I will pick you up from the office this eve-ning … would you like to take a walk on the jetty with me?"

"Yes, that will be nice … I will bring my white shawl because it is chilly outside … nothing compared to Boston, I imagine."

"We could also eat dinner together."

"I would love to," I smiled and hugged him, closing my eyes.

"I love you, Maxi," he said raising me to my tiptoes and placing his forehead on mine.

"I love you, too, Andrés Randal," I replied, feeling the tips of my toes rising off the floor. "I love you a lot."

El Tunel was a small *cenaduria* restaurant across the street from the Rubio Theater. They sold the most delicious *tostadas, gorditas,* enchiladas, *asado,* and hard shell tacos in the entire city of Mazatlán. My favorite dish was chicken enchiladas with sour cream and guacamole on top, accompanied by a cold Jamaica drink. Andrés's order was always the same: asado and a horchata drink full of ice. After dinner, we walked to the jetty. By the time we reached it, the sun was setting and presenting an unbelievably gorgeous display of colors. We found a bench to sit on and quietly watched the sky brighten and then fade to dusk.

Mazatlánians enjoyed their sunsets with a passion. People always gathered around the beach when the sun set and each day found the magic—a completely new panorama of colors and clouds and reflecting gems on the water. The sky artfully played with its brush and palette, painting the most amazing purple clouds dancing over the orange tinted sea one day and shyly hiding golden beams behind gray pinkish little clouds another and always ending with a darkening that announced the birth of the starry night.

Andrés and I were getting ready to leave when a loud party of four young men approached us. Andrés became alert and looked for my face when he recognized who they were—Gustavo Inzunza, Francisco Reveles, Teodoro de la Vega, and Orlando Sarmiento. Francisco and Teodoro greeted us with respect; I immediately noticed they had been drinking. Gustavo curtsied at me, and Orlando limited himself to a half smile. Andrés took off his hat and bowed good evening while walking me away from them, but Gustavo whistled a disrespectful sound at us, or rather, at *me.* Andrés stopped at once, and I asked him to let it go, but he returned to ask them what was going on. He asked me to stay put, a safe distance from the group.

"What was that?" Andrés asked them, clearly bothered by their attitude.

Teodoro de la Vega immediately answered, "Andrés, Gustavo is drunk; he doesn't know what he's doing … take Maxi home."

"MAXI? HA, HA, HA!" Gustavo exploded into laughter. Francisco lightly pushed Gustavo on the chest, asking him to calm down and shut up, but Orlando came to Gustavo's rescue.

"Leave him alone!" Orlando screamed, pushing Francisco back. A gossipy group was already forming, bringing more attention to the boisterous scene. Andrés then shoved Orlando away from Francisco, and Orlando threw a punch at him. He missed, but Andrés returned the blow and hit his mark, sending Orlando Sarmiento directly to the ground. Furiously he got up and wildly started throwing blows at Andrés, who avoided some but not others. Teodoro and Francisco separated them while Gustavo sat on a bench laughing at both of them. I wished they could have sealed Orlando Sarmiento's lips.

"What? Are you defending *her*? Has she told you of her visits to the balcony room every night with me?" Orlando said and then turned to me. "Have you told him? Have you told him that you came to my room in the house here and to this same beach at midnight? Have you told him everything you did with me? Have you?"

With dignity, I lifted my chin and answered, "Yes, I have. And I also told him that even though you had the *worst* intentions towards me, I was always smart enough not to let you follow through on them."

Teodoro lowered his head at my words, and Francisco shook it with mortification. Andrés kept quiet until Gustavo spoke.

"So you lied to this idiot? Because everybody knows you went to Alejandro and Domingo right after Orlando … Ha, ha, ha!"

Andrés tackled him with incredible force and sent him to the ground, but Francisco and Teodoro grabbed him by the arms.

"He is drunk; don't let his stupidity get to you!" Teodoro screamed.

They were arguing and did not notice Orlando Sarmiento walking in my direction. He looked at me with angry eyes and with grinding teeth said, within inches of my face, "Do you think you are a *lady* because you wear your hair like *that*?" and he rudely brushed my hair bun with his hand, "or because you now put shoes on?" he said while angrily kicking my foot with his boot. "You will always be an

Indian peasant from El Roble, wearing the costume of a—what?—a teacher?" He laughed with sarcasm, "You don't fool anyone … you are nothing but a stinky servant dressed as a pathetic lady … and you make me *sick* …"

I stepped back away from him, fearing he might try to hit me. But he came forward and continued, "Every time I remember I touched you, I am disgusted." He spit belligerently on the boardwalk. I walked around him to reach Andrés, glad that no one else had overheard his diatribe. Orlando tried to stop me by grabbing my arm, but I got rid of his hand in a second.

"Andrés … let's go, please," I said, and Teodoro agreed with me instantly. Andrés came, took my arm, and started walking away rapidly. With the corner of my eye, I saw Orlando Sarmiento sitting on a bench with his hands over his face, hunched over.

My legs were shaking when we started walking back to my apartment. It felt like an eternity to reach my place; and even though we walked in silence, Andrés caressed my hand with tenderness, trying to comfort me. Throughout the shameful scene, I had kept myself firm and not let Orlando and Gustavo see that their offensive words touched me. Nevertheless on the inside, my dignity felt battered.

When we arrived at my apartment, Andrés walked up with me, even though he never did at night, and stayed for a while until Agatha got home. As much for himself as for me, he kept repeating that I shouldn't pay attention to Orlando and Gustavo, that they were being plainly stupid. Deep inside, I was glad Orlando had said those biting words to me where no one else had heard them; it was too humiliating for anybody else to know he felt disgusted for having touched me in the past.

It was getting late, and I wanted to go to bed and lie down. Agatha came, and Andrés told her what had happened. She asked him to go home, that she would stay with me for a while. As soon as Andrés left, Agatha hugged me and went home; she said that, as a woman, she understood that I needed to be alone.

I closed the door behind Agatha and walked to my bed. Tears of unhappiness instantly fell from my weary eyes. Everything inside of me hurt; the armor I wore that let others think their slights could not hurt me anymore slipped off, and I saw it for the fantasy that it was, unable to protect me from such painful words. And such words he had spoken! He had devalued a time in my life that I had given with genuineness of heart, and each one of them had passed through my mind and settled into my very soul. I had only hope to grasp, that they would not stay for all time.

I fell asleep, listening to the wind of the sea and wishing for Orlando Sarmiento never to come back into my life again.

A blast of thunder woke me up, and lightning illuminated my bedroom with each strike. Thunderstorms still terrified me; I pressed the sides of my pillow to my ears, wishing for the noise to go away, but my wishes had no effect. I sat on my bed when the weak sound of a knock reached my ears.

It must be Agatha, I thought and walked to open the door.

"Agatha?" I asked, looking through the hole; it was too dark to see anything. I made sure the bar on my door was secure, and I asked again.

"Agatha … is that you?"

"Maximiana …," Orlando Sarmiento said on the other side, "open the door please … I want to apologize for what happened today."

"This is not the time or the place … go away."

"I can't; don't you hear the storm outside?"

"I cannot let you in …"

"Maximiana … please open the door," he said with a broken voice, "I couldn't sleep thinking of what I said to you today … and what I did, and I beg you, open the door."

"No," I firmly replied.

"I had never consumed beer before … I was drunk, and when I saw you with Andrés, I went crazy with anger because earlier you had rejected me … but I didn't mean what I said; I swear to God I didn't mean it." He broke into sobs, "Pardon me for kicking your foot and pushing your hair; please pardon me for what I said … I regret every word, I swear."

Resting my back on the door, I slid down to the floor and started combing my hair with my fingers, parted it in the middle, and begun braiding it in two braids, the way indigenous and *mestiza* women do, the exact way I used to wear it before coming to Mazatlán for the first time, before I knew who I was. I rose to walk to the window and held onto the iron bars, not fearing the lightning or the thunders that roared and made the paintings given to me by Agatha shake on the walls.

"Go home, Orlando," I said.

His back was resting on the door, and he fell backwards when I opened it. He got up but did not try to enter the apartment.

"Did you hear what I told you?" he asked, looking down.

"I did ... but as the saying goes, 'Only children and the drunk tell their real thoughts.'"

"Not in my case ... I was angry," he said in a low voice, "and I acted out of anger. Please forgive me."

"Why do you hate me so much, Orlando?"

"I don't know ...," he whispered, "but sometimes I wished I had never spoken to you that first time in the library ... other days you don't even exist to me, and I forget all about you and what happened between us, and then ... you suddenly reappear when I am least expecting it and make my heart palpitate as if it were going to jump out of my chest."

"Why don't we do each other a favor and try never to come across one another again? Let's stay as far away as possible from each other, and if we do cross paths, please do not talk to me. Very soon I will leave, and you will leave too ... and we will never see each other again, so in the meantime, try not to hurt me anymore."

"Where are you going?" he asked, taken aback.

"To sleep."

"No, I mean when you said that very soon you will leave and I will leave ..."

"I want to move somewhere else, where I can be at peace and angry women whom I have never harmed can be out of my life."

"But where are you moving to?" he continued, apparently astonished.

"It is really late ... I think you should walk home now."

"May I have a glass of water, please?" he suddenly asked.

I walked to the kitchen and lit an oil lamp; as usual the storm had cut off the electricity. Orlando walked into the apartment and sat at the table. I gave him the water as I placed the lamp on the table and, in shock, saw the dark purple bruises on his face and his right eye splattered with blood.

"Your face …," I said.

"I know …"

I sat on a chair and then rose again to bring him an ointment to put on his bruises, some of them had red spots of blood on them.

"Do you have a mirror?" he asked.

"Yes, in the washroom … you also need to put ice to bring down the swollen areas … your cheekbone looks like a bump."

I wetted a towel and gave it to him.

"Thank you."

He twitched his eye when he placed it on the left side of his face. Blindly he started putting the ointment on his bruises. I reached out for it, and stood next to him; with a trembling hand I softly touched his face with my ointment finger. Orlando closed his eyes; he embraced my waist with both arms and started to cry. Lightning announced a coming thunder, but still I jumped when it struck. I didn't know what to do with my hands, but compassion won in the end, and I placed them on the head full of brown curls I had loved so much not long ago.

"I am confused, Maximiana," Orlando said in sobs, "I don't know what I want anymore … do you believe me?"

"Yes …," I replied softly.

"Do you promise?"

"I do … if you weren't confused, you wouldn't be sitting here right now."

"I don't know what to do …"

"Forget about me; that is what you have to do. Stay away from me, as I told you before, and try not to harm me anymore …"

"I can't forget about you …"

"You already did several times, so this time doesn't have to be different."

Slowly I took his hands off my waist, and he stood up to look down on my face.

I looked up and said, "I will always be Maximiana Valdez, the *servant girl* who, for a long time, secretly jumped your balcony at night, Orlando, nothing more."

"You are much more than that …" he replied, penetrating my gaze.

"Not to you." I smiled with a hurtful sarcasm.

The warm yellowish light coming from the oil lamp softened his gloomy features when he asked, "May I hold you one last time?"

"You just did."

"I want to hold you like before … like the times when you wore your braids as you are right now and I spent my days and nights thinking about you and the moment when you were going to be mine."

"I *was* yours, Orlando."

But I know what you wanted from me, Orlando Sarmiento, I sadly thought and replied, "Those times are gone now and will never return … there is no point in hugging as we did before."

Ignoring my reply, he grabbed me as he used to when I was living the fantasy that we were a couple; his familiar scent entered my senses, but my arms hung on my sides.

"Good-bye, Orlando," I said, perceiving everything was now cleared between us.

"Good-bye, Maximiana," he replied with a heartbreaking tone while I extricated my body from his arms. He walked away without looking back.

I closed the door and placed the bar on it. Then I went to bed, wishing to forget that Orlando Sarmiento, my first love, had been in my apartment that night. Again, he had gone through the same story of asking for forgiveness for his insults. No matter what would happen, I would never be good enough for him to stop having doubts about my worth as a human being.

24

By Monday morning, it seemed as if everyone in town knew of the violent encounter between Andrés Randal and the foursome at the jetty. But few knew the facts. The story spread and grew into gossip that Andrés had beat up Orlando because of *me*. Nobody ever said, "They were drunk and insulted Maximiana Valdez."

In the office, everyone was as curious about the incident as they were about my new hairstyle of two very Mexican braids on the sides. Paula attempted to put a stop to the gossip from the beginning and explained to everyone that it had been an incident due to alcohol.

I told Andrés of Orlando's visit Friday night. It bothered him, but he did not make a big deal about it. But he did say, and I agreed, that I had taken an unnecessary risk in letting him in since I didn't know if Gustavo Inzunza was with him. Andrés was very intelligent and sized up situations rather quickly.

The Cactus had a meeting the following Friday. Usually our meetings had a potluck with different foods and drinks. However, this time someone also brought a guitar in celebration of a new ruling. According to Eduardo and Agatha, the bourgeois could no longer dismiss a person on whim—they couldn't use their economic power just to fire someone without due cause—and this meant conditions for the oppressed were starting to change in México.

Paula Randal told everyone present that Señor Joaquín Sarmiento, accompanied by his wife, Leonora, had come to the *Afternoon Mail* office to talk to the director. They had requested that the director fire me because, according to them, I had been responsible for the attack on their son. But Señor Rodriguez had ignored their request completely, to the delight of everyone present. I couldn't believe my ears! It was the best news I had heard in a long time. At last, I felt I had a chance to stay in Mazatlán and escape the harassment of those people.

"I propose a toast!" Paula Randal exclaimed. "For changing times! The day has come when people of México are beginning to understand that we cannot live life influenced by the bourgeois's commands over the proletariat."

"End to the firing of workers for unjust reasons!" Agatha said.

"For the people!" everyone exclaimed, raising their bottles and cups.

"And …" Paula continued, "I propose a toast for Maximiana Valdez's braids. Without words she is telling us how proud she is to be a Mexican woman!"

Andrés put his arm around my shoulder and pulled me close to him; he whispered in my ear, "You look beautiful." And I realized that he had never seen me with two braids before. I was secretly flattered by his words and felt pride in Paula's statements.

It was an unforgettable evening, but part of my heart went to Boston when they started playing the guitar and memories of Natalia's songs came to my mind. I desperately wanted to know how was she doing in that hotel room by herself, hiding from the Barraza family while her husband of three months was boarding his almost fiancé and her family, whose intent behind that trip was a reconciliation between the two.

Night came and everyone began to take off. Andrés stayed behind, noticing my distracted mind. He thought Orlando had returned, but I explained that I was worried about Natalia; we hadn't had a chance to talk in private in a long time.

"The Barrazas are in Boston, and Alejandro had to move Natalia out of their house into a hotel room to hide her," I told him while putting away the cups and dishes from the table.

"How long are they going to stay there?" he asked, clearly concerned and reaching out for water to help me clean the kitchen.

"I don't know … but Natalia must feel miserable. Besides, in her letter, she said the weather disagrees with her; it is too cold and gray and dark. She is not used to it, and now that she is alone most of the time, just imagine how bad she is doing. I have been writing to her every week since I received her first letter, but so far, I haven't gotten anything back, not even from Alejandro." I sighed. "I am very worried about Natalia."

"Is she expecting a child already?" he asked pensive.

My eyes widened like the moon. "Oh … I hadn't thought … I don't know … I don't think so. Oh my God! I hope not!"

"I know Alejandro; he knows how to do things right, so even if she is alone in a hotel room, I am sure she is very comfortable and they are constantly visiting her. There is no way they are going to leave your sister alone."

"I trust Alejandro, but still, I worry about Natalia."

Lightning started illuminating the living room.

"This is not the rainy season, but these days we are getting storms as if we were in the middle of summer."

Andrés shook his head.

"We are done," he concluded while putting away the broom.

"Thank you, Andrés." I hugged him with affection.

"I have to go now … it must be after midnight," he said, holding my face. "May I steal a kiss from you even though we are alone in your apartment at midnight in the middle of a lightning storm?" he said, wetting his lips.

"Yes, you may," I replied. "And I think you should spend the night. I don't want you to go into the street in the dark with this rain."

His cheeks took a reddish tone. "Really? Do you trust me that much?"

"With all of my heart, I do."

He stared at me intensely for a few seconds and smiled. He then kissed me with gentleness, knowing that I meant he would respect my decision to keep my fifteen-year-old virginity intact.

"Let's go to bed then," Andrés said, winking. I pulled out an extra blanket and pillow for him to use.

"As you will see, I am not exactly the type of girl who dresses up to go to bed," I joked when I came out of the washing room wearing my long sleeve white sleeping gown, hat, and socks.

"I will have nightmares!" he exclaimed. "Are you the Weeping Woman?"

"Aye, my childreeeennnnnn!" I sang to his face in a spooky voice. "Where are my childreeeennn?"

We both laughed. Andrés took off his shirt and pants; he was wearing long undergarments that made him look like a baby in cotton white pajamas. He made a tamale out of himself in the blanket but left his arms free to hug me when I lay down next to him in my own blanket. I turned my body to look at the window and sighed.

"Andrés … may I ask you something personal about your brother?"

"Sure … go ahead," he said, resting his chin on my back.

"What kind of relationship does he have with Agatha? They seem to be together as a couple, but at the same time, they are not."

"Agatha wants it that way, and he accepts it; they are together but free of compromise. Do you understand me?"

"Yes."

"Agatha questions the norms imposed by society on women so she thinks she lives on her own terms."

"And she is right," I replied.

"True …" He started laughing.

"What's so funny?" I asked, turning my face back at him.

"You agree but will not let go of the imposed ideas of society on you …"

"There are two sides to this rebellion, my little Andrés Daniel Randal," I said smiling. "I am rebelling by *not* doing something that I am *not* ready to do yet, just to please somebody else who wants to do it."

"Don't you desire *it*?" he asked seriously.

I sighed. "Of course, I have thought about it. I love you." Andrés's face intensified. "But we are too young. I am only fifteen years old, and you are eighteen … if we don't die tomorrow … there is plenty of time."

"Most people our age are already married …"

"I know … and I am sure that by age twenty they feel they are fifty because they already have children and the special attraction of *it* is gone …"

He passed his finger along the edge of my face and seriously asked, "How far did you go with Orlando Sarmiento?"

"I don't think it is correct to speak of such things with you or anybody … but if you think I have been lying to you—"

"No! I wouldn't care if you did. I would've understood it."

Surprised I replied, "But I didn't! All this time you have thought that I—"

"He was older than you and the son of your *patron*, if you know what I mean—"

"But I always respected my body, Andrés, and Orlando cannot say otherwise … we only kissed and hugged and that was all … but I thought our feelings for each other made us a couple, which mattered a lot to me in those days, but not anymore. So even though nothing else happened beyond *that* physically, for me, those kisses and hugs meant a big deal, as much as if I had gone all the way."

His face tensed. "It makes me jealous to think about you with him."

"What about you? Have you done it?" I bluntly asked. Andrés turned to look at the ceiling. He thought about it for a while before replying.

"I have."

Blood rushed through my body when he said that. "Many times?"

"No … only twice …"

"Twice?" I asked, shocked; twice was too much for me to hear. "May I know with whom?"

"You don't want to know that …" He cut my questioning short.

"Why not?" I asked, consternated.

"Because you know her."

A shaft entered my heart.

"So don't ask me anymore, Maximiana."

"When did it happen?" I asked, questioning his loyalty and respect for me.

"I don't want to talk about it—"

Tension rose to my face. "Why not? You haven't disrespected our relationship, have you?"

"Of course not! It happened when you and I were not together this way ..."

"Then why can't you tell me? Tell me when it happened then ..."

He gasped and replied, "The day I met you at the square and asked for the Central Hotel address, I was on my way to meet with her ... and days before traveling to El Roble, in December, when I was on my way to La Villa de San Sebastián."

I was speechless. It took me a while to react to what I had heard.

"You have the dates quite fixed in your mind," I finally said, biting my lip.

"Yes, because you have no idea how much I regret it."

"Why don't you look at me when you talk about this?" I asked, involuntarily getting upset.

"Because I am embarrassed ... it is really complicated."

"Who is she?" I asked, looking for his face. Andrés turned to the wall. "You are worrying me, Andrés ... what is going on? Who is she? Don't you trust me?"

"I don't want to lose you because of this ..."

"You will for sure if I find out later, and trust me, I WILL find out."

Andrés sighed and with resignation turned back at me and said the name in a murmur, "Catalina Barraza."

"What?"

The room started turning around me.

"The day at the Central Hotel we met, but I didn't know she was steady with Domingo ... and the second time she came looking for me at my brother's office, and Eduardo told Alejandro ... when he came from El Roble and got the blackboard for you. Alejandro asked me to tell Domingo, and that is why he broke up with Catalina Barraza ... and I stopped at El Roble to talk to Domingo again, but he was fine with me about the whole thing because I hadn't known they were steady. Supposedly she was going out with me secretly because her family did not allow her to go steady then, and since I had been in San Sebastián for three months, I wasn't aware of her relationship with Domingo Sarmiento, and the second time … she came crying to me, saying that she was being forced to go out with Domingo but that it wasn't real and Domingo knew about it … she was also doing *it* with him … Domingo later told me."

"My goodness … Domingo broke up with Catalina Barraza because she was cheating on him with his friend. I never thought things like that happened in *your* world."

"Maxi … I did not know they were going out—"

I interrupted him abruptly, "So … did you love her?"

Andrés turned his body back to me, and I turned my face to look at the wooden beams supporting the roof.

"Not as much as you loved Orlando Sarmiento."

"How can you know how much I loved him?"

"Because I know you, Maximiana, and you would've killed an army for that fellow."

"How much did you love her?" I wanted the answer he was avoiding.

"I liked her because she was beautiful, and I thought I loved her for some time, but when I realized she was just tricking me … I disliked her, and every time I saw her, I swear to God … I don't want anything to do with her."

"Now I understand why she was looking at me that way at the dance … her anger didn't make sense … is that the reason why you invited me? To make her jealous?"

I am jealous now, and I wish to strike you, Andrés Randal.

Andrés took his hands to his face extremely bothered by my words, "This is exactly why I didn't want to tell you about it … you are thinking something that is not true. Of course I didn't take you to the dance for such a stupid reason; I took you because according *to me* you are my steady girlfriend …"

"Do you think Domingo started going out with Natalia to get even with Catalina Barraza?"

"Of course not! Somebody like Catalina Barraza is not worth the effort. Max ... how can you even compare Catalina to your sister?"

"Catalina is beautiful and very rich ..."

"But she is empty-headed and boring," he replied. "When Domingo met your sister, he told just us, his friends, about her. If he had started going out with Natalia to get even with Catalina, he would've let everyone know about it, right?"

"Who knows!" I exclaimed visually irritated.

"Come on, Maxi ...," he softened his voice, "she didn't mean to me what I know Orlando meant to you, and you forgot about him ..."

I abruptly turned my back on Andrés, fighting tears of jealously. I wished a thousand times not to have asked him about that in the first place, but it was too late, and I didn't know how to react to that unbelievable truth just revealed to me.

"Maxi ..."

I covered my ears with both of my hands.

"Maxi ... it happened a long time ago before I met you, and you know I love you ... why are you taking it like this?"

I kept quiet for I didn't want him to hear my voice breaking down. Andrés moved closer to me and passed his arm under my back to wrap me in an emotional embrace. He placed his face on the back of my head.

"Maximiana ... forgive me for hurting you like this ... I can imagine how you feel because when I think of you in Orlando's arms, my blood boils ... but you don't have to feel that way about me with her ... it means nothing."

I reached for his hands and entwined mine with his. Andrés brought himself closer and kissed my wet cheek.

"I'm sorry for making you cry, Maxi ... I am very sorry," he murmured and kissed each one of my eyes with a gentle touch.

"I am sorry, too," I replied. "All this time, I hadn't thought much about how you feel about Orlando ... he means nothing to me."

"It is raining hard out there. You don't jump with the thunder anymore ... how come?" he asked in a sweet attempt to change the subject and hugged me tighter.

"I grew up, I guess …," I replied and huffed at my own answer. "My tall friend Daniel would probably say, 'You didn't grow up literally.'"

"Ha, ha, ha … who is Daniel?"

"Daniel Gutierrez Tiznado is my best friend in El Roble; I love him dearly."

"Is he handsome, this Daniel friend of yours?" he teased.

"Oh yes, he is … and the tallest man in El Roble, actually."

"Mmm … but he doesn't have a crush on you, right?" he asked, faking a concern.

"Nooo … we have been friends since we were children."

"Your nose is cold," he suddenly stated. I touched it, and he was right. He sighed and in a low voice said into my ear, "I want to lock myself with you in this room and hold you like this for eternity."

I had once thought those same words, a year earlier in the balcony room; it was the first time Orlando and I had kissed each other. It was an odd coincidence that Andrés Randal felt the same way about me. And the kisses on my eyes, those were two touches that I did not expect, but they made me believe how much he cared about my feelings and thoughts.

"I love you, Andrés; thank you for respecting my feelings." I kissed him on the lips.

"Mmm … thank you for understanding me, and let's not talk about the past anymore; it is gone already … there is no point."

"True … you are right."

"Good night, Maxi …"

"Are you sleepy?" I asked, giggling.

"Mmm … I don't think I will be able to sleep, having you so close to me, but I want you to rest … so go to sleep and every time lightning comes, I will hold you tighter to keep the thunder's roar out of your ears."

"You are a wonderfully charming man, you know? And incredibly handsome."

"Whoa … that was a huge compliment!" he laughed.

"Just don't let it go to your head," I laughed back. "Good night, Prince-look-alike."

"Ha, ha, ha! Hold on! What is that all about?"

"A friend of mine once told me that 'Prince-look-alike' Andrés Randal had a crush on me," I giggled, amused.

"Who told you that?" he asked, giving me a crooked smile.

"That is for me to know and for you never to find out," I winked.

"You are making it up … Aztec Princess."

"Hey! I thought I was the Weeping Woman."

"No … you look like an Aztec princess, a direct descent of Moctezuma."

"Who is that?" Now I was curious.

"Moctezuma was the Aztec emperor when the Spaniards arrived."

"I would like to learn about the Aztecs …," I replied, pensive.

"And the Maya, the Olmec, Toltec … Maxi there are many civilizations that we need to learn about—they make us who we are as Mexicans—and not just learn about the history of Spain."

"Were there civilizations like those here in Sinaloa?"

"Yes … the Cahitas, Tahues, and Totorames … mmm … and others … did you know there is a town south of here called Chametla?"

"I have heard of it …"

"The Totorames' most important town is Chametla."

"Do they still live there?" I asked.

"Yes, and we all have blood of these groups in us, you know? That is why we are *mestizos*."

"It is interesting how we don't learn about it …," I wondered.

"I know … we are taught to ignore that part of us and admire anything European."

"Sad, but it should change."

"Yes. As teachers we must make it change."

"Look at the window Andrés …"

The first rays of the sun were illuminating the sky. Dawn was coming our way.

"Should I get up and get the coffee ready, or should I try to go to sleep?" I teased.

"We should try to sleep …"

"Good morning, then."

"Good morning, Aztec Princess."

Tiredness finally took over, and I lost track of time and space to fall pleasantly asleep next to my best friend and lover in spirit.

Señor and Señora Patterson returned from their trip to the news that I had been fired from my position as their children's teacher a couple of days after they had left.

Señora Enriqueta sent a message, asking me to meet with her as soon as possible. I was happy to hear they were back in town because I could only imagine how much their children missed them. I gladly accepted to see her and presented myself in her house the following Saturday morning. Doña Ursula opened the door and greeted me as if nothing had ever happened. I walked in, and Carolina, Elizabeth, and George Jr. came running to hug me.

"Where are Ismael and baby Martha?" I asked them, full of happiness to see them again.

"Mother has Martha, and Ismael is napping," Elizabeth answered.

They held my hands and walked with me to meet Señora Patterson, who rose from her chair and gave me a hug. I happily took baby Martha into my arms.

"I am so sorry, Maximiana. I explained everything to Mother already, and she regrets profoundly listening to those women … how are you dear?" she asked, pointing to the seat for me.

"I am doing well, Señora Patterson; I found a job at the newspaper's office and rented an apartment. I am also tutoring a student once a week," I responded with pride while accommodating myself on the seat.

"Oh, Maximiana, the children miss you a lot. What can I do to bring you back to our house?" she asked in her pleasant voice while Carolina, George Jr., and Elizabeth jumped up and down pleading with me to return.

"I sincerely thank you, Señora Patterson, for asking me to return to your house. I want you to know that I was very happy working for you and teaching your children, but I have found a new way of life in which I have independence and I am learning many new things. I do not see myself living in a house under supervision anymore."

"You are still very young, Maximiana; you still need protection from older people until you are married. You will be better off if you return to live with us."

"I have learned to take very good care of myself. I am fifteen, but I feel older inside. But if you want me, I could come and work with your children on Saturdays as their tutor."

"What is your schedule at the *Afternoon Mail*?"

"From eight to one and three to five."

"It takes your whole day. Perhaps, if I talk to the director, they may be willing to let you work half-time, and that way you can still teach half-time. What do you say?"

"That would be great for me. I could teach from eight to twelve, and go to the office from one to five."

"Absolutely! You can eat lunch here before going to work. Would you consider moving back with us?"

"I'd rather keep my apartment, Señora Patterson. But, if you ever need me to stay during the evenings with the children, I will be more than happy to do that for you."

"You are such a sweetheart, Maximiana Valdez. I have no doubts that you are going to get very far in life."

"I hope one day to get to a university," I replied.

She smiled and winked at me.

"That might be easier than you think."

"I certainly hope so."

Doña Ursula brought us coffee and cookies. Carolina came down running with three presents that Señora Patterson had brought from Europe. They were a silk scarf to use in church that she bought in Rome, a fan from Spain, and a set of earrings and necklace from Paris. Elizabeth came running and put in my hands a beautiful box that had the best present of all: chocolates from Switzerland. The chocolates were a present from the children. They had gotten several boxes but saved one for me.

That evening when I arrived home, I felt somehow liberated from the injustice I had been a victim of three months earlier. I took a beautiful chocolate out of the box, and I slowly bit it, enjoying every single bite until I finished it.

It was good that the weather was cold now because I planned to save most of those chocolates to take them to El Roble to my family the following week.

25

22 November 1908
Boston, Massachusetts

My dear little sister,

I haven't received an answer to my letter yet but I am so sad and desperate that I need to tell somebody. That is why I am writing to you ... the person that understands me the most. Maxi, Catalina Barraza, my husband's ex-steady girlfriend, and her family are going to stay in Boston for two months. At our place. Alejandro and Domingo brought me to a hotel to hide from all of them, and they come to see me every day, but I am terrified that Domingo is going to fall in love with her again. Domingo comes every day before school starts, sometimes during his class breaks if he gets a chance, and after school, but I cannot stop worrying. And I don't know why, but Domingo is becoming very jealous if I go out because the young men look at me and greet me and I smile back as we do in El Roble, but Domingo gets mad. Alejandro found a voice teacher for me, but Domingo refuses to allow the teacher to come to my room if they are not here. Alejandro was very mad about that because the teacher is his friend and said that there was nothing to worry about. But Domingo did not even want to hear it! So Alejandro said he was going to be present in every single class, and Domingo replied that he had no business getting into our lives. I don't understand what is going through his head, but he is too worried about me doing something wrong. Thank God Alejandro found a woman teacher, and I started my singing lessons and English classes too; they keep me busy. I love my voice classes.

Forgive me, Maximiana. I know you do not like to talk about these things, but I have nobody else to talk to. I suspect I am expecting a baby, but I haven't told Domingo yet.

I brought the letter closer and read the sentence over and over again: "I suspect I am expecting a baby."

I don't know how to say it, Maxi. I don't know if he will be mad about it. I love him with all of my heart and soul, but lately he scares me sometimes. I talked to Alejandro about Domingo's jealousy (not about what I just told you before), and he said that all of their friends keep telling Domingo that I am extremely beautiful and attractive to them. And Alejandro explained to me that if they knew I was Domingo's wife, they wouldn't make such comments. But Domingo gets upset just the same. His friends think I am their cousin so they want to meet me as a "girl," if you know what I mean. And Alejandro said they have made comments about the way I look to Domingo but never disrespecting me.

Domingo told me the other day that he was very happy that I had to wear a coat all the time so that no one would see my figure. I told him that he is scaring me, and he apologized and told me that he loved me more than anything in the world and was too afraid of losing me. But I swore to God for him and my family that I will NEVER leave him. Because I love him more than anything in the world. I think he suffered too much when his mother passed away. I don't know, Maximiana, but lately I don't even think about the cold weather anymore. I am too concerned about my Domingo in the same house as that girl. Maxi, this was going to be our first Christmas together, and we are not going to spend it in the same house. That breaks my heart. And I cry every night when he finally leaves and I stay behind, alone in this room.

I finally saw snow. It is beautiful. Just as beautiful as we all imagined it to be when we were little girls. In the middle of the night, if it snows, everything looks bright, as if it were the day. It looks so peaceful. I sit at my window and sing endlessly, imagining that all of you are here with me and that Domingo is peacefully sleeping in our bed. Then I turn around and see that I am alone and he is sleeping far away from me. I took the pictures in Harvard that you asked. Alejandro will take them to you when he goes back in February. The university is impressive—so many majestic buildings in brick and covered with ivy. One day you will see it, too.

I cannot tell you if I am sad or happy because I have a mixture of all the feelings in the world. On one side, I miss you all, and my husband is not with me as before. But on the other, I might have a baby inside of me. And the feeling is inexplicable. I am also singing and learning new things that I always dreamed of learning. I just wish all of you were closer to me. I love you very much, Maxi, and I miss you. Please write soon. I need you, little sister. I need you a lot. If I am expecting a baby, I hope she is an intelligent girl like her Aunty Maximiana.

Your sister,

Natalia Sarmiento

I answered Natalia's letter before leaving to El Roble to spend two weeks with my family for the Christmas season. I left hers behind, and saved only the best news for my family. Andrés and his family stayed in Mazatlán instead of traveling to La Villa de San Sebastián for the holidays. I used the opportunity of a caravan going en route to Villa Unión to travel with them. Once in Villa Unión, I found another group that was taking the El Roble route to the Sierra Madre Mountains and dropped me off on their way. My family was thrilled to have me with them after almost seven months without seeing me.

The Sarmientos were already in the Grand House when I arrived in El Roble. I heard they had brought guests with them; unlike other years, this time they had spent the fall in the city and were returning to El Roble after several months of absence. I was too full of happiness to be with my family and friends to think about the return two weeks away or the Sarmientos being close to me.

I was gladly surprised to see the progress of my family, thanks to my humble help. My parents painted the house and fixed the porch. Mamá also bought a cupboard for the kitchen, and now we had a table with enough chairs for everyone. Rosaura and Lucia were waiting for me to help them set up the Christmas tree, so the same night I arrived, we took the task of decorating our cotton-covered delight. The girls jumped in happiness when I pulled out the small nativity set I had bought in Mazatlán for them to place under the tree. I saved the chocolate surprise for Christmas morning.

However, our house was not the same without Natalia. Mamá would brush her tears away when we mentioned her name. I told them about her letter that I "accidentally" forgot in Mazatlán in which Natalia described how beautiful everything was and how happy Domingo and she were in Boston. I kept the baby news for myself; after all, it was not confirmed yet.

On Christmas Eve, Augusto brought his fiancé to have dinner with us. She was very nice, and we enjoyed having her company for the celebration.

Daniel stopped by as soon as he heard I was in town and welcomed me with a measurement of my height. Then I teased him about his girlfriend Tomasa; it was very sweet to see him so much in love with her. I had never seen Daniel act so formally until I had a chance to see him walk by with Tomasa.

Otilia had closed the school for the holidays, but I was very proud to see their classroom decorated with winter displays made by the students. They had a bell, as we once dreamed of having, but the biggest news of all was to hear that Señor Joaquín Sarmiento was paying Otilia and Daniel a salary as teachers. I was stunned when I heard it, but I could put my hand in fire that such action had been Alejandro's idea.

Raimunda's baby was simply beautiful. Her head was full of long curls, and her nose was a tiny button. She looked a lot like Alejandro. I avoided saying that she looked like her father. Raimunda told me Doña Luisa sent them a basket of food every third day and a weekly allowance, just as Alejandro had promised. And to Raimunda's pleasure, everyone in town believed María Magdalena was Alejandro's daughter. She never denied it—and who could blame her?

The day after Christmas, Otilia and I walked to the arroyo to wash clothes. Being there gave me a sense of melancholy; things were different now, and I believed they were better. However, it is hard not to bring memories back. To my mind came the days we used to play as little girls in that same stream and Natalia would sing her impassioned songs to us. The memories of us enjoying the countryside view with Alejandro and his stories returned as a flashback. I wanted to walk to my roble tree, but Otilia was too tired.

"Do you mind if I go on my own?" I asked with begging eyes.

"No, not at all. Go ahead," she said; "I will take the basket back home. Be careful, and I will see you soon."

I started walking to my roble tree, pulling up my skirt and taking care not to let the thorns in the plants get through my shoes. I took deep breaths to enjoy the fresh countryside breeze that I missed so much in Mazatlán; everything here was quiet and calm. Only the small sounds of the grasshoppers and birds reached my ears. I lay on the thick branch that was my special spot and closed my eyes to feel myself floating over a beautiful sea of green. There is nothing more striking than the heavenly smell of the countryside, especially when detected from the solitude of a roble tree.

A collection of memories came to my mind, some sweet and others not, but they felt too far away to touch me. I missed Andrés. When I left, my heart shrank a bit from sadness. It was strange to know Orlando was close by, but it didn't affect me anymore; indifference best describes how I felt at that point. I turned my face towards El Roble. In the distance, on my right, I could see the magnificent back side of the Grand House, the hacienda of the Sarmiento family. The palm trees pointed to its exact location; next to it stood the overseers' house, then the church, but around it, the poverty the rest of the people of El Roble lived in was clearly visible.

December's air felt cold on my face on my way back to town. I encountered the workers coming from the fields; their tired faces greeted me with a facial sign of hello. I greeted them back understanding the injustice in their exploited existence. I reached the arroyo at dusk.

"Hello." The voice of Orlando came from my right side.

"Hi …," I replied and started walking away.

"Wait … when did you arrive?"

I stopped. "A few days ago. Have you heard from Alejandro?"

"He is coming back in February, at the beginning of the month, he said."

"When are the Barrazas coming back?" I dared to ask.

"Early January …"

"Good …," I gasped in relief.

"How is your sister?"

"Fine," I replied, avoiding any more explanations. "I have to get home now; take care."

"Yes, I do too. Take care of yourself … Happy New Year."

"I wish the same to you, happy New Year."

I walked away without looking back.

New Year's celebration arrived in an opening and closing of eyes. It had been a year since Natalia and Domingo had met for the first time, and now they were sharing a life in Boston. Things took unexpected turns. We celebrated at home, and on the second of January, I was on my way back to Mazatlán with a caravan of horses. I traveled by horseback because, this time, there was no carriage to take me. But what filled me with pride the most was the fact that my parents agreed without hesitation to my traveling with the caravan alone. It meant that they respected my independence and trusted my judgment. The trip was even entertaining because other women were riding as well, and I enjoyed listening to their conversation. Besides, to travel by horse made the trip feel a lot shorter.

When we arrived in Mazatlán, the city felt so familiar to me that it was an odd sensation to enter my apartment and feel at home. Soon the next day arrived, and I got ready to go to work; Señora Patterson had arranged with Señor Rodriguez, the newspaper's director, to shorten my hours to half-time, which allowed me to teach during the morning hours. My life was getting more interesting as time went by. January 1909 had come, and at almost sixteen years old, I was an accomplished teacher, newspaper receptionist, tutor, and independent girl.

Andrés told me before leaving for La Villa de San Sebastián that he was going to stay in his hometown until the third week of January. Three more weeks without seeing him made for a never-ending experience of sadness. My feelings for Andrés Randal grew stronger as time went by; I now laughed at my foolishness in thinking I would never fall in love again or that Orlando Sarmiento would never leave my mind and my heart. Time *does* cure all wounds and erases all traces of despair left inside by a broken illusion of love.

Señora Solorzano was gentle enough to get and save the letter for me. Yes, I had received another letter from Natalia. With shaking hands I opened it and started reading it as fast as my mind could process the information.

12 December 1908
Boston, Massachusetts

My dearest Maximiana,

I received your letter! I read it over and over again. Thank you, little sister. Thank you for all of your nice words for me and your advice. Alejandro also received his; he was very happy to hear from his Silly Face. I swear to God, Maxi, I honestly believe Alejandro likes you more than a friend. Domingo thinks the same thing. Maxi, today is the Day of the Virgin of Guadalupe. Do you remember last year? When I sang at church … I woke up remembering that day today.

Oh my God, Natalia. Enough! Tell me if you are expecting a baby or not!

Alejandro in love with me! Ha, ha, ha the snow is over-stimulating her imagination and Domingo's too!

Maxi, you have to send word to Mamá and Papá: I am expecting a baby! I told Alejandro first because I wanted to see a doctor and confirm it before telling Domingo. Alejandro took me to his friend's father who is a medicine doctor, and he said that, yes, I am going to have a baby! By the time you receive this letter I will have three months; he or she will be born at the beginning of summer. Maxi, I am so happy! Domingo was stunned when I told him, and then he went crazy with happiness, like me. We are happier than ever and promised each other not to fight anymore for stupid things.

He started his winter vacation last week and moved into the hotel with me; he and Alejandro invented the story that he had to travel to New York with his classmates. Now poor Alejandro is stuck with the Barrazas in the townhouse until they leave, all by himself. And guess what? We are going to spend Christmas together and New Year's Eve.

The only bad thing is that Domingo started a cold that he cannot get rid of; it is because it is too cold all the time. I am giving him remedies, but Domingo says it takes time to get rid of colds because of this weather. I haven't been out much for the same reason, but Domingo and I are having fun. He is teaching me English as well, but my singing lessons had to stop because of the holidays. I will be back with them in January; I miss singing too much. You know? My teacher says I will be able to perform in public soon, well … after the baby is born, of course. Do you think she listens to me when I sing? I wonder that. Just in case I am singing to her all the time, but in a low voice, and I call her my little nightingale because Domingo calls me nightingale, so I figured she is our little one. Alejandro teases that she should be named "Alejandra" after him and if it is a boy (but I doubt it because I can feel it that she is a girl), he should be named "Karl Friedrich" after two men he admires a lot, but I don't think Mamá and Papá would be able to say the names, don't you think? So Domingo thought we could translate them into Spanish as "Carlos Federico." However, it doesn't matter because her name is going to be "Alejandra Otilia Sarmiento Valladares y Lastra-Valdez."

For God's sake, I could picture the tiny baby with the endless name!

Maxi, I hope everyone over there has a wonderful Christmas and a very happy New Year! I send you all my love, little sister ... please tell Otilia that I miss her like CRAZY, give an enormously gigantic hug to my beloved Augusto, Lucia, and Rosaura. To Mamá and Papá, tell them how much I love them and miss them ... and that they are going to be grandparents of an American girl or boy ... hopefully a girl. He, he, he! Shhh! My secret.

Domingo sends you salutations and to my family as well. He says the baby is going to be a boy, not a girl. He is kidding; he says the baby is going to be as beautiful as his or her mamá. I think he will look like his daddy (that is English for papá).

I love you, Maxi!!!!!!!!

Your sister who never forgets you,

Natalia Sarmiento

My Goodness! What a beautiful letter.

Natalia sounded so happy and full of hope that her excitement became mine in an instant. My sister was going to have a baby, which was something to celebrate even when she was young and far away. I thanked God Domingo had taken it the way he had because once Alejandro returned to México, Domingo was the only person Natalia would have in Boston by her side. Hopefully, she would soon learn enough English to start making friends; everything was going to be all right. Nevertheless, I needed to find a way to let my family know of the wonderful news.

ndrés returned to Mazatlán the third week of January as he promised. He missed almost two weeks of classes at the German School, but he had nothing to worry about; he was an "academic genius," as I called him. As soon as he arrived, Andrés came to see me. He brought me as a present—a set of miniature wooden chairs. La Villa de San Sebastián was famous for making very beautiful wooden furniture, and their miniature versions made the best Christmas presents for children. I had wanted a set of them as a little girl. How had Andrés figured that out? I don't know, but he made me a happy almost-sixteen-year-old girl.

It was almost my time to go home from the office after a long day when Orlando entered the *Afternoon Mail*, his face as white as the piece of paper in my hand. My respiration accelerated, and a feeling of anguish entered my heart.

"What happened?" I asked him as I rose from my chair.

He stared back at me with the blank expression of a person who can't find the strength to talk. I walked around and out of my counter and moved towards him.

"Orlando … what is wrong?" I reached for his arm. "Please tell me …"

Orlando looked down. "I got a telegram from Alejandro—"

"Natalia! What happened to Natalia?" I exclaimed in anguish, knowing right away that something was very wrong. "Is she well? And her baby? Are they all right?"

Confused, Orlando asked, "Was she expecting a baby?"

"*Was*? What do you mean *was*?" My eyes expanded into two saucers.

Paula got out of her office when she saw what seemed to be an intense discussion. "Is everything all right here?" she asked, turning her eyes from Orlando to me and vice versa.

"Orlando … tell me. What happened?" I asked as I started to feel a dizziness that was making me see double.

"She became sick with a very bad cold that moved to an infection in the chest …"

I didn't know if I wanted to listen anymore. And then I knew I didn't and took my hands to my ears when he whispered the words, "Natalia passed away."

The pounding of my heart stopped for a few eternal seconds while the walls around me turned in circles. Air stopped filling my lungs, and I ran out, hearing, as an echo, the words, "Follow her."

My feet carried me nonstop until I reached the jetty. Without thinking, I jumped to the sand and continued racing towards the water, leaving behind torn fragments of my soul. I felt nothing but numbness. I collapsed in the water, and devastation began to invade my confusion. I wasn't sure if the salty water entering my mouth came from my tears of sorrow or the water from the sea. I didn't care; I just wanted to drown myself in my grief.

"Maxi," Orlando said to my ear while tightly surrounding my waist with his arms, "come with me." He started pulling me out of the water, but I kept moving forward. "Maxi, don't."

"I want to die. This is entirely my fault."

"How can it be your fault?"

"I brought her that night to your house when she met Domingo because I wanted to spend New Year's *with you* … if I hadn't taken her she would never have met Domingo and gone to that cold place." That was my childish answer.

He dragged me out of the water and sat me between his legs on the wet sand while the waves continued hitting us.

"I want to die," I said in sobs. "This is all my fault."

I tried to escape his grasp, and he pulled me down again.

"No, Maximiana, this is nobody's fault …"

"Let go of me!" I said and started hitting him with all of the force of my excruciating pain. He grabbed my hands, and we struggled. I managed to escape into the coming waves again, but he pulled me out, and we fell on our backs.

"If you go," he said, forcibly restraining my wrists, "I am going after you. And if you drown, I drown with you. And Alejandro will never forgive you for it."

I broke into desperation and turned around; the water hit me relentlessly and without compassion, as hard as life was striking me at that moment.

Orlando stirred his body towards mine and hugged me with force. I could hear him cry at the rhythm of my sobs, "I am sorry, Maxi … I am sorry you are *now* going through something like this."

I didn't respond to that; my mind was too dazed to feel consolation, but I felt his once familiar arms around my body shaking, as if with the strength of his hold, the pounding of his heart, and yes, the caring in his effort were jumping from his body to mine. I closed my eyes to hear the echoes of our sobs and the crushing of the waves against each other. It was unreal to be in the embrace of Orlando Sarmiento at the hardest moment of my life.

I don't know how long I remained lost in those eternal moments of despair, but Paula and Agatha's hands came to mine and softly asked me to rise from the wet sand. I looked up and saw the faces of the two women comforting me. In the confusion of the moment, I glanced at the people witnessing my scene of desolation, but the perplexed figure of Andrés Randal watching from a prudent distance struck me. His eyes were not showing his usual compassion or understanding, and a small frown lined his eyebrows when I walked towards him. He looked up when I finally reached his side. I threw my arms at him, but he didn't respond to my embrace as I would have expected.

"Oh Max …," Paula said, placing her hand on my shoulder, "we are very sorry about your sister."

Agatha hugged me from my back, "Yes, Maxi … it is such a tragedy … but we must go home now; you are wet, and it is cold; come on, dear … let's go home."

I allowed them to direct my steps. Agatha and Paula each held one of my arms, and in the distance I saw Orlando still sitting on the sand looking into the orange and grey horizon. Andrés walked behind us, never pronouncing a word. I guessed he felt hurt and rejected because I had allowed Orlando Sarmiento to hold me in my despair, never realizing Orlando had saved me from my own drowning pain.

I didn't want to be the one telling the news to my parents. There were no words simple enough to ease the pain they were going to encounter at the moment they heard their daughter was gone forever. I could picture everyone hurting with the news, but the pain my parents were going to go through was unbearable to imagine. We all loved Natalia, there was no doubt about it, but next to my parents' affection, ours was nothing.

Agatha accompanied me to El Roble to give the news to my family. I wished I had had more details to tell, but Alejandro didn't explain to Orlando what had happened. I had so little time to comfort their sadness because I had to return to Mazatlán to my jobs.

Bittersweet was the memory of a few weeks earlier when we had talked so excitedly about the baby and our family growing, but the opposite had happened. Silently, my mind replayed Mamá's words of concern over Natalia's body, that she was going to stay so far away from us, in a place where no one would ever visit her. Mamá wondered if they had offered her a mass, if she had received the blessings from a priest. Deep inside I thought there was no difference because if she was gone, she was gone. But I didn't dare tell her.

Upon my return to Mazatlán, Andrés was waiting for me. He seemed sad and concerned about something but refused to tell me what was bothering him. At that time I still mourned my sister and had not the mental resources to pursue it; it could wait. I didn't know how to feel; everything appeared to be unreal because in my imagination Natalia was still in Boston, expecting a baby, and taking English and singing lessons, happily married to handsome Domingo Sarmiento. I kept that fantasy in my mind until Alejandro arrived unexpectedly, on a cold afternoon. Then reality struck me … there was no alternate truth. My dear sister was gone for real, but I just couldn't accept it.

"We are back," Alejandro said at my door when I opened it. He looked older, and his face showed an indescribable expression of mortification and guilt. A torrent of tears rolled out of my eyes as soon as I had my dearest friend, Alejandro, in front of me; my first reaction was to crush against him as I always had when my heart was aching.

"Maxi … I am so sorry … so, so sorry …" Alejandro broke down. "We tried everything …"

"Please tell me what happened, Aleh, and do not spare me any details, for God's sake; I have been waiting to hear this for a long time …"

We sat at the table, looking at each other's teary eyes.

Then Aleh glanced down and, with quivering lips, began. "I never thought I would live anything like that, Maxi." His face collapsed into his crossed arms resting on the table and started to cry. "Maxi … I felt so powerless; there was nothing I could do for Natalia or Domingo … I brought different doctors, but when you get pneumonia, even they cannot do anything." He paused. "Domingo never moved from her side … not for an instant."

"What did she say?" I asked in broken sounds. "Did she suffer a lot …?"

"She knew she was dying … the last days she became aware of it."

"How long did it last?" I asked, glancing at the afternoon light filtering through the window and the dust particles traveling through the sun's rays. My mouth and throat went dry.

"Almost one week she couldn't get off the bed; it happened so fast, Maxi … she started with a cold, then a cough … then the fever came, and it wouldn't leave her … when the doctor told us it was pneumonia, the world collapsed under my feet. I thought of you, your family … Natalia knew she was dying and kept asking for her mother …"

"Did she lose the baby before passing away?"

"No … the baby went with her …"

"Oh …" The sound escaped my chest.

"You could see the bump; the baby already moved …"

"Oh, Aleh … this is such a tragedy …," I murmured.

"Maxi … we couldn't take Domingo off her when she passed away … he couldn't accept it. He kept screaming she was asleep and was about to wake up. He called her 'nightingale,' and when it happened, when she was finally gone, he kept shaking her and repeating, 'Wake up, nightingale … please, wake up …' Maxi, all of our hearts broke at that; I can't imagine witnessing anything like that …"

I buried my face in my arms, picturing each of Natalia's last moments and drowning in my own sobs. "Did you have a mass for her soul before the funeral?"

"We did …"

"Where is she buried?" I asked, confused, still not completely grasping reality.

"In Cambridge, but we brought her things back with us … I am afraid for Domingo, he is too confused with sorrow. We already told Father everything, Maxi; he reacted better than what I thought he would. He is even sending the carriage down to El Roble to take Natalia's things to your family with us … I need you to come along; I cannot face them, Maxi."

"It isn't your fault. I felt the same way at the beginning … that I was responsible for everything that happened to Natalia, but now I see it was destiny; she was supposed to meet your brother and live the adventure of traveling to that place so far away …"

Alejandro rose and passed his arms around mine, "I failed you, my friend."

"No, you never have and never will. Thank *you* for bringing Natalia's things back to us."

"Oh Maxi, nothing will ever be the same … I am very afraid for Domingo; he seems lost without her, and he is not himself anymore, Max. You will not recognize him."

"I am heartbroken for Domingo, too. In Natalia's last letter, she said he was very happy about the baby … even though I wonder if he comprehended what becoming a father really entailed."

"I think he did," Alejandro responded in a whisper.

"It makes it worse for him then … he also lost a child and his dreams for it."

"I know."

A sudden calmness entered my not-long-ago turbulent mind. Perhaps a resignation to the unchangeable truth was the only option available now if I wanted to keep my sanity. I offered Alejandro a cup of coffee, which he accepted. We kept silent, and then he offered a gift I did not anticipate.

"Maxi, Natalia recorded several songs before passing away."

"Recorded?" I asked, not understanding what he was talking about.

"Yes, on a record, a flat platter that has tiny marks on it. A special machine called a phonograph turns the record and has a needle that can read those marks and changes them into sounds." Alejandro smiled. "I am telling you this, and I can hear how silly my words must seem to you. You will have to see what I am talking about to understand. But believe me; you will hear your sister on the record. She had a chance to record several songs … she asked to record a message to all of you … when she learned she was very sick."

"Her voice?" I still asked in disbelief.

"Yes."

"But … where is it? I want to hear it."

"A friend of mine will bring it when it's ready."

"I see …," I replied, turning away.

"How are things with Orlando …?" Alejandro shyly asked.

"There is nothing … he never apologized nor did he change his mind about my worthlessness."

"Don't think that; there is no way Orlando thinks of you that way. He cannot be that stupid, Maxi."

"His behavior shows that, and you know it. But, Aleh, I don't want to talk about it; there is no point."

"Are you single now?" he asked, rounding the cup with his finger.

"No," a smile escaped my lips, "Andrés Randal and I are in a relationship."

Alejandro smiled back, "He is a lucky man."

"You always say the right things at the right time."

"It is the truth, and you shouldn't think the contrary, Silly Face."

"It is interesting how you and I became friends. When I think of my best friend in the world, *you*, Alejandro Sarmiento, come to my mind."

"Thank you, Max," he said, pulling my nose, "I feel the same way about you."

We parted that afternoon after hours of long conversation that made me feel some peace. Alejandro Sarmiento always had such an effect in my life.

"Andrés!"

I hugged him with enthusiasm when he stood at my door. Andrés had kept a prudent distance since learning of Natalia's passing away, and even though his attitude puzzled me, I didn't question it.

"How are you?" he asked, avoiding my eyes.

"Better. Alejandro was here yesterday, and he explained everything to me; it helped me a lot to know what exactly happened. I haven't seen Domingo though. I hope he comes today. I want to see him and … offer … say …"

"Yes," he responded.

"How are *you*? I haven't seen you in days"

"Fine."

"Please sit …"

Awkwardness hovered in the air, and our conversation took no direction. It felt like an exchange of empty words. I looked into his emerald eyes, searching for a reason underneath his attitude and discovered somberness in what used to be light.

"No, Andrés, you are not fine," I finally said, now concerned.

Andrés looked away. He rose from his chair and walked to the window. The breeze from the sea blew his hair away; he removed his glasses and cleaned them with a red and blue handkerchief. I took a deep breath because an uncomfortable premonition suddenly settled within me.

"Whatever it is … say it, Andrés Daniel," I said, standing behind him. This time I was not turning my back to whatever was coming.

"Later … you are going through too much already," he replied without looking back at me.

I gasped, "I can take anything … trust me on that one … just tell me whatever it is, but look me in the eyes."

Andrés turned around and stared at my eyes with a shy intensity and spit it out.

"I want to break up with you—"

"Why?"

"I think you still have feelings for Orlando Sarmiento—"

"Don't be silly, Andrés … please."

"I am not being silly. When you found out about your sister, you ran to him, not to me."

"I didn't run to him! He ran after me because Paula told him to do it … and I tried to throw myself into the sea … I could've explained this to you before, but I had no chance … I am very sorry, Andrés, if I offended you with that …" I put his left hand between my two, but he didn't respond to the gesture.

"I … think we should break up and be friends … maybe later we could start again."

"Andrés … this makes no sense." I let go of his hand. "You are using Orlando as an excuse to break up with me."

"I am going to México City in three months and won't be back for a year …"

"We knew that beforehand, Andrés. Why are you bringing it up now? Besides, I plan to take the entrance examination … Señora Patterson is willing to sponsor me to become a certified teacher in México City."

Uncomfortably, he turned away.

"What is *really* going on? Why don't you tell me once and for all?" I asked, losing my patience.

"Nothing else is going on; I just need some time for myself and to move on to México City without any compromise. I think there should be nothing else beyond friendship between us. "

"Compromise? Since when did I become a 'compromise'? You should've told me before, Andrés. There is no need to … look …," and I took a deep breath, "I understand … I hope we can still be friends."

Andrés' face pulled backward. My reaction utterly perplexed him. "Are you sure?"

"Yes, I am sure," I replied, aching inside but not showing a hint of my bursting heart.

"Thank you, Maximiana. I really feel better because for some time I have been thinking that I don't want anything else to be between us … that we should stay friends."

"Really?" I asked, confused.

"Yes, I have been carrying this weight on my shoulders for some time because I didn't know how you were going to react to it, but now I feel that it is the best thing to do, for us to be friends and not change that."

"Well … I am glad I could help you," I said with a smile.

He grabbed both of my hands and kissed them. "You are amazing."

"Thanks … now I have to get ready; Domingo is coming today."

"Yes, of course." Andrés Daniel Randal, full of an undeniable happiness, hugged me and kissed my cheek. "Good-bye, Maxi … I will see you soon then … when are we having our next Cactus meeting?"

"I don't know … ask Agatha on your way out; she is the meeting coordinator."

"I will!" he replied enthusiastically as he marched away.

He closed the door behind him; I locked it and rested my back on its shiny flat wood.

It happens again.

I strolled to my bedroom to place myself in front of the long mirror and carefully examined myself. For the first time, I paid attention to the exact way I looked—my big and long oval eyes, full of long eyelashes that guarded the darkest brown eyes … the long nose, with its Indian curvature … my thick lips … straight white teeth inside a medium-size mouth. I passed my fingers over the side of my rounded face; it was golden dark, burned from the sun. I was small in stature; no wonder Daniel always teased me about it. I pulled my stomach in and noticed my body showing the curves of a woman, not a little girl's body anymore. My hair fell down to my buttocks, long, black, and naturally straight but showing waves from the entanglement of my braids. I sat on the small bed, not knowing how to react to Andrés's sudden departure from my life. A knock on the door interrupted my thoughts and shied away the tears I felt pushing from within me.

"Come in, Domingo," I said, and the brutal reality of Natalia's death hit me again. His beautiful eyes held such sorrow and pain; he hugged me with force, and I hugged him back. Alejandro stood outside and said he would be back later to pick Domingo up. In no time, Domingo's sobs shook him with despair; I didn't know how to console him when I was broken into pieces myself.

"I miss her, Maxi; I miss her a lot," he said in broken sounds and words of desolation. "I don't know what I am going to do now."

I pulled strength from within to say, "Natalia would not want you to be like this, Domingo; you have to be strong for her and her memory … she loved you so, and you know it."

"But how can I live like this, without her? I took her there; she became ill because of me."

"No, Domingo, don't say that … it was destiny. It had to happen like that for some reason that, perhaps one day, we will understand, but for now we need to have resignation and accept reality; we have to move on, as Natalia would've wanted us to …"

"But I can't, I can't accept it."

"You have to … God put you two together for a reason, and now Natalia looks after you from wherever she is, and I believe it is heaven. She was an angel, Domingo, and she had to be with the angels."

"No! I want her to be with me!"

"Domingo come, sit here … I will make you some tea."

He walked to the washroom, and while putting the teapot to warm water on the stove, I thought of Domingo. He looked helpless in his pain and not ready to challenge what life had placed in front of his young life. He collapsed on a chair at the table.

"Why do they leave me, Maxi?"

They.

"Your mother and Natalia left for a reason, Domingo, and I think it is to make you a better person … at least that is how I feel about Natalia's death. I have so much to do in her name and so many battles to fight. For example this afternoon, not long before you arrived, my dear Domingo, Andrés Randal was here …"

Domingo raised his face and looked at me with intrigue in his eyes.

"What happened?"

"He was here to break up with me, without further explanations than he wanted to move on and be friends, just friends."

"Natalia never said you were going out with Randal."

"She knew; I told her, but she probably forgot. I really liked Andrés … I even loved him, I think."

"You think? What do you mean by that?"

"I am hurting a lot, but it doesn't feel as bad as when your brother did what he did."

"Andrés is an idiot."

"At least he was honest." I had to keep my dignity intact.

"Why did he break up with you?"

"I told you; he wanted to move on and felt a weight lifted from his shoulders when he broke up with me."

"Did he say that?"

"Yes, he did. Perhaps he is going back to Catalina Barraza," I casually mentioned.

"I don't think he is *that* stupid, Maxi."

"Let's hope not," I replied with honesty. "When are you going back to Boston?"

"I don't want to go back."

"Are you crazy? How can you even doubt it, Domingo? Natalia would never forgive you for not finishing your studies! You cannot do that!"

"I don't have the head to do it, Maximiana."

"Well ... get it back on, Señorito Domingo! Stop this silliness right now! We are all hurting, we are all heartbroken in a million pieces, but we must go on; that is the least we can do in Natalia's memory. Do you understand what I am saying?"

"No."

"Domingo ... please listen to me ... Natalia loved you and you loved her. The two of you lived a romance to inspire a book, honestly ... but now that she is physically gone, you cannot give up your life. She would never forgive you for that. Natalia would want you to go back to school and finish your medical studies; she would want you to become the greatest doctor and help a lot of people ... Natalia would want you to spread the recording of her songs so that others can hear her beautiful voice ... and ... she would want you to fall in love again."

This last phrase came out in a whisper, as if I feared Natalia hearing me say such a thing to her beloved Domingo.

"I don't think she would want me to fall in love again ..." He lowered his head.

"Yes, she would! Domingo listen to me ... I knew Natalia Valdez like no one else in this world. She was my sister, we grew up together, and ever since I can remember, she was a romantic soul flying in the warm winds of El Roble. Her entire life was filled with music and love; she thought of nothing else but her songs and the passion that love stirred within her ..."

He looked up at me with his beautiful dark eyes, realizing that, indeed, I knew Natalia as well as he did.

"Do you understand why she gave herself to you without question? Do you see now that she would *never* want you to forget about love and happiness?"

"No," he replied in the lowest voice.

"Domingo ... she *truly* loved you ... and when you truly love someone, you want that person to be happy, no matter what, and *I know* Natalia wants you to be happy because she loves you so."

Affectionately, I held his face with both of my hands. "It will take some time, Domingo, and I am not telling you to fall in love again right now, but the first step is to go back to school. Don't be afraid that you will forget my sister. You will never forget her because the sounds of nightingales are never forgotten," I whispered as the timid tears finally escaped my eyes.

"Thank you, Maximiana."

"No … thank *you* for making Natalia so happy and giving her a chance to see what she saw before leaving us. Thank you for recording her voice."

"She was a nightingale, and you are a gardenia," Domingo unexpectedly said.

"Gardenia?"

"You are a mysterious flower … beautiful in your very own way, and your hair gives off an indescribable and unforgettable fragrance."

From the heat I felt on my cheeks, I imagined I had turned bright red.

"I'm sorry, Max; did I make you uncomfortable?"

"A little bit. I am not used to those kinds of compliments, but thank you." I rose and brought the tea, swallowing my tears.

"Are you coming with us to El Roble?"

"Yes, I will. And I will be there when your ship takes you back to Harvard University."

"You don't give up, do you?" he said, smiling for the first time.

"No, never … I am your worst nightmare." I gave him a little push with my fist.

"Do you remember when we talked the first time?" he asked, showing a hint of amusement.

"The night Aleh pushed me into your room and said a ghost was sleeping there?"

"Yes … that was funny."

"I know! It seemed as if it happened ages ago!"

"True … Your tea is good. Thank you."

"Would you like a piece of sweet bread? I bought it on my way from work; it is fresh."

"Sure … where are you working?" he asked, taking the first bite.

"At the *Afternoon Mail* and also as a teacher in the Patterson house-hold, plus once a week I tutor a girl; she is almost my age, though."

"Awesome … someone is at the door. Do you want me to open it?"

"Yes, please, it is probably Alejandro."

Alejandro was apparently shocked at the scene of us calmly drinking tea. I offered him tea and bread. He sat down but kept staring at Domingo's new serene expression on his face.

"I was about to tell Domingo that I am planning to take the admissions exam to the National University of México. Señora Patterson wants to sponsor me to get a teaching certificate."

"That is great, Maxi," Alejandro said in a flash. "You deserve it."

"Yes, this is good news. Andrés is also going there, yes?" Domingo said.

"Yes," I replied and looked away.

"So the two of you are together?" Alejandro teased.

"No, we are not *together* anymore," I answered with a dignified tone. "He … well … we became just friends this evening."

"Are you fine with that?" Alejandro asked, clearly concerned.

"Of course … I have experience in that subject, remember?"

"What subject?" Domingo asked.

"I have experience in the subject of being tossed aside in a relationship without any warning," I replied, showing the pain of Andrés's words still gripped me.

Alejandro's face hardened and asked, "What was his excuse?"

"He said that he needs to move on or something like that but … Aleh, I don't care. I also want to move on. This time … I didn't even cry."

"Because I arrived," Domingo intervened.

"No, I didn't cry because I know by now that I will forget about him as I forgot about Orlando, and someone who disrespects my feelings that way does not deserve my tears."

"But you must be disappointed," Alejandro said with his sweet tone of concern.

"Of course, I am disappointed, Aleh … I invested time and energy in this relationship, and it ended up in nothing *again*. Even though this time I am not as surprised as the first time; I guess you get used to it, yes?"

Apparently, they didn't know what to say.

"When he left, I took a good look in the mirror, and I think I am beginning to understand what is going on," I continued.

"What?" Alejandro asked, frowning. Domingo seemed confused.

"I think that they will always find someone more attractive than I am," I said, raising my eyebrows with a pretended disinterest in the subject.

"Andrés didn't break up with you for someone else, Maxi. Why do you say that?" Alejandro asked, immediately refuting my words.

"He didn't need to say it, Aleh. I *know*."

Both of them looked down.

"You are beautiful, Maximiana," Alejandro said.

"Am I?" I asked, sarcastically.

"You are being silly now, Maxi. Stupid fellows break up with beautiful and wonderful girls all the time for any number of reasons. Sometimes the reasons make no sense at all, sometimes they have stupid excuses, and many times the explanations are completely unrelated to the girls they are breaking up with. Maxi, don't make such an assumption and belittle yourself that way for a man that may well have his reasons hidden."

"I am not belittling myself."

"Yes, you are," Domingo intervened. "You are saying that your heart will be broken all the time because any other girl will be better looking than you, and that is wrong, Maxi, I am sorry to say. There will always be someone more beautiful or less beautiful than you, and most of the time, the way you look has nothing to do with whether someone likes you or not."

"Also," I ventured, "I might be attractive to some and not attractive to others …"

"Yes!" both of them replied.

"So, what is this then? Bad luck?" I asked with sincerity.

"You haven't found the right person yet, that's all," Alejandro firmly replied.

"At almost sixteen, my heart has been broken twice in an unexpected manner. Most girls my age are already married."

"Marry me then, and the problem is solved!" Alejandro said jokingly.

"Thank you for the offer, but I'd rather not have the first one who broke my heart as a brother-in-law!"

We all started laughing.

"Natalia would've loved it if you had married Alejandro," Domingo said.

Alejandro's smile faded away. He looked at me with a shocked expression.

"Nah," I said, "she wanted me to marry the least handsome Sarmiento." Both chuckled when I said that. "And if I'd marry Aleh, I would win over her because Aleh is the most handsome Sarmiento in the world."

I winked, and they laughed again.

"At what time are we leaving for El Roble tomorrow?" I asked, remembering we had to plan the trip.

"At five in the morning, and we are riding, if you don't mind, to get there faster. Also you need to be back Sunday evening, yes?" Alejandro replied.

"Yes, I have to work on Monday. I am glad you changed your mind about taking a carriage just for me."

"We are set then," Domingo said while getting ready to leave. "Thank you for your words, Maxi."

We all hugged each other good-bye.

That night I couldn't sleep, thinking about how the next day would bring memories I just didn't want to face again. I would be taking Natalia's things home. "Her things." It never entered my head that what we carried in that beautifully detailed box were the last items left of my dear sister. Taking it home with the knowledge that we would have to go through those items stirred up all sorts of feelings—dread, sadness, helplessness, even bittesweetness. Never before had I had to handle anything so difficult. But as apprehensive as I was, I needed to do it for her. And from her, her memory and the legacy of the almost sixteen years I had known her, I found the strength I needed.

27

As I feared, the trip home brought up all of the pain I thought I had confronted and dealt with but had only swept aside. To be around so many others grieving made my own suffering worse, and I had little heart left to help my poor parents. After days of pouring out my heart, I returned to Mazatlán. But I felt suffocated. Yes, Mazatlán was a city far larger than El Roble, but it felt small and confining to me, hampering my ambitious spirit. I needed to venture beyond the realities that surrounded me. I wanted to see and live and experience more—what exactly, I did not know, but I did know I needed to break away to feel complete.

Weeks passed by quickly once I settled back in my normal routine. On one of those busy days, while walking back from the *Afternoon Mail*, I encountered my dear friend Josefina. I had not seen her in a long time and asked her if she wanted to walk to the jetty with me to have a soda. We sat on a rock facing the immense purple sea. Josefina told me her life continued in the same mechanical existence of serving the Sarmientos at the Grand City House. She appeared tired and without much hope for the future. According to her, at her age of "over twenty," her chances of finding a husband were diminishing, and having to be inside that house from Monday to Sunday seriously reduced her opportunities of meeting men. I was more worried by the fact that Josefina seemed to have no dreams in life, besides that of finding a husband. I debated if I should tell her about the Cactus and its meetings, and finally I did. I had been part of the group long enough to have the freedom of inviting a member on my own.

Josefina showed a genuine interest when I began describing the Cactus to her. The uprisings in northern México were not rumors anymore; they were a reality, a response to the upcoming presidential elections. Porfirio Diaz had been México's president since 1876 and planned to see himself re-elected in the July 8, 1910 election. But the system imposed on the majority of the Mexican people could not sustain itself anymore; signs everywhere hinted at something bigger than those uprisings on our way.

Without a doubt, if the revolution exploded, I would fight and give my life for it if necessary. Up to this day, in every part of my being, I know there is no more honorable dream than the one of fighting to death for your true beliefs of social justice. I could not impose those beliefs on my friend Josefina. But at least I could expose her to a world of new ideas, and perhaps she would find a way to escape the barriers she had been born into as a member of the working class, or as we called it in the Cactus, the proletariat.

The following Saturday our meeting took place in my apartment, and to my pleasure, Josefina joined us. Andrés, who had been avoiding me since our breakup, came, as did Domingo, who accompanied Alejandro. But Orlando was nowhere to be seen, as usual, around these meetings, and I was glad for it.

Later on, when almost everyone had left, Josefina came to me to express her gratitude for inviting her to the Cactus. She said that she felt inspired and hopeful that perhaps things were going to change for the better. She was older than I in age but not in knowledge or experience or understanding, for she had never realized, as I had, the *true* realities surrounding her. But I told her that our wishes were not good enough, that action had to be taken. She was surprised by the idea of *her* doing something that would make a difference.

"But, Maximiana, what can *I* possibly do? Don't be silly!" she said, laughing.

"My goodness, Josefina! There is so much you can do!"

"Really? Like what? Tell me, Señora Maxi; enlighten me!" she replied, teasing me.

"Start by reading a lot. Take classes with the nuns … I am sure you will be able to escape from work for an hour! And save a little bit of your money, a little bit, Josefina, at least five cents a week."

"How does that help the revolution, Maxi?" she asked, confused.

"By rising from your ignorance and dependency on the rich … that is how. You see, you escape your slavery if you have the means to live on your own. And, if you continue to save a little bit, when you have enough, you can finally start something on your own away from the oppressive bourgeois."

"It is not as easy as it sounds, Maxi. And, even if I would work on my own—as a seamstress, maybe—I'd still be working for *them*."

"Yes, but at least you'd have a say about whether or not to do it … you choose the ones you work for, yes?"

She smiled, "Yes! Yes, I see."

"We have our very own *revolution*." I winked.

"I see and I like it!" she suddenly said enthusiastically.

I gave her an enormous hug. At that moment, very few people lingered in my living room, and Andrés was among them. Domingo and Alejandro noticed his presence and said good-bye to me, smiling.

"How are you?" Andrés asked with his emerald eyes hiding behind the round glasses, when we were left alone in the apartment.

"I am very excited!" It was my honest reply, "I think Josefina has been inspired to do something to change her life, and that makes me very happy."

"That sounds good, that is what the Cactus is all about … so when are you taking the admissions exam?"

"In May. I am going to Caliacán for it. Augusto is going with me. I have been preparing really hard, so I think I will be fine."

Barely hiding his shock at the realization, he gasped in reply, "I'm sure you will; you will probably be the most prepared one there. You are always reading."

He followed me to the kitchen but stood by the door.

"I feel lucky to work in the *Afternoon Mail* because I can borrow books from their store and even read during work hours. They don't mind at all … right now I am reading *Little Women* by Louisa May Alcott. I love the fact that the story takes place in Massachusetts and that my sister Natalia lived there."

"How are you doing with that?" he shyly asked.

"I regret not reading it before," I answered, purposely ignoring the true intent of his question, "because it makes a lot of sense to me. Everything in that novel makes sense to me! What a coincidence that they are several sisters and one … passes away."

Andrés looked down and walked toward me, but I passed by him quickly to enter the living room.

"It was a good meeting today," I said. "If I get accepted into the teaching program, I will miss these meetings a lot!"

"Where are you going to live in México City?"

"In a boarding house for young women. Señora Patterson is already making the arrangements; she is very sure I will pass the entrance examination."

Andrés sighed, "Me, too."

"You don't sound very happy. You know? You have nothing to worry about, Andrés; you will not see me in México City if I get to go … and if we ever meet on the street, it is fine with me … you don't have to greet me," I told him directly to his shocked face.

"What in the world are you talking about?"

"You know exactly what I'm talking about," I gasped. "It is late; I want to go to sleep now. Good night."

"No, I am not going anywhere, Maximiana, until you tell me what you are implying." His voice had grown irritated. "Are you implying that I am ashamed to be seen with you? Is that what you're saying?"

"You gasped when you said that you are sure I will pass the examination! As if you were not very happy about it!"

Clearly perturbed by my words he replied, "I … I am tired … that is why I gasped."

"Yes, but of course," I laughed in hurtful amusement.

"Why do you laugh? This is not funny at all," Andrés said with a blank stare.

"It is funny to me but not for the reasons you or other people might think."

"Maxi," he lowered his guard, "you said we would be friends no matter what, but you don't sound like one."

"You don't sound very happy with the idea of my going to México City."

"I hope you pass the examination and go to México City. There … are you convinced now?" he exclaimed, holding my shoulders.

Gently, I took his hands down.

"It is late, and I am going to the beach with Alejandro tomorrow morning, so if you don't mind, I would like to go to sleep."

"Yes, yes … good night."

He smoothly kissed me on the cheek. I felt shivers in my body when his lips touched my skin, and involuntarily, I closed my eyes. I felt his warm breathing lift the loose hairs above my ears. Then I turned around to hide my obvious perturbation.

Andrés closed the door behind him, and I took a deep breath to let go. I promised myself right that instant that I would neither question nor wonder what had happened between Andrés Randal and me. Once, I had trusted him with all of my heart, as much as I had trusted Orlando Sarmiento, and he, like Orlando, had betrayed my feelings without any warning. Again I found myself asking life if I would ever fall in love again and realized that I surely would; I was only fifteen years and eleven months old. And, even so, falling in love was just a small portion of what I had going on in my life.

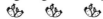

"Are you ready, Silly Face?"

Alejandro was at my door at 7:00 a.m. sharp; we had promised each other to spend the day at the beach that Sunday, and nothing would prevent it.

"I am almost done with the food basket. But this feels hot for April, don't you think?" I asked while filling the basket with treats for the day.

"I reserved a *palapa* so we will surely have shade for the day."

"How's Domingo doing?" I asked, locking the door behind me.

"Better, much better. Since his conversation with you, some of his optimism has returned. But Orlando is a bit dispirited."

I pretended not to hear his comment. "Are we walking or taking the carriage?"

"Since we are going far north, I brought the carriage. It is too bad Agatha and Paula didn't want to join us."

"I know! I begged them to come, but they already had plans to go to the Isla de la Piedra Beach; perhaps we should join them."

"We still can … let's take the carriage, and then we can rent a boat to cross us."

"Good idea!" I exclaimed full of enthusiasm, I had never been to the Island of the Rock before.

"You don't mind Andrés Randal being there?"

"Of course not! Why would I? Don't be silly, Aleh …," I scolded.

"Would you mind then if I stop at my house and invite Orlando?"

"I don't feel comfortable stopping by your house. Leonora doesn't like my presence around her property."

"It is my property as well," he replied sharply. "Besides, that is a misleading excuse, Maxi …"

I placed the basket on the floor of the carriage and smiled at Alejandro. "You should've invited Domingo."

"He has a cold," he responded with a frown. "When are you going to forgive Orlando, Maxi? It has been over a year since *that* happened."

The carriage started moving. "I don't want to talk about Orlando; I don't even think about him anymore, Aleh."

And you don't know how it feels to have your head pushed away and be kicked in public by him.

"Fine … but you shouldn't keep so many bad memories in you. Life goes on, yes?" he said a little bit irritated.

"I know, but it does not mean I want it to go on with him in my presence, yes?"

"No, but … fine … never mind!"

"Are you going back to the United States with Domingo?" I asked, hoping he would negate my question.

"No … I wish I could go with him, though, but I have to stay and work with Father. But Domingo is not going back until August. He missed this semester altogether already; besides this break is good for him after everything he's been through. Father agrees. I still cannot believe Father accepted the situation and did not kill us for what we did—Domingo marrying Natalia and us taking her to the United States." Aleh paused and then added with a bit of a smile, "Life goes on for him, too, I guess."

I nodded.

"Leonora is expecting another child; she is angrier than ever," he suddenly said.

"She is not a happy woman," I mused. "She married too young, I guess."

"Father is losing his patience with her, also," he commented, shaking his head. "He cannot stand her."

As we hit uneven roads closer to our destination, the bumps of the carriage kept us giggling because our jostling bodies could not utter a complete sentence without interruption. Soon enough, the sea breeze entered my lungs and told me we were close. Even at this very instant, the delight in the memory of those sudden encounters with the salty air hold strong within me.

28

I couldn't contain myself from giggling all the way across the sea to the Isla de la Piedra. When we passed the big rock that resembles a statue of a lion, the small boat shook so badly that I feared we might turn altogether or crash against the rocks; fortunately we didn't and reached the island in a matter of twenty minutes or so. Alejandro helped me jump off the boat and asked the owner to return for us at 7:00 p.m. I did not like that idea at all and refused to return so late. Crossing the sea at night was not my idea of an adventure at all. Finally, gentleman Alejandro agreed, and the man promised to come and get us at around four o'clock.

The line of coconut trees extended as far south as you could see on the edge of the sandy white beach. Isolated best described the landscape, and the Randals and other friends' absence made it feel more so.

"Do you think they are here already?" I asked, squinting to make my eyes see farther.

"They should be … or they are about to get here. I'm glad we told the man to return at four; I don't think it is a good idea for us to be here alone at night."

I found the loneliness around us disturbing. "But people live here, yes?"

"The town is very deep inside," Alejandro answered, also visibly uncomfortable with the empty scene before us.

"Perhaps we should go back; the *lanchero* is still in the boat."

"I think it is fine; the Randals and the rest of the group will be here soon, for sure."

Not completely convinced, I agreed. "Let's find some shade then."

꧂

I sat under the palm trees and waited for Alejandro who had to attend to a private necessity. I laid my back on the silky white sand and closed my eyes. The magical sounds of the waves reaching the beach floated me into a dream of sweet pleasures. I opened my eyes, and the rays of sun filtering through the palm leaves made me realize how lucky I was to be alive. And no matter how comforting the idea of my beloved Natalia being somewhere better, I regretted that she had not had the chance to be here … long enough.

I took a deep breath and told myself to work to be a better person, as I always did every time my Natalia came to mind. I felt Alejandro running towards the sea. I sat up and laughed to see him wearing short pants and jumping in. I stood up, pulled the back of my skirt between my legs to the front and tucked it in the front waistline; then I started running towards the fresh salty water. I don't know how many times I drank the waves, but it didn't matter; I kept laughing just the same. Alejandro was a great swimmer, he went far out to dive under, but I was not that brave.

However, my fun unexpectedly stopped when something grabbed my ankle. At first, I thought Alejandro was touching my foot underwater, but when the touch turned into a bite, my legs took me out of the water as fast as the current allowed. Once safe on the wet sand, I saw a bold little crab coming out of a wave, running sideways with the determination of a soldier to kill my ankle with his hard-shelled claw. I rose as quickly as I could and started running south along the beach, not even realizing that little Señor Crab could never match my elongated steps. Finally I had the courage to look back and discovered that the little crab had already returned to the sea and was probably laughing with his crab friends about the cowardly scene of my running away from something one hundred times smaller than myself.

I was out of breath from my race and took a seat against the closest palm tree amid several dried coconuts. My back rested on the trunk, and I began to unbraid my long hair to allow it to dry and take the sand off it.

A pleasant feeling grew within me. I wondered how it would be to write down stories that described scenes like the one I was just experiencing. This was a perfect place to live a love story, one where couples in love walk by the beach, holding hands, entertained by the waves crashing at their feet. A sigh escaped my bosom like a torrent of air full of romantic particles. I, then, imagined the adoring couple making love under the warming sun while the water reached their bodies and moved them inch by inch into the sea without them noticing, oblivious to the sounds of owls hooing in the distance. But in real life, nothing could make such love last forever. A story like that would not be realistic because all love that starts, sooner or later, ends. But readers would not be interested in a story that ends in empty feelings between two who once loved each other to the point of letting the waves of the sea drag them into its immense body of water.

Or would they?

If I were to become a writer, my love stories would be complete fiction, and I would tell the reader so. Yet, what would be the point of tales of everlasting love? They would only fill the hearts of readers with hopes of what would never arrive in their lives for such loves do not exist. I had no right to do such a thing.

I planted the soles of my feet against each other and pushed my knees towards the warm sand. I felt as if I were statue, a pessimistic and negative-thinking statue. Then I decided that I should become a writer, but a writer of non-love stories. I would write about my observations of everything and anything around me. I didn't know if such a profession existed. Journalists did that, but I didn't want to write as a journalist with impartiality; I wanted my bias to show, to write about the reality of people's lives from my point of view.

Here was a new destiny to my life. Not only was I going to get my teaching certificate; my goal was also to become a writer of life's realities. My first story was going to be the consequences of women not voting in México. Then, the second story was going to be about the importance of reading and how it changes a person's life forever. I had a million ideas for short stories ready to materialize on paper. But such stories had to be camouflaged with an entertaining touch; the brutal reality would come between the lines. Yes, I had set my goal, and my next step was to have the discipline to do it.

My optimistic thoughts were interrupted by Alejandro's screams to return to our beach "camp." Without realizing it, I had sat by that palm tree quite a long time because, by the time I arrived at Alejandro's side, my hair was already dry.

"What were you doing all the way over there?" he asked, amused.

Equally pleased, I answered, "I was chased away by a dreadful crab who tried to eat my ankle! It was hilarious. Then I rested under a tree … and drifted into a trance that took away the time … this is so beautiful …"

"Yes, it is. I miss this when I am away, the beach and the palm trees. From El Roble I miss the sugarcane fields and the Sacanta."

"I have had a chance to miss only El Roble because I haven't been farther than Mazatlán in my life … but you are right … the Sacanta is a part of El Roble that I also miss … and the sounds of the owls at night."

"Ah, Maxi, yes … I cannot separate the owls from the hacienda."

"Once, when I had just started working in the Grand House on a late fall evenings when it gets dark earlier, I went to the water tower to check if the clothing irons were off the heat, and I heard the sound of an owl above me. Her eyes were wide open, and she expanded her wings at me, as if fearing that I would take her babies away. Then she fluffed herself up to look even bigger and flapped her wings, and I ran out of the tower scared. Her ways scared me."

"Owls are mysterious."

"They do have mysterious ways … and at night, they also follow mysterious paths."

Alejandro turned to me; his cheeks were slightly burned by the sun, and he had traces of shiny sand on his wet hair. Even with those "flaws," he was dashingly handsome; his face reminded me of a picture of a Greek god I had once seen in a book. But his beauty went beyond a pretty picture. He was beautiful in a trustful way; I think that is the best way to describe Alejandro Sarmiento. The sweetness of his eyes perfectly complemented the purity of his smile. And his athletic, well-muscled body … well, I couldn't resist, and I passed my fingers over the bridges of his chest.

Alejandro giggled and took my hand to plant a loud kiss on it, and then he seized my face with his strong hands and pulled it towards his. He asked with his eyes closed, "May I kiss you?"

"Why?" I asked with surprising curiosity.

"I don't know …"

Without responding, I closed my eyes and felt the warm lips of Alejandro Sarmiento on my cheek.

"You are sweet," he said.

I opened my eyes and felt his loving half-opened eyes smiling at me again. He continued caressing my cheeks. I smiled while feeling his delicate touch on my skin.

"Your face is soft … and gorgeous … its bronze color makes it look even more beautiful," he said, softly gazing into my eyes. "You are the most beautiful part of nature on this island, Maximiana Valdez."

Alejandro's hands arrived at my hair and brushed it with tenderness with the very tips of his fingers.

"Your hair feels like silk in my fingers."

I felt the fresh wind roll over my bosom, and I took a deep breath. I was exposing my soul to Alejandro, but I did not feel any embarrassment for I knew he did not look at me disrespectfully. His affectionate touch and gentle words made me feel above all the rules and ideas imposed on me as a woman, rules that inhibited my sexuality. He made me feel what everyone desires—respect as a human being. I reached his hand and placed the palm of it on my warm cheek; then I closed my eyes to smell the natural aroma of salty water expelling from his skin. Opening my eyes, my gaze fell on his in a peaceful meeting of two souls who truly loved each other without restraint but who, nevertheless, respected each other's integrity of body, mind, and soul.

"Are you still a virgin?" he asked me in a whisper.

"Yes ... I am. But do not call it virginity," I said in a firm voice, "because virginity is too connected with *purity* and that is awfully unfair ..."

"I agree," Alejandro nodded.

"Are you ...?"

"Yes."

"Alejandro ... how come you never talk about love or the woman you love ... you always talk about someone who left you or didn't love you. I do not quite understand but ... why don't you tell me?"

He looked away. "One day I will ... but not right now. When I am ready, I will."

"Is it that grave?" I asked him, placing my hands on his knees.

"I don't know. You will decide once I tell you, I guess." He smiled with a sigh avoiding my eyes.

"Is she married?" I directly asked.

Is she Leonora Sarmiento?

"Stop it nosy girl! I won't call you Silly Face anymore ... I will call you Nosy Girl from now on!"

He rose from the sand and offered me his hand to get up.

"We have been friends for such a long time," I said rising, "and still you don't trust me with your heart, Aleh ... how can that be? I trust you with my life, if necessary, but you would not trust me with something as important as your feelings."

My complaint was genuine for I felt betrayed by his lack of trust in me. He held my hand and pulled me towards the sea. I tried to brake with my feet, but he dragged me just the same, leaving a deep mark in the sand behind us. In the distance, we heard the Cactus people setting camp on the beach and saw Andrés Randal standing close to where we had been sitting.

"They are here! Let's go!" Alejandro screamed and started running towards them. I followed him as fast as I could until finally, he let go of my hand. Everyone was excited to see us there, especially after

Alejandro explained that we had decided at the last minute to change our plans for our own beach picnic and join them on the island. Paula was always happy to see me around, I could feel it. She hugged me and said that I had made the right choice because they were going to spend the night there for a moonlight gathering. Eduardo and Agatha were already running to the water, followed by Teodoro and his sister Elisa de La Vega. All the others stayed behind, setting camp, while Alejandro walked to get our things from the site where we had left them.

Andrés was looking in the direction of the palm trees. I walked to him to greet him, but his response was accompanied by a blank expression that confused me. I wondered if he had seen me in the company of Alejandro Sarmiento's lips. The idea worried me a little bit, perhaps out of prudence.

"Hey, how are you?" I asked while braiding my hair on the side.

"Pretty good, and you?" he responded with an inevitable frown.

"Fine, I guess, glad to be here. I needed to get out of—"

He walked away leaving me in the middle of the sentence.

"Andrés!"

He stopped.

"Don't do that! You remind me of Orlando Sarmiento," I said with a sudden anger in my voice.

Andrés turned around to give me a violent stare that seemed to have the intention of blowing me up into little pieces

"What?" I asked with clenching teeth of desperation. "What?"

"You *never* allowed me to touch you, and yet, you are doing it with Alejandro Sarmiento … I guess Gustavo Inzunza was not so wrong that day at the jetty, yes? When he said Orlando was doing you right after Alejandro, he was right!" he said, almost touching my face with his trembling hands.

My respiration was cut in half.

"You are *stupid*. Do you know that?" I threw his hands off my shoulders. "You are *really stupid*!" I screamed at his face and started walking away from Andrés Randal, wishing to kill him with my very own hands, but then I stopped. He was right. I reflected for a second and realized that the scene Andrés had seen did not look good at all.

He had found me alone, on the beach with Alejandro, a man three years older than I and whose rumors about me being his *pastime* had been haunting me for years now. Pride aside and following my conscience of doing the right thing, I walked back to him.

"Andrés …"

"Leave me alone, Maximiana."

"No, I won't leave you alone because you have reason to think something like that … but you are wrong about your assumption. There is nothing between Alejandro Sarmiento and me, nothing but the purest of friendships … so pure that I could take off my clothes in front of him and he would treat me as if I were clothed."

He gasped and said in a sarcastic tone, "Yes, Maxi, and I still believe the Three Kings bring gifts at Christmas."

"You should believe me because I have never lied to you."

"You owe me no explanations; you are free to do whatever you want," he replied, victimizing himself in the most childish way.

"That's true … I am going to help others set camp. Did you bring your girlfriend?" I took him aback with my unexpected question. "Oh yes … I see her over there with Elisa," I concluded, pointing my finger.

I was referring to Venustiana Hidalgo, the girl he had been dating for the last two weeks and the one I suspected was the reason behind our breakup. Agatha had told me the news when they had started going out, but naïve Andrés apparently thought I would never know.

"She is very pretty. Congratulations," I said without a hint of sarcasm, I promise.

He looked down with apparent embarrassment and muttered, "Thanks."

"You better go to her because she is getting hysterical seeing you talking to old Maximiana Valdez all by yourself. I might *steal* you from her, you see?" *That* was pure sarcasm on my part.

"I didn't know you were going to be here, Maxi, which is why I brought her," he apologized with sincere honesty.

"No need to apologize. There is nothing between us, remember? Never really was," I said in a calm tone of voice.

"Don't say that," he interrupted exasperated.

"No? Even if Venustiana started seeing you when you were still going out with me as a boyfriend, I am not like her … so out of respect *for her*, I'd rather not talk to you about any of this when she is so close by," I sincerely replied.

"You are amazing," he said, smiling pleasantly.

No, I am stupid, not amazing! Why did I explain to you that there had been nothing between Alejandro and me?! Grrrr!

"You know whose body is amazing?"

"Whose?" he replied with a roguish half-smile.

"Alejandro's," I said, wetting my lips and looking in Aleh's direction.

His smile faded away.

"I like passing my fingers along the muscles of his chest; he has such a beautiful body," I replied in a dreamy voice.

Andrés was shocked with the intention behind my words.

"Just look at him," I said with a sigh.

Andrés stomped away from me with a cloud of sand flying out every time he took a deep step.

Take it Andrés Randal … now you know how it feels, I firmly told myself, and even though I didn't feel too proud of my attitude, for once I had fun getting even with someone who had left me hanging with nothing but false promises.

The smell of marinated meat grilling over the fire permeated the entire island. After our heavy lunch, we all took a nap, wanting to rest our full bellies and to hide from the blazing sun. I peacefully fell asleep next to my dear Alejandro. When I woke up, the sun was already setting. Agatha had nudged me with her bony fingers; she hadn't wanted me to miss it. We all sat at the edge of the waves to watch the glorious scene of shifting colors as the sun sank down in the distance.

"And to think that it is rising somewhere else," Agatha said in between expulsions of smoke from her mouth.

"It feels chilly," Eduardo Randal stated and got up to bring a towel to wrap around himself.

"Are you cold, Silly Face?" Aleh asked me with his usual generosity.

An odd silence fell over the group. Alejandro and I looked at each other and then at them. I couldn't resist looking at Andrés. His ego was hurting, and he could not pretend otherwise. Venustiana pretended not to notice, but the satisfaction of seeing Andrés paying back for his attitude towards me was too obvious in Paula and Agatha's faces.

"I am; please, bring me a blanket from Agatha's bundle," I said. We had not come prepared for a night at the beach, but they insisted we borrow what we needed from them.

"Thanks, Aleh!"

A murmur of gossip surrounded me when Alejandro went to bring the blanket. Dead silence fell once he sat behind me and wrapped himself with it as well. I rested my head on his embracing arm. Nobody made me feel more secure than my dear Alejandro. Unintentionally, eyes were fixed on Andrés Randal's face.

Finally, Agatha couldn't take it anymore, and she exploded, "What in God's name is wrong with everyone today? You are all applying a double standard to Maximiana! Andrés broke up with her for Venustiana, yes? Sorry, Venus, but you knew they had been together for a long time, and still you were flirting with Andrés without any respect for Maxi …" A funereal silence entered our little quarter of the Isla de la Piedra. "Then Andrés goes out with Venus without any respect for Maxi's feelings! Nobody says or does anything, but yet, just because Maxi was here with Alejandro, *by herself*, even though he is treating her with consideration, you are all looking at her as if she were a slut and poor Andrés a victim. What hypocrites!"

Alejandro turned to Andrés. "Maxi and I have been friends for a long time. I love her a lot, and everyone should know it … there is nothing to explain or any reason for you to feel humiliated, Andrés."

"I am not," Andrés responded, obviously distraught by being on the spot.

I looked at Venustiana. Just as I had suspected for a long time and Agatha kept repeating, Andrés had broken up our relationship because of another girl.

"I don't get why women do this kind of stuff to each other! How could you Venus?" Agatha scolded Venustiana, who was speechless in the embarrassing situation.

I took a deep breath.

"It is not only her fault ... it takes two to waltz," I said with a dignified tone. "But I don't think it is worth ruining our beach moonlighting because of this. Alejandro is my dearest friend, the one that I'd give my life for. Neither one of us is trying to hurt Andrés' feelings. Let's move on and forget about it, please. I already have."

Andrés was glancing in my direction but with a different intention in his mind. He shyly smiled at me and looked down. Apparently, Venustiana could not shake herself from the surprise she felt when I rescued her from a prolonged biting from idealistic and feministic Agatha Santos. Venustiana looked away when our eyes met. Alejandro kissed me on the back of my head, then on the cheek, and culminated his cuddling with a full arms-and-legs hug. As he rested his chin on my shoulder, I looked at him from the corner of my eye to discover the indescribable satisfaction he felt to be right there, at that moment, around me.

"Tonight," he murmured in my ear, "I will tell you what you so much long to know."

My hand climbed to the side of his head and buried itself in its soft wavy hair.

"Thank you ... I can hardly wait, my sweet Alejandro Sarmiento ... I can hardly wait."

29

When the members of the Cactus started playing the guitars and their singing became too loud, I moved away from the campfire. The required year without listening to music after a loved one dies had not yet passed. But even without the tradition, my heart still mourned my sister Natalia, and the idea of singing happy music around that fire with everyone else perturbed me. I walked away.

The full moon turned the night sky into a soft dark-blue blanket, illuminating a few wayward clouds with its shining rays. But it gave its most impressive effect on the sea with a giant white reflection extending all the way to shore where the waves merged into one another in their race to reach land. I could still hear the sounds of joyful music in the distance and barely make out the images of those around the fire. It wasn't long before Alejandro joined me.

"Max … why did you leave?" he asked while collapsing on the soft sand next to me.

"I don't feel like listening to music and singing; I am still mourning."

Alejandro hugged me, offering a silent message of support.

"Aleh …," I articulated in the most tactful way I could, "what happened to your mamá?"

A long silence fell between us.

Finally he said in a low voice, "To me … my mother was murdered."

Intrigued, I replied that I understood that she had committed suicide. Alejandro showed no surprise I knew about it.

"She was driven to do it; for that reason I think that she was murdered …"

"Why was she locked in the balcony room? Why did her family abandon her?"

"They thought she was a lunatic … according to everyone around, she was crazily demented."

"Was she?"

He shook his head, "No … of course not."

"It breaks my heart when I think of the three of you listening to her suffering inside the balcony room …" I rested my head on his shoulder with compassion.

"Oh, Maxi … it was horrible. Sometimes I could touch the tips of her fingers when I reached under her door, those fingers that used to have long nails that scratched our backs every night before my brothers and I went to sleep. Orlando was too young to realize what was going on, but Domingo and I knew it all, and we lived it and suffered with her."

"Who put her in the room?"

"Father … and her family agreed with him. They also thought she was demented."

I wanted to ask him *why* everyone thought she was demented, but I restrained myself again. If Aleh wanted to say it, he would say it but not under my pressure.

"Andrés Randal is dying up there; he asked me where I was going when I got up from the fire circle."

"Oh God, I don't understand Andrés; he broke up with me because he wanted freedom from our relationship, and now he is acting silly … his ego has been wounded, I guess."

"Yes … and also you are getting prettier, Maxi!" He tickled me with his usual playfulness, "You would've liked Mother … she was funny and read a lot of books. She was always in the library. As a matter of fact, she was the one who created the library in the hacienda and in the city house. When she was alive … when she was still allowed to be alive … each room in the house had books, even the parlors and the wash rooms!"

Excitement filled my mind. "Tell me more about Señora Magdalena, Aleh; she sounds very interesting to me."

"Call her Magdalena; she wouldn't have liked you calling her Señora Magdalena."

"Aha! So you learned *that* from her!"

"Exactly," he said, full of satisfaction.

"I heard she was unbelievably beautiful …"

"Oh yes! She was beautiful; Domingo looks a lot like her. Her face was like no other, and she liked everything that had to do with nature. She let her hair down and placed flowers in it and hated shoes … just like you."

"I love her already!"

"Yes … that was Mother." He took a deep breath and lay down on the sand, offering his arm as a pillow. I placed my head on it, and looking at the suns in the distance, Alejandro finally told me the secret …

"Maxi …"

"Yes …"

"Mother didn't love father," he said with a hint of embarrassment.

I am not surprised.

"She loved someone else, and he found out about it."

"I thought so," I honestly said; "I suspected that something like that had happened for him to do that to her … but still I don't understand her family. How could they agree to such atrocity? Her having an affair probably embarrassed them, that she would leave the husband they had chosen for her but—"

"Maxi … Mother was in love with a woman."

Rising from his arm, thinking I had misheard his words, I asked him, astonished, "What?"

"Father suspected Mother did not love him. She never did … her family married her to Joaquín Sarmiento for a business deal. They were both very young and—"

"I'm confused …," I said, placing the side of my face on his chest, my arm across his upper body.

"Mother had loved a girl since she had been a girl herself … and Father discovered it somehow; he started following her and told her family about it. When Grandmother Sarmiento heard the rumors, she also confronted Mother's family about it because she felt it was their fault somehow. It was a scandal … and everyone's conclusion was that mother was completely crazy."

"But—"

"Mother asked Father to allow her to leave, but her family didn't want her back either … and if she escaped on her own, she had to leave us behind, so I guess she couldn't do it. She loved us too much to leave us …"

"I don't understand why they thought she was crazy …"

"Didn't you hear what I said?"

"I did … but I still don't see how that made her crazy … she did not love her husband; she wanted to leave him, take her children with her; and she was in love with somebody else … what is so crazy about that?"

"Do you seriously see it that way?" Alejandro asked consternated.

"Yes … don't you?"

"What do you think of her love for a *woman*?"

"It happens … and as Agatha said it the other day; love is love … how can it be wrong? You cannot mandate your feelings for another person … I would think that she was crazy if you had told me she was in love with a chicken or a horse … or a tree … or—"

Alejandro couldn't contain his laughter.

"I am serious!" I exclaimed.

"I know you are! And you make me think …"

"It makes sense if she fell in love with a person who probably understood her better and made her feel special … I don't know how she felt, but I know how I feel when I fall in love with somebody."

Alejandro turned around to look at me directly. "Just imagine, Max, for a woman to leave her husband and children … and to do it because she is in love with another woman; it was too much for every-one to handle, especially Father."

"But it didn't give him the right to do what they did to her. Señora Magdalena was a good person; everyone says that she was like a liv-ing angel."

"Call her Magdalena; she didn't like titles, I told you already."

"Yes, Magdalena was fair and compassionate towards others; that is what Doña Luisa and Don Carlos say. They say that their memory of her is of a person who made them feel special … just as you make others feel, Aleh. You should be *very proud* of your mother because there aren't many people in the world like that."

His handsome eyes filled with tears that rolled down in tiny spar-kles illuminated by the moonlight.

"I loved my mother a lot … she was the best mother anyone could ever ask for … I miss her today as much as the first day she died because before, when she was locked in that room, I knew she was there, and I knew her voice would answer back when I called her from under the door; but when they took her that day after Luisa found her … you don't know, Maxi, how it feels for a little boy to see a body taken away from him forever, knowing that that body is not his mother anymore."

"Oh, Aleh," I hugged him with all the force my body could give, "I can only imagine such a pain. I am *so* sorry."

"She used to take us to the arroyo sometimes and get in the water with us. I clearly remember Orlando crying because he was scared—he must have been two or three—but she would sit in the water, hold-ing him so he would stop. Domingo and I would run around in our underclothes, and she would let us, and when we got tired … she would lie on the grass with us and look at the clouds. Mother would tell us all kinds of great stories … in her soft voice. She used simple words meant to be understood by little children … I liked that."

"Tell me more about her. Did she play the piano?"

"Yes, she did. She taught me more than Domingo because … she was with me the longest. I was always by her side. She also organized parties for us and invited some children from El Roble because she wanted us to play with everybody and have a lot of fun. She also told us that we were all equal, no matter what clothes you wear or what house you live in … she didn't want us to be spoiled, especially Domingo because according to everybody he was too beautiful and got all the attention."

I expressed amusement with that detail, "Well, the boy is beautiful!"

"Yes, I know. He looks like my mother."

"Aleh … who told you Magdalena was in love with a woman?" I asked cautiously.

"Nobody told me that directly, but as I grew older I heard conversations here and there, investigations I made … and finally I asked Father. But the one who had no problem in talking about it was Grandmother Sarmiento. To her, Mother was a lunatic … for her and everybody who knew her … I guess."

"So the woman she was in love with is supposed to be crazy as well?"

"Yes," he took a deep breath, "she had to move away from here."

"Really? Well, it makes sense. Just imagine how she felt."

"I heard she also tried to kill herself once … I don't know if the story is true, but according to my mother's sister, Aunt Evangelina … when the scandal broke out she was placed in a mental hospital."

"Alejandro … she was also considered to be a lunatic then …"

"Yes … she was a well-positioned lady … her family had money and power, and when they found out, they put her in a mental hospital, first in Tepic, then in Guadalajara … there … she …," he hesitated, "tried to hang herself out of desperation."

My heart stopped. "Yes … who wouldn't! She wasn't crazy, for God's sake!"

"Yes, I know. On the day of her birthday, her family came to visit her at the hospital, and when they entered her room, she was hanging from the ceiling but still alive."

"But, even after *that* they left her at the mental hospital?"

"After *that* they probably *knew* she was crazy, even though they had driven her to it … just as they had done to Mother."

"Aleh … is she still in the hospital? The mental hospital, I mean."

"I think so. I am not sure though," he said with a curious sound in his voice.

"What was her name?"

"Teresa Uvalde."

"My goodness," I exclaimed, "Alejandro, your Mother was very brave to be honest and tell the truth about her feelings. She didn't love your Father, and she wanted to go back to her own home. She was honest, and what happened to her is a crime. A terrible injustice."

"I wished I had been older to defend her, Maxi, but I was only a child when they put her in the room. She was there for years, years! At the beginning she could at least see through the windows, but then they put wood panels on the glass so she couldn't see outside, and nobody dared help her escape. Everybody was too afraid of Father and Grandfather Sarmiento, who hated Mother even more than Father."

"But … when all of you went to Mazatlán, couldn't Doña Luisa help her escape?"

"Grandfather Sarmiento left guards at the door day and night … nobody dared."

From the bottom of my heart, I said, "I am very sorry to hear the story of Magdalena … for a very long time I wondered … but out of respect, I never dared to ask you or Orlando about it. Now I understand many things, and let me tell you something, Alejandro Sarmiento, if I had been working at the hacienda when this happened to her, I would've waited until all of you went to Mazatlán. Then I would've given the guards a drink to knock them out, opened the balcony room, and helped her escape; and then she could've taken you all with her."

Alejandro's tears disappeared behind a smile. "Oh, I am sure you would've done that and much more, Maximiana Valdez, and Mother would've loved you as much as I do. You are very much like her."

"Am I …? Mmm … when you told me that your mamá taught you and your brothers that all people are equal, I realized that we have similar spirits. But she had a double spirit."

"What do you mean?"

"Well, she had the spirit of a mother and therefore a woman, and also the spirit of somebody who falls in love with a girl, instead of a boy."

"Do you think Mother wished to be a man?"

"I don't know … but someone once asked me why I wanted to be a boy."

Alejandro was surprised with my statement and said, "Really? Who asked you that and why?"

"It was my brother, Augusto. When I told him I went into the sea to swim, he asked me directly to my face and truly concerned," I imitated my brother's voice, "*Maximiana, why do you want to be a boy?*"

"What did you answer?" Alejandro asked, half smiling.

"That I didn't want to be a boy; I wanted to be a girl with boys' rights and chances and opportunities."

He hesitated before asking, "So, would you fall in love with a girl then? If she made you feel good about yourself …?"

I thought about my response for a while. "No, I don't think I would. I like boys and especially their boy bodies with muscles and all. I like the deep voices and masculine faces … I don't think I could be attracted to a girl that way … why do you ask?"

He didn't answer.

"Alejandro, why do you ask?"

"I don't know … I am just curious since you seem to understand all of this so perfectly."

I wished I could tell him that if I had been forced to marry mean Joaquín Sarmiento, I would probably have fallen in love with *anybody*, even a woman, due to the trauma.

"I was just thinking something," I said. "Leonora does not love him either."

"How do you know that?" By now, we were looking at the starry sky above us, and the water had reached our feet.

"Let's move back; the waves are getting to us!"

We crawled towards the palm trees, oblivious to the people around the circle, still singing in the distance around the fire.

"She does not look very happy with him, and didn't you tell me that she is miserable because she is expecting a child again? I suppose that if you love your husband and you are expecting, you would be happy, no?"

"True."

"And she always seems preoccupied with things she can't do anything about."

"Things like what?" he asked.

"I don't know."

Things like "She is in love with you, Alejandro."

"Do you like her?" I asked, hoping to get a hint for his real feelings.

"I do not care much about her. She is just Father's young wife, that is all, not my mother. And if I never see her, it is even better for me. However, I don't see her as if she took Mother's place because Mother's place in the family was never real, not as a wife. She was pretending out of an obligation."

"Now that you mention it … I think the same thing is happening to Leonora. Can't your papá find a woman on his own? Can't he meet a woman, then court her … and then marry her? He must marry only women that are chosen for him."

"I know … sad isn't it?"

Raimunda came to my mind. Poor Raimunda. She ended up being the target for Joaquín Sarmiento's rapist instincts, all of it created from his unhappiness.

"Yes, it is sad. But he is too old now to keep making the same mistakes."

"I guess he is paying for what he did to Mother."

We were interrupted by Eduardo Randal, who brought a plate of food for each one of us. He asked us to join them by the fire, and Alejandro explained to him that I felt uncomfortable around music because of my mourning. He reacted with mortification because apparently none of them had remembered that detail when the music had started. He apologized and went back to the circle. Silence fell, and Agatha came running towards us. I really wanted to continue this conversation with Alejandro, but with everyone around, it became impossible. Still, I felt blessed that my dear Alejandro trusted me so much as to tell me all those intimate details about his life and his mother. In my ear, he said we were not done with our chat and hoped to get up at sunrise and finish it. I agreed.

Venustiana did not look too pleased to have me back; she held onto Andrés Randal's arm as a little girl so afraid to swim that she is drowning in three feet of water. Apparently, she didn't understand she had nothing to worry about; Andrés had broken up our relationship to be with her, indicating that she meant more to him than I did. It was a matter of common sense, but perhaps a feeling of guilt invaded her egocentric self and produced that uneasiness. Besides, even without words I could read in their minds that they thought there was something going on between Alejandro Sarmiento and me. They did not know that my heart still felt so much pain of deception that the idea of starting yet another romance was out of the question at the moment. On the other hand, Alejandro was such an enigma to me. He was deliciously handsome, delicately soft spoken, yet strong and brave like no one I knew; there was a mystery inside of me as to *why* I was not attracted to him as a man. I guess some people are meant to be friends, real friends without the strains of a sexual attraction.

I couldn't read Andrés's attitude. He was very good at concealing his real feelings, and to be honest, I would've given a finger to know what was on his mind. Possibly, he anticipated drama on my part for losing him and whatever existed between us, but fortunately—or unfortunately—I had enough experience in the matter as not even to bother to engage in a drama over the break-up.

Everyone in the Cactus had many stories to share that night, with much talk of the changes coming, or so we hoped. Some guessed when Mexican women would finally be able to vote, and Agatha theorized that education was the only way to liberate not only women but poor men as well. I agreed. Women knew little of ideas and the world beyond their immediate experience. Europe meant nothing to them except, for some, as a place of proud ancestry or the source of French fashion. I observed the emptiness in their eyes, and I saw this in both rich and poor women. Just as Natalia had written me once that *the eyes of educated women look different.* Arrogance and rudeness were not synonymous with education, a true fact that the upper classes seemed to overlook constantly in México.

Of course, there were people like Alejandro and his deceased mother, Magdalena, who, even though born with economic privilege, treated everyone with respect and consideration. But they were the exception more than the rule. The women of the Cactus were considered by most people as strange and as bad examples to others; yet it was easy to see why we were identified as such because we were breaking the rules established for us.

Agatha had a way of telling stories that made you picture every single detail. Listening to her made me feel stronger about my decision of becoming a writer of reality instead of fiction. I held her as an example of the world's perfect future writer. Her stories, like her incredible paintings, made you think beyond what you were familiar with; they stretched your imagination. Even at the beach, she used her creative mind to bring humor into our carefree conversations.

"Listen *salty-feet* people of Mazatlán … you must accept the fact that Escuinapa, my beloved town, is in fact the navel of the world!" Agatha screamed, pretending to hold a glass of wine in her hands.

I protested, "Excuse me? Everyone present knows that the center of the world is El Roble … better known as *The Paradise.*"

"I second that!" Alejandro raised his hand. "Cheers to the paradise of El Roble!"

"There is nothing more beautiful than the Port of Mazatlán. What are you three talking about?" Elda Peralta y Peralta, the mysterious member of the Cactus and proud Mazatlánian intellectual, interrupted with pride.

"Ah, wait …," Teodoro de la Vega said in his quiet voice, "there is a city in the United States that we saw on our way to Canada that is truly beautiful. Do you remember Elisa? On our way to Vancouver … we stopped in the city of Seattle in Washington State?"

Elisa de la Vega responded with enthusiasm, "Yes! Seattle! It is full of pine trees, everything is so green, and the city is surrounded by mountains and lakes. The hardest part was pronouncing the name, though!" she laughed.

Seattle.

I repeated it in my head.

"Keep dreaming all of you," Eduardo Randal proclaimed. "La Villa de San Sebastián has no equal."

Each of us proclaimed the beauties and specialties of his or her hometown, trying to convince the others that no other surpassed it but not realizing that each one's town, no matter its true appearance, is for him or her the center, capital, and paradise of the world. How can it not be? One's first exposure to the world comes from its images, sounds, textures, smells, and tastes; they became the patterns of one's life, the base for all that one loves.

Later, Agatha suggested we play "blind little chicken," a children's game where a person stands in the middle of a circle, blindfolded. The others, holding hands, form a circle and move in silence around the one. The blind little chicken moves towards someone and the circle stops; then the blindfolded little chicken has to guess who the person is by touching his or her face. Obviously if the person guesses right, he or she wins.

My mind filled with long-forgotten memories of my own childhood. I stood in the circle, holding hands with everyone else, but my soul traveled to a not-far-away past where my sisters and I cheerfully played with our neighbors and friends. We had no interest but to have fun and get ourselves lost in our imagination. It was a time in my life when I was absolutely happy. I closed my eyes to feel the smile of my beloved Natalia in front of me, and I could hear her contagious giggling once again; my lower lip trembled at the memory, and more came to mind. I could see us running at the Arroyo de Constancia, picking up the roundest and shiniest stones to play the *matatena* and lose them all to Otilia, who was the best matatena player in recorded history. I smiled at my thoughts as a way of fighting the inner longing for those days that were forever gone but yet suddenly so vivid in my mind. I opened my eyes when I felt his hand on my face.

"It is Maximiana," Andrés said at the first touch of my face. He took off the cloth that was blindfolding him and gave me one of his profound glances; I involuntarily lowered my eyelids and then raised them again. Since he had correctly identified me, I became the blind little chicken. I clumsily stumbled to the middle, and while I struggled to walk in the soft sand, my hands reached the face of a person. I immediately knew it was a man because my hands touched his chest first. Cautiously I used both of my hands to feel the features of the face in front of me; the palm of my hand was tickled by pointy hairs sticking out of his cheeks. My mind raced trying to remember whose face had a growing beard, but I just couldn't recall it. It was harder than I thought it would be. The hair felt soft and wavy, and slowly the tips of my fingers touched the features of the mysterious face, but the explorations of my hands left me still clueless.

The giggles exploded into laughter when I couldn't figure out the person in front of me. I pulled down my blinding cloth, and surprised, I turned red to look up to the face of Teodoro de la Vega with his usual shy smile but ears red with embarrassment.

"Teodoro!" I said, genuinely surprised, "I am sorry I couldn't guess it was you …"

Teodoro smiled back at me with kindness, and the game continued. Eventually, one by one, the participants left the circle to get ready to sleep under the firmament. I fell asleep in the embracing sounds of a sweet lullaby of waves, loving each in the moonlight of a spring night.

30

Sunday morning was glorious. All the men ran into the water as soon as they woke up, and Agatha and I followed them. The rest of the girls stayed behind, brewing a delicious coffee, ready upon our return. The water was fresh and so clear that I could see the bottom. Alejandro came close to me, and we swam together for a while. Agatha was jumping waves, and I went to her. She showed me the trick to it; in order to break the wave, you had to jump under it as it approached you, then you could come up behind it. It didn't take long for my eyes to begin to burn because of the salty water.

I was too involved in my water game to hear the screams and signs coming from the people at the beach. Agatha noticed it first and signed to me to look at them. We all scrambled out the water, thinking that something was wrong on the beach, but Paula ran to us, screaming.

"Andrés! It is Andrés! He is drowning! Help Andrés!"

I looked back and saw Alejandro, Eduardo, and Teodoro turning back into the sea.

My first reaction was to try to help him, but Agatha pulled me back and told me I was not strong enough to fight the sea and that I would end up drowning, too. But everything in me told me at least to try to do something.

I don't want Andrés to die. God don't let him die.

With all my will, my feet struggled against the waves as I fought to reach Andrés, and then I saw Alejandro and Eduardo dragging his limp body out. As soon as they reached the shore, Teodoro took over and tried to revive him by pressing his chest and blowing air into Andrés's mouth. Paula was crying in desperation, seeing her baby brother lying in the sand, unconscious. Everyone else asked how could such a thing happen when Andrés was a good swimmer.

Venustiana Hidalgo stood there like a stone statue with no courage to respond to her own emotions.

I took a turn and kneeled and pinched Andrés's nose closed with my fingers while I blew air into his mouth as Teodoro had instructed. Finally, Alejandro pulled Andrés's arms and raised him from his lying position, and Andrés spit out the salty water trapped in his lungs. A loud cough exploded, and we all cheered in happiness.

"The undercurrent … pulled me in … I just couldn't … get out …," he said, gasping for air.

"Don't talk," Teodoro de la Vega told him. "Just take deep breaths, and you will be fine."

Teodoro de la Vega was a medical student like Domingo Sarmiento, but he attended the university in México City. I knew no one like Teodoro. He was always so pensive and philosophical in his statements. And he also seemed to be the one with the strongest spirit to fight for social justice. Several times, during the Cactus meetings, he had stated that the only reason for him to go to medical school and become a doctor was to help the poor and that he was more than ready for the time when the revolution finally exploded to take care of the wounded. Teodoro was always writing and taking notes of everything around him, and he wrote the most amazing poems I had ever read. Some of those poems rhymed, and others did not, and he explained to me once that he liked to write in free form because that way he could truly express his feelings without restraints.

Teodoro de la Vega had no girlfriend, and I had never seen him dating anyone. He claimed he avoided going out with anybody because he had too much to accomplish before thinking of getting married. However, according to Agatha, who knew the thoughts of all, Teodoro felt that marriage was just another social imposition on people to control them in every aspect of life. So Agatha suspected that Teodoro de la Vega would probably never get married, but she said whoever became his lover was going to be a very lucky girl. I couldn't resist, and I had asked Agatha why; I knew she was not referring to physical intimacy. She had said because he was true to his feelings and a loyal man.

Right at that moment, when those words came to my mind, I paid especially close attention to Teodoro de la Vega and his words. We all sat to drink coffee and share the scary experience of Andrés's close encounter with death. And I was dying to hear what Teodoro was going to say about it.

"Everything changes in a second when you least expect it," Teodoro said, looking at everyone. "That is why you should make each day count as if it were your last." We all agreed. This was the second time that I had encountered death or an almost death in less than a year. Eduardo Randal was very much concerned, and the shock still showed on his face. Poor Paula's eyes were swollen from crying, and I thanked God that nothing worse had happened to Andrés.

The drowning scare made us all return to Mazatlán earlier than planned. We all got on the boat, and as we departed the Island of the Rock, I realized how many lessons each day held for me. I was very grateful that I had had a chance to have that conversation with my dear Alejandro and felt honored that he had trusted me so with that hidden part of his life. What had happened to his poor mother had always intrigued me, but I still wondered about the woman he held so dearly to his heart.

On May 15, 1909, I turned sixteen years old, and my co-workers at the *Afternoon Mail* received me with *Las Mañanitas* and a birthday cake. I wished I could have gone home to El Roble for my birthday, but I had to leave the following day to Caliacán to take the university entrance examination. My brother Augusto was coming to Mazatlán that evening because he would escort me on my long trip to the capital of the state.

Alejandro had offered to take us to the train station the following morning. Shortly after we three arrived, Andrés, who was going to travel on the same train, and his family showed up. Andrés greeted us all very cordially when we sat in the same compartment. It was going to be a long day and night to get to Caliacán so I tried to keep my nerves settled and my mind focused on the exam in order to do my best. This was the opportunity of a lifetime. I had prepared for the examination for almost a year, thanks to Andrés Randal who had told me about it and allowed me to borrow his study guides and materials.

Augusto was usually shy, but that day he retreated further into himself because the train was full of strangers and he had never been on one. Neither had I. But I had no time to get excited; I used all the daylight to continue reviewing everything in my notes. When night fell, I placed my white shawl on my brother's shoulder as a pillow and fell asleep.

Caliacán was a city much bigger than Mazatlán. Augusto and I couldn't believe our eyes at the sight of so many buildings and carts moving from one side to the other. We even saw carts that moved without horses. I had seen one in Mazatlán once, but Caliacán had many more moving around the wide streets. Andrés rode the same cart with us to our hotel, which was located across the street from where the examination was going to be. We wished each other luck on the day of the exam, and before starting, I made the cross upon myself and asked God to help me pass with flying colors.

We returned the following morning, and this time, I was able to enjoy the trip; I felt very comfortable with how I had performed at the examination table. I recognized most of the questions and felt confident that I answered correctly. Andrés told me that he felt the same way, and I was glad for him as well.

The train ride was far more comfortable than the cart on the stone roads jumping with the horses, and its sounds and motions almost hypnotized me. A musical sound rose from the wheels sliding smoothly on the tracks, and the swaying of the train followed a calming rhythm. All created the perfect chance for me to daydream with abandon. As we rolled along, I saw the Sierra Madre Mountains to the east and the sea to the west. Less inspiring were many little towns on the road to Mazatlán, each one as miserable as the other; the poverty of the country was too evident to ignore, but people seemed oblivious to it. We were sitting in the middle-class section, a very small portion of the train, but even smaller was the upper-class wagon. When we took one of the curves, I looked back to see the tail of our train, and I noticed that people crammed the lower-class compartments, and many more were sitting on top of the train. The heat of May was heavy and relentless as usual, but no one appeared to notice it. The desire to escape poverty was stronger than any sunray burning their tired bodies.

I decided to write a letter to Otilia. There were things that I urgently needed to tell her.

Dear Otilia,

> *I'm writing to you on the train from Caliacán to Mazatlán. I wish you were here to know how it is.*
>
> *The examination was easy. I think I passed. You have no idea how happy I am with the possibility of attending the Normal School for Young Women. Señor and Señora Patterson will sponsor me. But I plan to work to continue saving money and helping you all in El Roble as I promised that I would always do.*
>
> *Oti, I cannot accept the fact that Natalia is not with us anymore. I feel that she's still in Boston with Domingo Sarmiento. I wonder if you feel the same way.*
>
> *How are Mamá and Papá doing with that? I can only imagine their pain.*
>
> *How is the school going? I hope everything is better.*
>
> *Otilia, there is something I want to tell you, and that is why I am writing ahead of time. I wish you would go to México City with me. I think we can both manage, and you can get a job there. What I want to make sure is that you get a chance to get*

out of El Roble because there is so much life outside of there that you need to see. Please promise me that you will think about it. I will not talk to you about Andrés because there is nothing between us anymore. He broke up with me just like Orlando did, but this time it didn't hurt as bad. I guess I'm growing up. I haven't seen Orlando Sarmiento in a very long time, but Alejandro continues being my dearest friend, and Domingo comes to talk sometimes.

Dear sister, I miss you more than ever. And I'm counting the days to go back to El Roble in July, right before my trip to México City if I get accepted to the university. If I get accepted, this time I will not see you all for almost a year because México City is too far away to come during vacation. It would be my first Christmas away from home. But I embrace the opportunity because it is for the best.

I will see you soon. Give a big hug to Mamá and Papá, Rosaura, and Lucia. And you as always receive my entire love, dear sister.

Yours truly,

Your sister
Maximiana Valdez

I folded the piece of paper to give to Augusto when we arrived in Mazatlán. I didn't dare tell Otilia, but I wanted her to get away from her trauma and the way the town saw her and treated her because of it. She was a victim, but nobody saw her as such.

During the rest of the trip, I caught Andrés looking at me several times, but he turned away when I looked back at him. It was an unreal scene to be sitting there in that train as two acquaintances and not the romantic couple we once were. I had planned and dreamed this moment many times; it had given me a lot of hope for the future. The idea of taking that examination with him, passing it, and then moving on together to México City to study was a big dream. I took a deep breath and turned away to observe the distant horizon; I wanted to avoid thoughts that would break my heart no matter how hard I fought against them.

"Orlando Sarmiento was taking the exam in the male section," Andrés finally said as if he had debated to tell me for a very long time.

"I didn't know you had to take an exam here to go to Harvard University," I responded, honestly surprised.

"You don't; he is not going to Harvard," he said, waiting for my reaction.

I asked confused, "He is not? Where is he going then?"

"He said he wants to attend the National University of México like us."

"Is Domingo going to México City as well?"

"I don't know … but Orlando is for sure," he replied with a pretended indifference. I knew Andrés didn't like Orlando for more than one reason, including Orlando's attack that day at the jetty.

"Are you excited about it?" Andrés asked, disregarding the fact that my brother, Augusto, was sitting next to us, pretending to be asleep.

"Why would I be excited?" I replied with a hint of anger at the intention behind his words. "You don't even know what you are saying, Andrés."

He sighed, "Yes, I probably don't."

"Then don't say it … and even *if I were excited about it*, I don't think that it is your business, yes?"

"*Everything* about you is *my* business."

I took a deep breath again.

Give me patience, dear God!

"You don't even respect your girlfriend," I said looking out the window.

"She is not my girlfriend anymore," he replied, staring out the window as well.

Déjà vu.

"Funny … your words are the exact words Orlando Sarmiento told me after he broke up with Virginia Del Rincon Valle, yes … right before he started a relationship with Señorita Inzunza. You men don't even know what you want, do you?"

"No, I guess we don't," he said, still avoiding my face.

"But I think it is fine, as long as you don't continue doing it when you get married. The only bad thing is that girls are not allowed to act the same way you do," I said with indignation.

A sharp silence fell around us. My brother opened his eyes and looked at me for he knew my words were probably disliked by those around us on the train.

Andrés turned to the side, also noticing the environment around us, and agreed with me, "I know; that is really unfair."

"Yes. Why is it that always the men end relationships whenever they feel like it? If we women did that, society would look on us as unworthy—or worse. It is completely ridiculous," I stated with a firm tone of voice.

Other passengers on the train had already started to stare at us and make surreptitious comments among themselves. Augusto looked at me as if saying, "Maximiana, please, it's not the time. For God's sake, be quiet for once."

I decided to stop and turned to the window once more, not only because I didn't want to cause the trouble that usually came from those types of discussions but also because I wanted to enjoy the view in passing.

When we arrived in Mazatlán, Augusto had to return to El Roble. I wished with all my heart that I could have gone with him, but it was impossible. I needed to continue working and save money for my schooling in México City. I was willing to sacrifice everything to real-ize my dream of becoming a certified teacher.

"Give Mamá, Papá, and Otilia, Rosaura, and Lucia a big kiss and hug for me. And give Mamá this …" I gave him a small bundle with some money that I had saved for them. "Oh, and this is a letter for Otilia." I hugged and kissed my brother good-bye, missing him already; he was the closest I had gotten to home in months. "Thank you, Augusto … thank you for going with me to take the exam."

"You are welcome, sister," he said, returning my hug. "I hope you did well in the exam."

"Me, too."

I saw him ride the horse until he turned at a corner so far away from me that he looked like a toy moving away. I sighed and walked into my home.

☙

The same afternoon, the salty breeze of the Pacific Ocean invited me to take a walk on the jetty.

As soon as I arrived, I took off my sandals and felt the soft, warm sand under my feet. I was lost in my thoughts when I saw Teodoro de la Vega sitting on the beach, staring at the horizon.

"Hello, Teodoro!"

He stood up and smiled at me.

"Hello, Maximiana. How are you? How did you do in the entrance examination?" he greeted me, and we sat down simultaneously.

"I am fine, and I think I did well … and you? How are you? "

"I am good, thank you."

A moment of silence hung in the air.

"So, what were you doing?" I asked.

"Just sitting here, thinking. I am going back to school in July so these beautiful places will be out of my reach for a long time! Until December!"

"How is medical school?"

"What do you mean?"

"Is it difficult? What classes do you take? How long does it take to become a medical doctor? Are there women in your classes …?"

"It is not difficult, I take different classes that have to do with the human body and diseases, it takes four years … and no … there are no women."

"Have there ever been women?"

"Yes … but not in my class. Why do you ask?"

"I don't know. So many things I want to learn and do. I wish I could go to medical school."

"You can do it. It is up to you."

"Yes. Perhaps later, after I get my teaching certificate. I can work and study, yes?"

He looked, intrigued, and nodded with approval.

"How much longer do you have until you graduate?"

He sighed, "I have one more year of studies, and then I'll have to do my practice."

"Well, you're almost done then," I said.

"Yes, you're right."

"You know, Maxi … I just hope the revolution starts after I finish medical school." Up to that moment, I hadn't thought about that, that if the revolution erupted, it would also disrupt university classes, and I might not finish school. Then I shook those ideas out of my head because no matter what sacrifices I had to make, the revolution would be worth it because it would bring a better life to so many.

Teodoro was very quiet most of the time, and this was no exception. Fortunately, my days of compulsive talking had passed already; otherwise, the silence would have embarrassed me. I studied him out of the corner of my eye and seemed to see Teodoro de la Vega for the first time. He had a calm and mellow manner, and the tone of his voice had a gentle ring to it. There was no doubt in my mind that Teodoro was going to be a great medical doctor, and a gentle one, too.

"I will introduce you to the México City Cactus," he suddenly said. "You will like everyone, even though they are a little bit more radical than the people here in Mazatlán."

The idea of getting together with Teodoro in México City had not crossed my mind up to that moment. I thought I would know no one—other than Orlando and Andrés—in the big city, and I had anticipated many lonely days. Teodoro's offer for company as well as the chance to meet others and continue work with the Cactus meant a lot to me.

"Thank you. That will be great."

And then, I realized that Andrés Randal was going to be in the meetings. But coming into contact with him didn't matter anymore. My feelings about him were staying in the past. Interesting enough, my memory of times with Orlando were also remaining behind, even farther in the past.

Long moments of silence fell between us, and I could understand why; so many thoughts passed through our minds that we had no need for words to express them. For the first time in my life, I felt comfortable keeping quiet, thinking, and just listening to the sounds around me and the soft breathing of Teodoro de la Vega.

When the sky started filling with the twilight colors of evening, a deeper peace filled my senses. No words can describe my awareness of being alive at that time in the history of the universe. And a question came to my mind:

"Teodoro …"

"What?" he said.

"How do you think this spot, where we are sitting right now, and everything around us, is going to be in a hundred years?"

Teodoro took a deep breath, "I, too, constantly think about those things, and I wonder the same question myself. How is it going to be in the year 2009?"

I turned my face to look at him and asked, "How would people dress?"

"Will it be better or worse than now?" he asked as a comeback.

"Do you think women will be treated the same as men? I certainly hope so!"

"You will probably have a great-great-granddaughter, named Maximiana after you," he said playfully.

"Or you will have a great-great grandson named Teodoro de la Vega. Who knows?" I said laughing. "But it's fun to think about it."

Then I kept quiet because with our conversation I also understood that I was not going to be alive in a hundred years.

"What are you thinking? Why are you so quiet?" Teodoro asked.

"Nothing. I just realized the little detail that none of us is going to be alive in a hundred years, unless you discover a vaccine to prevent death and then the world's population will be tremendous! Ha, ha, ha."

"I wouldn't try to find a vaccine for death. I think that everything about life is beautiful, death included. And that is something nobody can escape from."

"Teodoro, I think everything is going to be a lot noisier."

"Why noisier?"

"Well, there is going to be a lot more people, and there are going to be more carriages without horses going around."

"Yes, that's true. We might even fly."

"Ha, ha, ha. How can people do that?"

"Well, I don't know, but there is a chance."

"Do you know what would be better … if we could travel up there." I pointed up to the sky.

"That's what I just said. We could maybe fly."

"No. I mean beyond that … to the next sun and see if there are other planets."

"Ah, yes. I think you should be an astronomer. Like Galileo Galilei."

"An astronomer is a person that studies the sky?"

"Yes. Space and stars."

"Oh, I like that idea … I would lie here all day if I could."

"Yes … me too."

After a long time that felt like an instant, Teodoro de la Vega offered to walk me home. We took the sidewalks of Mazatlán in silence, but it didn't feel awkward because his behavior was usually calm and silent.

I was surprised to see Josefina waiting for me at the door of my apartment. It was late for her to be out of the Sarmiento house, but she explained that she had been sent to call a midwife because Señora Leonora was in labor. Josefina asked the midwife to rush to the Sarmiento house but took the chance to stop by my apartment to chat. Probably no one would notice her absence in the bustle of delivering a baby. We prepared a fresh pitcher of lemonade and sat to talk. I honestly felt sorry for Leonora Sarmiento, going through childbirth in such a warm climate. Many times I heard of how hard it was to give birth, and the idea of experiencing such pain in the heat overwhelmed me.

"Who would want to be in her skin!" Josefina exclaimed when I told her my thoughts about it. "When I left, you could hear her screams all the way to the corner, poor woman. There is no joy in her life, and on top of everything she is having more children with a man that she doesn't love."

"You know," I said with curiosity, "I was surprised she didn't have any more children before; the twins are already six years old."

Josefina moved her face close to me in order to speak in secret. "She's gotten pregnant before, but she got rid of them."

"She got rid of them? Got rid of whom? What … I don't understand."

Josefina rose from her seat and closed the door to finally tell me the secret words she didn't want anybody else to hear, or at least not to hear them from her.

"Señora Leonora has gotten rid of her other babies. Doña Tacha has helped her all along. But I think she couldn't do it this time; Señor Joaquín got suspicious about it."

"I cannot believe it. Isn't it dangerous? Do you know how they do that? Do they drink something or what?"

"Sometimes they have to drink something that will make them … mmm … get rid of *it*. But other times, I have heard Doña Tacha or even a midwife has to do something else; don't ask me what because I really don't know."

"Poor Señora Leonora, she goes through a lot. I can only imagine how she feels inside."

"Well … right now she is going through hell, that is for sure! Her mother and one of her sisters arrived when I left; at least she is not alone."

My mind wandered off to El Roble and my sister Otilia. After the rape, Mother took her to a town named Agua Caliente de Garate to get "her period back"; at least that is how Mother explained it to Natalia and me. It now made sense.

How hard it is to be a woman.

That night, sleep did not come calling. Too many troubling thoughts wandered through my mind, especially after Josefina's visit and our conversation about childbirth and everything that women must go through in their lives and how they have so few options.

I remembered the story of the baby by the water hole in El Roble. Mother told us, in one of those lazy evenings when we used to sit on the sidewalk to talk to our friends and neighbors, the story of a girl, Rosa María, from the town of El Bajio who killed her newborn. She carried her pregnancy without anybody knowing about it, and up to this day, there are different theories as to who was the father of the child. Poor Rosa María was only sixteen years old, and when her time came, she walked to the sugar cane fields and lay right next to the water hole. Nobody heard her cries when the baby arrived, but she tore off the hem from her long skirt and entangled it around her baby's neck; she pulled the string until the baby didn't breathe anymore. After that, Rosa María buried the baby girl under a pile of dry sugar cane leaves and walked back to El Bajio. When the evening came and the men coming from the fields walked by the water hole, they noticed the dogs going wild around the pile of leaves. It didn't take long for them to expose the baby girl's body. She still had the hem around her tiny neck and the umbilical cord attached to her bellybutton. One of the finders ran to El Roble to call on the hacienda and tell the Sarmientos about the discovery while another one followed the line of blood left by the killer. The trail led them directly to Rosa María's little shack in El Bajio; she was wearing the skirt, still missing the hem.

No legal action was taken against poor Rosa María. Some felt sorry for her and understood her desperation in a world that would forever stigmatize her for having a child without a father. Many more judged her as a killer who deserved their spit when they walked by her skinny figure, a young girl who became but a ghostly silhouette of someone who had once existed.

I thought about the baby girl and wished to have saved her because she was a victim as much as her sixteen-year-old mother. I turned in my bed and thought about it for a while. Perhaps I should never have children of my own. Perhaps I should take babies like that little girl, whose mothers didn't ask for them but are nevertheless born.

I suspected something was wrong when Alejandro didn't show up for our Cactus meeting. Neither did Domingo. During the meeting, we exchanged ideas and opinions, planned an event at the town's square to generate funding, and went home after a long conversation as to what step to take next in our movement for social change.

Agatha told me she had no idea where Alejandro could be; he never missed the Cactus meetings when he was in town. Fortunately, Josefina, although too late for the meeting, arrived in time to give Agatha and me a ton of news. According to Josefina, Señora Leonora's delivery turned into a medical emergency. The midwife couldn't handle the birth, and Señor Joaquín sent for the doctor who could not be located soon enough. Alejandro took to the street to find him and didn't return until he brought Dr. Rosales to the Grand City House. However, the difficult birth paled in comparison to a little but telling incident during Señora Leonora's labor. Josefina said Señora Leonora started losing consciousness, and in the middle of her agony, she called for her Alejandro to come and be by her side. Everyone in the bedroom pretended not to hear her cries for her stepson, and they especially ignored the stiffness in Señor Joaquín's face when Señora Leonora's words hit his ears while standing outside the door of her bedroom.

Alejandro did not enter her room; cautiously he stayed outside, waiting for his father's next order. Josefina heard Orlando telling Domingo and Alejandro about it; he had happened to be near the bedroom's door when Señora Leonora started calling for Alejandro. They were not amused, and Alejandro seemed mortified by it.

"But ... was he confused?" I asked, wondering if that would be an indication of Leonora being the girl Alejandro loved so much.

"No, he didn't look confused. Domingo and Orlando looked shocked and uncomfortable about it but not Alejandro; he was more worried about it as I told you."

"This is really serious, no? Can you imagine Señor Joaquín guessing why his wife was calling for his son and, to make matters worse, in front of a group of witnesses that will certainly spread the word about it?"

"I know. There was no chance for me to go inside but to change the water and bring more clean towels every time they asked, and I can tell you the mood in there was very intense and not just because of her difficult delivery ..."

"And how is she? I haven't asked you yet ... Is Señora Leonora fine?"

"She had a baby boy, and from what I heard, she will have to be in bed for a long time after this delivery … and Lupe passed the gossip that she was refusing to breastfeed the baby so Señor Joaquín asked for a nursemaid."

"My goodness," I replied, truly concerned.

I hope she doesn't end up in the locked balcony room.

"That is an unhappy household, Maximiana; you can smell the problems all around you," Josefina stated, shaking her head. "And the problems don't seem to have an ending in sight."

31

An indescribable feeling of happiness came to my heart when Domingo played the phonograph for me and Natalia's beautiful voice escaped from the machine to travel throughout the room like the winds of El Roble during the summer storm season. I closed my eyes to allow the sounds into my soul; I wished for them to stay within me for a never-ending time, and even though the words were sung in another language, I could clearly recognize my sister's voice.

"The next part is the words that Natalia asked to record for you and your family … before she …" Domingo couldn't finish his sentence.

The sound of her voice made me shiver. It was as sweet and melodious as I remembered, but she was struggling to put her syllables together.

Maxi … I know you will be the first one to listen to this. That is why … I made this special message for you.

Natalia's words came out softly and slowly as she was clearly struggling to catch her breath.

Domingo is here with me; he is holding my hand, my sweet and beautiful dragonfly.

I took Domingo's hand and placed it between mine.

I don't know if I will ever see you again, little sister; only a miracle could save my baby girl and me from going away from all of you. Do not cry too much, Maxi; life is too precious to spend it crying for the memory of someone who left. Smile when our memories together reach your heart, and laugh at our times together ... I will be with you forever, Maxi ... I will never leave your side because I live within you, for God made us sisters for a reason. We shared the same womb, remember?

I don't want you ever to give up your dreams. I don't know anyone in the world more full of dreams than you are, but the most amazing thing is that you are willing to go for them and fight for them ... I wished I had been more like you.

And I always dreamed of being like you, my dearest Natalia.

Be strong for Mamá and Papá and for Otilia. Don't stop educating Lucia and Rosaura ... do not stop fighting for everything you taught us to believe in. I love you with all of my heart, sister, and I thank God for every minute he gave me to live near the woman you are.

Do not leave Domingo alone. Love him as if he were I. Support him as a best friend; he will so much need it when the time comes for my baby and me to go away from him ... remember he made me very happy in the short time we had together. I love you, Maximiana; you are my best friend and the best sister anyone could ever ask for.

Natalia was overwhelmed by the sentiment and started to speak in between sobs. I looked at Domingo who now was sobbing with the record. I rose from my seat and passed my arm around his shoulders. We hugged and cried together, like the day in the balcony room when Orlando had just broken up with me; without trying, we had created the bond that had survived these almost two years. The recording stopped, but an empty sound kept going, flowing with time while losing itself in space.

"Do not cry, Domingo; smile as she says," I said into his ear, hoping to alleviate the pain I saw in him—and the same I felt inside me.

"I can't … not when I listen to her …"

I stopped the phonograph. "Then you should not listen to it until you are ready for it …"

Even though I know it will always make you sad when you listen.

"When are you going back to Boston?" I asked in an attempt to calm him down.

"I don't know … I am thinking of going to the National University of México with Orlando; the change will be good for me, I think."

"If I passed the admission examination, I will also go to México City. Señor and Señora Patterson are sponsoring me to get my teaching certificate."

"That would be good, Maxi; I will be able to see you there then."

"Yes … I like that."

"Do you talk to Orlando at all?"

"No, well … I haven't seen him in a long time."

"Max … is there something between you and Alejandro?" Domingo questioned me with sincere interest, now that his eyes had dried.

"Everyone I know asks me that same question … there is friendship."

"That I know but … never mind."

"Domingo, if I passed the exam, I will go to El Roble to see my family before taking the train to México City … do you think it is possible for me to take them the phonograph?"

"Yes, of course …" He thought about it for a while. "As a matter of fact I was planning on taking it myself. I couldn't leave without doing it. You know that."

"Yes … I do."

When Domingo got ready to leave, I walked him to the sidewalk. Life did take unexpected turns, I kept repeating to myself. We gave each other a tight hug good-bye that was interrupted by my dear friend Agatha. She grabbed my arm and begged me to accompany her to the Voice of the People, a department store on Principal Street that sold the supplies she needed for her paintings. Then she wanted us to march directly to Machado Square to buy a guava *raspado* with sweet milk on it. I couldn't resist the invitation and pleasantly took her arm.

"I have wanted to buy these things for a while now, but I didn't have the time! I'm a busy lady, you know that …!" Agatha exclaimed as we walked down the streets of Mazatlán, carefully tucked into the shade of the sidewalks, protected from the scalding afternoon sun.

The store felt fresh regardless of the heat filtering through its opened windows and even seeping through the walls. The heat and humidity of summer weather had begun.

We walked around the narrow aisles, searching for the supplies, and as usual, we laughed together at the random comments Agatha said. I would certainly miss her if I went to México City; she had become one of my best and most beloved friends.

"I am almost done. Then we can go get our marvelous and deliciously fresh raspado," she said, opening her enormous green eyes even wider at the thought of our treat to come.

"Take your time; I am in no rush to go back home," I told her.

In reality, I had no desire to go home and be by myself. Every piece of my body was fighting the melancholic feeling Natalia's recording had left in me. The sound of her song kept playing in the back of my mind, and tears threatened to flood my eyes.

As we walked out of the store carrying Agatha's supplies, we had the unpleasant surprise of encountering Dora Elena Mora and Catalina Barraza right in front of us. I had not seen them since the day I had accompanied Andrés Randal to the dance at the German Club.

And what a surprise she had for me: Dora Elena was expecting a baby. She was at least seven months into the pregnancy because her belly stood out like a hot-air balloon. Even though she should have been happy, clear misery showed in her eyes and, with her natural bitterness, exposed her smiles and laughs as poor attempts at hiding the truth.

Both women recognized me and tried unsuccessfully to put me down in the only way they knew how: looking at me and smiling with a sarcastic laugh that displayed their unequivocal superiority over my economic and social condition. I passed by them and ignored their bitterness. I didn't have it in me to waste time in such irrational quarrels. Dora Elena was probably proud to be married so young, but apparently the reality of some aspects of her new life gave her reasons to feel otherwise. I did not know what to think of Catalina Barraza. She had everything within reach to do whatever she wanted with her life yet evidently took advantage of none of the opportunities offered to her. I was glad they didn't say anything directly to me because this time I would have responded with something that would have truly hurt their feelings if I had no other option but to defend myself.

"I want to color my hair pink, dark pink … wouldn't it look beautiful?" Agatha asked me full of enthusiasm. She usually dyed her hair in a combination of red and dark orange that made heads turn.

"I have never seen anyone with pink hair," I honestly responded, "but it will go well with your eyes and skin … I think."

"Me too … oh, Max, I am going to miss you when you go to México City! We are all going to miss you!" she said, hugging me firmly. "Even idiotic Andrés Randal is going to miss you … no … wait! He is going, too! I forgot. I hope you don't go back to him again, Maxi, because if he didn't appreciate you then, he won't later on …"

"I have no plans of going back to him for several reasons, and even if I had such an interest, he has no desire in coming back, so there is no point in even thinking about it."

"Ha! I'm more than sure that he is. Eduardo told me he is very sorry for what happened with you—"

"No, he shouldn't be," I interrupted. "Things happen for a reason, and he shouldn't feel sorry for *me* as if he owed me something."

"Ha! So *macho* of him to feel that way; he makes me laugh … do you have someone else winning your heart, though?"

"No, right now I just want to make sure that if I pass the examination I will be fully ready for my trip to México City."

"May I ask you something personal?"

"Sure, go ahead."

"Is Alejandro Sarmiento … your secret lover?"

"No."

"Do you *wish* he were?"

I chuckled, "I don't know … he is so beautiful, yes? And no one has given me more support than he has. Sometimes I wish to hug him so hard that I would break him! Honestly … I love him that much, but at the same time, I cannot imagine myself kissing him on the lips … I can't explain it."

"You don't love him that way, that is the reason … it is fine. Your friendship with Alejandro is beautiful."

"Yes, and I don't know what to do if one day he gets married," I candidly responded. "Losing our special friendship that way worries me sometimes."

Agatha giggled at my words. "He is not even steady with anybody; I don't see that one coming anytime soon."

She pointed to one of the benches on Machado Square to start enjoying our guava raspado. A guava with sweet milk raspado is the best treat anyone can ever have on a warm spring afternoon in Mazatlán. The sweet ice melts in your mouth in seconds and cools your throat. The contrast with the heat made me gasp and then smile broadly at the memory of Andrés putting his cold lips on my cheeks to make me shiver.

"What's so funny? Tell me little rascal!" Agatha pinched my ribs with her thin fingers.

"Nothing … just stupid memories that came to my mind."

"Tell me! Come on!"

"Mmm … Andrés used to place his frozen-cold lips on my face to make me shiver, and I used to laugh about it."

"Aye, Andrés …" Agatha winked her eye. "If he could be like my Eduardo."

"What are your plans for the future, Agatha? Are you going to stay in Mazatlán forever?"

"No … when the revolution explodes, I will follow it to wherever it takes me, keeping in my mind all the images that will later be painted in my pictures. In reality, I don't care where I live as long as I have what I need the most—my freedom to create what comes out of my soul."

"But, don't you plan to marry Eduardo?"

"Hell no! No way! I will never marry anybody. I want to be free and live under my own terms forever. I don't care if it is in a small countryside town or the biggest and most sophisticated city in the world, as long as I have my paints and the freedom to be myself. And dream, Maximiana Valdez, dream of life without hurting others."

Her words resonated in my mind as if two buckets of water had been thrown at me and suddenly woken me up. I also wanted to live dreaming of life and enjoying every moment of it, on my *own* terms. Slowly, I started to grasp what it means to be alive and why what really is important has nothing to do with how much you have in material possessions. Life is about breathing and seeing beauty in everything that surrounds you. It is about having a place to sleep and food on your table without harming others to get it. Life is about letting your mind fly away into the words of a good book and remembering how to dream as you did when you were a little girl.

Life is about living to the fullest.

"And speaking about the king of Rome, here he comes!" Agatha pointed at Andrés Randal, who was walking in our direction with his good friend Ernesto Hernandez. He greeted us with enthusiasm. His presence made me nervous, but I tried to hide my tenseness and let Agatha help by talking nonstop.

Night was falling, and we said our good-byes. It was a blessing that Agatha and I were neighbors because we could always walk home together. Andrés and Ernesto accompanied us until we reached our building. Andrés looked as handsome as ever, and his eyes, so green and intense, made me tremble within, no matter how hard my mind and heart tried to avoid it.

Doña Ursula sent a boy to give me the message that Señora Patterson wanted to see me. My heart stopped for a second because it was time for the examination results to arrive and she was supposed to get them for me.

I got ready as soon as I could and left the *Afternoon Mail*'s office fifteen minutes early to see her. It had to be the telegram because I had been teaching the Patterson children all morning and their mother had said nothing to me; it must have arrived that afternoon while I was working.

My feet took me to Principal Street until I turned on the corner to the right and reached the Patterson mansion. I stopped by the window that used to be my bedroom and held onto the bars, resting my forehead on its warm iron. I closed my eyes and said a prayer in my head, begging God that Señora Patterson had the best news for me. This was my moment of truth, the one for which I had been waiting for the last year of my life and the main source of so many hopes for the future. For the first time, I felt afraid to walk forward; the fear of disappointment invaded every inch of my body, but I had no way to go but forward.

I let go of the bars and marched straight to the front doors, determined to ring the bell. Doña Ursula's stiffed face received me and pointed with her finger to the parlor room where Señora Patterson was waiting for me with her complete tea set ready and a plate of cookies. Perhaps in another time I would have felt excited to see such a display but not today because I didn't know if it was a plate of cookies to celebrate or a plate of cookies to console me.

"Come on in, Maximiana. Please have a seat right next to me."

Oh God, bad news.

"Good afternoon, Señora Patterson," I said. "I received your message, and here I am." I wore a faint smile on my worried face.

"Well," Señora Patterson replied with a huge smile on her face, "I have wonderful news for you. You have passed the entrance examination and have been accepted to the Normal School for Young Ladies. Congratulations."

I took a deep breath to avoid fainting from excitement. My dream was becoming a reality, and it was finally in front of me. No words can describe how much my heart cherished that instant of change in my life. Still, I found the strength to thank Señora Patterson with all of my grateful heart. How lucky I had been to meet such a wonderful woman who had cleared the path for me to take.

"I don't think there are enough words to thank you, Señora Patterson, for everything you have done for me. I will not let you down," I said with sincere affection.

"I know you will not let me down, Maximiana, and for that reason we decided to sponsor you. And your idea of having your sister accompany you is good, very good."

"Yes, as I explained to you, her situation is very bad in my town, and this is her chance to escape all of it."

"Definitely," Señora Patterson agreed.

"She will pay for all of her expenses as soon as she gets a job, but in the meantime, I have saved enough money for both of us."

"I will give her a letter of recommendation; it will help her as well."

"Yes, Señora Patterson, thank you."

Señora Patterson gave me a tight hug when I got ready to leave. I promised to come teach her children one more week before going to El Roble as a farewell trip. I had to be in México City at the end of July; I had no time to waste. My entire body felt as if it were floating on a cloud of cotton when I took to the streets again to find my apartment. My happiness was apparently contagious because everyone greeted me with a smile when I passed them. Even the sound of the carts' wheels made a melodious hum in my ears from the exhilaration within me.

"Maximiana!" A familiar voice called behind me. When I turned, the pleasant face of Teodoro de la Vega stood in front of me.

"Oh, Teodoro! I have the greatest news! I passed the exam and got accepted to the Normal School for teachers!"

"Congratulations," Teodoro said with his quiet smile. "I am not surprised, though; we all knew you were going to make it."

Embarrassment came to me when he said that. It never crossed my mind before that such illustrious people in my life talked about me.

"Thank you," I responded timidly.

"I'm on my way to your building; Agatha invited me for coffee. Let's walk together, yes?"

"Oh, yes!" I could not hide my enthusiasm. "I have so many things to do in order to prepare for the trip, and it's not even funny! First of all my family needs to know the news ..."

"Yes."

"I wish to stay with them at least one week before coming back here to take the train to México City."

"You should, especially because you won't see them for at least ten months ... that is how long it takes to finish the Teaching Certificate Program at the Normal School."

"When are you leaving?" The opportunity of traveling with someone as knowledgeable as Teodoro de la Vega was tempting.

"At the end of July. Would you like to travel with me?"

"I would be so grateful! My sister is also going, but neither of us has ever traveled farther than Caliacán."

"That is fine with me. I am in a group traveling together, so adding two more will not be a problem."

"Even better!"

"Is it true that you want to become a writer? Paula was talking about it the other day," Teodoro said.

"Yes, I have some writings already, but I'm not brave enough to try to publish them yet ... they need *a lot* of revision."

"Any time you want me to take a look at them, I'm more than happy to do it," his genuinely good face responded with a smile.

"How very generous, Teodoro de la Vega. No wonder everyone likes you!"

"Really? Let's see," he placed his hand on his unshaven chin, "I don't have a line of girls behind me, though." He winked.

"Don't worry, Teodoro de la Vega; when I turn nineteen, I will be more than happy to be your steady girlfriend!" I poked the side of his waist.

"Really?" he asked, surprised. "In three years, I will be twenty-three years old, not bad at all. I will wait for you then."

We both laughed at the silliness of my joke.

"It is a very long trip to México City; you know that, yes?" he asked after a long awkward silence.

"Yes ... it takes days to get there."

He nodded. "But the time passes faster if you go with a group; we try to have as much fun as possible on the slow road." He kept quiet for a while, as if hesitating to tell me more or not. "The train stops for inspections by the soldiers ... so be careful with what kind of literature you take," he whispered in my ear. "Hints of the revolution are everywhere."

Agatha jumped up and down when she heard the news. Señora Bernardina Solorzano couldn't contain her emotion either and promised to prepare the best farewell basket of food for the long trip. It seemed like an eternity, waiting to deliver the news to my family; that following week became the longest of my life.

Before I left, I tried to give Alejandro my wonderful news, but he had gone to El Roble on an emergency trip. Josefina updated me on his family: The Sarmiento brothers had traveled with their father to my town because the Presidio River had flooded again and damaged a significant portion of the sugarcane fields—and with it, the livelihood of many of El Roble's people. Out of desperation to find work, some people left town. But others turned against the hacienda's overseers. I was glad my family had the money I had sent them with Augusto and that father had managed to keep a piece of land for our own cultivation; at least their condition was not as bad as most people in town. Josefina said Señora Leonora stayed behind with the twins and her new baby boy who was named Juan Sebastián Sarmiento. They left in such a hurry that Alejandro and Domingo did not even have time to ask me if I wanted to send something to my family with them, as they always did when traveling to El Roble.

Finally, I was waiting for the carriage that would take me to my dearly loved hometown. The caravan was leaving at 6:00 a.m., but my carriage picked me up at 5:00, and I had been up and ready since 3:00 a.m

"Good morning, Teacher Maximiana," greeted the carriage driver enthusiastically before starting our long journey.

"Good morning, Don Ramón. How are you today?" I replied while he helped me put my baggage on top of the carriage and opened the door for me.

"More ready than countryside brides on the day of their wedding!"

"Or do you mean city grooms on the day of their nuptials, Don Ramón?" I replied with a laugh in my counter to his comment.

"Aye, Señorita Maximiana, you always have an answer on the tip of your tongue," he laughed, amused. "Are you planning on reading one of those books you carry around even with the bouncing on the road?"

"Oh yes! This is a good chance to read even if my eyes have to dance with the jumping of the letters!"

Cheerfully, Don Ramón opened the carriage window and closed the door. We still had to pick up two more women who were on their way to Villa Unión; right after that we were going to join the caravan that traveled en route to El Roble.

I liked the company of the other travelers; our chatting enlivened the journey, and sharing the food with each other made the trip even more amiable. The two women in the carriage were a mother and daughter. Unfortunately their trip to the port was to attend a funeral. Still, they had a positive attitude, especially because as soon as they arrived at Villa Unión, they would take another trip to El Rosario to witness the miracle of the Virgin apparition. According to the two women, the image of the Virgin Mary was appearing on the trunk of a tree, and people were taking long expeditions to the site and asking for miracles.

I had never been a fan of those stories, but I respected people's feelings and beliefs when they talked about them. Nevertheless, the tree that cried next to the Twins' Well does qualify as a miracle, even if it doesn't involve religious images. In my mind, it was nature crying for being a witness to such a horrendous crime. Now that I was older that is how I saw it.

Domingo had already played Natalia's record on the phonograph to my parents before I arrived. Otilia told me that listening to Natalia's voice was like losing her all over again, but at the same time, they felt blessed to be able to hear her once more. My family expressed their gratitude to Domingo when he gave them the phonograph as a present, saying that they could keep it forever. He had several copies of her recording with him and was planning on making more.

Domingo also brought them a painting he had made of Natalia. The image remains painted in my mind with as much detail and permanence as on that canvas. It portrayed Natalia sitting in a garden with a blanket on her legs and a small furry dog sitting right next to her, as if guarding her. Her delicate hands rested on her lap, and she looked into the distance, where fog and flowers surrounded the trees. You could see a building far off; I assumed it was one of Harvard University's towers but did not inquire about it. She looked pale, as if that cold weather had taken the crimson color from her cheeks. But at the same time, she looked more beautiful than ever, the grandest flower in that garden; her smile illuminated the entire picture, and those who had known her could almost hear her contagious laugh and coquettish giggling rising from the painting.

Otilia also said that Domingo cried in silence when he came to visit them and asked for forgiveness. Mamá carried him in her heart as if he were her own son and, crying along with him, asked him not to blame himself for anything. It had been God's will for Natalia to join him so soon.

Mamá later told us how strange she felt to have a Sarmiento boy at our house under those circumstances; it contradicted everything in her background and upbringing and experience. It just made no sense to her.

My dear friend Daniel came to visit as soon as he heard of my visit to town. He had continued teaching the children of El Roble along with Otilia and Raimunda. We sat on my sidewalk for a long chat that included his usual jokes that I loved and made me laugh so much. Raimunda brought precious little Magdalena to my house. She had a head full of light brown curls and a smile as beautiful as a little flower, just like her oldest brother Alejandro Sarmiento. I talked so much that I feared getting a sore throat, but they wanted all the details of my trip to the state capital, and more than anything, they were dying to get the details of my impending trip to México City.

Otilia mentioned that people in town were wildly gossiping about me and my trip to the country's capital. They saw my clothes as fancy even though they were simply clean and well-ironed skirts and blouses. My shoes that caused a sensation were, in reality, ordinary footwear. And the famous adornments in my hair, according to some, were extravagant presents from Alejandro Sarmiento. To everyone's mind, Alejandro had a concubine named Maximiana Valdez, whom he showered with presents, and just to complete the fantasy, Alejandro had planned my trip to México City to keep me hidden from whomever his family had chosen him to marry within the next couple of months.

The week was flying at a speed that I desperately wished to slow down, but I could not. In a closing and opening of the eyes, it was already Friday; our return was set for Sunday morning. Otilia was still in shock with the true reality that she was going to Mazatlán with me to take that train to México City. Mamá and Papá had accepted my idea, and Augusto was our number one supporter. Rosaura and Lucia felt sad with the idea of Otilia going away, but they understood after a serious conversation I had with them while sitting in the Arroyo de Constancia on a hot afternoon. Mamá was happy to see us go; I think she had it clear in her mind that going away was our only hope to escape the sure misery waiting for us there as peasant girls.

"Mamá, I want to see Doña Luisa before I go. I still have the little embroidered bag she gave me when I left to teach for the first time," I said, putting my hair up to keep the heat off my neck.

"That is a good idea; Luisa has been kind to you. She truly likes you and deserves your respect. But the Sarmientos are in town. I don't think you should go to the Grand House if Señor Joaquín is there."

"I will ask Margarita or anyone around to get Doña Luisa for me. I will not go inside the hacienda," I replied, finishing my curls.

"Take the umbrella!" Rosaura came running to give it to me. "It is cloudy; it's going to rain for sure."

"Thanks, Rosie," I said and took to the street towards the Grand House.

Margarita came to the door to tell me Señor Joaquín, Alejandro, and Domingo were out of town until late evening—they had gone to Villa Unión to send some telegrams—and Doña Luisa wanted me to go inside. I hadn't crossed those gates in over a year, but it felt as familiar as if I had been cleaning their floors and walls the day before yesterday. I went through the *glorieta* entrance as I had done for the first time at the age of thirteen. The smell of gardenias welcomed me, and the sprinkles of water that fell onto my face from the fountain refreshed me. Childish giggles came out of my mouth without wishing them.

I wanted to avoid looking at the balcony protruding from the bedroom, but my peripheral vision caught its lined white Roman pillars. I hurried to get to the kitchen through the main door of the house but stopped and went around the outside of the enormous grand salon through the gardens.

Doña Luisa was not in the kitchen as usual, so I walked to the water tower. Sprinkles of rain were starting to come down from the grey sky. I pushed its heavy door and several owls flapped their wings at me. Frightened, I jumped and tried to avoid their claws that seemed to reach for my face. I felt my heart throbbing like an excited drum following the musical notes of my emotions. More than startled owls, something about the water tower perturbed me—or perhaps it was the hacienda itself. In the distance I heard music from the piano, a song not playing when I had crossed the gardens minutes before. I took both of my hands to my chest and took a deep breath. My ears and heart followed the sound of the notes and led me to the grand salon, and without listening to the command of my mind and common sense, my feet—now those of a woman of profession and not those of a barefoot servant girl—took me directly to the source.

Orlando Sarmiento was playing a sweet melody with his eyes closed. I stood in the hall, the same one with floor tiles that gave an illusion of three dimensions, as I had done years before to witness my beloved sister Natalia's song on New Year's Eve. The side of my forehead rested on the door frame in order to support the overwhelming emotion of the moment. Unsolicited tears rolled from my eyes when I opened them to meet his. Orlando did not end his playing but moved from one song to another. He stopped when my body turned away to leave.

"Maximiana … wait!" he said while walking towards me. "Please."

Involuntarily, I stopped myself.

"Maxi …," he said holding my arm with tenderness, "I want to talk to you; I beg you."

"About what?" I asked without turning my face to him. "There is nothing to talk about."

"Please," his voice implored with gentleness.

Orlando took my arm and led my way through the living room. We crossed the twins' bedroom and the closet hall to finally arrive at the balcony room.

"Doña Luisa is not here … she is at the five o'clock mass so we have some time to talk. Please."

"But Margarita said—"

"I told her to tell you that … Doña Luisa is not here."

"But why in this room? Let's go to the garden then," I said, walking towards the door and seeing my reflection in the mirror. I felt terribly uneasy in that place with Orlando Sarmiento again.

"Maximiana, please … I have too many things to tell you, and I want to do it here in our room … in our place."

Our room? Our place? What are you saying Orlando?

"Maxi …," Orlando said in a low voice, "I now regret what happened between us—"

I interrupted abruptly, "Oh, I do too. Do not have doubts about it; I regret it as much as you do. There is nothing I regret more in li—"

"I acted as a real idiot … especially when I brought Virginia here and broke up with you that way."

I turned my back on him just as he had turned his on mine the last time we had been in that room as a couple.

"There is no point in talking about it anymore, Orlando; that is the past, and it will not come back to us … *fortunately.*"

"It is not fortunate for me, Maxi," he touched my arm with the tip of his fingers, "because I miss you so much."

Suddenly, lightning illuminated the balcony room. I scrunched my eyes and covered my ears to avoid listening to the coming thunder, which reverberated throughout the building.

"How can you miss me?" I asked, "You have kept yourself busy with different girls, one after the other … there is no missing in your attitude, only a joyful indifference."

And at one point, such indifference hurt me, too.

"But no one has ever been the way you were to me. Nobody has been the way you were in my life. No one … I swear to God."

"I guess those girls needed to be servants in the hacienda to be like me, Orlando." The words came out of my mouth automatically.

"You never acted like a servant with me …"

My body tensed expecting the thunder from another lightning strike as I cut Orlando short, "But you always treated me like one, Orlando; don't forget that."

"It is true, and I am ashamed of it … you don't know how ashamed I am of my stupid behavior, of the way I acted towards you."

"You should … because no one deserves to be treated like a servant in any way, even if she works as such at your house."

"I have never forgotten you, Maxi …" He came near me. "In my mind and in my dreams … you are always there," Orlando whispered in my ear with a trembling voice that made me shake inside as if the thunder had just exploded from within my small frame.

I didn't turn my back. However, deep inside, I realized how much I would have given to have heard those words in the past, when I was drowning in despair and feeling, just as Maríanela did when Pablo didn't love her anymore and left her all alone in the midst of her suffering.

"Do you still love me, Maxi?" he asked, almost murmuring.

It took me a while to answer, especially when he placed his strong chin on my shoulder and his soft curls caressed my cheek. "I do not love you anymore, Orlando," I replied as coldly as my voice allowed it to be.

He surrounded my waist with his arms and pulled me close to his body while speaking softly the phrase that I had cherished so much in the past, "I love you."

My heart shook with emotion even when every inch of my common sense told me to restrain myself from feeling anything.

"Please forgive me."

He moved around and stood in front of me. I hadn't had his expressionless eyes so close to me in years; his hands reached for my face, but gently I held them down.

"I love you," he said again without blinking his eyes, now moist with tears.

How much I desired to tell him that those words were arriving too late. I could hear the words resonate in my mind, but the emotion that my heart once felt was now gone, and I could do nothing about it. The phrase "I love you" sounded empty inside of me for I knew he had used it too many times, with so many others. Still, the words brought back memories of how I had once loved him, and they now made me feel nervous in his presence. But my passion for him no longer existed. What reason had I to shy from him? I said nothing. Inside, though, I battled those old, familiar thoughts of a love now lost. And slowly, they fell away from me. I no longer needed them. Something new began building within me, and as I stood there, admiring the lightning's flash, I began to look forward to the thunder's roar. *Yes!* I thought, the sounds of a war dearly won. A feeling of empowerment invaded my soul.

I reached for his face and pulled it towards mine; my mouth grabbed his and gave him a lesson of everything I had learned from Andrés Daniel Randal. His face turned red as a strawberry in summer, and he embraced me with more force than ever. I lost track of time, of how long I had him in my arms. At the rumbling of every peal of thunder, I would reach inside him even more. I made sure to caress his deliciously scented neck with my lips and kissed it until he was ready to take me, to give his life for mine, then I escaped from his arms and walked away from him, leaving only the shadow of my presence to taunt him. At the threshold, I turned back and with the words, "We should leave all of this behind us," gave him a friendly smile and closed the doors behind me.

The sweet wet gardenias greeted me in the garden. I sensed something above me and looked up to see a bird flying over my head; a beautiful owl soared in the distance, flapping her enormous wings, getting away from the hacienda gardens, fighting the heavy rain, lightning, and thunders.

"Tell Doña Luisa I came to look for her, Don Carlos!" I screamed before closing the grand hacienda's heavy door behind me. I ran home, drinking the drops of delicious water coming from the sky and feeling an inexplicable triumph inside my sixteen-year-old, radically rebellious heart.

On Saturday morning, I had the pleasant surprise of Doña Luisa's visit. She came with a huge plate of *panquequis* with butter and honey on them. Mamá made a big pot of delicious smelling coffee to accompany the sweet panquequis and my unavoidable happiness.

Everyone noticed my good mood and wondered about it. I did not even know how to explain it, but I felt release from everything around me. Doña Luisa was very happy to hear about my story of the sponsorship to México City and that Otilia was going to come with me. She congratulated my parents and told them that it was a blessing to have such a girl in town. I was genuinely embarrassed by her statements, but a hint of pride settled within me.

Doña Luisa also said that she had a message from my dear Alejandro. He was working this morning at the hacienda's office with Señor Joaquín and the overseer; but he was going to be at my roble tree that evening and was expecting me to come. I told Doña Luisa to let Alejandro know that I would be there; no way would I miss meeting with him before going to Mazatlán, especially because we would likely not see each other until I came back from México City the following year.

It was a blessed day, full of family, friends, and sweet memories. During the afternoon, Otilia accompanied me to the town cemetery to take a bouquet of sunflowers to Natalia's empty graveyard. Mamá had insisted in giving a sacred burial to her memory. I know Natalia would have liked that.

I passed my hand along the engraved words of her name while Otilia walked to the small waterhole to fetch some water to clean the headstone. We moved other flowers at the grave to the side in order to make ours fit in the stone vase and then sat there for a while and cried in silence, even though in our hearts she was still in Boston. Otilia and I were about to leave when Domingo arrived with a bouquet of fresh, fragrant gardenias.

"Good afternoon, ladies," he greeted us, giving us a tiny smile and taking the hat off his head.

"Good afternoon," we replied in a chorus.

He kissed us both with familiarity. Otilia became stiff with nervousness and shyly walked away to fetch more water.

"So, Maxi," he said smiling, "did you see Big Head yesterday?"

His question threw me aback.

"I did," I answered, trying to hide my perturbation. "Don't tell me Orlando told you what happened."

"He told me," he said casually, looking away at the Sacanta; it seemed closer while standing on the cemetery hill.

"Yes, I went looking for Doña Luisa, but she wasn't there. I'm glad that I am seeing Alejandro today," I said, thoughtfully changing the subject; "I couldn't bear leaving without seeing him."

"Oh ... Where are you going to see him?"

"At my roble tree."

"At your what?" he asked, confused.

"Do you remember the first time you and Natalia talked, and I was up in a tree and Alejandro came up there with me? When ... after ... Orlando broke up with me? That's *my* roble tree, the one I go to, to think ... or maybe not to think ... by myself," I replied in a low voice, accompanying him in viewing the Sacanta.

His eyes filled with tears. "Yes," he replied.

"Well ... there." I reached for his hand and put it in between mine. "Remember to smile, Domingo. Don't forget Natalia's words."

He forced himself into a smile, and I asked him to go back to town with us. I didn't want to leave him there, in the cold and lonely cemetery, all by himself. He agreed and walked with us to our house before taking the cobblestone street to the hacienda.

After eating two of Mamá's red tamales with sugar, it was time to go and meet with Alejandro. Once at my tree, I climbed up and waited for my friend to arrive.

"Maxi, are you up there?" I heard his voice call from below.

"Yes!" I waved my hand at him.

He climbed up and sat next to me.

"I can't believe you are already going to México City! You really did it ... and I'm going to miss you, Silly Face," he said while pushing my shoulder with affection.

"Oh ... I am going to miss everyone as well. I have mixed feelings about all of this. And I worry about leaving my family like this, without my help."

"I can help ..."

"No … thank you, but no; that wouldn't be right. I have a better idea. What if when you become the hacendado—one day you will, yes?—hand out your lands to the people, which is the only acceptable way to help … but then you wouldn't be a hacendado anymore, yes?"

"It wouldn't matter to me; those things don't matter to me. You are right."

"You know, Aleh," I said pensive, "since I walked for the first time into the Grand House now over three years ago … I have wondered *why* you have all those unnecessary things—furniture and decorations and rugs and all that space … I don't understand it."

"I don't know either … that is the only environment I have known. The first time I walked into a peasant's house was when I came to talk to your parents about letting you work in Mazatlán …"

I sighed, remembering that day that now seemed so far away.

He continued, "And to tell you the truth, Max, I felt guilty afterwards."

"Why?" I asked surprised. "You should've felt proud because you were trying to help me."

"But … the poverty around you, Maxi."

"Misery is not good looking … I know that. But simplicity—not poverty but only possessions that you need—is wonderful if you think about it. As long as you have food, clean water, a place to live that when it rains the water doesn't pour in, a nice clean bed, money to pay for remedies if you get sick, and education to be able to read … then what else do you need to be happy?"

"You need love."

"Of course!" I replied with a smile.

"I have neither … not simplicity or love."

"You are simple at heart because you don't enjoy all of those luxuries around you … and love? I am sure that more than one woman is madly in love with you, Alejandro Sarmiento! More than one, and if they are not … then they are a group of blind girls walking around the world without seeing who you are."

Alejandro smiled warmly at me and rested his head on my shoulder without saying more.

"Aleh," I finally asked, "why don't you tell me who is that woman you love so much that … is it an older woman? Is she married?"

In a low tone, as if wishing my ears not to grasp its sounds, he said, "It is more complicated than that."

"But … why can't you tell me? I have uncovered my heart and soul to you as my best friend; why can't you trust me the same?" My voice broke when those words came out of my mouth, my face turned to the Grand House. I could see the fainting light in the distance, the only artificial illumination in the dusk of the entire countryside.

"I am afraid of telling anyone about it …," Alejandro said, turning his sad face towards mine.

"*Why?*" I begged, "Why are you so afraid? Is it *that* bad?"

"I don't know."

"I will understand anything … I will even help you get *her*, Aleh … I promise. What wouldn't I give to see you happy?" I replied hugging him with both of my arms as tight as I could. He lowered his eyes to whisper the words hidden in the deepest chambers of his humble heart:

"I know you would … and what wouldn't I give for the miracle of making you *a man* to fall in love with *you.*"

His words echoed inside me like the bells from El Roble's church on humid summer evenings. I cannot deny his confession surprised me, but at the same time it helped me understand why my dearest friend had kept that secret to himself for such a long time. The world around us might recognize that Alejandro is the most wonderful person walking on earth, the one with the purest heart and the strongest soul. Yet people would not understand his feelings and passions, and they would reject him because he did not fit into the order of things.

"Do you think I'm crazy?" he asked, looking up to the sky full of tiny suns in the far-away distance, "just as they said of Mother?"

"No …"

"Do you think I'm a deviant … as people like me are called?"

"No, of course not," I replied, looking for his face. "You are not a deviant person; don't you *ever* say that again."

Alejandro's eyes filled with tears. "I feel ashamed of myself, Maxi, very ashamed. Sometimes I wish not to be alive."

His words hurt me deep inside; my heart was crying with him, but I didn't show it through tears. I didn't want my dear Alejandro to feel sorry for himself; there was no reason for it, and he had to understand that.

"Aleh … there is nothing wrong with you; you have nothing to be ashamed of. People who *hate* and *hurt* others are the ones who should be ashamed of themselves. But someone like you? For God's grace!"

"But I hurt my family being like this. They—"

"How do you hurt them?' I asked. "No … don't answer that. Look … you have thoughts and feelings, and nobody can take them from you. How can you hurt your family for *loving* a man? How does it hurt them? Those are *your* feelings, not theirs. They *cannot* take away from you what's inside … especially if those are feelings of love and they bring you happiness …"

"I know other men who feel the same way … but they have to hide it like me; you can clearly see why …"

"I do … but you don't have to hide it from me," I declared with an assuring voice. "Tell me … what happened with your first love? Was he handsome?" I asked pushing his shoulder with mine. His face turned red like a tomato about to be ripped from earth.

"I don't feel comfortable talking about those things, Maxi; I feel embarrassed," he replied with a shaking voice and looking away from my eyes.

"Did he have blue eyes?"

Alejandro looked at me puzzled.

"I ask because of your favorite poem … remember? *"What is poetry? You ask while nailing in my pupil your blue pupil? What is poetry? And you ask me? Poetry is* **you**.*"*

He couldn't conceal the truth but still shook his head as a sign of not wanting to talk about it. I insisted a little bit more.

"You don't feel comfortable because you are not used to it, but there is nothing more beautiful in life than talking about loving feelings," I said with a smiling heart.

"So are you in love with someone right now?" he asked, turning the conversation around.

"I don't think so; I have so much more going on in my life and many things I want to do that liking a man or loving a man is not one of my priorities at this precise moment. There is time for everything, I think."

"Others would be worried about time passing and not getting married …"

"That's the way we are raised, Aleh, to believe that we have no other destiny in life or that our lives are not complete unless we have a beau at our door."

"True."

"I know there is someone out there for me, and he will come at one point in my life. Now, changing the world around me is what matters the most; that makes me happy … and feel fulfilled."

"Me, too," Alejandro replied with a smile. "Do you think it is possible?"

"Of course it is! Everything is possible; right now we are changing the world with our conversation, aren't we?"

He took a deep breath. "Yes, we are. I feel a release within me from this conversation with you."

"I am sure that if you tell Agatha, she will tell you exactly the same thing. And I am also sure everyone in the Cactus would understand you because if they don't then they are a bunch of hypocrites who talk about revolutionizing the world around us but judge others who do not comply with their rules and standards!"

And don't they dare hurt you or make you feel bad about your feelings, Alejandro Sarmiento, because then they would see the violent side of me!

"I love you, Aleh; I love you with all of my heart," I said, hugging him with the force of that love.

"Oh, Maximiana, I love you more. You are my best friend and the one who understands me without restraint. What am I going to do without you?"

"I keep asking myself the same question … what am I going to do without you, Aleh? When you went to Boston, I missed you so much." Tears threatened to roll down my cheeks, but this was no time to break down.

"I did too, Silly Face … even though I have to confess that I like being away from Father and my family. I am freer to feel anyway I want."

"But do they know? Do your father and brothers know? Have you told them?"

"No … but I do know Father is suspicious of it," he replied with a sigh. "Do you remember the night you came into my room in Mazatlán and hid under my covers?"

"Yes …," I replied, remembering the night of my farewell to Orlando Sarmiento turned into a mess when I discovered Señor Joaquín entering Raimunda's room.

"Father thought I had somebody *else* in the room …"

"After that happened, I thought your father had believed," and my words turned into a whisper, "that his *wife* had been in there."

"Oh … yes … there is that issue as well," he answered, confirming my suspicions he was aware of his stepmother's romantic feelings towards him. "But, at that time Father didn't know about it."

And now he does.

"He probably thought a man was in the room with me, as if I had no respect towards my body and my house."

"He thinks you are like him!" I instantly regretted my assumption. "I'm sorry, Aleh … but he is mean sometimes. I understand he has suffered, too, but … others pay for it."

"Don't worry about it." He shook his head with resignation.

"So he now knows about Señora Leonora's secret love for you?"

Alejandro's face tightened when I said it, but it was too late to go back from my words.

"How do *you* know that piece of gossip, Nosy Girl?"

I didn't want to mortify him with the reality of everyone in that house knowing his stepmother's passion for him, so I played along with his name for me. "You know how nosy I am, and I always observed her more than the others, so her intentions became obvious to me. But I am a romantic and see love and romance everywhere; so don't imagine anybody else noticing it."

"Leonora cried my name and said she loved me when my little brother was born. Father heard her, and now, I don't even know how to look at him." He kept quiet for a moment, as if debating whether to tell me the rest or not, then he continued, "She screamed my name many times and said she didn't want to die before telling me she loved me."

"Oh my goodness! That is grave." My heart sank thinking about the scene. "Oh, Aleh … is he now jealous of you?"

A frown came to my face, thinking of such an injustice.

"No, I don't think so." Then he changed the subject, "Everything is so beautiful here … the quietness of the countryside is paradise itself." A profound sigh escaped both of our chests. "But it has become too small for you, Maximiana Valdez; you have the world in front of you and are willing to take it."

I rested my head on my friend's shoulder and closed my eyes. A hidden passage in my subconscious came to life as if I were living it again:

I walked into the hacienda's library for the first time and saw before me on a special stand a mysterious sphere, big and full of colors. I passed my fingers over its shiny texture and felt the ridges on it. What is this? *I asked myself, for I knew the big ornamented ball was not a mere plaything, not there in the library. I walked around it, trying to decipher the images in front of me, and somehow they started to make sense. The blue colors must represent water and the brown ones land. The lines among them were something that marked different places. And the squiggles all over—those I could not figure out at all, but I knew they held the key to everything. Slowly I turned the ball, and the childish smile of a thirteen-year-old girl came to my face when I saw the drawings and lines and squiggles passing in front of my eyes over and over again. How I wished to know what those little lines meant!*

Later I would learn that they were the names of mysterious and faraway places that I could visit at the turn of my fingers! Not just on geographic globes but also in books; words gave me the power to travel and learn and become more than what my birth had determined. That day a new emotion was born within me, and it stayed inside my mind, body, and soul forever.

My encounter with the geographic globe marked the beginning of my journey. I started taking the *ways of the owls*: exploring the world around me at night, reading, learning, expanding. I opened my wings to understand all around me and flapped them many times until I finally took flight on my own and started thinking for myself, by myself. I realized my birth as a peasant girl need not shape my destiny; other pathways lay before me. So it is for everyone; we choose which one to take and which ones to avoid.

"Are you asleep?" Alejandro asked in my ear.

"No … I'm remembering the past," I replied without opening my eyes.

"Listen to this poem, Maximiana Valdez:

Although poetry is not my strong note
Notes of beauty surge in my mind
When I remember the moments
You and I have shared
Now and forever, you and I …
Best friends.

"Oh, how beautiful! Who wrote it?" I asked, filled with emotion.

"I wrote it for you as a going-away present," he said with a shy crimson painted on his cheeks. "But you know I am not a talented poet."

Then, this poem was born in my heart, and I recited it to my beloved friend:

What would the world be
Without your beauty
Walking on its lands?
An empty sphere of opaque colors
And soundless hums.
A round globe turning and
Floating in space
Without meaningful motives to be there.
You are the meaning of words,

The giver of sense to those of us
Who had just discovered that every morning
The world we live in … turns around inspired
By such light.

"Those whose hearts and souls are just like yours create that light, Alejandro Sarmiento, and never think less of yourself than that fact."

EPILOGUE

Seventeen-year-old Maximiana Valdez received her Teaching Certificate from the Normal School for Young Ladies in June 1910. She graduated with the highest scholastic honors and was recognized by her professors and fellow students as the most promising teacher of her graduating class. She was also awarded a scholarship to start medical school in the National University of México the following fall, one of very few women. "Unfortunately," she replied when asked about the honor, "because there should be as many female students as males entering medical school."

She continued participating in México City's chapter of the Cactus where she met new people who inspired her in her never-ending desire to learn and change the world for the betterment of all.

Otilia found a job, love, and the desire to fight for women's rights and against sexual oppression. She was inspired by Maximiana and the women of the Cactus to start speaking out about the violence against women in México.

Maximiana filled herself with the illusion of love again with the young man she least expected, and it was like first love for both of them, even when the feelings were familiar enough to take them back to places both knew by heart.

The Mexican Revolution exploded in November 20, 1910. Maximiana was more than ready to dive into it, and her true and beloved friends joined her in the struggle. They fought with fervent passion along the ranks of the oppressed, and at the end of the victorious adventure, Maximiana Valdez became the writer of realities she had dreamed for so long to be.

One evening, after many summers, Maximiana found herself lying on the ground amid the sugarcane fields of her beloved town of El Roble … in the distance she could hear the murmuring sounds of the Arroyo de Constancia. The clouds of the Sacanta came down to her, and in the humid touch of its mist, she closed her eyes to perceive the familiar aroma of El Roble's countryside. Another memorable scent reached her senses. A presence lay next to her, and Maximiana extended her arm to entangle her fingers in the soft hair she had lovingly held before. He turned his face to her, and for the first time, his sweet eyes, no longer empty, expressed his love for her. He smiled, and she smiled back to embrace in the passion that for so long had pended within them.

They finally gave each other the chance to become one, and they did it under their terms, not society's imposed rules, while beautiful owls flew over the roble trees surrounding them. The wavering sounds of a radio in the hacienda arrived at their ears, and they recognized the melodious voice of Natalia Valdez singing for them in the near distance. She was celebrating their love through her voice. They both smiled again, without taking their eyes off each other. Then Maximiana closed hers as she felt herself flying in the arms of her beloved one. She didn't know if what they had at that moment would last forever, but she did know that her love for him was eternal.

AFTERWARD

The spirit of my great-great-grandmother Maximiana Valdez lives within the walls of El Roble's *La Hacienda*, a historic building that even today stands as the Grand House in the heart of El Roble town in rural Sinaloa, México. And even though the hacienda times represent an era of brutal oppression for the majority of Mexican people, from that arose the call for change and the struggles of an entire country's revolution.

This is the place where, in my imagination, Maximiana Valdez learned her worth as a human being. It is also at La Hacienda of El Roble where my heart started to follow the ways of changing the world around me through learning and writing. Like Maximiana, I also believe with all of my heart in THE WAYS OF THE OWLS.

Manoush Genet Castañeda-Vizcarra
Spring 2009
Seattle, Washington

GLOSSARY

agua – water
agua de horchata – a sweet rice drink
arroyo – a stream.
asado – a potato and meat dish
cajeta – caramel spread
cenaduria – a dinner restaurant
corico – a cinnamon cookie.
empanada – a turnover
glorieta – a round front porch
gordita – a thick corn tortilla topped with meat and vegetables
hacendado – the owner of an estate
hacienda – a large estate
huanacaxtle – the elephant ear tree
lanchero – a boatman
Las Mañanitas – a traditional Mexican birthday song.
matatena – a game with jacks and a ball.
mestiza – a person of mixed European and Indian blood
natillas – sweetened burned milk
palapa – an umbrella made of coconut tree leaves
panquequi – a crêpe
raspado – crushed ice sweetened with a flavor, such as raspberry
    or vanilla
roble – an oak tree
señor – a man; also a form of address; when capitalized, equivalent
    to Mr.
señora – a woman; also a form of address; when capitalized,
    equivalent to Mrs.
señorita – a young woman or girl; when capitalized, a form of
    address equivalent to Miss
señorito – a young man or youth
tejuino – a corn-based drink
tertulia – a conversation
tostada – a toasted tortilla topped with meat and vegetables